O|||o

SHORT FICTION

for Emily,
   with love and
   a writerly
interest.

James
         christmas '95

OHIO
SHORT FICTION

A collection of
twenty-two stories
by Ohio writers

Edited by Jon Saari

Introduction by James Thomas

N
Northmont Publishing, Inc.
West Bloomfield, Michigan

Northmont Publishing, Inc.
6346 Orchard Lake Road, #201
West Bloomfield, Michigan 48322

Printed in the United States of America
96 95 94 93 92 5 4 3 2 1

Permissions

"Getting Even" by Lee K. Abbott. First published in *Southwest Review*. Copyright 1991 by the author. Reprinted from the collection *Living After Midnight* (G. P. Putnam's Sons) by permission of the author.

"The Way It Comes Back to Me" by Ellen E. Behrens. First published in *Fiction*. Copyright 1991. Reprinted by permission of the author.

"An Introduction to Opera" by Robert Canzoneri. First published in *Southern Review*. Copyright 1985. Reprinted by permission of the author.

"Winter Term" by Robert Flanagan. First published in *Cornfield Review*. Copyright 1989. Reprinted from the collection *Loving Power* (Bottom Dog Press) by permission of the author.

"Throne of Blood" by Abby Frucht. First published in *Ontario Review*. Copyright 1990. Reprinted by permission of the author.

"Jerry's Insomnia" by Jack Heffron. First published in *North American Review*. Coypright 1990. Reprinted by permission of the author.

"On Vacation" by Richard Kraus. First published in *Gamut*. Copyright 1990. Reprinted by permission of the author.

"Little Night Creatures" by J. Patrick Lewis. First published in *New England Review and Bread Loaf Quarterly*. Copyright 1987. Reprinted by permission of the author.

"Rabbits, Live and Dressed" by Paul Many. First published in *The (Ohio) Journal* and *Special Report: Fiction*. Copyright 1987. Reprinted by permission of the author.

"Funeral Plots" by Jack Matthews. First published in *Southern Review*. Copyright 1989. Reprinted by permission of the author.

"Distance" by Eve Shelnutt. First published in *Western Humanities Review*

ISBN 1-878005-62-6

For Peggy
and
In memory of
Sherwood Anderson (1876–1941)
Author of *Winesburg, Ohio* (1919)

CONTENTS

PREFACE

Not too long ago a common bit of literary wisdom pronounced the death of the short story. The reasons were many, the most frequent being that there was no market for the short story, no writers of the short story, and no publications willing to devote space to it. The death of the short story, like the death of the novel earlier, was premature. The publication of John Cheever's *The Stories of John Cheever* in 1978, if one is going to gamble on a literary cause and effect, and I am, changed all that. As the quintessential short story writer of the world War II generation, Cheever brought the short story full circle. Surely minimalism, K-Mart realism, Donald Barthelme's exquisite experimentation, and Raymond Carver's controlled precision characterize the varieties of short story writing over the past fifteen years, but Cheever's sixty-one stories in one volume were a confirmation of the classicism of his prose and the durability of the form.

In the 1980s the short story flourished more than any other literary form. Although the informal essay reestablished itself, it was the short story that stood apart. New small magazines came into existence, long-standing literary quarterlies reasserted themselves, and new writers of short stories came into their own. More short story volumes by single authors were receiving attention by reviewers. A new generation of writers learned the craft of fiction from M.F.A. programs where some of the nation's best writers now taught and used as their professional base. Explanations were offered for the revival of the short story as a literary form, such as the relationship among the short attention spans of Americans, the similarity [!] of sitcoms with short stories, and the relative ease of writing short fiction. But this equation is false and facile. Any writer of short fiction knows the degree of difficulty of this form, and any close reader of the short story comes to recognize the subtleties of the form—of how the short story's suggestiveness demands the reader pay strict attention to a world both revealing and restrictive, apparent and concealing.

No one talks about regional writing today, not with a national popular culture that brings a uniformity to the outward conditions of life. Television has flattened a genuine regionalism into quirky oddities or convenient visible symbols as false as they are misleading. Short story writers use literary technique and a sophisticated knowledge of language to write about the common and uncommon experiences of Americans. Writers use the form of the short story to present individual experiences that startle readers into conscious awareness of recognizable patterns of cultural life. Writers come to know intimately what unites and divides us as a nation, what constitutes our diversity and similarity. Their understanding puts them both into and above the fray, to borrow a word from George Bush, of what has been labeled the debate over political correctness. The art of the short story penetrates below the surface of personal troubles and public life. A generation ago C. Wright Mills called upon the sociological imagination to "make a difference in the quality of human life in our time." So too must the literary imagination, and it does. The true test of the short story is the believability of the story and the understanding by the writer of human psychology. This believability is not limited to a new realism in short story writing; even stories that deliberately play with formal characteristics ring true. Characters in a Madison Smart Bell or a Rick Bass story may live in the South, but we recognize their inner conditions—their humanity—as similar to the midwestern characters in a Mary Grimm or an Eve Shellnut story. Short fiction today is largely existential, although we do not tend to describe it as such. Popular culture has helped displace regionalism, but writers of short fiction depict a common internal reality we all recognize. Today writers are not self-consciously existential as Albert Camus's *The Stranger*. The stranger phenomenon in fiction is a typical state of mind and exists as a shared unarticulated assumption—a recognition of a common inner life.

In *The Green Hills of Africa* Ernest Hemingway offered the opinion that "all modern literature comes from one book by Mark Twain called *Huckleberry Finn*. . . . All Americans writing comes from that. There was nothing before. There has been nothing as good since." But everyone knows that Hemingway owed a debt to Sherwood Anderson and that *Winesburg, Ohio*, as Malcom Cowley pointed out, influenced a generation of writers—a roll call of modern American masters that includes, besides Hemingway, Faulkner, Steinbeck, Saroyan, Wolfe, and Miller. Anderson's plain, unadorned style is deceiving, hiding an emotional core that becomes compelling through the reading of *Winesburg, Ohio*. But the other point, the one I want to make and one easily ignored, also comes from Cowley. Anderson, wrote Cowley, "was essentially a story teller, as he kept insisting, but his art was of a special type, belonging to an oral rather than a written tradition." The link between Sherwood Anderson and the writers in this book is one that melds the written and oral. These stories can be enjoyed read aloud as well as savored as words on the page. The silence of hearing words in your head can also be experienced and appreciated spoken aloud to others.

The writers in this volume live and work and write in Ohio (a few passed through the state long enough to end up in this book) and practice a contemporary American short story that links them to a tradition best represented by Sherwood Anderson and one they are changing as they pay honor and homage to it.

In his *Memoirs* Anderson wrote about revisiting the house in Chicago where he wrote *Winesburg, Ohio*. He wanted to recapture the experience and had brought his wife along to impress her with that magical time in his life. Instead, Anderson found the house to be seedy and unattractive, nothing like he had remembered. But he found something more important, something vitally important, when many years before he sat down at a table in his Chicago rooming house and started to write: "There was a story of another human, quite outside myself, truly told," Anderson wrote. "The story was one called 'Hands.' It was about a poor little man, beaten, pounded, frightened by the world in which he lived into something oddly beautiful. The story was written that night in one sitting. No word of it ever changed. I wrote the story and got up. I walked up and down in that little narrow room. Tears flowed from my eyes. 'It is solid,' I said to myself. 'It is like a rock. It is there. It is put down.'" There Anderson "found what every man and woman in the world wants. A vocation." These stories are by writers who, like Anderson, have found and practice a vocation—the vocation of writing. They too are like rocks—like Anderson's literary rocks that exist as they are with no words changed.

Jon Saari

ACKNOWLEDGMENTS

Many persons have contributed to this book. First I want to thank Robert S. Fogarty, who recommended me to Robert Mandel. Bob first introduced me to the possibilities of literature when I was a student and recommended that I read *Winesburg, Ohio*.

James Thomas and Anne Shafmaster served as an editorial board for this book. Anne read hundreds of stories, and the three of us argued over, against, and for stories in a process that makes this book more than just the isolated choice of one individual. As editor I claim ultimate responsibility for the choices herein, but I could not have made the ones I did without James and Anne. All of us came away with a sense of discovery of the writers of Ohio and certainly a richer knowledge of their talent.

Bob Fox of the Ohio Arts Council was most helpful in my securing a grant for this project.

Vickie Hitchcock provided keyboarding services, as did Amy Elkins. Alan Maurice provided scanning services, and Sue Maurice scanned a number of the stories. David Comstock contributed invaluable computer assistance, as did and my wife, Peggy. Bill Clark, Cathie Apgar, Pam Burton, and Jenny Cowperthwaite provided additional computer assistance. My sons, Stephen and Aaron, helped me at the very start of this project, as did Dennis Bailey.

All the writers in this book were patient in the time it took to publish this book. To them I owe the reality of this book as well as a recognition of their regard for the special powers of the short story. Any reader of this collection will come to recognize what I mean.

INTRODUCTION

by James Thomas

"On the Edge of a State of Mind"

The state and the place of Ohio, it can be said with a certain curiousness, has been *especially* hospitable to and supportive of writers, particularly fiction writers. Curious because such a statement seems to belie the mundaneness and celebrated ordinariness we associate with the state, where average often feels like a goal. And also curious because such a statement would seem to call some kind of explanation, some reasoning to account for the exception, and such answers are hard to come by. Why Ohio?

But the facts are there. Ohio has produced, along with politicians (including eight presidents), an inordinate number of past and present fiction writers. Perhaps there is a connection. And it has also attracted them, a great many of them, though we can be sure it is neither because of weather nor scenic vista of mountain or sea.

To try to satisfy that curiosity, perhaps the *best* we can do is make some connections, both historical and contemporary, and even if sometimes tenuous or shadowy. In that spirit we might consider Ellen Behrens, one of the authors in this book, who grew up in the small town of Clyde, the actual locale of the fictitious *Winesburg, Ohio*—grew up between Sherwood Anderson's house on Spring Street and the church (on Forest Street) he made so famous, and played at Waterworks Pond. Her first job, when she was in high school, was at the little museum and library that housed Anderson memorabilia. While she would be the first to say that we can credit neither Clyde nor Anderson for her story that appears here, who can be so certain what effect that atmospheric place—with Anderson studying her, from his photo on the wall, on quiet Wednesday nights—had on her future artistic sensibilities?

Another of our authors here, Michael J. Rosen, grew up in James Thurber's Columbus—in a sleepy suburban township, for him a "personal geography, zoned in memory not square miles . . . a repository of individual experience," which, having evolved, has produced "a text of connotations that I continue to read and interpret and write." Which sounds remarkably like what we understand of Thurber's approach to *his* work, his almost obsessive use of his own local history and familial situation. It is no doubt merely coincidence, but nonetheless an Ohio coincidence that could be read as *some* kind of connection, that Michael J. Rosen is now the literary director of The Thurber House *in* Columbus, which is home not only to Thurber memorabilia but many programs and activities that continue to invigorate the Ohio literary scene.

It would be fruitless if not laughable to try to establish personal literary ghosts such as these for all the authors in this book, particularly since few of them did not grow up in Ohio; but it does seem useful to allude further to the state's rich literary heritage to which we all connect. Besides Anderson and Thurber, Ohio can claim such major American fiction writers as Harriet Beecher Stowe, Ambrose Bierce, Zane Grey, Hart Crane, William Dean Howells, O. Henry, Louis Bromfield, Kay Boyle, and, still living, James Purdy, Herbert Gold, Virginia Hamilton, and Toni Morrison. Indeed, though most of the authors in this anthology are situated early in their careers, several of them are already emerging as major figures, certainly Jack Matthews, Eve Shelnutt, and Lee K. Abbott among them.

Ohio, as a cultural entity, has been supportive of its writers in many ways, both publicly and privately. First of all, it has respected them, past and present, and has a strong tradition of celebrating its literary heritage. The Anderson Library and the Thurber House, both privately funded, are only two examples; another is the Ohioana Library in Columbus, which for nearly fifty years has been collecting and cataloging books by and about Ohioans, tracking and keeping up with that history. Now holding forty thousand volumes, it is believed to be the largest privately maintained collection of its kind in the country. Its parent Ohioana Library Association also produces the *Ohioana Quarterly* in which appear reviews of recently published books, along with literary commentary and criticism; and each autumn the organization presents Ohioana Books Awards for the best books published the previous year—Jack Matthews and Lee K. Abbott have been recipients.

Each year in Wooster, at the bustling Buckeye Book Fair, an annual event perhaps as much social as business in nature—publishers and writers and readers connecting with one another—one may observe the ever-increasing number of books published by Ohioans, as well as books published *in* Ohio, by such publishers as Carpenter Press, Pig Iron Press, Bottom Dog Press (which has a book series dedicated to Ohio writers), Swallow Press, and F & W publications where Jack Heffron, one of the contributors to this anthology, serves as a book editor—and these presses are to name but a few.

Directly supportive too of writers, providing outlets for their work as well as a sense of "community in print," are the many very fine literary magazines in the state. These include (and again to only partially list) *Ambergris, Artful Dodge, Field, Heartlands, The Journal, The Mid-American Review, Nexus, The Ohio Review, Oxford Magazine,* and *The Vincent Brothers Review.* There are also several of significant importance to literary history: *The Antioch Review* and *The Kenyon Review,* which for many years have practically served as reference texts of "where we are now" in American literature, and the recently revived *Story,* the first magazine to publish some of this century's finest fiction writers, including Carson McCullers, William Saroyan, John Cheever, Norman Mailer, and J. D. Salinger.

All of this publication points to the vigorous good health of the literary arts in the state—a life further nourished by the Ohio Arts Council through its many programs. The Arts Council, a public agency funded directly by the state legislature, doesn't just announce its goodwill and applaud literary efforts in Ohio, it puts its money where its mouth is. Through individual artist's grants, through its artists-in-the-schools residency program, through financial support of readings series, literary magazine publication, and various other special projects (including support for this book), the council has not only been part of the "accreditation process" for Ohio writers, it has literally helped sustain them financially. Only the state of New York, with twice Ohio's population, spends more on the literary arts—which to the minds of many makes Ohio number one.

But if we were trying to establish the single most identifiable connection between Ohio writers (or the Ohio "literary scene") and the state itself, by way of its institutions, we would probably have to point to the state's colleges and universities (both public and private), which historically have supported not just the study of contemporary literature but have literally supported contemporary writers by hiring them to teach that literature, and also to teach creative writing. Some call it the late-twentieth-century form of "patronage," this kind of "state support," and maybe it is; the point is, Ohio provides it in abundance.

Julie Brown, who grew up in Oregon, knew Ohio (from her wooden puzzle of the country, with pictoral symbols on each state piece) as the state that produced (not cotton or coal or cars or pine trees, but) *tires*. She was hired, a few years ago, to teach literature, composition, and fiction writing at Youngstown State University. Paul Many came from Long Island to Ohio because he thought he was in love with a woman who went to Ohio State, discovered he loved the state, and, after earning an M.F.A. at Bowling Green State University, has ended up teaching at the University of Toledo. Lee K. Abbott now teaches at Ohio State, having originally been lured from New Mexico to teach at Case Western Reserve, in Cleveland—where Mary Grimm, a native Clevelander but writer of *The New Yorker* fame, now treads the halls.

And on it goes, because the higher-education connection must be conceded: Ellen Behrens teaches at a variety of schools, including Bowling Green State University, her alma mater whose M.F.A. program in creative writing (just mentioned) is one of the oldest and most respected in the country; Robert Canzoneri is professor emeritus of English at Ohio State; Robert Flanagan is the director of creative writing at Ohio Wesleyan University; Abby Frucht's novel *Licorice* has as its "real" setting the community that is the home of Oberlin College; Richard Kraus has only recently retired his professorship at Denison University; Jack Matthews and Eve Shelnutt teach at Ohio University; Constance Pierce teaches at Miami University in Oxford.

Ohio universities support writers directly, treating them with professional respect and providing them with incomes—but even more important, through the courses those writers teach, they promote a lively and continuing interest not only in contemporary literature but also in the process through which it is created. A. W. P. (Associated Writing Programs) lists eighteen universities in Ohio that offer undergraduate programs or degree emphases in creative writing, while additional schools simply offer courses in creative writing, so that each year literally thousands of students are given the opportunity to write stories, to *be writers,* within a community (class) of writers, and get academic credit for it. What a gift to the literary life of the state!

There is a growing sense of a statewide community—as writers come together, in print and in person, at universities and at book fairs and at award ceremonies, at The Thurber House and at the Arts Council, and at the growing number of literary art gatherings, such as the Antioch Writers' Conference in Yellow Springs and the Midwest Writers' Conference in Canton. Indeed, perhaps we should not be surprised by a bimonthly publication, founded in Cleveland in 1987 by Mary Grimm and her sister Susan, called *Ohio Writer,* a publication that fosters that community by informing it, further defines it by discussing it, and awakens it with each new issue.

One may still ask, rightly, why Ohio? Why, among the states, even the Midwest states, should Ohio stand out as so particularly supportive of writers? There seems to be no truly good answer, and steadily we seemed reduced to a sort of historical and mathematical observation. Ohio was once "the West," and attracted huge populations from the Southeast and the Northeast. Ohio was once the *new* "melting pot" of this nation, a status it has never given up. Ohio, with its hills and Honda plants and vineyards and vast stretches of road bordered on one side by cornfields and the other by computer companies, but no seas or mountain vistas, seems insistent on being the harbor of the central— okay, maybe even "the average." Columbus and Dayton, it is said, are the best test markets in the country for new products, new programming, new ideas. New ideas?

There it is! . . . maybe. Is it possible that centrality and gravity, identity and a lack of it, can itself account for this curiosity? It seems as good an answer as any. Ohio is sort of everywhere and nowhere at the same time, or as Louis Bromfield said (in *Pleasant Valley*), the state ". . . the farthest west of the east, and the farthest east of the west, the farthest north of the south, and the farthest south of the north." Where better, than on this interior edge of the country where the average may be elevated to the unique, to anticipate support for what is at the cutting edge of any culture: art. In this case, literary art; and at *its* edge fiction, the art form that directly and through narrative informs us about ourselves, how we live, the culture *in which* we live.

Please read, enjoy, and learn from these stories. They *are* about us.

In one way or another they are all about Ohio, whether set here or not, because Ohio is the central place in which we all live, from which we are all listening. Read and enjoy these stories, which come to you *by way of* Ohio.

ORDINARY LIFE

by Mary Grimm

Once we dropped acid. It wasn't anything much, some laughs and the walls came closer and farther and some of the usual, I guess. We were at Janie's house, I was staying overnight, and her dad came home. So we went to bed because he yelled at us.

We tried to sleep, but it was like there was a movie running in my head, and I just lay there with my eyes open in the dark. But after a while I went to sleep. And then I woke up because Janie was screaming and screaming from outside on the front porch. I ran out, and her dad ran out in nothing but his shorts and we held her arms where she was standing at the top of the steps looking down. I was still flying and it was like there was a mist around my ankles, like the air was getting solid from the bottom and there was a mist at the bottom of the steps. I thought if there was something down there that made Janie scream I wouldn't be able to tell. There were only five steps. "Hold on, hold on," Janie's dad kept saying.

Later in the dark in bed I said to Janie, "what was it?" We were coming down then finally, and it was so cold, I could feel the cold coming like a real thing from the windows, and the street light was such a cold color. We were together in Janie's bed because we were afraid, and I held her hand and begged her to tell me what it was she saw. "What was it you saw down there?" I said, "please Janie, please." But she wouldn't. She said, "nothing." I lay there with her all night as close as we could, and she didn't sleep. I could feel what she saw in her mind, that it kept her from closing her eyes and letting go.

But that's all in the past now. I don't do that stuff now, and I don't drink all the time either. I don't live over the bar anymore, where Janie and I lived later when we were on our own—not that I think the less of anyone who does. It's a place, isn't it? And the bar had a lot of nice people who went there. Everyone asked after each other, and we all had our own mugs, the regulars did, hung up from a hook with our names on them. Where I live now is a half a house with an old landlady downstairs. She's all right. She watches the kid sometimes when I have to work late. You can't live by a bar with a kid.

I've got my friends and they're perfectly nice. A lady next door, older with four of her own. We go to bingo together, and sometimes I babysit for her. Two girls from down the end of the street at the apartments. We go to the movies or on Fridays to a real nice bar with music and then out to breakfast at Denny's. And there's some girls at the plant I eat lunch with—they're from on the line and I'm in bookkeeping, but we get along. I don't talk to anybody who looks weird or like they don't care what happens.

And I don't think about Janie or those times hardly ever. They were hard in some ways, it was a hard life. Before I lived with Janie I lived with my ma, but I don't remember much about that. I only saw her in the day, or she'd come in and yell at me when I was asleep. What'd she want? I had a job—my first job—on the line. I was giving her money. And after that Janie and I got the rooms over the bar. We were pretty happy then for a while.

So it was hard, not much sleep or ever enough money, but we had some fun, we had some good times then. And when I say that I don't mean just that we were drunk or doped up all the time, or driving around in smooth cars with strangers, or guys giving us presents and buying us dinners. There was something else.

You never knew at breakfast what would happen by dark. We met people and went off with them forever, and we came back the next day or the next week. I'd get out of work and take a shower to get the plastic smell out of my hair, and Janie would get back from this great job she had where she was receptionist for a doctor and a dentist. We'd do up our hair, I would give Janie different styles, like curls all down one side, or swept up. And we'd eat just a little something, sitting at this round yellow table we had in our robes or just underwear—a hamburger or a cheese sandwich, or maybe donuts, and we'd talk about who we were going to see, or who we saw the night before or last week or whatever.

About seven we'd start getting dressed. Everything had to be just right. I had one outfit that I really loved—a pink sweater with beads on it in a pattern and puffed sleeves that I wore with white pants and a special pair of earrings. Every time I wore it I felt like a star, like my hair was extra blonde. I only wore it about once a month.

In the summer, the windows would be open and we could hear cars outside and people yelling to each other and the back door of the bar downstairs opening and closing, opening and closing, while Ray the owner did stuff to get ready for the crowd. The air would come in hot and smelling already like cigarettes and perfume. As soon as I put on makeup I'd start to sweat.

In winter there'd be frost on the windows so you could only see out from the middle, and we'd dress in front of this little heater that was in the big room. We'd have to wear our coats over our good clothes. We'd run down the stairs and around the side yard where there was always ice on the bricks and step from one dry patch to another like a dance so as not to fall in our heels and good clothes. Janie was always ahead of me, dancing faster from one red brick to another and sliding sometimes across a whole white sheet of ice that I crossed in tiny steps.

Inside we'd stop and walk in slow. Sit at our regular spots at the bar—slow. Order a beer and sip. Sometimes you could figure out your whole night right then. You knew you'd just hang around with the old standbys, nice guys who you knew everything they would do. And this was all right. But other times we felt wild, and someone would come in that was wild too, and those were the times that anything might happen.

On a regular night we drank beer or seven-and-sevens or a silly drink for a change, one with cream or sweet stuff in it. But when it was the other kind of night we drank gin on ice in a boot mug, with a piece of lemon in it. Ginny the barmaid knew what we liked. And then we'd watch. We'd sit in our spot at the end of the bar where we could see the door. It was always different. Sometimes a guy would look at me like he knew I'd be there and I was the first thing on his mind. And I'd look back, and away, and he'd walk all the way along the bar like I was pulling him on a string till he was right behind me, where I could feel him an inch away from my back. I'd look at Janie and she'd nod. Or Janie and I would pick some guys out and work it so that they'd come over to see what was up. Or sometimes we'd even go over to them—

Janie liked to do this more than I did. She'd go over and ask them right out for change for the juke box. If they said yes, she'd ask them what their favorite song was. If they said no, they didn't have any, she'd say, "Well, it's time you did." Those nights we'd stay until twelve maybe. "Let's go someplace else," one of the guys would say, and him and his friend and me and Janie would go out into the night.

Or sometimes it would be a guy we knew, but someone who was really wild, with a life where it was always strange, like Rocket. Rocket was a stripper at those bars for women, and he was crazy, crazier than Janie and me ever were. When he came in you had to think if you were up to it. "Are you psyched?" Janie would ask me. With Rocket, we didn't stay but until eleven. Rocket always had a plan and you had to go along, you had to hang in there with him.

What did we do? Let me just tell you this once. Rocket comes in one night. "I got a party," he said. "Are you girls ready for some high life?" So Janie said to me, "Are you psyched?" And I said sure and off we went in Rocket's car, a black Mustang that according to him, some woman gave him. "So what is this party?" I said. And he said it was for some old rich woman, a surprise birthday present from her bridge club that he should strip for her. "You can say you're my assistants," he said, and Janie and I figured what the hell.

We'd seen him strip before, at the club where he was a regular. His name was outside in pink lights, second on the bill after Colt-45 Cody. I'd always thought it was a little scary, how all those women grabbed at him and yelled. But that was nothing like it was at this rich woman's house with no m.c. or bouncer and all their husbands gone. It was in the basement, but the basement was like a whole other house, nicer than the nicest parts of any house I'd ever seen. Everything was in smooth colors, creamy-looking greens and pinks, and everything was soft-looking and curved. But all these women in like pearls and hundred-dollar dresses—they were high as kites and out for a piece of Rocket. "Why doesn't he mind?" I said to Janie. Watching them yank or feel up whatever part of him was close made me feel strange—pulled apart, with a dry feeling at the back of my throat so I could hardly swallow. Rocket said we were his sisters, and we had anything we wanted to eat or drink and no snotty remarks. We sat behind the bar that was all along one side. Come on over here, the women said to us, but I felt funny about it, and Janie stuck by me.

So it was crazy, but Rocket could handle it, and Janie and I were just sitting back and eating things we didn't even know what they were. You don't look like Rocket, a woman kept saying to me. "You're so pretty, but you don't look like Rocket," she said. "Your hair is so pretty, but it's not like Rocket's." She leaned over the bar with her back to all the screaming and dancing and kissing, and looked right into my eyes and I was glad of Janie. Then the woman's husband came home. It was out the back door with hardly our coats and Rocket in his silver underwear. He had the money though—two thousand plus tips, think of it. We partied the rest of the weekend.

But things changed. They looked better because then was when I met Carter and we saw each other all the time. We tried to stay away from each other because he was engaged to someone, had been for four years, ever since junior year in high school. But we couldn't. For a while his fiancee would follow us in different cars, just follow us around. She never did anything but I didn't like it. We'd be at the movies and she'd be there when we came out. Or eating burgers and she'd come in and sit at the other side of the room. I hated it. She was like a ghost, like we were being haunted. I felt she had no right to hang over me and Carter like that. But then she gave up and it seemed like Carter and I had nothing to do but be happy.

That was all he wanted, Carter said, that I should be happy. We had matching shirts and rings. He was always bringing me something, and for Janie too. One time we went to the bar, it was our six-month anniversary and he ordered me one of every drink they had. When he had to go to Columbus once, he had his buddy follow me around to see that I didn't get bothered by anybody. I felt like a rock star, with my own body guard. When it was over, I used to think about all that stuff, and it was hard, because I knew nobody would ever take care of me again like Carter did.

The last time I saw him he hung on to me like he would never let go or go away, but what he was telling me was that he was gone. "Think about me, don't think bad things about me. Promise me you won't," he said. He was drunk out of his mind and he broke the mirror on the closet door that Janie and I used so we could see how we looked all over. When he left I went to bed and slept for four days, like a dead person, Janie said. She got scared and tried to wake me and finally when she couldn't she called my ma. I couldn't blame her. My ma wasn't so bad about it. I had to have somebody then, and what was Janie supposed to do? She had her job and you have to have a life of your own.

After Dusty was born I thought somehow things would go back to like before, but it wasn't just my shape that was different. I can't complain. Now when I go out, I am careful. I'm saving up for appliances and a car. Things are really pretty good. I thought about this when I went to Peg's, my married friend's house, for a party she had—a Christmas decoration party. She is so solid in her house, where everything there is hers, she can put her hand on anything in it and know whose it is or what it's for. The party was nice, matching paper table cloth and napkins and all little bits of food that you could eat with your fingers and punch with sherbert and rum in it and party favors for everyone—a pin with red berries and green leaves on it and your name. You didn't have to buy anything, but everybody did because we all like Peg. I bought an angel with crinkly blonde hair and a star on her head to put at the top of the tree.

Really, I had a good time. I ate some of everything and I had a little talk with Peg's mother-in-law who told me how it used to be in the old days and about her dead husband and all. I got the recipe for her chocolate Christmas tree cookies from Peg. At the end, when everybody was silly from the punch and didn't want to go home, they had fortune-telling, a game where you could play with this board and it would tell you the answers to questions, like would your husband be faithful, or would you meet someone out at bowling. It was fun, but when it was my turn I said, "no, not for me." I couldn't, even though they probably thought I was nuts or afraid. What it was though was that I'm not sure I want to know what is going to happen.

I took my cake pan and the angel home with me, and crossing the street I looked down at the bricks and thought about Janie. "Why don't you come down to the bar and party?" she'd ask me sometimes after Dusty was born and I'd always say I would. But I didn't. Or she'd remind me about something that happened when we used to hang out together, like the time when a cat got in to the bar and ran around like it was crazy and Ray the owner caught it and threw it out like it was a person—"Get out and stay out," he said.

And then two years ago she was killed, run over by a car in front of her house, in a second. When I came, there was only her blood in the spaces between the street bricks. And for a while I thought that this was what she saw that long time ago when she was standing on the porch steps with her dad and me holding on to her arms, was herself, dead, with blood spreading out from her hair. And I thought she should have told me. I felt like if she told me we could have held it off, together we could have done something. She was always like that, even though we were best friends, she kept things back. She'd hold on to it until it didn't make any difference any more.

But now I think it wasn't that. That she didn't see it ahead, didn't know—and this is worse—that maybe I didn't know her so well as all that. We neither of us looked ahead or even tried to, because what was going on right around us seemed like all there was and all we wanted. But if she'd known? And then I think, what good has it done me?

I know what I want now, and this is a good thing, even if I don't get it. This is it: what I want is a house and more kids, a little girl especially, and a nice yard. I want to brag to the girls where I work how big my kids are getting, and how they wear out their shoes and clothes faster than I can go out and buy them new ones. I want a washer-dryer and a dishwasher and a freezer as big as a boat. I want things that match and things made to go together. I want things that I made myself because I couldn't find any readymade that was just right. I want things that are just the right colors and sizes and shapes. I want for someone to come home all dirty from his job and for him to take a shower and we will make love and eat the dinner that I kept warm for him. I want all these things. I want them all even if I can only have them for a little while.

GETTING EVEN
by Lee K. Abbott

The ruckus started while I was on the phone to my fiancée, Mary Ellen Tillmon, attempting to explain why I was in the El Paso Airport Hilton Hotel instead of in her arms there in Denver.

"I got bumped," I told her. "Continental said they'd get me on tomorrow's flight. Promise."

"Oh, Walter," she said, "you just naturally find ways to foul up, don't you?"

That's when we heard it, the hooting and shrieking, and if I'd known then that out in the hall, that August 1968, was a kid named Alton Corbett—"Buttermilk" to those in our fraternity who knew him better—then there'd be no good versus evil to tell you about, and I'd be just another grown-up here in Deming, New Mexico, concerned only with the beef cattle I raise, the dues I owe the Mimbres Valley Country Club and the bad rings that cause my Jeep to go *chuck-chucka-chug*.

"Get up, you sons-of-bitches," he was hollering, running from one door to another, banging and kicking and stomping. "Watch what's going on!"

"Who you got in there with you?" Mary Ellen said. "You're in the bar, aren't you?"

There was screeching that was neither jet planes nor the Clyde and Jim-Bob cowboy music from the lounge on the first floor.

"Wait a second," I told her, half scared. I had nearly three thousand dollars on me, down payment on a shipment of yearling shorthorns my daddy had sold to Del Norte Packing, a feedlot outfit.

"Out of bed, out of bed, out of bed" is what I heard when I eased my door open, and what I saw, flying at me an arm and a leg at a time, was a young person, hair like a haystack, wearing Beach Boys swimming trunks and hurling himself against every closed door on his way.

"Turn on your TVs," he was ordering, smacking a wall a few paces from my own. "They're beating the living shit out of us."

"Buttermilk?" I said, not loud enough to be heard. A Senior, he'd been the pledge chairman when I rushed Lambda Chi as a Freshman, and back then he'd looked like my mother's idea of a bank teller.

"What is it?" Mary Ellen said.

I had switched on the TV—to what the next day's papers would describe as the "overreaction" of the Chicago Police Department to the demonstrators, people more or less my own age, protesting at the Democratic party's national convention. "Ladies and gentlemen," an announcer was saying, "Ladies and gentlemen—"

"Walter, answer me," Mary Ellen was saying. "You still there?"

"Yes," I said. "I'm here," I said.

On the screen, people were being chased by Jeeps with barbed-wire barricades attached to their bumpers, and out in the hall, harsh and spooky and impossible as the images CBS was showing me, raged Buttermilk Corbett.

"I gotta go," I told Mary Ellen.

She was yapping about her own father, Harvey ("Hootie") Tillmon, and what he expected from a son-in-law, which concerned a character upright and stubborn as a tree stump, when I heard Alton Corbett calling a West Texas hotel guest a retrograde, neo-bullshit Fascist fuckface.

"Listen," I said, "I'll call you tomorrow."

"You don't get involved, Walter," she said. "You hear me?"

I had graduated from New Mexico State University in Las Cruces the previous May, but what I knew about Vietnam and foreign policy and LBJ or Hubert Horatio Humphrey and The Vietnam Day Committee was vastly inferior to what I knew about Natural Resources Economics, Agricultural Materials Processing Systems and Field Crop Breeding, the courses I'd taken so that I could inherit my father's ranch and thus be as carefree, raw-boned, tanned and well-regarded as he. That's what I was thinking about when Alton Corbett slapped my door—what crop-drying and soil conservation had to do with riot and turmoil and head-banging.

"I know you're in there," he was hollering, thudding at my door. "Channel four. It's happening, the revolution."

I'd been face to face with Alton exactly once: He'd stopped me out-

side Young House, the English building, snatched off my Derby Days
hat, and told me to recite for him—backwards, for crying out loud—
the Greek alphabet. "Now," he'd said, and that was all until, when I
sputtered between omicron and tau, he shrugged and muttered, with
more sympathy than malice, "Good God, what a geek."

Down the hall, in front of the room that turned out to be his, Alton
was engaged in a dramatic finger-pointing and head-wagging conversa-
tion with a man built like an Amana refrigerator, while across from me
a woman in a poofy cocktail dress red enough to glow in the dark was
saying, "Get him, Billy Puckett. Punch him in the nose."

"See?" Alton hollered. "This is what it's all about."

Up and down the corridor, folks, like bystanders at a car wreck, were
peering out their doors, abashed and aghast, why-mouthed or huh-
faced, and maybe—I'm not sure—I had the idea to shoo them away,
or turn this off like the TV Alton had ordered us to watch.

"What're you looking at?" Alton was saying. "I'm an impassioned
man, that's what. You people are weasels."

You couldn't hear much from Billy, the big man, except a kind of
growling and, given the fury his size could be, the oddest, most inappro-
priate phrases, like cussing in church: "Pipe down, son. Put a lid on it."

Alton's head jerked up and down, hands waving. He shouted a sentence about brutality and injustice and what would come around if it
went around. "Go ahead, clodhopper. See what happens."

"Aw, Jesus H. Christ," Billy was saying. "Why me?"

We'd come to a point where that hollering woman's boyfriend (I
found out later that they'd known each other about five hours) had decided—with real reluctance, I believe—to coldcock my former frat
brother.

"Son," Billy began, his fist up for everyone to see. This was less to
hurt than to get Alton Corbett's much-divided attention. "Why don't
you go back to your room now? You got everybody excited here."

"Go on, Billy," the woman shouted. "Mash that little bug. I hate
them when they grin like that."

She had a cigarette going, her face as shiny as an eggplant, and I
thought how nice it would be to see her catch fire and disappear in a
cloud of smoke; and then my attention shifted to Alton Corbett and
how his eyes, now fixed on mine, had filled up with light and recognition.

"What say, geek?"

Something hot shot through me at that instant, I swear, and my instinct was to throw up my own hands and wave all of them—Alton, Billy, the woman, that man in his baggy pj's and that lady in her pink bathrobe—into never-never land.

"What're we gonna do with this here proto-dipstick?" Alton said. "I recommend we give him kisses then turn him loose with a grin and a way to go."

Here it is, when I play these actions back in my mind, that what happened becomes less a movie than a slide show, each image sharp and surprising, violent as a nightstick: Sighing as if extremely tired, Billy punched; Alton Corbett collapsed; Billy said something intended to be the final word; Alton Corbett took exception and, from his knees this time, toppled over in a heap; and then, with Billy trudging back to his girlfriend—"I'm sorry, folks," he was saying, "I'm normally real peaceful myself"—three El Paso policemen appeared, and Alton Corbett, a welt on his cheek and his lip already swollen, arranged himself on the carpet, crossed his legs at the ankle and folded his skinny arms across his chest as if for a nap.

"Hey, Walter," he called. "This is what's called passive resistance. We go limp and think about being communists."

"Yes," I had said on the phone. "I am here," I had said.

"You know that shithead?" This was Billy's girlfriend again, her face a puzzle of pride and contempt, and I saw in her then what I eventually saw in Mary Ellen Tillmon when, over the next six and a half years, I screwed up.

"Outrage, repression, lies," Alton was saying, less his innermosts than an *i-before-e-except-after-c* recitation. "Shame on you bozos. This is a bourgeoisie insult."

In the woman's room before the door slammed shut, Billy was slumped at the foot of his bed. Behind me, my TV was going, the shouts and screams from it tinny and too cowboys-and-Indians to be real; and down the hall, a cop holding each wrist and the third grabbing his wriggling legs, Alton Corbett was being dragged toward the exit.

"Hey, Walter," he said. "Are you gonna help me or what?"

Then it was over, everybody else back indoors, nothing to indicate who'd done what or why. I felt cold, I remember, and took in the interesting way goose bumps came to my arms then disappeared. I could hear my own breathing, not ragged or quick, and wondered what hour it was, what day.

Something happened to me that night, I have concluded. Something as dire as death—or marriage or childbirth or bankruptcy—is for others; but as these events took place—when I was twenty-one, smart only about what multiple-choice and fill-in-the-blanks can teach you, and stuffed with facts the value of which I couldn't have said in a million words—I didn't know what to think; or, having thought, what to do. Instead, feeling sneaky, I tiptoed to his door, pushed it aside and stepped in, my conscience, which I imagined in the Hibbs and Hannon cowboy hat and Tony Lama boots my father wore, saying, "Walter Junior, you dumb peckerwood."

Alton Corbett's room was the mess a whirlwind leaves behind. Plus it smelled like four dogs had been in there, stale and close and wet. The linen from the twin beds, mattresses shoved sidelong, was flung everywhere (I found a pillow in the bathtub), and the towels, soaked and knotted, were piled on a chair. This had been a place of panic and frenzy, as wrong as an umbrella blown inside out. What clothes he had—Levi's and socks and two button-down shirts like lawyers wear—were scattered on the floor, his Converse tennis shoes atop the TV, which was on but silent.

On the screen, crowds were running helter-skelter, as my cattle do when heat lightning strikes. A kid who looked like Wally Cleaver was dragging a sawhorse and pumping his fist, his mouth gulping air after air after air. In another scene, junk—ashtrays and trash cans and an easy chair—came hurtling down from the upper floors of a building that was itself a Hilton Hotel. The pictures kept coming, jagged and bouncy and tipped over. You heard not words, I was sure, but grunts and moans independent of thought, not from the brain but from other corners of the body.

Alton had a case of Coors beer in there, and I drank a can, the first mouthful tangy but still cold. Outside, it was quiet, eerily so, as if, were I to peek out the curtains, I would find myself upward toward heaven, my company the twinkly faraway stars children wish upon. "Alton Corbett," I said, not the last time I'd say his name to myself. I wondered how he'd gotten his foolish nickname and recalled that he lived in Raton in the north near Colorado. He could flat-out shine a shoe, I'd heard, and owned the first waterbed in the frat house. His pals were named Mink and Univac and Rubberman, and his car—I don't know why I remembered this—was a Chevrolet Monza Spyder, gold with wire rims; and then, at the moment I noticed his half-eaten room-service hamburger, next to his Longines wristwatch on the dresser, and observed a squad of blue-helmeted Chicago police charge willy-nilly into a line of boys and girls, I felt myself seize up inside, as if the engine of me had clicked and clanked and stalled, nothing in America to start me going again.

"Aw, Christ," I muttered, my words those Billy Puckett had used when he too realized he had unpleasant business to do.

Alton was being held at the Stanton Street precinct house, a cinder-block box that now is a Bob's Big Boy restaurant; the man I had to talk to sat at a counter in the booking room. Behind and above him hung video monitors showing what was going on in the cells: Alton was curled up on his cot, still barefooted but now in a too-small T-shirt.

"Been like that since we brought him in," the man said. "Did some singing for a while, then zonked out. Real polite."

I held up Alton's overnight bag.

"Could you see he gets this?" I asked. "Personal articles."

The man passed me a property sheet to fill out. *A comb,* I wrote down. *A Norelco electric razor.* I watched my hand on the page, noticed the pen I was using so badly. I was having trouble spelling, which I am usually expert at, and could not scribble my address down without getting the Star Route backwards. Overhead, like a ghost, Alton lay on his back, his dreams evidently agreeable enough to make him smile.

"How much is bail?" I said, and this time the sergeant showed me another clipboard of papers, an arrest card smudged with Alton's fingerprints, plus information regarding hair color and date of birth. He was a flyweight, I read. He had brown eyes. He had a vaccination, smallpox, on his upper left arm.

"Let's see what we got here," the man said. It was a list of misdemeanors that seemed little-related to what I'd seen hours before: disturbing the peace, public nuisance, interfering with something-or-other, assaulting an officer, fourth-degree vandalism, failure to this and that, giving false witness—

"What's that for?" I wondered.

The sergeant smiled. He had forearms like Popeye's and one tooth brown as saddle leather. "Claimed he was Fidel Castro."

Alton's had been the last room in the back of the frat house, over his door a hand-lettered sign: ABANDON ALL HOPE YE WHO ENTER HERE. It was Dante, he'd told everybody, a name laughable in my sophomore World Lit lecture for ideas of hell that didn't include sand and sun and wind, the natural elements we were familiar with.

"How much?" I asked, wondering why my head hurt.

"Almost two thousand. Which he forfeits if he doesn't show for court."

I was thinking of a course I'd aced, Principles of Animal Nutrition, and the joke-minded professor who'd taught it, then looked down to find my wallet in my hand. *What do you get when you cross a gorilla with a vulture?* we'd been asked once. *Who's buried in Grant's tomb?*

"You a relative?"

I shook my head. "Acquaintance."

This wasn't anything, I was telling myself. This was merely Walter Seivers Johnston, Jr., all six feet of him. This was but one person helping out another, much as strangers will do. This was only money and did not involve, like love or friendship, other things that can be given back and forth.

"You gotta sign," the sergeant said. "A receipt."

I made the *W* and *J* of me readable from across the room, and was almost out the door to the parking lot when the man asked if I was going to stay. "Be a half-hour," he said. "More paperwork."

Omega, I thought, suddenly as Greek as Aristotle. Psi. Chi. Phi.

"You can pick him up around back," the man said. "Gonna be real difficult to get a taxi."

"No," I said, and, a dozen giant steps later, I was gone.

Almost six years would pass before I would indirectly hear about Alton Corbett again, during which time mine was a life that proceeded fecklessly from A to whatever B was. I married Mary Ellen Tillmon in 1969 and lived four entirely blissful years as the ramrod for the Double H spread northeast of Colorado Springs. Every morning I showered in cold water, ate with a he-man's heartiness and hollered "how-do" to the outdoors before me. Then, in 1973, as my father was campaigning for the state senate in New Mexico, he had a heart attack and, according to my mother, after cursing himself and every derelict Democrat he knew, he died, which brought to the ranch me and Mary Ellen (then almost a mother herself to what is now the most helplessly beautiful girl in the Southwest). In the next year, notable in public affairs because of Patty Hearst and the resignation of President Nixon, my mother moved out to town, a tidy Victorian house on Iron Street (where she still resides and from which she calls me nearly every day to learn how her wealth is doing).

I liked this life, I am telling you; I was content doctoring spavin and founder and worms and wolf teeth in my wide-ranging livestock, and congratulated myself on knowing what grasses are edible, what not. I liked my foreman, a Jalisco wetback named Rojo, and my mostly good-humored roached-mane cutting horse, Skeeter; and there was much pleasure to be found, in our Julys and Augusts, in just floating naked in a stock tank, my brain as uncluttered and calm as the horizon, any notion of Alton Corbett as far from me as the moon is from Miami.

"I'm an old cowhand," I'd sing, my warbling weak in the wind, "from the Rio Grande."

I liked, too, sitting in my office, an outbuilding I'd converted, where I studied graphs of the stocks I owned, seeing how, in a pattern heartening to behold, my BioGen and PolyTch had gone mainly up and up and up. I had my *Wall Street Journal,* rousing shoot-'em-ups by Eric Ambler and the man who gave us James Bond, plus what reached me via the *Deming Headlight* and *Sports Illustrated,* and conceived of relations among folks to be as straight and true as a surveyor's section line. Hell, I was even pleased to learn—from KTSM, the only TV channel my antenna could pick up in those days—that Billy Puckett, the man who'd whacked Alton Corbett, was a coach with the University of Texas-El Paso Miners. I was pleased with all close and not, until Mary Ellen, citing irreconcilable differences (which had to do, I think, with the seductions towns are and how shopping is at the malls in Albuquerque), moved out, taking our daughter, June Marie, with her—whereupon I went from stunned to baffled to very, very quiet.

And Alton Corbett entered my life again.

It was a small item really, six lines in the "Transitions" section of our alumni magazine—that page where we learn the bad luck liver cancer is or who married or what had become, say, of that chunky cheerleader who, on a dare, did the splits in Intro to Natural Philosophy. Alton Corbett, I read, was employed in Chicago, Illinois, as a financial analyst for Arthur Andersen & Company. He had married Bonnie Shaker, of Philadelphia, and they were living in Lake Forest (where, I have heard, the movie star Mr. T has a mansion).

"Well," I said, "isn't this a fine turn of events?"

I remember perusing that entry several times—the "married" and the "financial" and the "Chicago" parts—and then meandering into my kitchen to have a swallow of Jack Daniel's. I was not jumpy, or particularly smitten, as if I were no more connected to Alton than I was to the others on that page—that '71 graduate who now attended law school at UCLA, for example, or that woman who'd been appointed superintendent of the Belen Consolidated School District.

"Hang the Key on the Bunkhouse Door" was the song uppermost in my mind, by Wilf Carter.

Like an ordinarily nosy person, I had "Who" questions, and "What" and "How." I wanted to know, in detail, how he'd gone from radical (if that's what he'd ever been) to Republican, what breakfast was like in jail and even how it was to wear a coat and tie for the do's and don'ts in life. I could hear my house ticking and observed what plantlife I could see—brittlebrush and fireweed, monkey flower and beaver tail—and then, while I stood at my sink, my jelly glass empty, I thought to make that long drive to the El Corral bar in Deming and, for the first time since Mary Ellen departed, raise some pure-D, grade-A, washed-behind-the-ears Cain.

That was the night I met Jean Furgeson and fell enough in love to be her steady companion for the next four years.

"It was just one of those things," I sang, plopping onto the barstool next to her, "just one of those fabulous flings."

We'd known each other in high school, and she still looked as lively as she did in the Wildcat marching band she played trombone for—a woman whom the years had not robbed of her desire to toot, toot, toot.

"I know you, Slim?"

Hers was a suspicious face, to which, over the next few minutes, I aimed to bring a chuckle or a tee-hee-hee. Onstage Uncle Roy and his Red Creek Wranglers were providing a twangy background, a potent mixture of slide guitar and yodeling that came at you like a truckful of turkeys.

"Would you like to dance?" I asked.

Her eyes shifted to and fro, and it occurred to me how life-affirming it would be to breathe the mist or gel that made her hair so upswept and Spanish-like.

"Now, why would I want to do that?"

I managed a left-and-right with my rump, which showed I wouldn't be coarse on the dance floor, bowed as a humble servant might and at last opened my mouth to say I was filthy rich.

"Well, well," she remarked immediately, and sashayed into my arms. "This is my lucky day, isn't it?"

I want to tell you now, without meaning evil by the contrast, that Miss Jean Furgeson was as different from my former wife as gunfire is from gargling. What's more, she had virtues too—not the cooking and sewing and small-talk kind—some of which I understood while we mo-seyed round and round, Uncle Roy crooning to us, and to the citizens who were our confederates that night, his hand-me-down sentiments about love and the losing of it.

"*Bueno*," I said, when she told me that after high school she'd gone to Hollywood, where, in a slasher movie titled *Hanging Ten,* she'd played a coed especially photogenic at blood-curdling. *"Bueno,"* I said, when she told me about the bungalow she rented on Olive Street and how, cross her heart, she enjoyed her cashier's job at Meachum Chevrolet-Toyota near the interstate. "Bueno" was my word to her sign, which was Scorpio, and to her secret ambition, interior design. *"Bueno,"* I said, us sliding back and forth, the balance of her well-fit for my arms, her lips the real-life equivalent of moon-June-swoon lines you can read for yourself in ancient poetry.

And then her brow knit, and her eyes took on the telltale glimmer that is Oh-my-goodness itself.

"Why, you're Walt Johnston!" she cried.

I was, I said. I truly was.

"Hell, nobody's seen you in a long time." She gripped me by the arms, like dry goods, twisting me this way and that, looking me over. "I heard you were in Montana—maybe Wyoming."

Well, I wasn't, I said. I truly was not.

"I like you semibald," she insisted, poking me in the roll that is my stomach, and, strange to say, I felt compelled to speak about my personal life—the hollow it had lately been, its sockets and hinges, the quakes and boom-boom-boom it sometimes was.

"I like your moustache too," she said, adding that I resembled Burt Reynolds, as large a compliment as it was a lie. "You look downright jaunty, Walter Johnston."

Here we stood, cheek to cheek, cowpokes and cowgirls spinning past us in a clip-clop that is one form of music too, and I said, from the deepest parts of me—the parts that had been too long lonely, and the parts, I ignorantly believed then, not linked to anything Alton Corbett meant to me—"Miss Jean, with all respect, why don't we go to your house and be sweet to each other?"

Minutes later, separated by a squeaky brass bed and as charming in our undies as we can be, she declared, "Walter, this is for pleasure only, see?" I was watching moonbeams pour off her body and thinking unmistakably glad thoughts about the world and what we're here for. "I've been married," she said, "to Buster Levisay, you remember him?" I did not: She could have been talking about a poinsettia. "Anyhow," she said, "I'm looking to kick up my heels for a time, just have some fun, okay?" I could grasp the wisdom in what she was saying and, in a paragraph, told her so.

"Good," she announced. "I knew you were a gentleman."

She stuck her hand out and it was no effort at all for me to lean forward to shake it.

"I'd like to do some kicking too," I said. "Maybe high as yours."

These are the years—before I heard directly from Alton Corbett— that whooshed by as swiftly as years can. For my birthday that April, my thirtieth, I hired a caterer from El Paso, over a hundred miles away, who erected a tent under which, for three noisy days and nights, ca- vorted and romped virtually everybody I knew in Deming. Even my mother drove out, escorted by our banker, Mr. Dillon Ripley. The Aggie Ramblers played for me, fast tunes and slow, and a thousand times I had to drink to my health or, like the ability to juggle, another piece of good fortune. We hunted jackrabbits at night and cooked up enough beef barbeque to feed most of Luna County. Miss Jean gave me golf clubs I had no innate talent to use (like a parasol to a penguin!) and made a speech about my best point, which was honesty, and my next-best point, which was—har-de-har-har—the singing voice of a chicken.

"Mr. Johnston," she said to me later, "you're not very serious, are you?"

We were watching Buddy Merkins, the manager of the Ramada Inn, do a handstand on a picnic table, and from the scrub beyond my tack room we heard Bob Pettigrew yell about nitpicking he wouldn't any- more put up with.

"What do you mean?" I asked.

"I mean, I'm trying to figure out what I've got myself into."

I considered her and me and what there was yet to know in the world, and I decided, I think now, to take what was then my usual way out.

"Miss Jean," I confessed, "I'm just a college-educated shit-kicker with a big bank account and an open mind."

In the next years, we bet the horse races at Sunland Park and tried snow skiing at Cloudcroft and twice drove over to Arizona to see the spring version of major league baseball in Tucson and Scottsdale (dutch treat, of course). I introduced her to my daughter and was, in turn, in- troduced to her ex-husband, Buster Levisay, a lineman for Southwest- ern Bell. We were together no more than three days a week and, as the Bible says we should, I endeavored to avoid the backward glance: She had her personal business, I mine. Still, I was happiest at sundown, extreme and too stark for any artist I know, when I stood on my patch of lawn, heedlessly whacking golf balls into the hinterlands—my swing a tragedy of flying elbows and unruly knees—while behind me, on the porch, Miss Jean Furgeson, mirthful as fireworks, blasted out Beatles songs on her gleaming King trombone.

Then, as we'd begun, we ended.

"Riley Meachum has asked me to marry him," she announced one day. "And I have accepted."

She'd driven up my dirt-and-gravel road, and from the moment her red pickup pulled off the Farm-to-Market highway over a half-mile north of my house, I'd felt a shift in me, slight but as definite as what tides make.

"Hey," I said, waving good-naturedly. "What're you hungry for?"

She was stopped near my front gate before it registered that the truck bed was full of boxes and, wobbling back and forth, the wicker rocker I'd given her.

"C'mon in," I hollered. The radio was going—yakety-yak about the Ayatollah, I think, and our embassy hostages—and I had nothing to fret about but fly rubs and the quality of steel T-posts.

"You stay right there for a second, okay?" she said. "I have to compose myself."

Here it was I had a thought, too scattershot to be complete yet, and the desert, from the parched hills that looked like bumps in the distance to the crooked, scrawny mesquite bushes nearby, appeared remote and inhospitable—too farfetched to be any place but a planet like Mars.

"I have your stuff," she said.

I could see that, I told her.

"I kept the coat, all right? Sentimental reasons."

She was referring to a fox stole, her Christmas gift, and I remembered the flip-flop my stomach did when she wore it at Sylvia and Marv Feldman's New Year's Eve party.

"You should keep it all," I called. "I'm a generous guy."

In those boxes, which one by one she unloaded by herself, were other presents and necessities it had given me genuine satisfaction to buy her: stoneware and matching crockery from Sweden, the *Encyclopaedia Britannica,* porcelain figurines she'd oohed over at the White House department store, a Mickey Mouse desk lamp, a Yamaha cassette player with buttons to satisfy every need related to the playing and recording of music, a portable RCA color TV so fancy it took me a Sunday to hook up—and now the whole of it, haphazardly piled and teetering, looked like, from pictures I've seen, what those pathetic dustbowl Okies used to tote toward wherever it was they ran out of gas.

"Don't get up, Walter," she ordered.

I had made a step forward and so, good at following directions, backed up to squat on my porch. I had two wishes: for a cigarette, which I'd given up, and a bourbon, which I hadn't.

"I'll be done in a few minutes," she said.

A name had occurred to me, Alton Corbett; and, in ways central to the explanation that this story is, I felt only curiosity—not despair or fracture or anger—about what was to happen next or after that.

"You want something to drink?" I asked.

Riley Meachum, she said. Sober-minded Riley Polk Meachum. Who didn't pace at night. Or spill on himself. Or get crazy quiet. Riley Meachum, who was so chubby and wholesome it was impossible not to like him.

"This isn't strictly personal, Walter. I hope you see that. I got to be looking out for myself now, that's all."

I considered the far and near of my place—the tumbledown bunkhouse, the corrals there and there and there, one windmill yonder creaking round and round—and immediately I understood: there was a hole in me, she was saying, a fraction of me that was void as space itself. I was not a hundred percent anything, she said. Not lover or friend or daddy—not, leastways, like Riley Meachum, who was one hundred percent himself, which could be sad or gleeful or plain old humdrum, and consequently not unsettling whatsoever to be with.

"*Bueno,*" I said, a word still meaningful between us.

My possessions were now tottering against the fence and she'd swung her truck around, its polished chrome the last of her I'd see.

"Maybe I could kiss you good-bye," I said.

She looked doubtful, then aglow with an insight.

"Let's shake hands," she said.

Up close, she did not appear riven or otherwise rent inside. This was the end, is all, and we had reached it.

"Maybe you ought to lose some weight, Walter."

A wind was whistling through the center of me, bitter as those in Alaska, and for a second I was saddened that she did not feel frozen too.

"*Adiós,* Miss Jean," I said, releasing her and standing aside so she could speed away.

Many, many months would pass before I'd hear from Alton Corbett, but I did not—gossip to the contrary—become addled or crumble to pieces. I was being prepared for something, I felt. I was waiting, alert like a sniper. In the meantime, dawn to dusk, I was your common *i*-dotter and *t*-crosser. By day, I herded cattle from one scrub-flecked range to another, their mooing and hoarse bawling as sensible as any phrase from my ranch-hands. I paid for hay, fifty-pound blocks of iodized salt and the services of Dr. Weems, our vet; I rode fences and set traps for coyote. In need of shirts or pants, I marched into Anthony's department store on Zinc Street and afterwards treated myself to chicken-fried steak at Del Cruz's Triangle Drive-In. I talked on the phone to my mother, said "yes" and "no" as appropriate, and comported myself like a citizen with a serious private life.

"Alton Corbett," I said to myself. "Butter-goddam-milk."

By night, I played Nintendo Donkey Kong or watched movies like *Rambo* and anything featuring the Pink Panther. I forsook alcohol entirely, even beer. I took up reading, finding hours of delight in the crackpot vision of us offered by Sir Walter Raleigh, as well as what opinions a Dallas author named C. W. Smith had concerning good and bad. I was not shattered, I say, nor in distress nor modernistically dark-minded. Alton would phone, I felt. Or he would drive up my road. He would have a respectable haircut, shaved at the neck. And shined wing tips to see yourself in. He would be softer, spongy in the belly the way we all are, and more mindful of authority. He would have his kids, Marvin and Roylene; his wife, Bonnie Shaker; his poodle dog, Fifi. He would tell me exactly what he'd mumbled to Billy Puckett, the gent who'd clobbered him, and how fistfighting felt. He'd tell me what he'd been doing at the Hilton Hotel, specifically the circumstances that had sent him howling into the hallway. He would have words for me—dozens and dozens and dozens—and afterwards the hole in me would be filled up and gone forever.

News of him reached me in March, while I was scrubbing dishes and ruminating over such crossword clues as "lark or light preceder" (three letters, across) and "saturate" (six letters, down). I saw Cash Corrum, our mail carrier, park his Buick at my box next to the highway, heard him honk to tell he was done, and—saucepan there, coffee cup here— I did well to ignore the clatter and jangle and rattle my feelings were.

"I'm an old cowhand," I sang, riding my Honda trail bike over three cattle guards to a stop beside blacktop that ran east and west into nothing.

I could smell rain, I remember, and noted the cloudwork rumbling my way from California.

"Okay," I told myself, and opened my box to find what I knew would be there.

In typeface fussy as that Miss Jean had bought to announce her nuptials almost two years before, it was an envelope from Hewey, Stone, Tyler & Dowes, "Investment Counselors" on Montrose Street in Houston. An alarm had gone off in me, wicked and whiny, and I wondered naturally how Alton had gotten from Illinois to Texas. I thought about his wife, whom I imagined to be as tall and red-headed as Dr. Kissinger's Jill St. John, and the thousand-dollar smile she could turn on and off. I'd visited Houston and found it to have not one downtown but several, as though its people—those who needed counseling and not—were restive or too heat-soaked to make up their minds.

Sitting by the roadway, my motorcycle making a putt-putt that an hour of tuning can't reduce, I regarded the other mail Cash Corrum had delivered: catalogues to thumb through (Sears, Monkey Ward's, Horchow), bills to pay out of pocket-money, a notice about who was appearing at the Thunderbird Lounge, and a rolled-up poster that said Rob Pettigrew's goods—his four-wheel-drive Ford, his portable troughs, his ranching-related etceteras—were up for auction (courtesy of Milton Wolf and Sons).

"Goddam," I muttered, the word from me that stood for, in six letters across or down, misery and silliness and time.

It was a check, nubby as braille, plus a sheet of stationery on which interest had been calculated.

This is for your trouble was the first sentence.

A face bushwhacked me from memory—not Alton's, but Mary Ellen Tillmon's, my ex-wife's, and I heard again what she'd called me in divorce court. "Lunkhead," she'd said. "Foolhardy," she'd said. And "supercilious," an insult I'd had to buy a Webster's dictionary to check on.

At the bottom of the page was his signature, more a doctor-like scrawl than penmanship you'd recognize as heartfelt.

This isn't about him, I was thinking. This is about me.

We're even now was his second, his last, sentence.

Inside me, crude and thick, valves opened and closed.

Astride my motorcycle, I sought to concentrate very hard; and, if it helps, you can imagine Walter Seivers Johnston as an Alfalfa-like grade-schooler faced with a three-page math problem and a half-hour time limit.

Alton Corbett was even with me now, yes. But I was not even with myself.

Like a starved dog to a soupbone, I went to Billy Puckett—who had, I am happy to say, risen over the years from coach of the UTEP Miners' secondary to offensive coordinator and associate professor of physical

education. The morning after I'd read Alton's letter, I filled my Jeep
with gas and told my foreman, Rojo, that he was in charge. "This could
take a day or two," I said. "Maybe longer." In a nearly singsong state of
mind, I was joyous to see sunshine and inclined to honk "howdy" to
those I-10 motorists who zipped past me in a hurry; and hours later,
light-footed and what-have-you in spirit, I presented myself to Mr. Puckett's secretary, in his field house office, with the news that I was a reporter for the *Headlight* of Deming, New Mexico, eager to hear how
his football team might fare the following fall.

"He's in a meeting," she said. "That man is a meeting fool."

I could believe that, I said.

"Would you like some coffee?" she asked. "We have Coke too."

"That's very considerate of you," I said, scooting up a chair to talk
personal to her.

Elaine Brittle, mother of two boys (though now separated from their
tomcatting father, Archie Lee), was just tickled as all get-out to be working for a man like Billy—who, by the by, preferred to be called that
instead of his whole name, which was William M-for-Murphy Puckett II.

"Do tell?" I said, mine the other cheerful voice in that room. "That's
just like him, I hear."

On the walls hung photographs of athletes past and present, the
constant in each a smiling or serious-seeming Billy Puckett. Dressed in
shorts or long pants, wearing a gimme cap or headphones, in hooded
sweatshirt or orange pullover with UTEP stitched on the breast, he
seemed as huge as I recalled, his a personality that boys and men alike
wanted to stand next to, like a shade tree.

"You want some candy?" Mrs. Brittle asked me. It was a Valentine's
gift, she said, from Billy, and the one I chewed into, though old, was
itself as gooey as her point of view.

I was cool, my smile as disconnected from my inner organs as shit is
from Shinola. Billy was another work of wonder to me, like magic to a
kid. He had a wife, Maureen, and three children, the oldest of whom,
Lilly, was a sophomore music education major and as show-biz on the
piano as Van Cliburn. He had a house in the north valley and a mem-
bership at the Coronado Country Club, El Paso's sagebrush Beverly
Hills. He was Baptist—"though not the rednecky kind," Elaine whispered—and a Rotarian, not to mention a man who could read, well,
Henry David Thoreau and tell you what was cockeyed about selfish-
ness. "You ought to see that man fish," Elaine Brittle confided. "He'll
drop a line in a sewer, I swear."

I was collected, an ice cube inside, and mentally removed enough from myself to be in the other corner of the room, plotting; and by the time he walked in, as large in life as he was in time, and we were formally introduced, I knew his boot size, his allergies to the milk family of foods, and what year he'd received his master's degree from Louisiana State University.

"We're gonna be miserable this season," he laughed, my hand thoroughly buried in his. "I got athletes out there with only one leg, or blind."

He had aged, yes, but not as remarkably as some I knew from back then; he had a face like a cupcake, plus the fine, square-cut hair you can find on a shoebrush.

"How's Harley Edwards?" he asked, referring to the editor I'd claimed to work for; and then, in Billy Puckett's office, him camped behind his desk and me in a chair next to a window that opened onto several basketball courts a couple of stories below, a look came to his eye—a glint as important, I think, as my own—and he said, "I know you, don't I?"

His was an office spacious enough to wrestle in, and I struggled to put in order all thoughts unique to my mission here.

"Names, I'm no good with," he said. "Where I know you from, son?"

So I told him—about Alton, about the Hilton, about that night and all that had descended from it, about the sour-minded shrew he was with—

"Rita Bates," he said, his mood a bottom condition entirely, as though she was a mistake he wasn't yet through paying for. "I wasn't married then, you understand? It was a matter of oat-sowing. A matter of bad judgment."

"Me too," I said. "I was engaged."

He had put his feet up on the desk and was, with the deliberation of a traffic judge, studying what the ceiling could tell him. The air-conditioning had switched on, a frigid blast on my face, and I was waiting for some pops from my chest, something to say the cords in there had finally snapped.

"So what can I do for you?" he asked, which made it my turn to look up and down for inspiration.

"If it's all the same," I began, finding breathing easier than expected, "I'd like to slug you one."

We shared a moment then, fraught and time-filled, pointed as a nail: his feet slipped slowly to the floor, his chair groaned, his fingers went tat-tat-tat on his blotter, and there were, in the eye-to-eye we had, about ten thousand things to think about.

"Friend," he said, "your leg is shaking."

I grabbed my calf and, soon enough, brought my limb under control.

"This is important to you, I guess."

I admitted that, given the givens I was stuck with, it was.

"Holy moly," he said, not for a second speaking about God or righteous living. "Holy damn moly," he said about eight more times, and I could see his mind, as betrayed by his eyebrows and pursed lips, confront my proposal and race around it at a dozen speeds. He was bemused and taken aback and perplexed, as if I'd suggested he push a pile of peanuts across the room with his nose. I had learned from Elaine Brittle, his secretary, that he'd majored in sociology and that once he'd bench-pressed nearly four hundred pounds, and now these facts were as plain in the tilt of his head as the facts of how he slept at night and what he hollered in defeat.

"Lordy," he said, "I hate politics, don't you?"

I hastened to agree with him.

He had stood now, his shirttails tucked in, and moved his Rolodex to a spot by his phone, which was by his pencil holder, which was by his stopwatch. You could tell that, however peculiar, a decision had been reached.

"Is here okay?" he asked.

Modestly, I assured him it was.

"Hellfire," he laughed, "it's been ages since I had anything lunatic to talk about at the dinner table."

Alton Corbett wasn't with me when I hauled myself up: he was as meaningless to me as most science or what suffices for entertainment in darkest Africa. Instead, I was arguing with my knees, which seemed rusted stiff, and was tempted to apologize for the tight trousers I was wearing.

"You ever been in a fight before?" Coach Puckett said. "I mean, one with blood in it?"

I had not, so, patient as a preacher, he showed me how to make a fist, thumb outside the fingers.

"Thank you, sir," I said.

I felt like a player of his—or a former waterboy, say—who had, unaccountably but profoundly, lost his obvious way in the world.

"Call me Billy," he said.

He arranged himself then, hands on his hips, his chin thrust out palooka-style, eyes wide as if this were the Memorial Day pie toss, and I took a step back to wind up. There was only one more question to ask and, without hemming or hawing, I mustered the courage to ask it.

"You wouldn't want to get on your knees, would you?"

He tsk-tsked a bit, looking inexpressibly sad. "They're all busted up, plus there's my dignity, you know."

I knew, indeed, and stepped back again to gather myself from the million places I'd been.

"Ready?" he said.

And, for the first time in a slew of years, I was.

AN INTRODUCTION TO OPERA
by Robert Canzoneri

"Little bitty chicken pies," she sang out, closing the glass-paned door
behind her. "One apiece. Did you ever see anything like it?" She was
a large woman in a still larger print dress, thin white sweater thrown
awkwardly over her shoulders. "Not round, neither, but kind of what
you'd call oval." Jimmy had watched her come up from the sidewalk
past the barber's pole, one hand holding the sweater, the other on the
iron railing. Not a minute before, Madden had billowed out the red and
white striped cloth like a sail and let it settle down Jimmy's front. "You
want that thing run up through the opening in the back here?" Madden
had asked.

"Doesn't matter," Jimmy had said; when Madden fastened the cloth,
Jimmy could feel the wire that ran to his ear from the radio in his shirt
pocket tighten within the paper collar already around his neck.

Madden was shaking his head. "Got to have that rock and roll
twenty-four hours a day." His voice was gruff.

Jimmy worked his hand from under the cloth to unplug the earpiece
and turn it upward.

Madden leaned over to it but did not let it touch. "Huh?" He pulled
himself upright, shuffled backward a step. "What's that? Some of that
there. . . ." a glance over at Raymond, trimming away on old man Gray
in the other chair, "opera?"

Jimmy had stuck the smooth plastic back into his ear. The baritone
hunchback and his daughter the soprano were singing sad little things

back and forth in Italian. "Rigoletto," Jimmy said. The last act had just started.

"Regal what?" Madden had snipped the air with his scissors. "Wouldn't matter much if I was to slip up and cut that wire, now would it? Prob'ly be a relief."

The woman stopped in the middle of the barbershop, set herself firmly there upon the rubber soles of her low shoes. "How many little pans that must have taken I hate to think." Her voice carried within it a high trill, like a bird trying to break loose and sing. "If it was me, I'd just set out big pies and let them help theirselves."

"Sit down," Madden said to her. "No use to stand."

She shook her head. "I can see for myself he's not here yet, but if I got settled in I couldn't get up when he does come." She glanced over toward Raymond. "My husband," she said. "It's easier for him to meet me here than going all the way back to my daughter's."

Madden pointed a long tapered comb toward her. "That there's my grandmother." He held the pose, waiting. In Jimmy's other ear, the Duke and the assassin had taken over, tenor and basso; Rigoletto and his daughter, Gilda, would be looking on from outside, through cracks in the wall.

"Grandmother!" She laughed. "Cousin," she said toward Raymond. "Younger'n *him* by a year or two."

Raymond's voice was high and thin, like a wire. "She's been here before." His eyes did not waver from the delicate interaction of silent comb and humming clippers.

Madden snorted out what he seemed to intend as a chuckle. "Comes into town as much as twice a year."

Jimmy gave an involuntary jerk of the head. He had known that the Duke was supposed to go off into a song about women being fickle—Mrs. Deville had made sure he knew that—but he hadn't expected it to be music he'd heard before.

"Got to keep still there," Madden growled. He had given Jimmy every haircut he'd ever had. "One of them fat women give a screech?"

"Little what you might call individual chicken pies." The woman no longer looked from Madden to Raymond; she seemed to sense a larger audience. "A whole one on every plate, and I reckon there was a hundred people, counting me that hadn't no business there at all except my daughter had me come as what you might call a guest. Working women's luncheon, only they say it with some kind of initials that never would stick in my head, and if *he'd* known Evie was taking me to one of them kind of things, he'd of never let me off at her apartment this morning and drove on to load the pickup truck so we don't have to come in off the farm more'n once a month or so—which is not just twice a year, but feels a mighty like it sometimes after thirty-one years come the fifth of June—and her making more cash money in a week selling what they call real estate than he ever come up with in pocket, so to speak, let alone me get a chance to look at."

The Duke held a high note just long enough, Jimmy decided, to show that he could do it as long as he wanted to; now he slid off it and let his voice go bouncing downward like a ball dropped on the stairs. The orchestra gave a couple of lifts and let him bounce it down again, and then brought it up once more to let him toss it high in the air for a minute before bouncing it all the way back down into the orchestra, which caught it and went charging into the whole song all over again. Jesus, Jimmy thought; he'd felt goose flesh all down his spine. What if I get to where I like this stuff?

"And some green peas pretty near big as marbles, and a cooked crabapple so full of red dye it looked plumb unreal, that and coffee— oh, I forgot them soft little bakery rolls set out in baskets and a square of what you might call butter on a piece of cardboard—and instead of cream what they call coffee whitener in some funny-shaped cardboard, and sugar substitute in paper squares, and real sugar, too, with bird pictures like the little cards we used to get with baking soda when I was a girl."

Madden turned off his clippers, stepped toward her, stood as planted as she was. "I've got a complete set of them cards over at the house. Only one I'm missing is the Cedar Waxwing."

The Duke had ended off his second time through, not by holding a high note, but by playing around as far up there as you thought he could get and then punching it through the ceiling, the way Jimmy could toy with all but the best players at the club—let them just get a forehand, just get a backhand, barely reach another forehand, then whip it past them off the baseline.

Madden stepped back to the chair, bent deliberately toward Jimmy's free ear, said, "You wouldn't know where I could locate a Cedar Waxwing baking soda card, would you? I guess you wouldn't," and started his clippers again.

"And then for dessert they had these little glass things like candle holders, or bud vases maybe, with this kind of pink and brownish fluffed-up kind of mixture which Evie said was par-fay, with some of that what they call whipped topping on top, and it's no wonder the dairy farmers is having such a time. Did I tell you he'd sold his cows?"

Madden stopped everything again and took his deliberate step toward her. "Sold 'em?"

"Every last one, down to the littlest heifer."

The Duke was already off into another song. "Tenors get it all—in opera," Mrs. Deville had said, flecked green eyes directly into his own across the little bar table in the lounge. "Are you a tenor?" This was after she'd said, "*Mi chiamano Mimi.* They call me Mimi—a lie, but you call me that anyway," but before he'd been able to make himself think of her as Mimi, much less say it. It had irritated him that she spoke in Italian. How many times had he seen her at this same table with Harry Maggio in one or another of his expensive suits with their intricate woven figures and every line a flare?

Madden was a white-smocked statue in front of the woman. "How come him to do that?" he said finally.

Now the Duke had the contralto singing back to him. That would be the assassin's sister, who didn't know it was the Duke, of course, but seemed to know anyway that he made it to bed one way or another with every woman he saw.

"He's not the only one up our way," Madden's cousin had said. "It's all because of the new inspector they put in up there that's a woman instead of a man, and she tells them what to do, too. Told several of 'em, You got to do this and this—and mad? That's the maddest bunch of dairy farmers I ever came across, I'll tell you that for sure."

"She put him out of business, you mean?" Madden moved back toward Jimmy, lifted his arms aside, took up the position of cutting hair.

"She never got around to him. He sold out first. Said he'd gone more than sixty years on this earth without letting any woman tell him what to do, and he wasn't about to start in now." She laughed, tugging at the thin white sweater over her shoulders without budging it. "And I can stand here and tell you for a fact that he wasn't telling no lie."

Mimi Deville had watched Jimmy's reaction to everything she said with as keen an eye as his upon her backhand volley in the lesson they had just completed. ("Now, tu-r-r-rn and *punch*. Tu-r-r-rn and *punch*.") "You're unusually bright, or I wouldn't be fooling with you, but you don't know Italian, do you? Of course you wouldn't, with a name like Jimmy Rigan. Nor opera? Do you know what *opera* means in Italian? We'll just have to acquaint you with Italian opera. Which we may want to interpret as how Italians *operate*, mightn't we? The way Italians go at . . . what Italians do."

"Deville's not an Italian name, either," Jimmy had said.

"Nor is it, of course, the name I was born to." She didn't say what was. "No matter. I acquired my taste for opera. You might develop a passion for it, too, with the proper exposure." Her eyes did not waver from his. "They're doing *Rigoletto* in Cincinnati next month. Would you like to go?"

The thought of tooling down the freeway beside her in the Ferrari she always drove to the club made Jimmy bold. "Wouldn't that be an overnight trip?"

She had leaned back in her chair and laughed. "Wouldn't your mother let you out?"

"Used to be," the woman had been saying, "we got out a good bit and saw people, but you think I can talk him into budging out of that house now? Not an inch. Joined the Eastern Star long time ago and went to meetings all over this part of the state, but I guess that just what you call wore thin after a while and sort of petered out."

"You think you've seen enough that flying you did there for a while?" Raymond was asking Mr. Gray off to the side. "Or are you still at it?"

"Well, I'll tell you one thing for sure," Madden said directly into his busy hands, "he's starved for talk. *Both* of 'em's starved for talk." He backed off and looked as if in astonishment at the hair he had been shaping. "I stopped by the farm there, must have been . . . , well, it was before the trees begun to bud, and I thought I'd never get away, both of 'em talking as hard as they could go."

Mr. Gray had cleared his throat. He was the grayest man Jimmy had ever seen; had been ever since Jimmy could remember first going into Gray's Appliance Store with his mother; did everybody grow fit his name? he had wondered. "Well, yes and no," Mr. Gray was saying. "I've gone over from airplanes to gliders."

"Gliders?" Raymond said. "You mean flying around up there without no motor or anything?" He stopped cutting hair and turned toward Madden. "He taken up airplanes after his big heart attack, oh, two-three years ago. Now he tells me he's gone over to gliders."

"I know when he taken up airplanes," Madden muttered into Jimmy's free ear.

Jimmy tried to shut out the voices around him and figure out what was going on in the opera. He had studied the libretto Mimi Deville had brought to the club for him, but it was easy to get confused in the talky parts. Probably lost forever, he told himself, when off the Duke went into a song he knew about: "'Bella *figlia dell'amore,*'" Mimi had said. "Listen for that. You'll never hear a more lyrical attempt at seduction. Then try to hear the other voices come in, the contralto putting him off, the soprano heartbroken because of his betrayal, the baritone vowing revenge." She'd sat back in her chair and lifted the small glass of Amoretto she kept always before her, but did not put it to her lips. "I tell you, Jimmy, it's like being pulled apart by thoroughbred horses. It's like . . ." She did take a sip, then, eyes slowly closing so that the faint green eyeshadow lowered like a curtain. "It's the way I live."

"You'd a thought he'd a been here by now," the woman had said. "But it's a fact, you let anybody, friend or stranger, come up to the farm and him and me will just what you might call take one ear apiece and talk it black and blue. Now, me, I'll talk anytime, anywhere—ask Evie how many times she had to shush me at that lunch thing so she could hear what the speaker was about—but get him out, and not a word. You'll see, if he ever gets here to pick me up. Not a word."

Madden stopped dead still, his back to her. When Jimmy looked at him, he said, "Not a *word*?" and held his mouth open as though astonished until she spoke again.

"Not a word. And the same thing day and night with just me and him out there on the farm. He might of talked to them cows, but not a word to me, so it's all stored up and when somebody does stop by, well, you might say it's like taking a bulldozer to the dam with the pond lapping at the edges."

"It wasn't that I didn't enjoy flying," Mr. Gray had said, "but they have these regulations, you see, that at my age and with my heart condition, I couldn't get a solo license."

"Well," Raymond said, "as they say, rules is rules, I guess."

"I always had to have another pilot with me." Mr. Gray's lips scarcely moved; his face was expressionless. "And I found out that it's different with gliders, and after so many hours of instructions, I'll get to solo."

The Duke was rounding into his lilting seduction song again: "*Bella figlia dell'a-a-mo-o-re.*" That was the only phrase Mimi Deville had taught him to listen for except the one about women being fickle. "'La donna e mobile,'" she'd said, and her mouth quirked up at the corner. She had good full lips. She was, in fact, a damned good-looking woman, no matter that she must be nearly twice Jimmy's nineteen years—maybe more. Her legs were firm and tan, agile beneath the

short white tennis dress that just barely covered the white panties.
When she'd first come to him for a lesson, he had been startled at what
seemed to charge the court space between them. Months before, he
had quit even bothering to wonder where all the irresistible and unre-
sisting females were that tennis pros were supposed to have their pick
of. Now Mimi Deville had aroused in him what he had to think of as
Lust. It was like nothing he'd felt even in his fantasies about Beth
Shreiner, not only at the perfect age of seventeen, but with figure and
face so flawless and strokes so pure that the club manager claimed she
had sprung full grown from the forehead of their public relations man.
You could walk into the lounge and tell by the knot of men at the long
window overlooking the courts whether Beth was working out on three
or four or five. "'La *donna e mobile,*'" Mimi had repeated. "They
translate it sometimes as 'How fickle women are,' which fits the music,
but it's really, 'Woman is fickle.' In Italian you say *the* woman to mean
women in general." She'd given the liqueur glass a careful half turn on
the smooth table top. "The woman is fickle. Does that bother you?"

He knew exactly what she was talking about. "Yeah," he said.
"Yeah. I have to admit it does."

"Did you ever think, though, that if the woman weren't fickle she'd
never have gotten around to you?"

Madden had spoken across to Raymond as though since Mr. Gray
was Raymond's customer, he had to go through him. "I reckon he had
to wait, you know, till his kids was raised and gone before he could
afford to take up flying. Me, I might be able to get an old second-hand
bicycle, or something, when it comes to that."

Jimmy could keep the Duke and Rigoletto pretty well apart, but the
contralto and the soprano kept blending and separating. He tried to
concentrate. Mimi had told him, "We're in luck. It's going to be on the
air, this Saturday, and the more you hear it the better. I think you'll
discover that wondering what it's like is nowhere near the pleasure of
becoming so familiar with something really good, and, well, proven,
that you can appreciate every. . . ." She laughed. "Shall we say, exquisite nuance?" The green eyes had held him; despite the amusement
in them, Jimmy had felt as though he would not be able to draw his
next breath.

"Well, not really," Mr. Gray had said. "I'm still sending the second
boy to school. Wanted to study philosophy, he decided, and I figured
what does it matter that he'll never see thirty-five again? If that's what
he wants. . . ."

"You'd a thought," the woman said, "that with them cows gone he'd a wanted to get away *some* time or other and do something. Travel, maybe. I'd like to see what Florida looks like just once, but he just works around the place as much as he ever did, and don't even hear anything I mention unless it's come get your dinner."

Madden had stepped back, thinning shears and comb out to his sides like the tips of wings. As he turned his head this way and that, studying Jimmy's hair, he lifted first one leg and then the other as though his pockets were leaking change that he had to shake down to the floor. "Wish somebody'd call me to dinner," he muttered just to Jimmy. "Get me off my feet. First time all day somebody hasn't been sitting in that chair right there, waiting."

"No." Mr. Gray always spoke with muted precision. "When I was coming around after that heart attack, I just asked myself what I wanted to do in my life, and I knew that what I wanted was to be there all by myself."

"Now, that there speaker they had at that luncheon was a woman." Madden's cousin was facing a window, but although on its outside ledge a squirrel was busily nibbling at sunflower seeds ("Here," Madden had said to Jimmy. "Just look at that!"), she seemed not to see it. "I never heard a woman make a speech before—oh, a little welcome thing at Easter Star, I guess, but not a whole speech. And Evie said she was some kind of . . . femist? How you say it?"

"Feminist," Raymond piped up.

"Feminist, she told me she was, and, now, I don't know about all that, but of course it wasn't me she was talking to."

"My only disappointment," Mr. Gray went on, "is that I haven't flown by myself yet. What with the weather and finding time to get all the way over to Marion to the glider field, it's going to take me till up in the fall." His gray face came to rest for just a moment. When he spoke, it was with great care, as though any movement of the head would cause Raymond to make a terrible mistake. "I do want to get up there all by myself."

"There he is," the woman said, pointing out the door. "That's him, all right enough."

The four voices had been working their way through the intricate number, the tenor soaring out with the melody now and then, or the soprano topping them with a long high note. Now they all melted together in final harmony, like the muted Amen to some anthem Jimmy had sung with the glee club back in high school. Baritone; he had not answered when Mimi asked, "Are you a tenor?"

A man in overalls had come as far as the steps and stood waiting. "You see," the woman said, going out the door. "Not a word."

"Tell him he better get him some chickens or something to talk to," Madden muttered after the door had closed, "now that them cows is gone."

"I think I've done what I can to you." Raymond's voice was a single high thin note, unwavering. He folded the striped cloth up from the bottom and down from the top, then stepped aside. Mr. Gray slid forward in the chair, planted his thick crepe soles on the floor, raised himself above them. He drew thin-lensed rimless glasses from the side pocket of his gray sweater, settled them on his nose, thumbed the curved wires behind his ears.

Rigoletto had told his daughter, Gilda, to go home and disguise herself and escape to another city. Now he was paying the assassin to kill the disguised Duke, inside; he would come back for the body at midnight. Who is he? the deep sinister basso was supposed to be asking. He is Crime, Rigoletto was to sing in Italian before the storm broke, and I am Punishment. "Tell your mother you're going with Walter Malde, a student," Mimi had said, and Jimmy had had no idea, of course, until he'd read the libretto, that "Walter Malde, a student" was who the Duke said he was when he sneaked into Gilda's courtyard, and then he'd set it up for her to be abducted and, as Mimi had said, "deflowered. A very strange term, don't you think?"

"I'm going to step over to Vernon's for a cup of coffee," Raymond told Madden. "I'll be back in a few minutes." He laid his white jacket in the barber chair Mr. Gray had just left.

Madden stopped and looked at him. "You remember I hadn't got off for lunch or nothing yet."

"I'll be back. I wouldn't expect you'd want to eat this late, anyhow. Just ruin your supper."

Madden watched him all the way out the door and down the steps before he grunted and turned back to Jimmy. The contralto was singing to her brother the basso that they should spare the young man they did not know was the Duke, and the basso was singing back about being paid to kill him. "There's those that thinks the world owes them whatever it is they want," Madden said, "and then there's the rest of us. You still what they call a pro over at that club? Playing tennis?"

"Sure am," Jimmy said.

Madden grunted again. "That ain't going to last. Not even long enough for you to get too old for it."

The orchestral storm was over and midnight was striking as Jimmy went out into the spring afternoon. He walked under maple leaves small as the hands of his sister's tiny baby spread out to grasp whatever was in reach. He skirted broken glass upon the sidewalk, a beer bottle thrown from a car by some high school kid out on what he thought was a drunk. Gilda had returned in the guise of a man and let them stab her in place of the Duke, whom she still loved despite his perfidy, as the summary with the libretto had put it. Rigoletto had paid the basso the rest of the money and was hauling the body off in a sack, exulting in his revenge. Now the Duke, who was supposed to be in the sack, broke into song, faint and clear from the distance: "*La donna e mobile.*"

Jimmy rounded the forsythia, its long yellow spires interrupted with green leaves, and came in sight of his house. The Devilles have asked me to go to the opera with them, he would tell his mother. That's nice, she would say, but pay your own way; don't impose on their hospitality. Meanwhile, the hunchback had opened the sack and he and his dying daughter were singing final sad things back and forth to each other.

RABBITS, LIVE AND DRESSED

by Paul Many

When I was ten I got a rabbit for Easter. It was tiny and white and the lady next door gave it to me. The lady was old and smelled like bandages when you first take them out of the box. She said her rabbit had a litter and I could have one of her "little babies" if I wanted it.

I kept it in a cardboard box lined with shredded newspaper. It was kittenlike and fun to play with. I named it Booju, and fed it out of a toy bottle my sister used for her dolls. Then it got bigger and bigger and my father built a hutch for it from two-by-fours and chicken wire out in back of the house.

I kept it for a year, until it got fat and sluggish on its water-and-wilted-lettuce diet. Then it was Easter again and the lady next door said she would trade me Booju for another little baby. I was glad to be rid of the old sleepy rabbit, for the tiny toylike one. I named the new rabbit Jimbo.

The lady made the same trade with me four years in a row. By then I was old enough to figure out what was going on—I broke into a cold sweat the day it hit me. The fifth year when she came over, the cute little bunny in the palm of her hand, I said no, I liked the old one just fine.

In one town we lived in, we rented a hundred-year-old farmhouse. The landlord, who was a great-grandson of one of the original settlers of the area, lived next door. He had an old Labrador mutt named Cinder. Cinder was nearly blind from the bluish-white cataracts that covered each eye, and hard of hearing, but she was nimble enough for her age.

One day she flushed two rabbits out of the landlord's vegetable garden. They tore hell-for-bunnytail out of the back yard and through the side yard, heading for the road, Cinder lumbering behind. Just when it looked like they were safely out of her reach, one suddenly came to a dead halt. The other kept moving, throwing in a few extra zigs and zags and high kicks for effect.

Cinder ran right past the stalled rabbit, which must've stopped its heart so its blood vessels wouldn't pulse. As the other rabbit reached the road, it made a 180-degree hop like an Olympic swimmer doing a flip turn and ran right between Cinder's legs.

The dog changed direction about as well as an ocean liner, and by then the two rabbits had joined up again and were halfway back to the garden. Cinder closed the distance, but just as it seemed she might have them, they slipped through the fence at the back of the yard and she had to screech to a four-paw stop to avoid mashing her muzzle on the wire.

To save his garden, our landlord had to start letting out the cat.

Rabbits run across the road a lot out here in the country. It must be partly sport. Sometimes they lose their nerve halfway across, though, and try to run back. That's usually when, despite some fancy driving, you hear a thud and somehow through all that vinyl and carpeting and steel and rubber you feel them squirm as you roll over them. Then you get a feeling in your stomach, like you've just swallowed a ball of fur.

A friend of mine told me what to do for your peace of mind in such cases. When you get home, he said, find a quiet spot to sit. Then close your eyes and call up the rabbit's spirit—"soul" is actually the word he used. Tell it you certainly didn't mean for this to happen, that it was just one of those things and you are sorry.

Then release the spirit so it can go wherever rabbit spirits go. In its rush it will take along its hot, furry guilt.

I was raking leaves late last fall. It was a cold, rainy day, but leaf pickup was scheduled for the next morning and I didn't want a truckload of tree droppings mouldering in the yard all winter.

As I raked the wet leaves onto a tarp, I saw some movement under the hedges that surround the yard. I went for a closer look, and saw it was a rabbit sitting in under there looking at me. He didn't move. That's when I saw that his magnificent hind legs were splayed out flat. There was no blood, but apparently he'd been run over.

I went back to raking my leaves. It was getting dark and there was nothing I could do for him. He crawled out from under the hedges and began dragging himself across the yard, apparently following his own special vision of where he had to go to die.

He stopped every five feet or so and collected his energies. I thought of getting the shovel out of the garage and smashing his head.

He crawled within a few feet of me and off down the driveway. I hoped he would find somewhere secret.

When I'd raked enough leaves on the tarp, I dragged it around front to dump it in the street. The rabbit lay on the front lawn. When I came back with the second and third loads, he was still there.

I poked him with the rake. His body was still supple. I flopped him over on his back and he lay unmoving.

I got the shovel, scooped up the body—tinier and lighter than in life—and took it to the back yard. I was going to dig a hole under the hedges and bury him, but I saw there was a hole there already. I slid him into it, and the earth swallowed him up.

When I lived in the city, I had a friend whose family was from Malta. They ate strange foods, compared to our pork chops and mashed potatoes. One day while my friend and I were hanging around his house, his mother gave him a few dollars and told him to go to the market and buy a rabbit for stew.

The market, whose main business was selling live chickens, had a musty, hot feather-and-dung smell. In the cloudy shop windows over the wooden cages of squawking chickens hung small steel cages, each containing a rabbit. My friend pointed to one of the cages, and the butcher—a short, balding man in a blood-stained apron—reached in, took out the rabbit, and held it up by its hind legs.

It struggled slightly, then was still. We stared blankly.

Then, not waiting for us to say anything, he took the rabbit into the back room. A wooden wedge propped open the door allowing us to see in. The room's walls were of white tile and at its center stood a couple of sinks, a row of stainless steel hooks running above them.

The butcher tied the rabbit's hind legs together, then slipped them up over one of the hooks so the rabbit hung by the intervening bit of twine. As before, the rabbit struggled slightly, then was still.

Then the butcher picked up a slat of wood the size and thickness of a ruler and quickly and sharply smacked the rabbit a glancing blow off the base of its skull. The rabbit went completely limp and blood dripped out of its nose and mouth and into the sink.

A few deft cuts with a razor-sharp knife and the blue guts plopped in the sink; another few cuts and the butcher peeled off the skin and fur the way you might pull off a sweater in a steam-heated room.

He next tore a length of white paper from a large roll, neatly wrapped the carcass in a crisp bundle, and handed it to my friend. We walked out the front door past the cages, one of which now swung empty in the sun-etched window. The whole process had taken less than five minutes.

When we got out in the street, my friend handed me the package: "Here, feel this," he said. The flesh was still warm beneath the stiff paper.

We were very careful crossing streets on the way home.

My wife and I were visiting a childhood friend and his wife back East. I had been his best man the year before and now we were getting together at what was to be a quieter time when we could really talk.

My friend believes in being a perfect host, and (I suspect) the demands he placed on himself in that respect, along with the other complications of modern living, conspired to give him a migraine. A bad one.

He told me a story he'd heard on the radio about a waitress who was taking an order in a restaurant when a workman, renovating a shop next door, accidentally shot a nail out of a nail gun clean through the wall and into her skull. My friend said he knew exactly how she felt.

So he had to lie flat in a dimmed room, while my wife and I sat out in the back yard and spoke with his wife. We got to talking about how nice and secluded the yard was and she said it was so quiet that they would often see a rabbit out there sunning himself.

This was fascinating to them, having grown up city folks, and they would peek out the window and marvel at him—peaceful and calm, legs stretched out in front and in back, eyes blissfully closed, drinking in the sun.

She told us how my friend's father—a gentle man who would walk me home by the hand when my friend and I were children and I had stayed playing late—came out for a birthday dinner my friend and his wife had prepared for him. They told him about this rabbit and he was very interested, and talked about how he and my friend's mother had kept pet rabbits and how he held onto them after my friend's mother died—so he couldn't ignore, he said with a wink, how life went on.

At one point they left him sitting out on the patio, drink in hand, while they went in to tend the meal. When they looked out the window, there was the rabbit, sitting under the old man's chair, quiet and blissful as usual.

"It was a miracle," said my friend's wife.

They tiptoed around trying to keep quiet so they wouldn't scare the rabbit away while they finished their kitchen chores. When they went back out, however, the rabbit was gone.

When they asked if he'd seen the rabbit, the old man said no. "But it's funny," he added, "with all of your talk, you got me to thinking, and I'm sure I was humming the little tune your mother used to calm the rabbits when she handled them."

They still see the rabbit from time to time. "But he seems uneasy or something," said my friend's wife. "He hops around sniffing and twitching. He can't seem to get settled."

SWEET BREATH

by Jaimee Wriston Colbert

He's cruising along Route 315 going nowhere, and there she is. Her thigh is what he notices about her first. Long, really long, tight jeans, she's stuck it out then curved it in and around a utility pole like a backwards question mark. She's blond, same as his wife, only, his wife's hair is short. Everything about his wife is short. This hair swirls out and about like an animal's tail, like something with a mind of its own.

As he lets up on the accelerator, braking, coaxing the Plymouth Fury to an uneasy stop beside the girl, she whips her arm behind her head and yanks at the hair, stretching it down in front of her neck like a shield. She leans into the window he rolls down, passenger side, takes her sweet time about it too despite the line of cars building up behind him. "What do you want?" she asks, peering in at him like he's the one with no right to be here.

"Shit," he mutters. An ache of something neglected tugs at his groin. She's barely more than a kid. Her blue eyes burn with newness. "Excuse *me,* but do you or don't you need a ride? I thought you were hitchhiking." His voice seems strange, a sound apart from the rest of him. It's been awhile since he's spoken to anybody.

"Depends. If you're a weirdo or a creep, forget it. Are you some kind of a pathetic loser?"

The driver of the car behind his leans on the horn. He flips him off in the rear-view shaking his head, his own hair black as the road but for a slow creep of premature, just-over-thirty grey at his temples, and cut in an uneven line at his neck. He feels a surge of anger, the girl, the car behind him, it's like a conspiracy sometimes. "I didn't know hitchhikers were so bloody picky. Take a bus, why don't you?" A semi, emptied of its load, barrels by like a warning. The horn-blaster behind him, white car, probably a BMW or a Volvo, is writing down his license plate; he'd just bet on it. The girl shrugs, tugs open the door, and climbs into the car.

"Just take me anywhere," she says, as he forces the Fury back into traffic, out of the right lane, shooting into the left where things flow a little freer. "Anywhere that's away from here." She tosses her hair over the seat so it's drifting into the back of the car where recently his whole life has been kept, a bag with his toothbrush and shaving stuff, his quilt, a clean shirt, and HOLLYWOOD—the book he's reading, about a guy who doesn't live his life the normal way but people love him, he makes a movie the way HE wants to make it, it's a success, naturally, and he lives forever with lots of money.

His eyes leave the road for a second traveling quickly over the girl. Her hair is the color of the moon and just as showy. A hank of it has blown across his arm that rests tenuously on the seat near her shoulder. She's left the window open even though the wind has teeth and it's about to rain. Not a yellowy blond, he rolls his eyes, stares straight ahead at the street again; she's hardly a real blond at all.

"Can't you get off this damn highway? I hate this highway. My last ride was an asshole and he left me here." Her eyes, a hard blue, search his profile. Eyes like mint, he thinks, cool and cutting. "I'm into your regular roads, country roads. I hate highways. They go on forever."

"You know," he starts, then tightens his lips. He remembers he didn't brush his teeth this morning, does his breath stink? There was no fresh water in the park he stayed the night in, just a mud hole—Fishing Pond, the sign said. He shrugs. "Hell, how old are you, anyway? I mean, isn't this kind of thing pretty dangerous, you telling me to take country roads, away from civilization and all? Who am I? You don't know, I could be a mass murderer."

"Civilization, hah!" She throws back her head, her sleek neck long as a horse's. "Ain't this Ohio? I'm from Honolulu. The bars in Waikiki are open till 4:00 in the morning. THAT'S civilization."

"Yeah? So what. You're too young for bars." He shakes his head. Why did he even stop? Not that he was going any place in particular, but *this* is supposed to give his afternoon meaning? He fiddles with the station tuner on the Fury's radio, sliding it up and down like scales, music, news, chatter, numbing and drab. He flips the power off.

"My father picked up someone in a bar. He brought her home and screwed her. I think he screwed her into something permanent, like maybe a light socket, because she's been with us ever since."

He smiles and sees she's smiling too, a little. He feels that ache again, the stirring that starts deep in the pit of him, swells and announces itself, proud as a flag. Something about the way she talks. Tough kid. He glances at her thighs, longer than his, longer than anyone's. "So, what are you doing in Ohio? You look like you should be in high school."

"School's bullshit. I'm going to stay with my mother. My REAL one. She lives around here."

He maneuvers the Fury around a fallen tree branch. The roads away from the highway are rain-soaked, deeply pitted in places, the pavement maybe as ancient as the trees. Not many trees though. Field mostly, dull and beaten by winter, by constant rain. The sky is huge and grey as an old man's face, the grass bent and wheat colored. He takes his left hand off the steering wheel, laying it subtly upon his lap. He sees her, silver hair, legs wound around him tight as a vine. He'd be everything to her, lover, brother, though of course she can mean nothing to him. He means nothing. His loathing, his self-pity, this is what's alive in him. He'd put it in her, and then he'd be free.

She shuts her eyes, tilts her head back against the seat, its upholstery warm and familiar, a rich thick smell of plastic. The motion of the car under her is the motion of the world around her. It jerks, it moans, it whines, it moves forward too slowly, like a breath, like a sigh, like something broken.

The car door slams, "I'll be right back," he tells her. The sudden quiet is like the silent place inside her, empty, waiting.

Iron crow, her mother's letter said. 'I've got this iron crow in my yard, Sarah, it's *so* quaint.'

"Don't you know," her father told Sarah, "your mother loves her *things* more than us." But this was the way they had talked about each other, her father, her mother. And then her mother was gone.

A tiny yard, hardly a yard at all, she lives in a trailer park, said the letter. No room for you, Sarah. A trailer, in central Ohio, no return address.

Iron crow. Sarah pops open her eyes as if one might be perched on this dashboard, cold metal stare, leadened feathers. The dog in the trailer next to hers barks all night long, the letter complained. Sarah can hear her mother's voice underneath her scattered, jubilant script, breathy, a lingering sigh.

The man climbs back into the car, his face pink and mottled. "Sorry. I had to use a bathroom, a user-friendly bush as my wife used to say." Sarah stares at his hand as he shifts into first, reddish fingers, beefy, weathered, like her father's. But her father's are sun-damaged from his years lifeguarding at Waimea Bay. That was when he was young, just a little older than Sarah is now. His last good years, he told her once. Her own hands are smooth and long-fingered.

"The woman my father keeps in our house doesn't let me keep pets. Not after the guinea pig incident, that's what she calls it. She marches into my room, doesn't even knock, says she wants to 'throw open the windows to the ocean breeze.' Can you believe that? Like, we live in Manoa, a valley not the beach. Then she says, she's got this shrill, bitchy way of talking, 'Your guinea pig's gonna be dead by morning. Look at it! The cage is filth, pure filth. Do you ever feed it? You don't take care of it so good, yeah?' What a major bitch."

"What's your name, anyway? Mine's Wilson." He stares at Sarah, she knew he would. While she's been talking to him she's unsnapped three snaps on her jean jacket. She's wearing not a thing under it.

"Wilson. Sounds like a last name. What's your last name, John?"

He shakes his head, pulls at his chin, gazes fiercely at the road in front of him. "So, what, you're probably all of fifteen, huh?" He pushes the gearshift into third, accelerates, slips into fourth. "I have no life," he says. "My wife's gone, and she's got our apartment. I quit my job. There's nothing so-called respectable about me, but I've never done a thing I can't at least live with myself about, if living is what I do."

Sarah sticks her foot up on the dash, short black boot, candy-cane striped sock, drums her fingers against her knee cap to the tune of the rain that falls suddenly hard. "I'm seventeen," she says, "almost. I'm a model. Did you guess that? The woman my father keeps sent me on this shoot in San Francisco. My father said maybe I was too young to go alone, and she said Oh, don't be stupid. It was a fashion spread and the photographer kept feeling me up in the different outfits. He's 'arranging me,' he said. When it was over my agent took me to the airport, left me there, and I cashed in my Honolulu ticket for a ticket to Columbus." She unsnaps the last snap on her jacket, pulls it wide open. "You want me, right? Go ahead, why the fuck not?"

The Fury veers toward a ditch at the side of the road, dips, bounces back. Sarah feels it's return like a curse. One whole week, nights alone in cheap motels, days spent riding busses, hitchhiking, through all those flat little towns in the middle of Ohio, all those trailer parks. In seven, maybe eight of them she sees iron crows on yellow lawns, between patches of dirt, of dust, of mud, standing staunch and vacant-eyed like the real birds, only, who wants crows in the first place? And iron chipmunks, iron squirrels, deer, horses, in every other trailer's yard, even on top of a couple tinny roofs there's imitation animals; nobody's heard of her mother. With the sleeve of her jacket Sarah swipes ferociously at the tears rolling down her cheeks, onto her bare breasts.

"Maybe we should go find us a place to eat at," says Wilson, his eyes looking straight ahead. "I'm starved."

"Well," says Wilson, watching Sarah inhale a hamburger like it's her first or maybe her last meal of the month. He's taken her into Moynihan's, a little cafe in the middle of nowhere. Like a father he made her close up her jacket, comb her hair. A father, he thinks, that's what the others are thinking, staring from their tables, at her, at him, then away again. He hates them, their smug, shut faces.

He imagines feeding Sarah until she's all satiated and content. It would be dark when they go back outside, she'd lean against him as he leads her to the Plymouth—she'd be his willow tree and he her roots; he'd drive them to some park for the night that doesn't close its gates, that doesn't have gates. Some park that has water so he can brush his teeth.

Then, he'd say something completely outrageous to her, like, "See this belt? (He'd whip it off his pants in one slick movement, the strike of a snake.) Hit me with it, OK?" Something really outrageous so he can remember he's alive.

A terrible taste swells into Wilson's mouth, like his own food coming up again, like venom. He covers his lips with the napkin, bites his tongue until it bleeds.

He says to Sarah after a slug of coffee strong as tar, his second cup—she's attacking an ice cream sundae—"So, you got a boyfriend in Honolulu?"

Sarah snorts, slaps at a drift of snow colored hair near her mouth that threatens to mingle with her ice cream. "Oh, yeah, lots. Hundreds. They all like me just as far as they can see me."

"That business in my car, with the jacket? What was that about?" He signals the waitress for more coffee, it's bleak taste a punishment he no doubt deserves.

Sarah lowers her eyes. She slurps the remaining ice cream, mostly liquid, up with a straw, picks up the long-handled silver spoon, turns it against her tongue, sucks. He thinks about her long legs under the table almost touching his, her bony knees, her hair hanging down around her heart-shaped face. A sadness sweeps through him. "OK," he sighs. "So, what?"

"You mean *this* jacket," says Sarah. "This fucking denim jacket? This jacket belongs to the woman my father keeps. Yeah, well, isn't that what everybody sees when they look at me, anyway? I just figured it's what you wanted, that's what you picked me up for."

Wilson's face is hot. He stares at his fingers, stretching them out and around his coffee cup. The room they are in is dingy, colorless walls, and he sees himself as blending into it perfectly, a part of its walls, its ceiling, space, air, its nothingness. "Why should you do what *I* want, if it's what I want?"

"So you'd help me."

"Meaning what?"

"So you'd help me find my mother. But, forget it, because I changed my mind anyway."

Wilson cups his chin in his hands, it's scratchy, a two day beard, nothing about him is fresh anymore. He closes his eyes. Last month it would have been his wife sitting across from him, her cold, vacant stare never seeing him, always looking around, down, out any available window. "It's dead," she had said finally, one night, handing him his suitcase the minute he gets home from work. "I can't feel myself when I'm with you. I feel more looking at your dog then I do when I look at you, and your dog drives me crazy. Always shoveling his nose around the carpet, always smelling bad. But, at least I feel *something* when I look at him."

That's when he quit everything—his job (it was a nothing job, selling other people's property, nothing solid, nothing built, nothing gained past his paycheck), his friends (they were *their* friends, couples, a way to get through the weekends), even his dog (he left his dog with his wife!), just gave it all up. To prove . . . what? It seemed so pointless now. As though when one part of your life falls apart you can just shrug off all the rest to emerge clean and free as something else. What is he but the same old Wilson without a life? "I wish I at least had a kid," he says to Sarah. "I think I could have loved it, I'd have done a good job loving it. A kid makes a person more permanent."

Sarah's eyes, the blue of some distant sea, study Wilson's face. "You know what?" She leans toward him. The smell of vanilla ice cream surrounds her like perfume. "You know what my mom used to call me, when I was a baby? She used to call me Sweet Breath. Of course, I don't remember, but she told me. She said she would throw me up in the air, to startle me because I cried a lot. Then, after she got my attention, she'd hold me close. She said I had the sweetest breath. Like a new morning, she said. Like something perfect."

Wilson takes Sarah's hand lightly in his. Her fingers are cold, and he feels bad about this. "Oh God, oh God, oh God," she says, not wailing it, sort of matter-of-fact. "I hate modeling, could you guess that? I'm going to be an anthropologist. I'll travel thousands of miles away, and I'll dig up remnants."

"Remnants?"

"Things from past civilizations, hundreds and thousands of years ago."

Wilson nods, solemnly.

"I'm not dumb, you know. People think because I look the way I do I'm lolo. That means stupid in Hawaiian."

"Where do I take you now?" he asks, "I don't know where to take you."

Sarah shrugs. "To the airport, I guess."

Wilson hands the cashier his VISA, feeling a strange satisfaction at paying for Sarah's meal along with his. Outside, in the parking lot, he puts a tentative arm around her shoulders. She's taller than him and he laughs. Because he's the one who's leaning on her.

THRONE OF BLOOD

by Abby Frucht

It is early evening of the day of the birth of Cara's second child, Max. Max was born at noon, and Cara is waiting to fall in love with him. She didn't love him the very instant he was born, as many women say they love their babies, or during pregnancy, as other women do. In fact her inclination all along has been to ignore him entirely, so that the changes in her body during pregnancy seemed to her to be just that, changes in *her* body, not in anyone else's. She barely thought of the baby at all until the labor began, and then her recognition of him was clouded by pain. She hasn't forgotten the pain, as women say they do, but she is trying to forget it. Still, she can hear someone down the hall in the throes of it, screaming, "I can't do it, I can't do it, I can't do it," until Cara's entire body clenches in agonized, convulsive sympathy, and only on reflection can Cara say to herself, I did do it, I did do it, I did do it, it's over.

Cara's gown does not fit properly. Either that or she hasn't got it on right, because it doesn't cover her. She doesn't care. She has license to be half-naked, lazy, depraved, steeped in strange, uncommon relief. She is pleased with herself, and she is pleased with her baby twitching in sleep on the high, wheeled, glassed-in cart at the foot of her bed, where she can gaze at him as if through a window. He is knobby and pink, unconscious, detached. She hasn't counted his fingers or toes, as mothers are said to do, but she knows they're all there because the nurses would have said something if they weren't, and she knows he is breathing. She can see the uneven rhythm of it through his blanket, unless that's his heartbeat, so fierce in so tiny a body. No matter what, he's alive. She has said to Douglas several times since the delivery, "He's alive, he's alive," meaning, "I'm alive, I'm alive, I'm alive."

Cara still hasn't gotten out of bed but knows she'll be expected to soon, to go to the bathroom. The nurses all want her to move her bowels. Now that the labor is done, that is what scares her the most. She might split apart, pushing it out. She has stitches where she tore and where they cut her. Besides, she feels shaky even four hours after, but nothing like when he was born. Then she was afraid to hold him she was shaking so hard, and her breath thumped under her ribs. She could see that they were holding the baby above her, still wet and unwashed, bloody, with the white, pasty stuff still on him, but it did not occur to her to take him in her arms and when they lowered him onto her chest she said to Douglas, "Hold him there, don't let me hold him." The baby was warm and wet and she didn't welcome the feel of him the way women were said to. It was too distracting. She wanted only the sensation of the pain being shaken off of her, limb by limb.

"I feel like I'm going to die," she said.

Douglas smiled. "Well, you're not."

"Yes, I am. Look at this." She held up a hand that was shaking so hard that its outline was blurred. Beyond it she could see the nurses clustered around the baby on the cart against the wall, cleaning him, clipping him, tapping here and there and examining. Then the doctor was sitting between Cara's legs with a needle and thread, peering critically at the ragged edges needing to be mended. So calmly, so confidently did the doctor thread her needle that she might have been sewing on a button. She gave Cara a shot of novocain meant to last five minutes, but the stitching took five and half. Douglas held Cara's hand, but how eerie it was, because the hand was not part of her body. Rather, she *had* no body. She was all system, no flesh, all blood rushing this way and that in narrow humming channels that seemed never to reach her brain. When someone cranked up the head of the bed on which she was lying, it was only like a change in the weather as if after a rain when the air thins out. Cara thought she might stay that way forever, all effect and no substance, even while the nurse palpated her belly to make sure her uterus was shrinking.

"That's very good," commended the nurse, as if Cara had anything to do with it. This is not a bad way to be, Cara thought—buzzing, buzzing—but already it was starting to fade. For a while she was all pins and needles, and then she was only someone lying on a bed in the hospital room. Now the pain was like a ball of yarn unraveling, as if the nurse across the room were drawing it to her to be wrapped up and taken to the neighboring room where the next woman lay in labor. Cara's room was pleasant and large, with tangerine walls and a dense, mauve carpet. Over the sink, a mirror reflected Cara propped up on pillows, and she could see the baby there too, looking more remote than ever. There was a bathroom, which she avoided looking at, and just next to the bed a table with a water pitcher on it. She was reaching for a cup when Douglas said, "I can get you some ginger ale or juice from the hall," startling her because she hadn't seen him in the mirror. He was sitting in the arm chair reading the newspaper.

"You were asleep," he said.

"No, I wasn't."

He raised his eyebrows.

"Ginger ale," she said, "and a tooth brush, please."

Douglas said he'd help her to the bathroom.

"Never mind," Cara said.

"It's okay. I can walk you."

"It's not that."

"What?"

"It's what I'm supposed to do when I get there. I can't."

"That's okay. You don't have to."

Her feet were bare, and she laid them flat on the floor all at once just to feel the ground against the soles, before putting any weight on them. In the bathroom, she didn't look at the toilet but took a moment to look in the mirror where she noticed how vivid she looked; how red her lips, how dark her hair, how pale her skin, like Snow White, only her gown had fallen wide open so you could see her pubic hair and the elastic belt around her hips, that held the sanitary pad. It would have to be changed. It was heavy with blood and hung loose between her thighs, and as she took it off she got blood on her fingers and on the toilet seat. She rolled the pad into a ball, wrapped it in a strip of toilet paper and was dropping it into the garbage when she realized that she didn't have another. She called out of the bathroom to her husband but he was getting the ginger ale. Instead there was a nurse in the room, hovering near the bathroom door.

"I don't have any pads," said Cara.

"Did you go?" said the nurse.

"What?"

"Did you go to the bathroom? Have you moved your bowels?"

"I don't have to," said Cara.

The nurse brought in a stack of pads and a squirt bottle that she filled with warm water at the sink.

"You clean yourself with this," said the nurse, gesturing with the bottle, "and then pat yourself with these," holding up a bag of cotton balls.

Cara said nothing. She was in awe of all the blood, as she had been years ago after Georgie was born. It had run down her legs, and when she wiped it, the soaked cotton turned immediately crimson. No man can ever bleed like this and still be healthy, she thought, but she didn't say it to her husband when he came in carrying the can of soda. He would think she was insulting him, and maybe she was. She climbed gingerly back up on the bed, then took the straw in her mouth and sipped, concentrating hard until she thought she could feel in her body the very spot from where the blood began to flow, like the start of a river. It was like sun beating down on ice, and the ice clopping off in big chunks that released just a drop, then trickled, then gushed. It was like sitting on hot ice. She was reveling in this when a nurse wheeled the baby in on his high wooden cart. The baby was waking, the edges of his blanket beginning to tremble, a high wail escaping. Douglas picked the baby up and brought him to Cara, but the nurse had started taking Cara's temperature. After that there was the blood pressure to be taken again, and the palpating of the uterus, the baby mewing all the while as Douglas rocked him. Cara hadn't nursed him yet, and thought of letting Douglas feed him with a bottle; they made a snug-looking pair, and she would keep a safe distance and watch them together, today, and maybe tomorrow as well, and maybe the day after. But Douglas put him in her arms before she had a chance to speak. What a shock it was; Max was practically weightless, yet in a moment he managed to find her nipple, all by himself.

"He has a strong suck," Cara said after a while.

Douglas bent close to the nipple and said he could hear the stuff coming out of it; it made a sound like the fizz of champagne.

"I could go buy us some champagne," he said. "But I'd rather stay here if you don't mind."

"I don't mind. I want you to. Can you bring me a couple of pillows? Put your finger in his hand; see how he grabs hold."

"He's really cute."

"He's so small. When's the doctor going to come and look at him? He's tinier than Georgie ever was."

"No, he isn't."

"He looks like Georgie as a baby. He's so red. I wish . . . Oh, look, he's opened his eyes."

"He's looking at you," said Douglas.

"You take him and feed him with a bottle and then he'll look at you," Cara said boldly.

"I'm not worried," said Douglas.

"I am."

"What?"

"I am worried," said Cara.

"Because why?"

"I don't want to say it."

"Don't worry. It'll happen."

"What will?"

"You'll fall in love with him," said Douglas. "Soon enough. You said the same thing with Georgie."

"I'm not just saying it," said Cara.

"I know. I mean the same thing happened. It took a while."

"It's already been an hour!"

"No, it hasn't. You're exhausted, Cara. You're too tired to fall in love."

"But what if I don't?"

"You will," said Douglas.

"You will," said a nurse, who had been there all along, stacking towels at the edge of the sink.

The timing of this second labor had been the same as the first; Cara had wakened at three in the morning and given birth at noon. At three-fifteen the first time, she woke up Douglas; now she'd waited until quarter to four.

"How far apart?" Douglas had asked, both times.

"Fifteen minutes."

"What do they feel like?"

"Like fists clenching and unclenching." She got up on one elbow and looked at the clock. "I don't know. Fourteen minutes that time. And they don't really hurt. It's just pressure. It's just a squeeze." She was thinking it was probably false.

"That's what it felt like the last time," said Douglas. "It didn't hurt at the beginning."

"It's premature."

"It's two days before the delivery date," said Douglas.

"I know. But I was planning on being late. Remember?"

"Well, doesn't look like you're going to be late."

"I don't know. I don't think this is it. Fourteen minutes again. Shit."

"Did that hurt?"

"No. Listen."

It was the dog. Whenever anyone woke up in the middle of the night, she woke up too and needed to go out. She was sitting at the base of the steps, shaking, tail thumping on the carpet. Douglas sighed and climbed out of bed. The dog was a point of contention between them—Cara didn't want her around anymore.

"You'll be okay for a couple of minutes?"

"Sure," Cara said, and then she watched him get dressed in the light from the hall. Half in and half out of it, his nakedness glowed and dissolved, glowed and dissolved. He had a muscular belly and heavy, muscular thighs, yet a way of stepping gracefully into his jeans, toes pointed, a little wiggle to the hips when he pulled them up. Snow had fallen that evening and into the night; now she knew it would lie deep and unblemished even on the street, for she hadn't been wakened by the scrape of the plow.

"Don't hurry up," she told him. "Just have a good walk."

The dog yelped excitedly when Douglas started downstairs, and Cara thought she heard their other child stirring in the room across the hall.

Other child, she thought, horrified, *already I said "other* child."

There was a window above the headboard of the bed, and when she pulled herself up and looked out, she felt the fist again, sharper than before. She nearly yelled. But she looked at the clock instead. Fourteen minutes, same as always. Not much later, she heard her husband kick the snow off his boots, then sit down to untie the laces as he talked to the dog. "There's some water in your bowl," he said personably, and the dog tick-ticked to her bowl in the kitchen. Not since the birth of their first child had Cara said even that to the dog. Long ago she used to sing to her, and lie on the floor with her head on the dog's soft ruff while stroking her paws. Now the dog was just an animal needing meager helpings of affection that Cara doled out begrudgingly if she had a little extra. Cara wasn't one of those big-hearted women like the one who lived just down the block. If you knocked on her door it was opened by children and dogs all sizes shapes and colors, not one at a time but all at once, ten or eleven of them, crowding the steps and front hall. After visiting there, Cara felt stingy with love. She was worried she would use it up. Pregnant, she kept looking at her son, thinking, What will happen to us? Even then she kept getting lost staring at him. He was nearly five, so she needed to examine him in order to know who he was changing into, so she would love him for who he was now and not who he had been before. These days he was Bilbo Baggins, on his way to Murkwood. He wore Cara's big fuzzy slippers and a magic ring she had made out of foil. The ring was supposed to make him invisible, so she would pull him onto her lap and pretend she didn't know he was there. "Bilbo! Bilbo Baggins!" she'd call, and set him down in the chair and get up and go from room to room looking for him, from closet to closet, all the while hearing him giggling against the arm of the chair until she came back in and sat down right on top of him saying, "Forget it, I can't find him, he must have gone to Murkwood." Ordinarily he was playful but once he grew very still and worried there underneath her so that at last she got up and took his head in her hands exclaiming in an adoring voice, "Oh, you're back, I've found you," taking a risk and calling him not Bilbo but by his name, Georgie. He didn't want to let go. They stayed in the chair as the room grew dark while she let the soup burn on the stove. She could feel the baby hiccupping inside her in jumps and starts as it did every day at this time. Her son seemed unaware of them. Cara did an experiment; she told herself the hiccups were a baby that she needed to love, and she sat there and loved it and felt how much love was left over for her son in her arms. Almost nothing. It was terrible. When she wanted to start loving Georgie again, she had to stop loving the hiccups.

"I called Georgie *our other child,*" she said to Douglas when he'd come upstairs.

"How are you feeling?" he asked.

"I don't know. It's still every fourteen minutes."

"You still think it's fake?"

"No."

He unbuttoned his shirt and in that same graceful, unconscious fashion let it slide from his body. In bed, he put his hand on her belly so the cold temperature of it was like a balm on top of the next contraction. She took his hand in her own and moved it in widening circles around her navel and then up over her breasts to her neck and chin. She was scared about the labor because she hadn't read any books this time and had forgotten the breathing techniques. Throughout this pregnancy— early on when she was tired, then later when she'd felt so light and buoyant—Cara had insisted, had believed, that this delivery wouldn't hurt. But now she knew that it would. She was being made to prepare herself. It was like some hand reaching in, grabbing hold of her guts, squeezing hard, withdrawing, only later it wouldn't withdraw, it would knead and twist, it would dig in with knuckles and nails.

"That was nine minutes," she said after a while. "They're getting harder. I think we should call the doctor. I'm taking a shower."

In the shower she shaved her armpits and her legs although that was difficult because her belly was in the way and because she didn't want to be already doubled over when the contraction came. Soon her son padded into the bathroom, unzipped the long zipper down the front of his pajamas, stepped to the toilet, peed, climbed up on his step stool, washed his hands, climbed down to dry them, climbed up again to get a drink of water out of his cup, all this with his pajamas down around his ankles.

"You're all grown up," said Cara, who was drying herself while standing in the tub.

"I know."

"Get Daddy!" said Cara, but Douglas was in the room already with a pile of clothes that he helped her get into.

"What should I put in the bag?" he said breathlessly.

"Get breakfast for Georgie. Call Deena and tell her to come by for him. I'll get the bag. I'm okay," said Cara, who when the contraction faded felt cool, organized, able. She packed a robe, two books, three pairs of socks. She forgot underpants, a toothbrush, and everything else. The next contraction took the breath out of her and forced her to stand absolutely still as if to acknowledge its presence.

"Okay, okay," Cara said to it, and then, to herself, "If they stay like this I can make it. I can deal with this."

The hospital was just down the street five blocks and she imagined she and Douglas might walk it together, red-cheeked, arm in arm along the uncleared sidewalks, stopping every seven minutes to look at the snow on the telephone wires. But then she found she'd put her coat on and was standing at the door, waiting, her hands on her belly, her bag packed but upstairs where she'd left it. She was like someone trying to stay calm in an air raid. But for the sake of what? It was only going to get worse. When at last it was time to go, she made straight for the car without so much as a glance at the sidewalk. In the car she said, "I'm not going to do up my seatbelt." There was nobody else on the road just then, and Cara had the feeling that everything in the world was being put on hold so that she could have her baby. She felt singled out. The windshield was free of snow but she didn't think about her husband having found a minute in their hectic morning to clear it. She only stared at the hood of the car as it brought her closer to the hospital.

"This might not be the real thing," Cara said to the nurse examining her. "They seem to be subsiding. I think if I go home and rest, get in my own bed, read a little or something, clean up a little, do some—"

The nurse said that Cara was four centimeters dilated, that it was certainly the real thing, that the baby might hold on til nightfall, and that if Cara felt she would be more comfortable at home in her own bed, then she could leave the hospital and come back around five.

"What do you think?" said Douglas, in such a way that Cara knew he was thinking of Georgie and of how fast that had happened, faster than the nurses had predicted.

"I don't know," said Cara. "Why don't I sit down a minute and we can wait a while and get my breath and see how things go and if I'm okay for a while we'll go."

There was an armchair recliner in the corner of the room, big and sturdy looking with just the right amount of yield when she put her weight in it. Just as she relaxed there was a contraction long and painful, not like the ones before it.

"This is a really bad one," Cara said, and no sooner had she said it then she felt something pop and then a gush of fluid. Cara was astonished, but the nurse was unconcerned.

"Well then. You better go to admitting," she said to Douglas before mopping it up, then changing Cara's gown. "Here. You're okay. But it will speed things up if you walk around a little."

"I don't need to speed things up," said Cara.

"It distracts you a little, if you walk around."

The nurse fitted some paper slippers onto Cara's feet, then took her arm and led her slowly out into the ward. It had been a busy weekend, so the ward was nearly full. The nurse led Cara to the window of the nursery where together they looked in at the babies all sleeping except for one who stared back through the glass.

"I'll take that one," said Cara. "Oh, no."

"Just relax. Breathe deep. Look at me." The nurse took a long breath, then let it out just as slowly.

Cara inhaled, her eyes on the nurse's eyes, her arm linked through
the nurse's arm. When it was over she could remember from the other
delivery this same childlike awe she felt for the nurses, who looked wise
and even lovely in their white costumes, and whose sensible calm was
their greatest virtue along with the fact that they all seemed to know
precisely how much it hurt. They never made apologies or told you to
be brave or said it would be over soon if it wasn't going to be. They said
things like, *Let me know if you think you're about to faint,* or, if you
urinated on the delivery table, *Don't worry about that, that's nothing
compared to what's coming.* They never showed worry or impatience, and they might at any minute walk straight up to you and stick
a thermometer under your tongue in such a way that you didn't even
flinch. Then there you'd be with the thermometer in your mouth while
a second nurse began taking your blood pressure and a third cranked
the headrest one notch higher. They were like gypsies, Cara thought
as she lay there among them; one of them could pick your pocket in a
second. Except the gown didn't have any pockets. It was white with
black medallions, so soft and loose you barely noticed it was there,
which was fine because then you didn't notice so much when it wasn't.
Twice it had slipped off her shoulders, and now as she lay on the delivery bed it fell open over her breasts. She didn't know for how long she
had been lying on the bed, knees up, head raised, Douglas stroking her
arm the way she liked during foreplay, shoulder to wrist with the very
edges of his fingernails. The contractions were back to back with no
more than a minute between them in which to drink a little water and
tell him to keep doing what he was doing although she knew very well
he would keep doing it anyway. Another thing she said, when she had
the time, was "You don't have any idea what this is like."

"You're right," said Douglas. "But I can imagine."

"No, you can't imagine," said Cara.

"We called the doctor," said one of the nurses. "She said she needed
to do a few things and then she'd be on her way over to check up on
you. Hang in there."

"A few things!" said Cara.

"Shhhh," said the nurse. "Breath. Good. Slow. Slow. That baby
won't be out for another two hours."

"Yes, it will," said Cara.

"You're doing fine," said her husband.

"I'm doing terribly," said Cara.

"You'll forget about it when its over," said one of the nurses, which was as close as they ever came to downplaying the pain. *Serene as glass,* Cara thought reproachfully, looking at the nurse. It was a challenge.

At once she yelled, "I'm pushing!" and gripped the edges of the mattress.

"No pushing!" said the nurse and Douglas at once.

"I have to," said Cara.

"You won't."

"I'm going to!" she yelled. She had to. If she didn't she would split apart. Rather, the thing that had become her would split apart. For it was no longer her body. It was hers and the baby's together. The two of them were like a padlock trying to get itself open. And there wasn't a key. They were steel. The nurse had taken hold of Cara's wrists and was staring her straight in the eyes saying, "No, you WILL NOT PUSH. IT IS NOT TIME TO PUSH."

"It IS time to push," Cara protested, knowing all the while that she wouldn't push, that if she did, she would split apart, just as surely and horribly as she would split apart if she *didn't* push, so that the only thing to do was scream at the nurse and thrash at her husband and so keep herself locked in this noisy limbo between not-pushing and pushing, between pushing and not-pushing, between splitting apart and splitting apart again.

The nurse was no longer serene; that battle was won, anyway.

Near eleven-thirty the doctor came, tugging on some gloves and whipping her hair up into a cap. Then she was between Cara's knees, pushing them gently apart while gazing firmly and sympathetically at Cara's face. Cara screamed, "I can't do it," and then, "I want drugs, I want drugs, I want drugs. Douglas, I want drugs," turning victoriously toward him as if he were the reason she hadn't said anything about drugs in the first place. He wasn't. Cara had had no thought of drugs, ever, during either this pregnancy or the last, and the very idea of drugs now was so amazing and so surprisingly, unexpectedly welcome that she nearly burst out laughing in the middle of her screams.

"Demerol!," she cried, "Demerol, Demerol, Demerol," while her husband raised his eyebrows at the doctor. The doctor frowned. She pulled her hand out of Cara, then stood up and called for a gown.

"Not quite," she said, and then something that Cara didn't hear because Cara was screaming again at the words Not Quite. *Not Quite What?* she wanted to know, screaming and screaming, in the back of her mind still thinking about the breathing that had worked a bit with

Georgie's delivery and that had seemed, for a while, to be working with this one except that the screaming seemed more responsible. It was like being hit with a train; you didn't lie there deep-breathing if you'd had your legs run over, did you? No, you screamed, and everybody accepted it, and if you didn't they'd be begging you to do it.

"I want Demerol," she yelled, "I can't do it, I'm pushing," and then something happened, at least Cara thought that it happened although she couldn't quite believe it. That is, the doctor did or didn't place the tip of her index finger directly and purposefully between Cara's legs creating such a shock of pleasure, like a slap in the face of the pain, that Cara quit screaming all at once for the second that it lasted and locked eyes with the doctor in a gaze so intense that between them it made a tightrope that the baby might walk across from one to the other. Then the doctor said, "Okay Cara, you can push."

"I have to tell you all that I screamed," Cara confesses to her friends during visiting hour that evening. Someone has opened a box of chocolates and they are passing it around.

"You're excused."

"You look beautiful."

"You're glowing. Your hair, it's like a halo, and your face is so pale. Translucent, practically."

"I mean I didn't just shout. I *screamed*. The breathing didn't work, or else I didn't want to be bothered. I couldn't help it. I wasn't *even* embarrassed."

"Oh, they don't care."

"They're used to it."

"Did you have an episiotomy?"

"I tore, and then I had an episiotomy."

"I've never heard of anyone who hasn't had an episiotomy, personally."

"Oh, I have."

"Really Cara, he's so beautiful. He was the only one in the nursery who wasn't asleep."

"He was the only one who wasn't crying."

"He was the only one who really seemed to know what was going on."

Her friends all laugh. Cara laughs, too, but she knows that her friends don't understand quite how loudly and persistently she had screamed during the labor. That's okay, only she doesn't know if she should be ashamed or not. Just a little. From down the hall where that other woman is in labor come screams more guttural than Cara's but with that same shocked pulse as if every second of pain were somehow unexpected. Cara can hear it through the wall, the way the moaning reaches a pitch and then tables out, and then the other moments when the woman starts to argue as if with the pain itself, with the clutching, tearing hand, saying "Oh no, oh no, oh no." How perplexing it is, to be listening like this, and to be sympathizing but not feeling, as she had before, that sympathetic, agonized contraction. For a moment, for the third or fourth time that evening, she thinks of describing for her friends what the doctor did, or what the doctor didn't do although it felt like she did it. Cara could swear that she did it. But then again . . . it's unbelievable. Isn't it? One of her friends would believe it, one of them wouldn't, the third would be skeptical. And Cara doesn't feel like getting into a discussion about it. She doesn't feel like talking much at all, for that matter. Still, she gets nervous when the nurse comes in and says visiting hours are over, because that means she gets the baby back. Visiting hours he has to stay in the nursery, the rest of the time he can stay with her. Not that she isn't impatient for him. She is, for his tiny soft warmth right up against her through the thin cotton of the gown, and for his strange smell so similar to the smell of sex. But she's not in love with him yet, at all. In fact, after Douglas went home to have supper with Georgie, Cara fully resigned herself to the notion of not ever really loving this child but getting simple comfort from his smell and proximity. "I'll be a good mother to him," she supposed. He'd never know. No one ever would. She'd stroke him, nurse him, teach him, show him. But not as she does with Georgie. Never in a whirlwind of need and sensation. Inside her will be only patience, and fortitude, and this same, resigned magnanimity.

Cara's bed is equipped with padded metal armrests that can be pulled up on either side of the mattress or dropped down. Cara pulls both of them up. She asks the nurse for extra pillows to be propped up against the armrests although that will make it harder to get in and out of bed. Indeed, when the baby awakens needing to be held, she has to pull herself down to the foot of the mattress before sliding off the edge of it, her stitches tugging at her crotch, and when she's picked the baby up gently and carried him back to the bed, she finds it impossible to pull herself back up the length of mattress while holding onto him. But if she puts the baby down at the top of the bed and then shimmies up after, she'll have to swivel around and pick him up without falling on top of him first, and then she'll be stuck half-way up and half-down, anyway. It all seems so impossible. And the baby is wailing. Down she sits in the arm chair to nurse him, hoping that one of the nurses will come take him away from her so she can get back into bed. But the nurse doesn't come. Through the wall, Cara hears the heavy, angry panting of the woman in labor, but the sound leaves her curiously empty and unimpressed by anything but her own afterpain spreading over her inch by inch. She begins to cry, purposefully at first and then helplessly so her tears fall on the baby's arm and slide under the loose plastic of the bracelet printed with his name.

Max, Cara reads, in a moment of lucidity.

"Look at me, Max," she says.

But the baby doesn't look. Instead he grunts, squeezes his eyes shut, and defecates. The stuff fills his diaper then oozes like tar into the folds of his blanket and onto Cara's arm. At that moment, Douglas walks into the room so Cara holds the baby out to him with every bit of her strength saying, "Here. This was a mistake. This was a terrible mistake."

Wide awake now, the baby gazes at Douglas who explains to him who and where he is and how he got there.

"Your name is Max," says Douglas, "You have a brother who isn't here right now. And a dog. This is a room in the hospital. Your mother did all of the work and that's why she's so exhausted and disoriented that she forgot how to get back in bed."

"I didn't forget how to get back in bed. I told you that. I just can't get back in bed when I'm holding him because I won't be able to grab hold of the armrests and pull myself up without splitting myself open, Douglas. I want the doctor."

"Cara, I've never heard of a single woman splitting open from having a baby. I'll stay with him, you go take a sitz bath. You remember how good it felt last time."

"I know," Cara says, but she stays in the chair, and then at last gets up and climbs slowly, ever so slowly, onto the bed, knee by knee, hand over hand, like someone climbing onto an inflated raft in a swimming pool. "That hurt," she says, just as the nurse comes in with a fluted paper cup. Cara downs her medication before reaching out her arms for the baby. Holding him, she finds that the head of the bed is too high, so she gives the baby back, lowers the bed, then takes him into her arms again. He is cross-eyed. If Cara moves an index-finger back and forth above his upturned face, one eye stays put while the other tries to follow, lagging behind and then skipping ahead. Gradually he closes his eyes and is asleep in such a way that he appears to be just hovering on the surface of his own unformed consciousness. Cara watches him a while aware of her own eyes closing and of Douglas getting up out of the armchair, kissing both her and the baby, shutting the light and leaving for home.

"Douglas," she says.

"What?"

A pause.

"When can I see Georgie?"

"Tomorrow at lunch, I'll bring him," he says.

"Douglas."

"Yes."

Another pause.

"I'm still not in love with him."

"Just go to sleep, Cara."

"Goodnight."

"Goodnight."

"Goodnight, Max," says Cara, relieved that the room is not totally dark, that there is still a dim light over the sink and a little from the hallway through the half-closed door. Then she sleeps, too. First she feels the pleasant warm weight of the baby on top of her but soon she is spinning in a dizzy fatigue that makes their two bodies seem to clasp each other equally as if falling together through space.

At three o'clock that morning, when the nurse comes for   Max to check his heartbeat and temperature, Cara won't give him up from his place against her under the blankets. There's a sleepy tug of war before the nurse finally takes hold of Cara's fingers and gently but forcibly dislodges them from their hold on the baby. "Go back to sleep," she says. "When I'm finished with him I'll bring him back all clean and diapered and you can wake up and nurse him. He's due for a feeding. When did you feed him last?"

"Eleven," Cara guesses.

"How long on each side?"

"Five minutes," Cara says, although in fact she has no idea. The nurses insist on five minutes per breast and that you have to rub lanolin onto the nipples to keep them from cracking.

"Have you been using the lanolin?" asks the nurse.

"Yes," says Cara. She hasn't, but she finds it in its tube on her nighttable, next to the ginger ale. It smells like sheep in a barn, and when the baby comes back for nursing he first nibbles at the breast experimentally, licking and tasting. Then when he tries latching on, he slips off, over and over again. It's like getting a rocky start on sex, Cara thinks, before they finally settle into a good rhythm. At last he sucks firmly and hungrily. The nurse tells her to please put the baby back in his bassinet after feeding and not to sleep like that with him lying against her chest, and Cara nods but knows she'll keep him with her. For one thing, in order to put him back in his bassinet she'll have to climb out of bed again, and then, once out, she knows she'll have to go to the bathroom. If she stays put, she'll be able to hold it in. For how long, she doesn't know. She might talk to the doctor about it. She is thinking about this when the baby stops sucking and lifts his face openly towards hers as if to say, "Here I am." He is utterly, unfathomably calm.

Throughout the very early part of the day, the nurses keep coming in to ask if she's alright and occasionally to take the baby away from her. Each time before giving him back they make some comment about the soaps and shampoos and lotions in the basket in the bathroom, but by nine they have stopped coming in so much. Cara eats breakfast while the baby watches blissfully and then blankly and then thoughtfully every move of her hand as it travels from plate to mouth.

"This is orange juice," she explains. "This is a muffin. I'm taking a bite."

Max is lying on a pillow on her lap, and she thinks that to remain like this and watch him drifting in and out of sleep would be enough for the rest of the day if she didn't need to learn how to bathe him. She's forgotten how to do it. There are parts of him—his umbilicus, for one, his fresh circumcision—that seem too vulnerable even to look at. Also, his breathing is somewhat uneven: one-two, one-two, giving way all at once to a speedy vibration or else stopping altogether for two or three seconds during which Cara places the palm of her hand on his ribcage and waits, patiently. In the mirror across the room she can watch herself unmoving under the blanket—knees up, hair uncombed, one shoulder unclothed. Her eyes are bright, her face is pale, she has a coy, cool, secretive smile. She hasn't mentioned to the nurses that her baby stops breathing occasionally. Simply, there is no way to say it without making it sound horrible when really there is something delicate and necessary about it, as if it's his way of coming to grips with the fact that he is now, whether he likes it or not, part of the world.

Just before noon, the nurse comes in and asks hopefully if Cara has moved her bowels.

"I haven't had to," says Cara.

It's a lie.

"It would be a good idea. You don't want to get constipated. We might give you an enema in an hour or so if nothing happens, before the doctor shows up. Are you planning on having a shower before your husband comes?"

Cara says no, thank you, she is perfectly comfortable.

"I'll change the linens, then," says the nurse, who has a stack of fresh sheets already in her hand, white as can be, and a thin yellow blanket.

"Oh really, don't bother," says Cara, sliding deeper into the bed until she no longer can see past her knees to the mirror. The nurse, making a face, drops the clean sheets onto the armchair and, before turning to go, pulls open the blinds on a window looking into a snowy courtyard. Only then does Cara begin to wonder, and to notice the smell. She's grown accustomed to it, sitting in the middle of it for so long, in fact it is rather interesting in the way certain wild animal smells are interesting if you can be objective about them. Cara sits for a while just taking it in before she notices the strange texture of the sheets underneath her, which are sodden and crusty at once, while between her thighs the big sanitary pad feels as dense as a sausage. Looking under the blanket, she can see that the pad is black all through but no blacker than the sheets she's been sitting on. Everything is saturated with blood, and everything smells. Even a corner of the blanket is stiff with blood while the hems of the pillow cases propped here and there are soaked through as well with a fresher, redder color. The only thing not stained is her gown, which has ridden up completely over her hips. Now she presses a corner of it gingerly between her thighs, and having satisfied herself that the blood is thick and crimson, she holds the baby desperately, kissing him and kissing him.

WINTER TERM

by Robert Flanagan

It is nearly eleven when he turns off the gravel road to nose the car into the leaning barn they use as a garage. Killing lights and engine, he hauls out his bag of books and crosses the frozen yard. The tin-roofed farm house, which belongs to her family, needs painting and rewiring, but the rent is so cheap that he can't bring himself to complain.

As he opens the door he thinks he catches the sound of singing. He dumps his bag on the deacon's bench and listens, but hears nothing.

He finds her in the pantry on a stepladder. Her back is to him and he leans against the doorway looking at her. She's wearing jeans and one of his old shirts, red flannel, with the tail hanging out. Her coppery hair is caught up in a blue kerchief.

She twists about on the wobbly ladder. The expression on her face teeters between hope and worry, or maybe he only imagines it.

"Watch yourself," he tells her. "You'll fall."

She gestures at the wall with a paint roller. "Look."

"Gold?"

"Van Gogh yellow." Her generous smile is a bit too toothy to be pretty. "Like it?"

"Bright"

"With no windows, you'll want bright walls, won't you?"

He shrugs. She likes redoing things. First it was their bedroom, then the smaller one as a nursery, although after her miscarriage and his tenure denial they agreed that a baby would have to wait. Now she's gotten it into her head that all he needs to get back to his dissertation is a place of his own to work.

"Don't you like it?" she asks.

"Did I say that? I said it's bright."

He backs from the pantry and opens the refrigerator. "Jesus, I'm beat."

"That won't help, you know."

"I'm wound up, all right?" He takes out a bottle of beer and twists off the cap.

"Why it's called a pick-me-up, I'll never understand. I read where it depresses you." Backing down from the ladder, she empties the paint tray, caps the can, wraps turpentine-soaked rags around the roller and puts it into a plastic bag which she seals with a green twistie. "When we get your books and typewriter in there, it will look a lot nicer, really."

Her good spirits in dealing with the rubble life dumps at your door amaze him; he fails to see how anyone can be so cheerful with so little cause.

"The car's stalling out again," he says.

She follows him into the chilly kitchen. "Didn't we just get it tuned or something?"

"Back in September. Sixty miles round trip to the main campus every day, fifty twice a week to the pen, you think that doesn't add up?"

As she washes her hands at the sink her head is framed by hanging plants. The little house is a jungle of spider plants, wandering Jew, peace lily, Chinese evergreen. She believes they clean the air.

"If it breaks down for good," he says, "then where are we?"

She dries her hands on a sunflowered towel.

"Stuck," he tells her. "That's where."

"I bet you're hungry."

He drops into a chair. "I could eat something."

She begins scrambling eggs at the stove. The only sound in the room is the clicking of the spatula on the pan. She used to sing bits of songs while she cooked, he remembers, and he would needle her about not knowing any one piece all the way through.

The day's mail has been opened and left on the table. Looking at the bills, he calculates how tight their money is this month. He finishes his beer. His body feels like lead. Maybe he spends too much time reading and brooding, and reading other men's broodings. But no, actually he spends too few hours studying and making notes on Conrad's stoic vision, and far too many in Columbus or Marion badgering illiterate freshmen or convicted manslaughterers to put predicates in their sentences. That it isn't in her to complain, he thinks, makes him seem bad-natured simply because he has a common sense awareness of their trouble, and the world's.

"Coming home tonight, I couldn't help thinking." He twists the bottle in his hands, then taps its neck on the chrome edge of the table. "I don't know, it sounds crazy."

"What's that?"

"I could do something terrible," he says.

"What?"

"That's what I kept thinking, that I could do something terrible."

"Why even think something like that?"

"You don't think so?"

"No."

"But I could," he says.

"Here you are, here's your eggs."

"If I was locked up like that, I don't know what I'd do."

"Well, that's different. If you were in prison."

"You don't know what you could do, not until maybe it's too late." His voice sounds flat to him, as if the room had been emptied of furniture for moving, or like that of a man reciting his serial number. "The prisoners, they're losers, sure, but not *bad* guys, not all of them."

She puts wheat bread and margarine on the table. "You want toast?"

He shakes his head, and starts in on the eggs. "Some of them act like high school kids. Last week when I said they had to finish *Heart of Darkness?* You should've heard them. 'Aw, Teach, do we have to?' Then there's the others, the bad asses. They don't say a word, just lean back with their arms crossed on their chests and look right through you. What they're doing in class, I've no idea. They look like wrestlers, pro linemen. All they do in there, except eat and do God knows what to each other, is lift weights. They wear workshirts, like denim but thinner, this washed-out blue with the seams all split at the shoulders. You should see them, you wouldn't believe it. They're like monsters."

She lays a slice of buttered bread on his plate, then steps behind him. He expects her to rub his neck, but she doesn't touch him. "You're not really scared, are you?" she asks.

He knows it's not the truth she wants to hear, not if it's hard to live with. "I don't really think about it. It's a job." What she wants is for them both to be happy. It's a heavy load for him to carry, but he tries, though he can't hope to compete with her Mom and Dad, beet-farmers, square-dancers, church-goers, married for forty-two of the happiest years of their life. And he can't help but think that she's less happy now than when she was a part-time secretary at the college, taking on extra typing jobs at night, like his dissertation when it still looked as if he might finish it in time to land a permanent appointment there.

"It's just, you're so worn out when you get home."

"Three straight hours. Plus the drive. And they're no help. I'm the one does all the talking."

"It must be scary," she says, "I can imagine."

"No, you can't."

She sits across from him at the table, as he pictures wire mesh keeping them from touching all but their fingertips.

"You know what I mean."

"No," he says.

He goes to the refrigerator and opens the door to stand looking into its bright cold interior as though he's forgotten what he's after. The ceiling lights dim, as the refrigerator motor kicks in. He takes out the second beer he knows he can have without getting anything serious started between them and, feeling her eyes on him, sits down. He forks up another mouthful of eggs before opening the beer. "Tonight," he says, "I'm right at the place, you know, where Kurtz says, 'The horror, the horror.'"

"I never read it." She points to his eggs.

"No, and you don't want to." He takes a bite of bread, then shoves the eggs around the plate with the fork. "'The horror, the horror.' I'm just going to explain it to them, when Czuba starts in. He's got his head in his hands and he's rocking back and forth and I think he's having a seizure or maybe somebody slipped a knife into him."

"They can't have knives, can they?"

"Who knows what goes on in there? Nobody tells me anything. I'm just the man with the books, an outsider."

"But they search them."

"They're supposed to, sure. All I know is, Czuba could be dying, and the rest of them sit there looking at me like 'So what now, Teach?' He's rocking back and forth, groaning 'Oh Jesus, Oh fuck, Oh Jesus, Oh fuck' So I go to his seat, squat down beside him, and ask what's wrong. How about him taking a deep breath here, trying to tell me what's wrong. What else am I going to do, send him to the principal? But he can't stop, or won't, and I can feel the others getting restless. I tell them please tear a page out of their notebooks and, this counts as a quiz now, write a paragraph on 'What does Marlowe learn from Kurtz?' Then I kind of pat Czuba's elbow and he gets up. He's a big guy, one of the weight lifters. I get him out into the hall. He just stands there, sobbing. I can't see any blood on him, and I don't know if I should put my arm around him or what. Maybe it's against their code. So I just stand there."

"What was wrong with him?"

"I'm telling you, all right? He keeps going 'Oh fuck, Oh Jesus,' then looks right at me, his eyes are running with tears, and he says, "That's just how I felt when I blew away my fucking wife.'"

"What?"

"That's exactly what he said."

"But why?"

"Like Kurtz. The horror!"

"He said that to you? No!"

"Yes. I had no idea what he was in for. All the office sends me is the enrollment sheet. Now he wants to tell me the whole damn story. We're standing by the water fountain; he's got my arm and it's like the ancient mariner, there's no way I'm getting free. The others are hunched over their desks trying to write a paragraph; most of them can't put a sentence together yet, and all I can think is, How the hell did I end up here? So Czuba tells me he and his wife split up because he brought his work home with him; he couldn't help it, even when he didn't talk about it, it was there, his attitude, his temper. They were always fighting over it. Then she started seeing this psychologist."

"Because of him probably."

"I guess so. Anyhow, he said that's what did it."

"But she was only trying to keep them together, wasn't she?"

"What? No. *Seeing* him meaning *sleeping* with him."

"Not her psychologist."

"A psychologist. They met someplace, at a bar or in church, who knows. He's a man, all right?"

"She wasn't trying to get help?"

"She was fucking him was what she was doing."

"Don't."

"I'm just telling you what Czuba said. 'She's fucking this guy,' he says. 'So, okay, we're split up, what right have I got complaining? Then this Sunday I run into her in the parking lot, at the shopping center.'"

"This was here?"

"Akron. He went to church that morning like always, he's Catholic, and that afternoon, he says, he's supposed to direct traffic at a shopping center, for extra money. I look at him, I don't get it, so that's when he tells me. He's a cop! *Was* a cop. You see what I mean? This guy spent nine years on the force and got two commendations. So he sees her getting out of their station wagon, and goes over. He says something, she says something, the next thing you know his service pistol's in his hand and she's down on the blacktop."

"She died?"

"He shot her, sure."

"No!"

"Then, he says, he sat down right beside her, in the parking lot, in his uniform, and waited for the other cops to come run him in."

"Oh my God, the poor woman."

"It drove him crazy, her running around."

"But still."

"Now he's doing twenty to life."

"He'll get out, won't he?"

"Maybe. He's done eight. But they crack up; they kill each other."

"Think of his wife."

"All right, I realize."

"At least he's got a chance. What chance does she have anymore?"

"Any longer. You had to see him, the way he was crying."

"But . . . Oh, they didn't have children, did they?"

"How should I know?"

"Didn't you ask?"

"I just listened. He didn't say. I didn't ask him anything."

"But if they had children, he'd tell you, don't you think, what happened to them and all?"

"I guess so, I don't know."

"Then I bet they didn't have any."

"Look, all I know is what he told me."

"You think he was telling the truth?"

"Why wouldn't he?"

"Don't they lie?"

"Doesn't everybody? Jesus! Not about something like this."

"Maybe he likes getting attention, wants you to feel sorry for him."

"You don't believe it?"

"I believe he told you, but I just can't . . ."

"What? Because he's a cop he can't go crazy? Oh sure, like the psychologist, right? He's a *doctor,* he wouldn't fool around with the wife of a *police officer.* Sometimes, you know, I really can't believe you."

The overhead fluorescent tubes put purplish shadows under her eyes. "Your eggs are cold," she says.

He puts down the fork. "I'm finished."

"No, you're not. Look."

"I don't want any more."

"She gets up, takes his plate to the sink, and runs water.

"Look," he says, "it's just the whole thing, I'm worked-up is all."

"I know it must be scary for you there."

"Did I say I was scared? When did I say that? Tell me." He twists about in his chair. Her back is to him and she's washing the day's dishes. He tells her, "I'm locked in too, you know."

"Do you have to be?"

"That's the way it is."

"But what would you do if, if there was trouble?"

"I told them, the first class, I said, 'I don't expect any disciplinary problems here, understand.'"

"Good."

"They laughed."

She turns to face him. "How do you mean?"

"How what? If you have to explain a joke, you know, then . . ." He lets out a short, barking laugh, surprising himself. "Once I came home from school with this history assignment, and I asked my dad, 'Were you alive during the great depression?' He's in his chair, like always, half-crocked, and he looks up and says, 'The economic one?' It was a joke, the only one I remember him telling. I didn't get it for years." He shakes his head. "Look, with the class, I was making a joke, that's all. And they laughed, all right? *At* me maybe, but I think *with* me. I might as well joke about it. They could break me in two, there's nothing I could do."

"You said there were guards."

"I'm on the second floor." He turns to empty his words onto the table. "The classroom's open up there, and so's the toilet, but the corridor itself is locked. The guard shack or whatever, the room with all the electronic gear, is down on the first floor. It's locked up tight. The guards stay in there, mostly. They stick together too. You don't see any of them going into a room alone." Like me, he thinks, but leaves it unsaid. It could be courage on his part, or only a failure of imagination.

"Well," she says, "at least you won't have to do it much longer."

"Teaching? About thirty more years is all."

"No, I meant at the prison."

"Four and a half weeks."

"That's what I mean."

"That's not long?"

"Is it?"

He shrugs. "Winter term always seems longer."

The dishes dried, she hangs the yellow towel on the wire rack beside the sink. "Why don't you go to bed?" she says.

"No. You go on."

"I thought you were tired."

"Wound up, I said. Wound up is not tired."

"I didn't tell you to do it, you know."

"Do what?"

"Teach there. It was your idea."

"My idea?"

"Well, it wasn't mine, I know that."

"Paying off bills was my idea, right. Being caged up with killer apes was not my idea, believe me."

"They told you, didn't they, what it would be like."

"Forget it."

"No, I sympathize."

"You do?"

"But remember, you said that's why the other teacher didn't do it, why you got the chance."

"Fine," he says. "Whatever." He scrapes the label from the empty bottle with a thumbnail. "All I was trying to say, when this whole business got started, was that you never know what you might do, maybe you could do something terrible."

"I know, but you're . . . it's late, and I think really it's that policeman you're talking about."

"No, *I* could do something terrible."

"If you were in prison, yes, but then you already would have."

"That's not what I'm talking about!"

"But I'm saying, don't you see?"

"Logic," he says, "takes you only so far."

After a moment she touches his shoulder. "I'm going up."

He sits in the bright, chilly kitchen hearing her weight creak the floorboards over his head. Even if he called her back and said something to smooth things over, his apology would be tainted by resentment. What's done is done. And he can think of nothing to stop him from doing it, despite himself, day in and day out.

When she was helping out in the department, he'd hear the sudden bubbling up of her laugh, and would find some excuse to drop into the main office. She'd be done laughing when he got there, but sometimes would give him a smile. He married her, he thinks, because he wanted to be in the room where that laughter was.

After she's stopped moving above him, he turns off the lights and sits looking out the window at the snow-dusted fields under the full moon. In the center of his view there is a flaw in the pane that distorts his vision. He shifts his head, and recognizes the crystal prism she's recently hung there. Days, to her delight, it refracts the sun about the room like a school of rainbow minnows. He cups it briefly in his hand, a cold lump of cut glass. Stepping to the refrigerator, he opens the door, then closes it without taking anything out.

When he goes up, the stairs squeak beneath his stockinged feet.

She sleeps with a pillow over her head. The hall light throws his shadow across her legs, so dark that it looks heavy, and it surprises him that she doesn't wake up to see what's in the room with her.

HOME
by Julie Brown

After five years of attending night school, Don finally graduated with his degree in chemical engineering. Darlene was proud of him—it hadn't been easy going to school while managing an apartment building. After graduation Don started looking for work. There didn't seem to be much in the Milwaukee area, so his advisor suggested he contact companies further east, in the industrial belt of the Midwest: Chicago, Gary, Cleveland, Detroit, Pittsburgh. Finally, a paint manufacturing company in Ohio took an interest in him.

Darlene splurged for a second ticket and flew to Youngstown with Don, waiting for him in the hotel room while he was being interviewed. Sprawled out on the queen-sized bed, drinking room-service coffee for the first time in her life, Darlene skimmed through the *Youngstown Vindicator.* A quick look at the Help Wanted ads told her she wouldn't have too much trouble finding some kind of job. If she wanted to, she could probably even find something at the paint plant where Don would work if all went well today. But the real estate ads interested Darlene most. She read these with a green pen in hand, circling the houses that she wanted to see.

Darlene knew exactly what she wanted—she was a subscriber of *Victorian Homes* and had her dream house planned, right down to the way she'd hang the Austrian lace curtains and how the Oriental rugs (as yet unpurchased) would look on the newly refinished hardwood floors. Oh, they'd have a family room with comfortable chairs and a

TV set (tastefully hidden in an antique armoire), but the rest would be
furnished with authentic period antiques. She even wanted the accessories to be just right: antique frying pans and a flat iron in the kitchen,
old linens draped over a wicker chair in the bath. For the five years
they'd managed apartments in Milwaukee, Darlene made herself
happy this way, planning how things would be in their first house.

> "As standardized housing became more accepted, the social implica-
> tions of this architectural uniformity were often discussed. Reformers . . .
> were especially eager to champion the need for common architectural
> standards. Such a vision of similarity would, they believed, reinforce a
> balanced, egalitarian social life for a community. Nonetheless, there was
> a certain resistance to uniformity. Most architects believed unquestion-
> ingly in the unique, custom-designed dwelling for those clients who could
> afford the expensive experiment. Because all people in a community are
> never alike, [some argued], standardization of settings and of social ex-
> pectations would lead to misfits and wide-spread maladjustment."

> (Gwendolyn Wright, *Moralism and the Model Home,* 1980)

At first it was fun being apartment managers. Right away, Darlene
had a brass MANAGER sign engraved to hang on their front door.
Then she transformed their second bedroom into an office with a desk
and swivel chair, and bought a filing cabinet for the files she made on
each unit. She even bought an answering machine in case tenants had
problems while she was out cleaning or gardening. That first summer,
she asked Don to hang window boxes in which she planted geraniums.
During the holiday season, she had Don string lights around the front
door. Little touches like this, she reasoned, made the tenants feel more
at home.

But as the five years went by, managing began to take its toll on
Darlene. It didn't bother Don that tenants sometimes lost their keys and
had to be let in at 3 A.M. Don kept his cool when the older tenants
complained about rent increases. But Darlene found herself getting
edgy. For her, the tenants came to represent intrusion, entrapment.
She'd find herself avoiding them in the halls and laundry room when
she did her cleaning. When the phone would ring she'd let the machine
answer for her. She would find a note under her door that said "please
send exterminator next month have found cockroach in kitchen" and
throw it down the garbage disposal.

Life at the Charleston East didn't really count—it was a sort of dress-rehearsal for the real show that would follow. Their savings had grown and would surely help them turn their dream into a plan. The dream was simple: to find good jobs, buy a house, have children, and be happy. The house was a crucial part of this plan—it was a necessary part of living happily ever after.

Grandmother's House

My grandmother lived on the Oregon coast when I was growing up. From her front porch it was a five minute walk to the windy Pacific Ocean. My brother and I would play in the sand, filling our buckets with treasure: oval pink shells like angel wings, rusty crab claws, milky agates, sand dollars warm from the sun. We scattered crumbs for the squawking gulls and chased, but never caught them. We were often the only two on the beach, especially when it rained, a cold drizzle that burned our hands and turned the ocean a steely gray.

From her back door it was a five minute walk to the edge of a forest so lush and green it sheltered us in a cocoon. My brother and I would hike through the woods in search of trilliums and animal tracks: raccoon, deer, sometimes elk. We waded barefoot through the creek, holding still for the curious tadpoles, black watermelon seeds that came to graze our ankles.

The house itself was ordinary: two cozy bedrooms with gingham curtains, a kitchen paneled with knotty pine. She had coffee cups with our names on them: Julie in pink, Jeremy in blue, that only we were allowed to drink from. The rooms were heated by a large wood-burning stove that Grandma fueled with logs she split herself.

This house of my grandmother's must be my Eden. The homeland I have lost in all ways but one: memory.

Good Starter Home

Bring your hammer and paint brush to this little charmer. On 1/2 acre conveniently, located at intersection of 2 interstate highways. Owner will help finance—must sell!

My mother lives in a mobile home. I begged her not to sell the old house but she said with you kids gone now I don't need the space and I can sure do without the headaches of home ownership. She has already replaced the roof, the pipes, and the stove in her mobile home. The whole house quakes when she washes a load of clothes. "Get ready for takeoff," she says, laughing. A native Oregonian, my mother is partial to the "Western" motif—she bought a wagon wheel and a wooden plow to display in the front yard (chained to the mailbox so no one would steal them) and put up a split-rail fence. In her kitchen, all counter top appliances have quilted dust-covers featuring hearts, animals, and cartoon barns.

My father lives in a condominium. His unit is sandwiched between neighbors to his left and to his right. They share a common roof, a common yard, and a common parking lot. My father lives in this condo with his third wife, who has furnished the entire place in "Oriental." Gold foil wallpaper provides the backdrop for expensive black-lacquer furniture. Potted bamboo and jade plants pose indifferently, silhouetted behind a rare silk folding screen. "This condo is just what we were looking for," my father says. "Except we could use one more room. And a fireplace."

Darlene and Don celebrated with champagne when the paint company called Don to offer him the job. Darlene was proud of Don for all he had accomplished—she was also thrilled to be moving out of the Charleston East into a house of their own. She had saved seven thousand dollars for the down payment.

Don's company gave him a house hunting allowance, and in July Don and Darlene drove to Youngstown, staying in the same hotel they'd stayed in when Don interviewed. While Don unloaded the car, Darlene called a real estate company to set up appointments for the houses she had circled.

Monday morning, the real estate lady's heels clicked on the stairs as she led Darlene and Don to the front door of the first house Darlene wanted to see. "I know you'll like it," the lady said, fiddling with the lock box. "It's an authentic century home." Darlene and Don followed her into the house.

It was a century home, if you could see through the surfaces each owner had successively layered down. Three kinds of linoleum—gold, green, and blue—were visible through the worn area near the sink. The window in the dining room was dressed in layers, too—brown velvet drapes over musty lace curtains: beneath it all, a shade pulled down. When Darlene lifted the shade she found a cracked window that someone had pieced together with electric tape. "You can replace that window," said the real estate lady. "Think of the potential this old gal has."

Don crossed through the house and flipped on the bathroom light.

Red bath mats nestled on blue shag carpet. The walls were papered with a daisy print and over the paper, shards of broken mirror had been glued in a kaleidoscope pattern, reflecting their images back in a hundred bits of color.

"I couldn't bring myself to use this bathroom," Darlene said. She opened her purse and fished around for her Tums. She handed a pink wafer to Don and chewed two herself.

"It's certainly an original concept," said the real estate lady. "I've never seen anything quite like it."

By Friday, Darlene and Don had looked at 30 houses in the Youngstown area, ranging from two-bedroom ranches to three-story tudors. None of them seemed to fit their needs exactly. Or rather, their desires.

Suburban Special

"Wood look" aluminum siding renders this lovely house maintenance-free. Newly remodeled kitchen boasts easy care faux-marble countertops with z-brick backsplash and red vinyl floor in "classic tile" motif. One owner—three years new!

In 1883, Pasteur demonstrated that germs were responsible for causing disease. This led to a revolution against richly patterned wallpaper, heavy velvet drapes, and thick layers of carpets, all of which were thought to harbor germs. With the new fear of germs and the diseases they brought, housewives wanted interiors that looked sanitary and were easy to keep clean. Living rooms and parlours now featured white plastered walls and white curtains. Bathrooms were tiled in white, and white porcelain sinks and tubs made their debut. Kitchens also sparkled with white tile and enameled white appliances. The ideal kitchen was thought to be one you could "hose down" every night to a germ free shine.

After tirelessly viewing so many homes, Darlene and Don finally found one they liked: a five bedroom century home in a village outside of Youngstown.

Darlene thought it was the most elegant house she had ever seen. A three-story Queen Anne beauty, this home was richly fitted with oak floors and woodwork, a magnificent staircase that swirled up to a stained-glass window at the second-floor landing, and bathrooms with claw-foot tubs. Darlene fell in love with it the moment she stepped onto the wrap-around porch. "It's so pretty!" she said. "It's what I've always wanted! Look at the tower—it would be like living in a fairy tale." She ran from room to room, breathlessly describing in words what she was seeing: "A pedestal sink! A bay window! A fireplace in the entryway!" The real estate lady smiled and said nothing.

Darlene and Don discussed the details of the purchase with her over coffee at a local diner. Don had a few qualms about the house. For one thing, the house had been broken into a four-plex. How hard would it be to reconvert it to a single family dwelling? The real estate lady assured him it was only a matter of removing a few walls and rewiring the electric meter. Don was concerned, too, about the location of the house—wasn't this town a bit far from Youngstown? A quick half hour, she said with a wink. It will be worth it, coming home to this beauty. Don also wondered about the street. This house was on Main Street, and it carried business traffic to and from downtown. "We'll get used to it!" Darlene said. "We won't even hear the cars after a week!"

"Let's think it over," Don said. "Let's go home and come back next weekend to see it one more time."

"If it's still for sale," said the real estate lady.

"It might be gone!" said Darlene. She grabbed Don's arm. "We have to act now. Oh, please," she said. Tears filled her eyes. The real estate lady gave Darlene a concerned, sympathetic look, then excused herself to the lady's room.

"You've got a degree, you've got a job, you've got everything you want," Darlene said. "I need this house. We could be so happy here together. I'll be miserable if someone else buys it," she said. "It already feels like it's ours."

"This is the true nature of home—it is the place of peace; the shelter, not only from all injury, but from all terror, doubt, and division. In so far as it is not this, it is not home; so far as the anxieties of the outer life penetrate into it, and the inconsistently-minded, unloved, or hostile society of the outer world is allowed by either husband or wife to cross the threshold it ceases to be a home; it is then only a part of the outer world which you have roofed over and lighted fire in. But so far as it is a sacred place, a vestal temple, a temple of the hearth, it is a home."

(John Ruskin, *Sesame and Lilies,* 1864)

All the places I have lived:

1. the woods of Northwest Oregon
2. St. John's district in Portland

3. San Francisco
4. my grandmother's
5. a cottage on the Oregon Coast
6. a ranch house in Portland
7. low-income housing in Beaverton, a Portland suburb
8. a dormitory in Corvallis, Oregon
9. a professor's basement
10. my father-in-law's 1854 mansion in New York
11. a duplex in Corvallis
12. an apartment in Corvallis (we managed it)
13. rental house in Portland
14. a Victorian apartment in Missoula, Montana
15. a duplex in Milwaukee
16. an apartment in Milwaukee (we managed it)
17. our first house in Salem, Ohio

I am 29 years old.

Moving day was like Christmas for Darlene. Wednesday morning she woke up at four, even though they hadn't planned to leave until six, and she woke up Don as well. "We're on our way! It's moving day!" she sang to a silly tune. All the boxes and furniture had been loaded into the U-Haul truck, and their car was attached to the rear of the truck for towing—they wanted to ride together in the cab. They had their donuts and thermos full of coffee, their Brewers baseball caps, and their small bag of coins for the tolls. This is it, Darlene thought as they pulled out of the driveway into the dark morning. This is the part where we live happily ever after.

Although it was a ten-hour drive, time passed quickly for Darlene. She chattered as Don drove, telling him how she would evict the tenants first thing, then tear down the wall that separated apartments one and two. She told Don how she wanted to replace the kitchen floor with black and white tile, find an old woodstove, change wallpaper, the works! Room by room she decorated the house as they drove, smiling when Don asked her if she had a banker in her back pocket. "One room at a time!" she assured him.

A strange thing happened to me two years ago. It was finals week at the university and I was walking home, my mind tired after a difficult final exam in French. The air was winter dark at this evening hour, and

snow was falling heavily from the salmon-colored sky. I pounded my
mittened hands together as I trudged through the drifts, grateful I had
my new boots on. All I could think of was going home.

I was shocked to realize, however, that I couldn't remember where I
lived. When I tried to picture it—the house, the apartment, whatever it
was—my mind was as empty of image as the snow-covered sidewalk
before me.

Where did I live?

I kept walking, unable to visualize the place toward which I was walking. I could remember other houses I had lived in. Many of them quite
clearly. I conjured up the last green-carpeted apartment I lived in, one
of the ranch-style houses I lived in as a child, my dorm room. But I had
no idea where I lived at that moment. I worried that I might be walking
a long, long way that night. Or maybe I was out of my mind. Would I
freeze in the snow like the man in "To Build a Fire"? I became panicky.
I started to cry.

To my surprise, after four blocks I saw the duplex I lived in and all
memory returned. I knew I would find our chipped oak table in the
dining room, our stained yellow couch in the living room. I knew the
shape of the entryway. I walked into the kitchen and my husband
smiled and handed me a mug of hot chocolate.

There is my necessary angel, my home.

It's the promise a fog horn makes, calling to sailors through cottony
darkness: HOME, HOME, HOME. Dresses you sew in home ec class—
"homemade," an insult. Cookies you bake—"homemade," a compliment. If you aren't pretty, they say you are homely. Homegrown, ho-
mebrewed, homespun virtue. The homeowner who keeps a tidy yard:
homeproud. The homemaker keeps things clean and homey inside.
The books you study on the kitchen table, homework. Dusting the
same table, housework. Homefree, home run, things you do well.
Homesick when you move away, homecoming when you return.

By Friday afternoon the truck was unloaded and returned to the U-
Haul station in Youngstown. Darlene and Don carried boxes to the appropriate rooms and arranged most of their big furniture pieces. While
Don set up the stereo and TV, Darlene cleaned the sink and tub and
disinfected the toilet. While he changed all the burned out lightbulbs in
the house, she wiped out the kitchen cupboards and scrubbed the fridge

and stove. Darlene whistled along with the radio as she put away the dishes. "I never saw you whistle cleaning an apartment," Don teased. Darlene smiled.

"I'm almost done unpacking the kitchen," she said. "Let's celebrate tonight. Let's cook a nice meal."

"I'll get a good bottle of wine," Don said.

"We'll have a nice quiet evening at home," she said. "We'll light candles."

That night, Darlene cooked a big tray of lasagne and Don made a tossed green salad. They put on a favorite record and dimmed the lights while they ate. "Let's toast," she said. "To the people who built this house one hundred years ago."

"They don't make 'em like they used to!" said Don.

After dinner they carried their glasses into the living room and snuggled on the couch. Darlene was about to tell Don how perfect everything was when she heard the blaring of rap music so loud it affected her heartbeat.

"What the hell was that?" she asked.

"Tenants?"

"I guess it's someone driving by," she said. "What a rude person."

Darlene kissed Don and smiled. Nothing could spoil this perfect evening.

Until a second car drove by, its stereo blasting heavy metal. This music was so loud it rattled the dirty dishes in the kitchen sink.

"What's going on?" Don asked.

"Maybe a movie just let out? I don't know. What do you think?"

Throughout the night, cars crawled by one after another, all with stereos howling loud. When the traffic light at their street corner turned red, cars backed up until they were nine or ten deep. When the light flagged green, the first two or three peeled their tires as they screeched ahead. One car would recognize another car and honk till the other honked back. Their motors were seething in the sticky darkness of the summer night.

Darlene became very quiet on the couch. Her scalp felt prickly, like it had separated from her brain. She didn't want to say it.

"Cruisers?" Don asked.

"Looks that way," she said.

"Maybe it's just this night. Maybe a party just ended or something."

"I hope you're right," said Darlene.

Every year the motor vehicles department in the small coastal town where my grandmother lived takes in 200 California license plates for Oregon plates. The Californian's new houses are expensive *Sunset Magazine* homes, the kind with angular cedar decks and wood siding stained "sienna" or "umber." The new houses feature large windows facing west, the better to view the Pacific. Each year the houses are built one road higher up the coast mountains, to optimize this viewing potential.

The trees that covered the foothills have been clear cut, as high as the newest houses could be built. The forest is almost gone. Because of this, many species of animals have left the area. Some, like owls and frogs, are in danger of dying out.

On my grandmother's street below, the houses have been bull dozed and replaced with a trailer park. These are the weekenders from Portland, who perch plaster of paris gulls on their roofs and artfully arrange driftwood along their gravel driveways.

Experts predict that erosion will carry the topsoil off the mountainside. Heavy rains will cause serious mudslides. It would only take one such mudslide to bury the trailer court below.

> LOVE CANAL (AP)—State of New York housing authority recently announced that the Love Canal district has been cleared of hazardous waste and is now safe for human occupation. Early next month, homes in the area will be sold at 65% of current market value. A list of would-be buyers is currently being compiled in the county office. John McDonald, first on the waiting list, said to reporters, "The government says it's safe, so I believe it's safe. I'm going to move in this summer. Hey, the government wouldn't let us move there if it wasn't safe, would they?" No guarantees are being issued as to the possibility of future leaks.

Total Self-Sufficiency

in this geodesic dome with eight multi-purpose rooms. Well water, solar panels, septic tank. 1/2 acre organic garden included. Why pay bills each month?

Monday morning, Don got up and readied himself for his first day on the new job. Darlene cooked him a bacon and egg breakfast, and smiled when he kissed her goodbye.

"What's your plan for today?" he asked, handing her the folded newspaper from the front porch.

"I'm going to hang up our posters," Darlene said. "That ought to brighten this place up."

After Don pulled out of the driveway, Darlene skimmed the head-lines of the paper. A creek that ran through their village had been poi-soned with a chemical spill a month earlier—citizens were reminded not to fish or swim in the creek. Residents with wells were still urged to drink bottled water until further testing could be done.

Darlene crawled back into bed and pulled the blankets up over her face. She closed her eyes, and started to cry. Saturday night had been worse than Friday, and Sunday was almost as bad. She feared that the worst was true—the cruisers would be back next weekend, maybe sooner. How could she bear to live on the cruising strip? And what about the chemicals? Why hadn't somebody warned them? Curled up under the covers, Darlene cried and cried. She was homesick and she missed her mother.

Eventually, she forced herself to get up and unload boxes. It wasn't the same without Don around, but at least if she got something done today she could surprise him when he got home. She busied herself with the kitchen. She thought she could at least get that room unpacked all the way. But why should I unpack if I'm going to paint? she won-dered. So she took everything out of the cupboards, deciding she'd try to paint the kitchen that afternoon. She lifted the plates down. Two cockroaches tumbled off the shelf. She reached under the sink for the bug spray and felt cold water drip on her wrist. How had they missed that leaky pipe?

Darlene crawled back into bed.

So many things went wrong in the first house my husband and I bought. For one thing, the roof leaked badly, though the sellers had assured us that it was sound and the stains on the wall were from a previous time. When a downpour struck, we situated five buckets under the drips—they made a kind of music, PING pung PONG deet deet, PING pung PONG deet deet. The house was also infested with ants, big black shiny ones that I worried might be carpenter ants. I called the man who had inspected it. "You said termite inspection," he explained. "That's all you paid for, that's all I looked for. Termites." Then there was the chimney—when the roofer came out, he alerted us that the chimney was ready to tumble at any moment. Until he could schedule it in, he warned, better put up a fence around the area so no one gets killed. In the basement, we hauled away a mattress that the old owners had left behind. We found that the bricks in the foundation behind it were crumbling. There seemed to be no end to our troubles.

Welcome to the joys of home ownership, my mother said.

The cemetery is a kind of home—a tiny garden space, your name and numbers etched on a stone: your address. Your stone arranged in a row of stones, the rows grouped into sub-divisions. Footpaths carry visitors to greet you, carry them away. You buy a space in a community of souls—quiet, peaceful, and the grounds are well-maintained. As always, you worry about location and price.

The following Friday, Don fixed breakfast for himself before going to work. He brought Darlene toast and tea in bed.

"You haven't done much with the house," he said gently. "What's wrong? You were so excited before." He sat beside Darlene on the bed and rested the toast on a cardboard box they were using as a night stand.

"You know what's wrong," she said. "It's the cruisers. They are making my life miserable. I can't stand it."

"It's only a little noise a couple days a week. We'll get used to it," he said.

"But they cruised last night! Why would they cruise on a Thursday?"

"Let's go out to dinner tonight," he said. "Tomorrow we'll paint the kitchen together, OK?"

Darlene smiled. "OK," she said. "I'll choose the paint this afternoon."

"I have another idea," said Don. "Why don't you call some people about this cruising problem? Call the Sheriff, the mayor, call city council, call the newspaper. Maybe you can do something to change it."

"That's a good idea," she said, brightening. "I'll do it. There must be others who can't stand this noise."

"That's the spirit," Don said.

COME HOME TO SERENITY . . .

15 homeless in Salem.
At Southington West Downs. An Exclusive Planned Neighborhood
    80 homeless in Columbiana County.
Community featuring spacious, elegant Homes on wooded 2 acre
    140,000 homeless in the state of Ohio.
lots. Prices starting at $200,000. Traditional Values are

3,000,000 homeless in the United States of America. reflected in every detail. Call now for Private Showing.

That evening, they went out to dinner. Darlene pushed her salad back and forth across the plate. She didn't touch her wine.

"Any luck with your phone calls?" Don asked.

"No."

"Couldn't get through?"

"I got through," she said. "I got through."

"Well?"

"It seems that cruising is an institution in this crummy town. Teenagers have cruised our street for two generations. The sheriff says there's no law against it. The mayor says there's nothing he can do. Our city councilman said he regrets the situation and wishes we had bought a house in a quieter part of town. He meant the new part of town."

"Nothing we can do, huh?" Don asked.

Tears fell down Darlene's cheeks. She took a sip of wine, and still the tears kept falling.

"Don't cry," Don said. "We'll think of something."

"There's nothing we can do," Darlene sobbed.

"Nothing. I hate that house. It's dark, and cold, and the whole thing smells like a wet basement. I can't fall asleep at night, and when I do I have bad dreams. One of the tenants told me a woman was murdered in our house."

Don took Darlene's hand. "What do you want to do?" he asked. "Would you like to sell the house and move?"

Darlene stopped crying. "Could we?"

We can put it on the market tomorrow, if you like."

Darlene sniffed. "We could find another house. Oh Don, you're so sweet about this."

"It may be a while till this house sells," Don said. "It's sort of a white elephant. Don't forget, it sat on the market for two years till we came along. We'll have to make the best of things till then, OK? Maybe we'll even have to keep the tenants."

Darlene smiled and nodded. She knew just the kind of house they would buy when this one sold.

Dear Mom,

In answer to your last letter, no, we haven't sold the house. It's been on the market for six months now, and no one's even made an offer on it.

Every week at least one family comes to see it—I think they just want to see if the inside matches up to what the outside promises. This house has history, charm, and grace, but people want wall to wall carpeting and aluminum siding.

Meanwhile, we're cold, lonely, and tired. We still don't know anyone. Last night when we were reading we heard a loud crash—three bricks had fallen off the chimney. I think a few roof slates were broken.

The drive to Youngstown every day is really wearing me out. Bob's drive to Warren is even further. Winter will be worse, no doubt. Everything just feels like such a mess right now, and all of this is my fault— I'm the one who had to have this house. If it was up to me, I'd sell it at a ten thousand dollar loss. ha ha.

More than anything else, I'm sorry to live so far away from you. It hurts me that I can't be there when you go into the hospital next week. I want to take care of you as you always cared for me when I was little. I promise I'll come for Christmas. I promise I'll move back to Oregon as soon as I can find a job there. I want to come home, I really do.

Love, Julie

THE WEST

by David Teagle

At daybreak, Mignon saw an apparition—a man, dressed in a long gray coat, like the ghost of a western outlaw, at the edge of the thin line of bushes that separated her yard from the Morrisey's wheatfields. His hands were clasped in front of him, pouring a thick spray that produced a cloud of steam as it landed on the ground, as if he were dousing a campfire that was invisible to her. He finished and walked away through the brush, fading into the early morning. She stared at the place he had been standing, convinced that he was an important omen, a sign.

She had been sitting for most of the night, nested in among the embroidered pillows on the wooden ledge by her upstairs window, a "reading nook" her mother had called it when they were planning the house. She was writing a long, serious poem, untitled as yet, that began:

> I exist
> and what of that;
> it does not seem to matter.
> The clouds are torn
> by moonlight,
> shredded by desire.

After the man disappeared, she set down her pen and put her face against the window. The glass was cold on her cheek, damp from condensation, and her breath made patterns of fog that vanished as quickly as they appeared. She got down from the ledge and stepped back, continuing to stare out the window with her arms crossed tight across her chest.

Each pane of glass was edged by a ring of frost, making the backyard seem like a cheap Christmas card—the barn, the trees, and the split-rail fence, all coated in fresh snow. The parquet floor chilled her bare feet, and tiny goosebumps formed on her skin under the thin cotton nightgown. She enjoyed the feeling, half cold and half fear, and stood there for a moment before getting into bed. She pulled her grandmother's quilt up over her knees and closed her eyes, going over the vision in her mind until it solidified into certainty.

With her eyes shut, she could hear every sound in the sleeping house. The far-off thump of the central heating unit turning on, followed by the faint puff of the warm air blowing through the vent in the ceiling. The quiet hum of the refrigerator and the ice-maker emptying downstairs in the kitchen. The clock on the mantle in the living room, a metronome for the rhythm of her life.

At 6:45, the automatic coffee maker on the kitchen counter began to bubble, and ten minutes later, she heard her mother's alarm clock go off. It rang for a long time before someone stopped it.

She dressed and went out into the upstairs hall. The water was running in the bathroom, and as she passed the open door, she saw Bill, her mother's friend, standing in front of the mirror with his back to her, brushing his teeth and admiring himself. He was wearing only a pair of jockey shorts, a bright white stripe that made the tan seem darker across his body. He spit into the sink and saw her in the mirror.

"What's up, kid?" he said.

Mignon frowned at him and went downstairs. In the kitchen, she took a bamboo tray out of the cabinet and began preparing breakfast for her mother—grapefruit, toast, and black coffee. She arranged the plates neatly and folded a linen napkin into the shape of a swan, an art she had practiced from her book of Origami. Lifting the tray, she carried it upstairs and stood in front of her mother's closed bedroom door.

"Room service," she said, knocking at the door.

She set the tray down on the carpet outside the door and walked down the hall to her room, where she sat at the foot of her bed, kicking her feet against the frame, until she heard her ride pull into the driveway and honk the horn.

Her mother picked her up after school in Bill's Mercedes, and they rode home, surrounded by the smell of hand-treated leather and the

muzak her mother enjoyed. They drove through town, past the shopping centers and the clusters of brick houses that encircled the city,
until the highway merged to two lanes and began to curve more often,
winding out into the country where the houses were spaced farther
apart—square farmhouses surrounded by empty fields of gray-brown
dirt. The land seemed to roll on forever, broken only by the feeble wind-
breaks, lines of stubby trees that fought to keep the soil in place when
the winds turned hot and dry in the summer.

Mignon watched the ground off to the side of the highway. She
imagined that she was riding her horse alongside the car, dipping and
rising through the gullies and small hills, laughing into the cold wind
with her hair flying behind her. For a moment, she could almost feel
the bite of the air and the jarring gallop, but she lost it, drawn back into
the car. She felt cut off from the outside, secure in a comfortable shell
of plush seats and warm air blowing onto her feet. Her mother
hummed along with the radio, tapping her manicured fingernails on
the steering wheel.

As they turned off the main highway onto the road that led to their
house, Mignon saw him again. He was sitting on the big flat rock near
the mailbox. The same rock that she used to sit on everyday, perched
like a waif, waiting for her father's letters that never came. She turned
around in her seat, staring at him as they passed. It was the same man,
the same coat, stained and faded by weather and age. It had been at
least two years since she had sat there on the rock, but she could still
feel every imperfection in the stone, as if her fingers were tracing them
in tandem with his.

"Did you see that man?" she asked her mother after they had
passed him.

"What man?"

"That man sitting on the rock back there—by the mailbox."

"What rock by the mailbox?"

"Mother, what is wrong with you?"

Her mother eased the car over to the shoulder and stopped near the
one tree on the road. Besides the Morrisey's farm, there were only six
houses on the road—six houses, one tree, and thousands of acres of
bare wheat fields. The tree was sad even in summer, but now its bony,
leafless branches and stunted trunk, twisted by the wind and sagging
against the wire fence for support, seemed unbearably depressing.
Mignon noticed how the thin wire cut into the trunk, leaving deep gashes.
It seemed strange to think of a wounded tree, and she suddenly felt a great
empathy for it. Time never healed, she thought; it only dug in deeper.

"Mignon, honey." Her mother's hands fluttered between the steering wheel and her lap, "Bill asked me to marry him. Isn't that great?"

Mignon continued to stare at the tree, thinking of the sap, frozen
inside the black branches.

Mignon watched the sunset from her spot at the window. Somewhere over there, not too far away, the real west began in the purple
and orange streaks that crossed the sky. The farms dried up, replaced
by gnarled bushes and thick-leafed, thorny plants, and the dirt turned
loose, crumbling to sand. The ground ruptured with sharp rock forma-
tions, jutting upwards like the teeth of strange animals. Winter became
different over there—cruel and mighty, a force rather than a nuisance.

She went to her closet and brought down her grandmother's photo
album, bound in dry, cracked leather, clumsily tooled in simple patterns
and closed with a rawhide strap. She carried the thick book over to her
shelf by the window and set it down, then opened the drawer on her
nightstand, removing a short candle and a tarnished brass holder. She
placed the candle in the holder and lit it with matches from the drawer,
sheltering the flame with her hand before setting the candle next to the
album. Her face was framed by the candlelight and reflected back from
the blackness of the window.

"Mignon, honey," she said, "I'm giving you this book now. Your
mother isn't interested in it, so it falls to you. I want you to take good
care of it and remember the lives it holds."

She opened the book in her lap and began turning the pages, touching each picture as if her hands could see better than her eyes. The
pictures were faded into dull tones of sepia, but she didn't need to see
them clearly. Each photo carried a story with it, one that she had memorized long ago.

"Now this was your great-grandfather Caleb," Mignon said to her
reflection in the window, "a wild one, he was, filled with poison. He left
us when I was a baby and went off to the Dakotas, up to the Badlands.
Wanted to be a train robber like Butch Cassidy. Nobody heard from
him for years. Everyone thought that he froze his fool self to death."

She turned the page. This was her favourite picture—a thin man,
his gaunt face staring out through the time-bleached photo, standing
with a stern woman next to him. In the background, there was a sagging cabin dug halfway underground and patched with scrap boards
and earth. The man wore a common slicker, like any other range rider,
a thick leather coat, worn soft and comfortable. A young girl stood be-

tween the man and his wife, looking away from the camera, stiff and formal in her high-necked dress.

"But he came back. One night he just showed up at the door. Mother let him in like he'd just been down to town or something, like he'd only been gone a couple of hours. She never asked him once about where he'd been, and she never said a word when he left again. I used to hear her crying at night sometimes, but she kept on working, raising us kids and running that farm until the day she died.

"Oh, he'd come back every now and then, just appear out of nowhere. He'd hang around for a while, mend a fence here and there or fix the roof up some, but then he'd just be gone again one morning. I wanted to hate him, but I couldn't; he was such a sad man. It was like he couldn't help it, couldn't stop the things inside that made him do what he did. Sometimes at night, I'd wake up, and he'd just be sitting there, looking into the fire with those eyes, like he looks in this picture here."

Mignon paused and held the book to her chest for a moment.

"And that little girl there," she said, "that was me, your old grandmother. That picture was taken in 1908. I was 14 years old, scared to death of my own shadow. That dress I'm wearing—he brought that to me one Christmas—he brought Mother one, too. I remember him coming in that night, tracking the wet snow through the door and smelling like the great wild outdoors. Mother fixed us a big dinner, and we sat around the table with the wind howling outside, eating Christmas dinner almost like a real family. That was the last time he came around. We never heard another word from him. I guess he died somewhere out there, wandering around."

Mignon fell asleep, leaning against the window, and dreamed of faceless people who walked in the distance, masked by the shadows of a barren landscape. The people turned towards her, exposing the dark, blurry regions where their faces should be, and waved at her to come and join them. One figure stood out larger than the others, a face that she could almost make out.

In the middle of the night she sat upright, wide awake. The air vibrated as if someone had just spoken, but the house was still and silent. She looked out into the yard, but it was empty, a white expanse of untouched snow. She put the book down and closed the strap, leaning forward to see better.

He was there at the side of the barn, looking up at her. She rose up on her knees, pressing against the window, drawn to the cold glass as if magnetized. He came around to the front of the barn and opened the door. She watched as he stepped inside, and then she jumped off of the ledge, rushing over to the closet.

Her nightgown lay discarded in a heap on the floor, and she had one leg halfway into her jeans when she stopped. She reached behind the rest of her clothes and removed a dress, wrapped in dry cleaner's plastic. Laying it flat on the bed, she removed the plastic carefully and smoothed it out.

Mignon felt the fragile lace collar, browned with age, and unbuttoned the line of buttons down the front. She stepped into the dress, smiling as she fastened the front, and then put on her snow boots. Gathering her hair in a loose bun, she secured it with the antique pin from her dresser and stood looking at herself in the window.

Outside, the moonlight had risen, draining the color from everything, leaving sharp black and white outlines of snow and shadows. The horses were restless in their stalls, and Mignon hesitated at the entrance to the barn, letting her eyes adjust to the dark interior before stepping into the blackness.

"I'm not afraid," she said.

"Don't be."

He struck a match, sending misshapen shadows across the walls, and raised it to light a cigarette. His face was like the coat he wore, gray and beaten, scarred into lines that she wanted to touch. A tiny flame reflected back from each of his eyes.

"What are you doing here?" she said.

"Nothing. Looking for a place to sleep. If it's a problem, I'll be glad to leave."

"No, I didn't mean it like that. I mean what brought you here?"

"I don't understand."

"Never mind. Of course you can stay—I've been waiting for you. I was just wondering what made you decide to come. That's all."

"What do you mean 'waiting for' me?"

"It's okay. Don't be afraid. I'm just glad you came."

"I'm not afraid. Can we just back up a minute here?"

"My grandmother died in June," she said, "She wasn't afraid of anything—not even dying."

The match went out and he lit another, holding it out to see her face.

"I brought a candle," she said, "What's your name?"

He passed the burning match to her and watched her light the candle. She turned it sideways, letting the hot wax drip onto a slat in the empty horse stall next to them. She held the candle in the melted wax until it dried, staying in place.

"My name's not all that important. Why don't I just go? There's a place just down the road."

"No," she said, stepping forward, "Please tell me. It's important to me."

"I don't ever use the name I was given."

"You don't like your name?"

"No, not really."

"Why not?"

"Look . . ."

"You're trying to separate yourself from the past?"

"Yeah, I guess you could say that."

"And your name ties you to it, weighs you down."

"Yeah."

"My name's Mignon. My grandmother named me, and I don't mind the weight at all."

"Somehow I believe you. You're a very strange little girl—do you know that?"

"I am not a little girl. I'll be fifteen in two weeks."

"Sorry, no offense intended." He leaned forward to feel the collar of her dress. "That's a nice dress."

Mignon could think of nothing to say. She stepped up and placed two of her fingers on the wrinkled lapel of his coat, a pantomime of his gesture. The two of them stood still, each holding on to the collar of the other, without talking, only their shadows dancing in the candlelight behind them.

She felt as if her body had divided, half soaring upwards, looking down at the two of them as the scene grew smaller and smaller, and the other half falling inward, being absorbed into the blank eyes of the stranger in front of her. She kept moving out until the house and the barn were specks on the ground and the sky drew back into points of light, and at the same time, she moved deeper into his eyes, shrinking down through the skin, into the smallest of particles. The two directions fused into nothing—a dance of light, and then she was in front of him, releasing his collar and stepping back.

"Who are you, really?" she said.

"Nobody. I'm just moving through here."

"You're just a man?"

"Sure. What else would I be? I ran out of money a couple of days ago. I've just been hanging around, trying to pick up a job here and there. Sleeping in barns to stay out of the cold."

"An outlaw?"

"No. I'm just a guy, trying to survive. Look, can we talk about something else?"

"Do you like to ride horses?" she said.

"I don't know. I've never ridden one."

The night was clear, almost brittle, but the stars were muted by the bright moon. They rode across the empty wheat field, Mignon in front, holding the reins, and the man behind her, stretching his coat around her to keep out the wind. She smiled into the cold as she let the horse run, feeling the man tighten his grip around her waist. The air froze her cheeks, a sharp pain that almost burned, and she laughed out loud as the horse began to gallop.

"I dreamed this once," she said, shouting above the wind.

"It's a good dream."

She led the horse around the perimeter of the Morrisey's nearest wheat field, following the thin tracks of the dirt roads that the farm machines used, a path that was clearly visible in the moonlight. Near the back of the field there was a small depression in the ground, a shallow ditch that stayed dry for most of the year, and a thin stand of trees. Alongside of the ditch, an abandoned thresher lay half on its side, broken and rusting into the ground.

Mignon slowed the horse and circled the machine.

"It's like a giant insect," said Mignon, "It's been there since before we moved here."

"It's beautiful. The moonlight makes it look alive."

"What keeps you alive? I mean, how do you eat?"

"I work when I can. Sometimes I steal things, things that people don't really need. Usually people like your parents."

"That's just my mom. And Bill. My father's gone."

"Yeah, but people like that, people who can afford to lose things."

"You are an outlaw."

"Look, I'm not Robin Hood or Jesse James. It's not like that. I'm just trying to stay alive."

When they returned to the fence between her yard and the Morrisey's, she got down from the horse, leading it through the gate and back into the barn. The man dismounted and watched as she put the horse back in its stall.

"My face is frozen," she said.

"Here." He put his hands on her cheeks, flushed red by the air, and held them against her skin.

"Your hands are colder than my face."

"Wait." He struck a match and lit the candle, holding his hands cupped around the flame.

"Why do you have to wander around? Did you do something bad somewhere?"

"No, not really. I used to think that home was a terrible place, so I left a long time ago, looking for this place that I imagined, a place I built in my mind. Only it didn't really exist, or, at least, I've never found it."

He came over to her and put his hands back on her face. They were warm now and smelled like wax.

"I'm in a terrible place now," she said.

"Oh, are they still cold?"

"I don't mean right here and right now. Your hands are wonderful. I mean my life."

"Your life seems pretty good from where I'm at."

"It's not very good. I hate it."

"I'd stay around here if I were you." He tilted her head back and kissed her, then walked across to the door and looked outside. "You better go inside now. It's almost sunrise."

"You're leaving, aren't you?" she said.

"Yeah, pretty soon."

"I'll stay if you'll come back and see me. I'll stay here and you'll always have a place you can come to when you need one."

"Yeah, maybe I will. That'd be nice."

At the door to the barn she turned around. He was standing in front of the candle, so all she could see was his silhouette.

"Give me a name that I can call you," she said.

"Why don't you find one for me. Whatever name you like."

Back in her room, Mignon took her Bible out of the small bookcase by the dresser and turned to the back, where there was a long list of Hebrew names. She read through the names until one made her stop and laugh.

"Your name is Sarid," she said, "It means 'the survivor.'"

The next night, Mignon watched at her window, but he didn't come back. In the morning, she came downstairs as usual and prepared her mother's breakfast. As she finished and walked towards the base of the stairs with the tray, her mother's bedroom door opened, and her mother rushed out into the upstairs hall. Bill shouted from inside the room.

"I didn't leave the god-damned thing anywhere. I put it right there in the dresser."

"Okay Bill, okay," her mother said as she came down the stairs, "but I didn't move your precious Rolex. I haven't seen it. Maybe you wore it to work by mistake."

"I don't wear that watch by mistake. I put it in its case right after we came back from the dinner party at the Barton's. I haven't touched it since."

Her mother passed her on the landing, said "good morning," and headed for the liquor cabinet.

"Jesus, that son of a bitch drives me crazy. Mignon honey, what are you doing?"

"Your breakfast."

"Oh, I'm too pissed off to eat. Leave it here on the table for now."

Mignon put down the tray and started up the stairs just as Bill came out of the bedroom, dressed for work.

"Fuck," he said, "My overcoat is gone."

"Bill, said her mother at the foot of the stairs, "It can't be gone. Just look around; you'd lose your head if it wasn't attached."

"Don't you fucking tell me to 'look around.' That coat cost me fifteen hundred bucks. It was Italian—wool and leather, for Christ's sake."

"Don't you talk to me like that. I won't have that language in front of Mignon."

"Listen, my watch and my coat are fucking gone. Somebody has stolen them, and I don't give a shit about the language I use."

Mignon closed the door to her room and leaned against it. The words couldn't penetrate through the door, only the muffled tones of the argument. She held her breath to calm herself and curled up in her window with her knees pressed tight against her jaw. The empty candle holder lay next to her foot, rocking where she had brushed it as she got onto the shelf.

She picked up the holder and thrust it through a pane of glass in the window. A cold breeze pushed through the hole, blowing a small fragment of glass back into the room. It landed on her leg, just below the knee, and as she brushed it away, it made a tiny cut on her shin.

One by one, she broke all of the panes, watching the glass as it burst out of the window in shards, falling to the roof and sliding down, some reaching as far as the edge and dropping to the ground below. Looking out the broken window,she took in a deep breath of the freezing air, leaning back and closing her eyes.

As she moved off of the shelf, she saw something on the door of the barn, a piece of cloth, moving in the wind. She ran from her room and down the stairs, past Bill and her mother as they stood facing each other across the den.

"Mignon, where are you going?" said her mother.

Mignon was already out the back door, running across the yard to the barn, where a long coat hung from a nail on the half-open door. It was Sarid's old coat. She jerked it down from the nail and hugged it tightly.

"You are an outlaw," she said, "You really are an outlaw."

She twirled around in the snow, hopping through the cold in her bare feet.

"People like that," she shouted as she made her way back to the house, "People who can afford to lose things."

She rushed back up to her room and unfolded the coat, holding it in front of her and waltzing around her room. She stopped in the center of the room and buried her face in the coat. It smelled of wild things— highway underpasses, bus station benches at midnight, cigarettes and tequila, rocks, sand, and cold cement—and the countless possibilities of the past and the future.

She fell forward onto the bed, hiding her laughter in the folds of leather. Bill would go now—she knew it. Her mother would go to the city to recover, sharing her misery with her old friends back there, just like when Mignon's father left. Time would pass, and Mignon would stay. It would become her home. She felt strong, afraid of nothing.

SMALL TREASURES
by Anne Shafmaster

For the past few weeks Joe Nolan has been leaving work early. He drives to a little town which is known throughout the state for its liberal attitudes, twenty miles away from the cement-mixing business which he just recently purchased from his wife's dad, who is now retired and living by himself in a progressive community out in San Diego where once a week everyone gathers together to meditate and then, afterward, to attend a macrobiotic dinner.

Joe parks his car, never locking it, although he keeps his tapes out on the dash where anyone could steal them, in the large lot behind the grocery store, and walks up and down Main Street for ten minutes, admiring the newly-planted young trees spaced every few yards apart on both sides of the sidewalk. From years of being a Boy Scout, Joe knows what most of the trees are, if not by their bark, then by their leaves, although each tree has a clear plastic tag, by which to correctly identify it, affixed to one of its lower branches, much like a Christmas ornament. There is always at least one friendly dog for Joe to stop for a moment and pat, or to roughhouse with if that seems more appropriate, tied either by leash, or by chain, to a mottled gray tree trunk.

While Joe looks at young trees and at the same time window shops, he sees pictures of his life inside his head. These pictures he sees look exactly like photographs, except that for some reason they are in black and white, not color. No one in them ever smiles, or laughs, or seems to be having a particularly good time either. Today Joe watches his wife and his two boys, Billy and Scotty, eating breakfast together at the kitchen table. Everyone looks about five years younger than what they are now. Sharon hasn't gained any weight yet, and her hair is still long and pretty, not ruined from her best friend Carol perming it whenever the two of them get bored and have no extra money to go shopping together at the Mall.

Joe has not made love to Sharon for over four months now, nor does he want to, and although he thinks that he should probably feel bad about this, he can't say that he does. He misses not having sex; but he doesn't miss not having it with her.

By everyone's standards Sharon is a very attractive woman. She is a genuinely nice person too, cheerful by nature, except for right before her period when she has PMS. She always says *hello* to people who say *hello* to her, even if they are complete strangers, and sends Hallmark cards to family members on all the holidays, including the lesser ones like Flag Day and July 4th.

Sharon is a domestic wonder: she sews, knits, and crochets, and, in a matter of minutes, can whip up a good dinner. She also has a green thumb and their house so resembles a tropical rain forest with flowers and plants everywhere you look that the local newspaper once did a story on it.

She loves to dress in pastel colors and wears chiffon and ruffles and lace when she does housework, or bakes his favorite lemon drop cookies on Monday night after dinner.

Main Street seems particularly busy to Joe today, but he thinks that perhaps this is because it is Friday. He watches the out-of-town people, with whom he in no way identifies although he himself is one, nonchalantly purchasing the little oddities which the local shops so generously provide (and which he, also, finds so charming), compete for precious sidewalk space with the locals, who are dressed in flannel shirts (male and female alike), down vests and blue jeans, as if they all intend to go camping together somewhere soon. One man, who stands in front of Joe at a store called the Emporium and who at first appears to be speaking nonsense, repeats over and over again in a monotonous whisper just loud enough for Joe to hear: Muscatel, hazelnuts, and hickory smoked mustard.

While Joe waits for the person who talks to himself in public places to write a check out in the amount of thirty-two fifty for the three expensive items he has purchased, he decides that it is hardly a coinci-

dence that in a dream he recently had a snake come out of one of
Sharon's nipples and bite him on the forehead. As much as he used to
love to suck on her large breasts—and god knows she'd always liked
that—he feels something akin to repulsion every time he looks at them
now. Not only has he developed this unusual aversion to what is un-
doubtedly his wife's best physical feature, but his attitude toward sex
has also drastically changed. Whereas eroticism used to mean orgasm,
both his own and Sharon's, now it seems to imply his desperate desire
to kiss, suck, touch, and lick the fingers and toes, earlobes and knees,
anklebones and wrists of attractive women other than his own wife.
Earlobes particularly intrigue him.

Each time Joe is in town he buys something special for himself. Yesterday he saw some black and white postcards that he liked a lot, two
for a dollar or sixty cents a piece, of silent film stars from the twenties,
pretty women with bow ties for mouths and pallid-looking young men
with slicked-back hair. He also took a chance on some Darjeeling tea,
never having tasted it before (Joe doesn't even like Lipton) as he fell in
love with the picture on the box of an elegant-looking, dark-skinned
Rajah riding on top of a gray elephant whose ivory tusks curved like the
front runners of an old-time horse-drawn sleigh.

Other recent purchases include a crystal that has a distinctive chip
in it, which he selected from dozens of others displayed at random in a
black enameled tray, and which he intends to hang from the rearview
mirror of his car if ever he can locate the spool of twine which should
be, but isn't, in his tackle box out in the shed; a colorful window decal
with a red, yellow, and blue circular design on it that looks medieval
and might even please some of his somber employees, or better yet
elicit from one of them an inquisitive remark as to its meaning and ori-
gin; an incandescent green stone of oval shape the color of sea water,
small enough for his coat pocket, yet large enough not to fall out, that
he holds in his hand when he feels nervous or wants something smooth
to touch; and a five-pound bag of IAMS dog food bought on impulse
from the hardware store because, even though he doesn't own a pet
and felt rather ridiculous when he paid the cashier too much money for
it, he might (one of these days) buy himself a dog, besides which he
hoped that the *I AM* part of the name might serve to remind him
to behave in a more forceful, straightforward manner than what he
usually does.

Whereas Joe likes everything about this town and the people who live in it who are so friendly and unpretentious, he finds himself to be increasingly annoyed with the suburban women who shop here and who, in their suede or leather pumps, with their nylon stockings barely protecting their smooth legs although it is quite cold out (not a degree above twenty, Joe thinks, while tucking the long ends of his wool scarf around his face), leave a trail of perfume behind them so nauseating that it makes him sneeze. He is not any more pleased either with their male counterparts of tight jawbone and pursed lips who seem to have unanimously agreed to select the same dark gray pin-striped suit to wear today, when none of them look particularly good in it. It is their fastidiousness, their way of letting everyone else know, mostly by the expensive way that they dress (Joe hastily decides) that they have risen above it all, it being the everyday concerns of a normal life which still keep him in line.

But what is normal? Joe asks himself, wondering if, in fact, this is an important question and one he should attempt to answer before more mundane thoughts fill his head. Perhaps, after all, what is normal for one person is abnormal for someone else, he decides, remembering now how when he had first explained to Sharon how important it was to him that they try something new for a change in their lovemaking, she coldly refused him, saying she was ashamed of how dimpled her skin was and certainly didn't want him going over every inch of it with his tongue.

Although Joe would never describe Sharon as a particularly sensitive person, he thinks that she is thoughtful and knows that she tries hard not to be hurtful to others. Rarely, if ever, does she try to imagine what someone else might think, or be feeling, however.

Yet she is a good mother to their boys, although lately he can't help but to notice that she has some strange ideas about things. For instance, just the other day, he overheard her telling the mailman that if Nell O'Brien, their next door neighbor who is pregnant for the first time, continued to jog the way she did her baby could be born with a birth defect. Also, as nice as Sharon is, she remains, despite endless discussions they've had about the nature of prejudice, uncomfortable with black people, Puerto Ricans, and Jews. As a matter of fact if she senses that someone might, in any way, be different from most of the people she knows, she gets an edge to her voice that he doesn't like and clams up so that he can't reason with her. He knows that she only acts like this because she is a small town girl who, except for one brief visit to the White House her senior year in high school, and a miserable trip they took to Florida early in their marriage, with the temperature well over one hundred degrees every damn day they were there, who has never left the state she was born in.

Joe wishes that Sharon would read the newspaper, even if only the Sunday edition, but after she has cut out all of the coupons, seen what sales are on, and looked at the comics, she is finished and puts on her leotard and tights and does aerobics in the living room: there goes his peace and quiet! Of course there are lots of things he'd like to change about her, but then he knows there are things she'd like to have different about him too. But his not making love to her has nothing to do with anything that has any logic to it. That's why he suspects that their marriage might really be over for good—because if thoughts are rational, and therefore can be altered with good intention and hard work, feelings exist in a realm where human wishes are rendered powerless. Joe desperately wants to love Sharon again and has done everything he knows how to do in hope of reclaiming this loss of affection. He can't imagine a life without her. He tries to catch every negative thought of his and replace it with a positive one. He *makes* himself think well of her. Yet his irritation increases.

In his heart he wants Sharon to miraculously disappear. He'd like nothing better than to come home from work one day and not have her be there. There really is no logical explanation for the way he feels. Nor is there an explanation for why this window shopping he does helps him to reconcile himself to the fact that, for the time being anyhow, he must remain married to his wife.

How stooped over I am, Joe thinks as he carefully observes his own reflection in the window of a jewelry store he has never been in before, not being one to purchase accessories, either for himself, or for Sharon. Tomorrow I take vitamins, he decides, unhappy with the way he looks: stiff like a wooden puppet that some inept craftsperson hastily designed, using cheap paint for the watery blue eyes that stare back at him blankly, utterly devoid of any interesting expression, and the washed-out complexion, a hideous chalk-like color. Sexiness, why hast thou forsaken me? Joe asks aloud, immediately feeling both embarrassed (What if a passerby heard him?) and guilty (What if God is listening?). In all truth, Joe cannot reconcile himself to what he sees. The light, of course, both inside the store and out on the street, plays tricks with him. After all, he is in good physical condition, and his clothes are neat and clean. Does he not look athletic and intellectual at the same time? Removing his deerskin glove from off of his left hand, Joe brushes some hair back from his face. It is at this precise moment that he catches a glimpse of the loveliest-looking woman he has seen in years; and, recognizing in an instant that everything about her pleases him, resolves to meet her.

Joe is surprised at how self-conscious he feels once he is inside the store. He doesn't even remember ever having been in a real jewelry store before. It was eighteen years ago that he bought Sharon's diamond engagement ring at Service Merchandise in a well-lit alcove from which he could see aisles of small household appliances, colorful tablecloths, silverware, and dishes. A few weeks later they purchased their wedding bands there, also.

As he moves silently from one case to the next, ostensibly viewing jewelry, but actually stalking his prey, he is overwhelmed by the huge selection of earrings, bracelets, and rings so artistically laid out before him now on black velvet cloth. He sees things he has never seen anywhere before. People must like snakes better than I do, he decides, as he counts dozens of sterling silver pieces in that spooky motif, some of which have red or green gemstones for eyes.

The woman he so desperately wants to meet is busy waiting on another customer, a young girl about the age of his own son, Scotty, who may or may not decide to have her ears pierced today, she explains in a half-joking, half-serious way that fails to mask her nervousness. Overcome with shyness, Joe is thankful that she is otherwise occupied for should she approach him now the way salespeople in stores are trained to do and ask—Sir, may I help you?—he'd be sure to blush, or worse yet even, to be rendered mute. Really though, he decides, things are near perfect, for with her attention so thoroughly focused on someone else, he is free to observe her while remaining unobserved himself.

Because she wears a ring on her right hand, but not on her left, Joe concludes that she cannot be married. And that, as pretty as she is, she is most likely divorced. He guesses that she is a good ten years younger than he is, which would make her just short of thirty, but when he hears her speak to the young girl who has decided not to have her ears pierced today after all, he changes his mind, increasing her age five or six years, because although she talks fast in a clipped tone of voice that instantly conveys to Joe a seriousness of purpose that he likes, there is nonetheless something soft and maternal about her too which one seldom finds in a younger woman who has not yet had children and which Joe likes very much.

He gets aroused just watching her walk gracefully around the store. He thinks to himself that, at some point in her life, she must have been a dancer. She is small and round and has creamy white skin that he wishes very much to touch. Her dark hair is loosely pinned up in back with a tortoise shell comb and wispy tendrils frame her sweet face. She wears funny-looking, thick-soled black shoes which, light as she is on her feet, cannot possibly be orthopedic, he reasons, but must rather be something avant-garde to do with health, for that's the kind of town it is.

"I'd like to get my ear pierced today," he suddenly hears himself say.

"Your right or your left?"

"Left please."

Amazed at his own boldness, he sits on a wicker stool next to a jewelry counter that has wooden sides trimmed with silver plate and appears antique. Not knowing what to do with his hands, which seem unusually large and awkward to him, he clasps them nervously behind his back. The store is empty now except for the two of them. All of his senses are amplified and strange thoughts fill his head as he waits for this wonderful deed to be done.

"Do you mind if I light some incense?" she asks.

"Go right ahead." He wants to suck on the back of her neck while she lies on her belly face down on the bed, a pillow beneath her hips to raise them up for his pleasure as he enters her from behind.

She turns on the radio and the five o'clock news comes on. "I don't want to hear that," she says. "Do you?"

He shakes his head, no.

As she takes her time selecting a station, shiny silver bracelets resonate like wind chimes on her slender wrist. For Joe it is as if a door has closed on a room in which he was confined all of his life. Everything feels different to him now, although he understands nothing. While she concentrates on finding music that they will like, he takes deep breaths and the smell of incense everywhere around him is so strong and the feelings inside him both of power and powerlessness so great, that he wonders if he might faint.

"Are the Everly Brothers okay?"

"Yes." He can hear a furnace shutting on and off down in the basement and a clock ticking loudly somewhere behind him. The urge to grab her is so strong that he bites down hard on his lip and, with both hands stretched out behind him, grips the bottom of the stool.

"Relax," she says, opening up what looks to him like a white cassette made of plastic, and removing the tape that keeps it sealed, she explains, matter-of-factly, as if she is reading instructions in a manual that she has read before and finds completely boring, so that the earrings inside, one of which she will use to pierce his ear, remain sterilized.

She rolls up her shirt sleeves and he sees that there is an iris tatooed on the inside of her arm. This both alarms and frightens him. With a felt tip pen she marks the spot on his ear lobe that she will pierce. As she leans over him the front of her oxford cloth shirt pulls away from her, billowing in and out like a blue sail, close to his face, and exposing her collar bone which he wants to suck on with his lips, mouth, and tongue. As she rubs alcohol on his skin to sterilize it, she brushes up against him lightly; and through her winter clothing he can feel how slight of build she is.

"It doesn't hurt much," she says, positioning the piercing gun against his ear, moving it first this way and then that. "Ready?"

"No." Turning his head sideways so that he can look directly into her almond-colored eyes, which, though narrow and close together, have cast him into a vortex of abandonment and desire from which he never wishes to escape, despite the consequences, he gets a hard-on almost immediately which he hastily covers up with his sweater. Giddy and self-conscious now, he turns away from her. "I'm very sorry," he says, "that was extremely stupid of me, as you were all set to pierce my ear."

"Don't move again or I'll miss," she says rather abruptly although she remains standing so close to him that their sides touch.

No pain. His ear burns afterward.

She offers him a small mirror. As he takes it from her, he slides his hand down hers intentionally, but just quick enough for her to wonder if it was an accident. His features appear swollen, except his lips which are tight and dry; and the highly polished gold ball looks more to him like an evil eye than a harmless piece of decoration. He wants to see a man who is sexy, intelligent, and kind. Unfortunately, his blue eyes confront him mercilessly with the truth: that, in fact, he has nothing to offer her.

The phone behind the cash register rings, and she answers it. "One minute please," she says politely to the person who has called. Then to him in that succinct tone of hers, "Eight ninety-five plus tax." She mo-

tions him over to the counter where she writes up a receipt. He hands
her a twenty-dollar bill and she counts out the change. Finished with
their transaction, she rattles off store hours over the phone, her back to
his face. "Monday through Saturday, ten to six. Sunday, twelve to five."

Joe tells himself that if by some trick of fate he can make love to this
woman now, whose breasts he'd like to cup between his hands and,
into that deep and dark crevice of flesh so miraculously formed, blow
love gently like a child's first song, he will never complain about anything in his life ever again.

"Thank you," he says, not knowing whether she hears him or not.
It seems to him that he has been inside the store for hours, and he has
a sudden urge for a cigarette although he gave up smoking a long time
ago. Just as the thought—What am I waiting for now?—passes
through his head, she gets off the phone and all of her attention is his.

"Mycitracin for the first three days," she says, carefully instructing
him. "Turn the earring around once at night and leave it in for six
weeks." She passes her tongue once quickly over her lips, pauses, then
says, "If you run into trouble, you know where to find me."

Joe's arms hang awkwardly straight down by his sides, and when at
last he buttons up his coast his hands shake. As the girl lowers her eyes
and begins to straighten up some bracelets that hang from a wooden
dowel in the case behind which she is standing, he watches her carefully
for a moment or two, then, without knowing why, laughs. She laughs
too, but she does it in a way that suggests to him that she simply thinks
this is the right thing to do.

"Maybe next week I'll buy my wife a bracelet like one of yours," Joe
says, for although it seems enormously important for him to tell her
what he wants from her, he can't find the words. He cannot say what
he means. Sick of himself and filled with fatigue, he waves good-bye,
and without waiting for her to reply hastily leaves the store.

Outside it is as if the sidewalk is no longer stable, but is instead a
series of choppy waves that undulate. As he lurches toward the car, to
lift each foot is to carry a weight no less than a ton. He is late now for
dinner and he knows it.

Throwing open the trunk of his car and shoving aside a red plaid
blanket that he and Sharon used to make out on in high school, he
takes out a briefcase of his so old that it is missing one of its handles
and some of the leather on one side. In his haste to leave town quickly
he accidentally drops it and his small treasures from other days scatter
on the ground. The medieval decal glares at him like a face full of

bruises. The crystal is small compared to a radial tire. Tea doesn't brew in a puddle of cold water. In that hollow holy place between what was once real for Joe and now no longer exists, pain resides. Feeling a terrible loss of strength and virility he is finally aware of how depressed he is. Without a moment's hesitation he rips the small gold ball out of his ear and flings it across the open lot.

On the way home Joe accelerates, rather than slow down when he sees he is driving fifteen miles above the speed limit; and is acutely aware of the trickle of blood that drips down his neck, onto his white shirt collar, even though the hole in his ear is so small as to almost not be there.

PARDON OUR DUST

by Michael Rosen

Just before treating herself to "The Mummy's Revenge" and a bowl of buttered popcorn, Darlene sandwiched the lamppost with the matching bulletin boards she had decorated for her children twenty-five years ago. Both bore her delicately brushed script, "Don't Forget" across the top. On her daughter Jacqueline's board, she had daubed a criss-crossing pair of hobbyhorses; on her son Denney's, a one-sailed sloop among billowy clouds that surprised Darlene with their ominous (or was it a simply unskillful) quality, as she mounted an additional phrase across the cork of both boards: THIRTY YEAR SALE TODAY 12–6, thumbtacks pinning the legs of each mammoth letter.

Darlene had designated Sunday as goodbye-and-good-riddance to the too many sad things that had, like unwanted pounds, accumulated in thirty-one years of other attachments. And while things themselves weren't the culprit, Darlene did maintain that things were a weight that stood in the middle, if not always in the way, of other things. She had planned to sleep late, abandon the whole possession-packed day to the Volunteers of America and the volunteers of her own lucky circle, and return from a drive in the country as from a spa with rejuvenating springs.

But Darlene was awakened at eight in the morning by the commotion of the garage door just under her bedroom, closing, crashing into something, jerking open, then closing again. When Darlene appeared at the doorway to the garage, two ladies, both older but roughly her own size, were prying her dresses from an overcrowded rack. Darlene's empty trashcans, previously uncrimped and crowded out by the sale items, were now crowded in behind the shoppers as though they had already been selected to cart home the women's other finds.

"You'd think they'd make them so as a person can tell a garage-door button from a door bell," claimed the older shopper, hoping for an assent from the winter coat Darlene had worn, off and on, since her first time at college.

"What kinda early bird specials you got?" asked the younger woman, momentarily draped in Darlene's maternity robe.

"Just worms," Darlene said, although she wasn't awake enough to know if the remark had gone unheard or ignored. The younger woman climbed over the riding lawn mower to join her partner at a table layered with clunky vases that Darlene had marked *25 Each, $10 They're All Yours.*

"Didn't you get a lot of these same kind when John died," the younger woman asked her friend, whose nod indicated that she, indeed, had. "You didn't get any of those 'Get-Well-Soon' bouquets that come in the chicken-soup bowl?" she asked Darlene. "I got a set of seven bowls. Had eight."

Most of the vases remained from the last two years of Darlene's mother's hospital stays. There happened to be a few good vases among them, but Darlene didn't distinguish those. Personally, she was through with cut flowers, through with the discovery of mortality's little message hidden along with the packet of preservative, among the dissembling arrangements.

Darlene punched the garage-door button and closed the door to the house, sealing her patrons inside. She watched for the women's exit behind the sheers of living room bay window. Her lamppost, strapped with the bulletin boards, hadn't turned itself off. The day threatened to be a grey, potentially depressing one when the lamp's photosensitive eye insists that nothing has changed since yesterday evening, and, as far as it can see, nothing might change until tomorrow. After ten minutes, Darlene returned to the garage to find that the women had selected a number of Dane's cardigans, her winter coat, a few peasanty housedresses she couldn't believe she had even chosen or worn, and the ice skates that had brought her no small recognition in high school. All this had been draped over the tandem bicycle, which, if they intended to buy, posed a problem: Darlene didn't know what to charge, couldn't remember what Dane had paid for the tandem. It was brand-new, his last anniversary present to her, and had come with Dane's pledge to take better care of their lazy hearts, which she had taken as well.

Now one woman—the mother?—spread a sequined jacket across the other's shoulders. Darlene remembered wearing the jacket to several weddings while Dane was finishing his degree. She could name the couples, and did, in her moment of hesitation. She also recalled—why she couldn't say—that none had divorced.

Finally Darlene said, "But didn't the paper say twelve to six?"

"For regular stuff, maybe, but early bird stuff is always earlier," the woman trying on the jacket explained.

"Oh," Darlene said.

"Didn't you have shoes to match the jacket?" the other woman asked, plucking at what must have been a loose sequin.

"One time I did," Darlene replied. "I'll make some coffee."

"Coffee's always nice," the younger woman replied.

A year ago Darlene had accepted a position with the Adult Literacy Council and her husband Dane had accepted the fact that his wife was not the woman he had married thirty-one years earlier. Dane was a meteorologist. Towards the end, Darlene liked to say that his divorcing her was the only accurate forecast he had ever made. She had even tried saying that she, on the other hand, *she* had seen it coming from day one.

During the finalization of the divorce, Darlene's mother had come to live and then, die with her, Dane had found a post at a cable TV station half a state to the east and simultaneously moved in with the station's entertainment reporter, and Darlene had put down a deposit on a condominium in Winding Hollow, a rural development adjoining an old golf course, whose entrance signage proclaimed, *Winding Hollow, It's only natural.*

At ten o'clock, Paula, Jeanette, and Nora, Darlene's three oldest friends, arrived at the garage sale. Calling themselves her "divestment specialists," they had offered to spare Darlene at least the day's haggling. Nora, who was still grieving the death of her own mother, had confided, "Friends are only good for the detail stuff, anyway."

In the too little time before noon, the sales team needed to count out a bank from an Easter basket into which Darlene had seemingly dumped a life's worth of small change; affix the remaining "Your Price" stickers that Nora had brought from her own parent's tag sale; and tape up the fluorescent signs at the street corners, which Darlene would have put out days earlier had the rain stopped. But once Darlene escorted the trio into the two-car garage, her friends were, for the first time, daunted by task's magnitude.

"Wait, this is the stuff you're keeping, right?" Paula said, spreading her arms to hold everyone back.

"It's *all* going," Darlene said, pushing through, "and ninety-six dollars of it already went with a couple nice ladies claiming to be early birds."

"Those were vultures, sweetness," Jeanette said.

"Don't you know, it's a hobby, picking over the remains of the dead," Paula added.

"You're awful," Darlene said.

"Hey, you don't mean to sell your mother's community-plate?" Paula declared, lifting the snug mahogany lid of a satin-lined box.

"What can you get for silver anymore? Who the hell has time to polish silverware?" Darlene asked.

"No way," Jeanette interrupted, "not your mother's baby-pearl sweater. And this one with a year's worth of hand-stitching—you're crazy, Dar—"

"Everything goes—the kid's junk, Dad's junk that Mom made me hold on to when Dad died, Mom's junk, my junk that won't clutter the condo just so I can clean it—and, of course, the junk Dane hasn't moved though he's known for two months that today was D (for "dump-it") -Day. Everything goes but the freezer. And if you can get a hundred bucks for it, it goes."

"And why aren't you keeping your tea cup collection? Or Jackie's swimming trophies? She might want them," Nora protested.

"Jackie wants them all right, as long as they're in my basement. I just don't need to hoard all that crap. It'll just sit in my new basement and get all dusty and sentimental again."

"That's right you'll have a basement," Nora said, seizing Darlene's shoulders and trying to squarely meet her eyes.

"Read the signs, Paula," Darlene said, shirking free to raise a fluorescent green posterboard on which a blur of barbecue paint spelled: *Everything Goes Today.*

"But Dar, nobody can pay you what this is worth," Paula said, pointing across a card table at the monogram on a set of napkins. "You're never going to find linen this . . . lineny again."

"But you *can* find paper napkins at any carry-out," Darlene replied.

"Since you're not taking back your initials, you're keeping these,"

Paula concluded. She gathered the napkins and brought them to Darlene who barricaded herself with another sign, a fluorescent pink one that read, *My Loss Is Your Gain.*

"What loss? You don't need to lose anything else," Nora said. "A mother, a husband, a house that, incidentally is going to bring a small fortune—that's about enough losing for one year."

"You're acting like this stuff is haunted," Jeanette agreed.

Make Good on a Marriage Gone Bad, Darlene lifted.

"What! That one's too much," Paula shouted, grabbing the sign.

"That one's just a joke," Darlene conceded, tossing it aside. "I was just practicing with the spray paint."

"No, no, put it up. Tell the world everything," Jeanette suggested, "Why not 'I'm having a cutting-off-my-nose-to-spite-my-face sale?'"

"'To-spite-my-friends sale,'" Nora revised.

"Cute," Darlene said, raising a sign, *Selling to the Bare Bones.*

"'Bare *walls,*' dearie," Jeanette said.

Darlene's friends failed to convince her to withdraw a single item from the sale. In a moment of urgent conspiracy, while Darlene showered and dressed, the women decided to overprice anything they knew Darlene didn't really mean or want to sell. But when Darlene peeked into the garage to announce her departure, she also mentioned that at exactly six o'clock the Volunteers of America would be arriving. "Whatever isn't sold I'm writing off on my taxes. So, sell it soon or it goes later."

"You win, Dar," Nora said, "No unreasonable offer refused."

"You know I never realized how many diets we tried," Jeanette said, hugging a cardboard Vodka box of diet books. "Remember when we were on this one, *You Are What You Eat.*"

"That was the problem," Darlene said, "You aren't what you eat, you are what diet you're on. You are what you cut out one month and then you are what you're eating twice as much of the next month."

"That means I've been celery sticks and grapefruit halves since I've been twenty-two," Jeanette said.

Darlene wedged her way through the clutter to give a quick hug to each of them. "I'll see you at seven, and no bargaining over dinner. You pick the place, I treat. If I can't thank you enough, I'll at least try."

"I just want to say," Nora said, "even though we're going to do this and we all love you and all that, you're behaving like a spoiled brat." Darlene accommodated by sticking out her tongue. "You want to have

your cake but you want to give away the nice cake plate and your heir-
loom silver server that—" Nora's remark was censored by the opening
doors of a packed car pulling up Darlene's driveway.

"Just ask for a price, we're getting a late start," Jeanette urged the
patrons. "Now, you, where can we reach you if we need you."

"Don't need me. I'll be antiquing in Waynesville and I might stop in
at an auction—"

"Great! You're giving away all your old things so you can go buy
other people's old things?" Nora said, "That's good business."

"I want things that don't know me from Adam that I can just sit in
and relax."

"Happy trails, Eve," Jeanette called, as Darlene pretended to make
her stomach skinny and slide toward the exit.

"How much you want for this wood thing?" A lean gentleman
blocked Darlene, pointing to a small tier of right-angled shelves that a
boy waved overhead like a torch.

"That?" Darlene asked, threading back between the bumper pool
table covered with linens and the milk crates packed with 78 RPM rec-
ords. "*That* happens to be a twenty-year-old plant stand that my only
daughter made in Girl Scouts. It's priceless," she said, grabbing the unit
from the boy, turning it right side up, and passing it back to him. "Make
me an offer."

Darlene returned from her outing much too early, antiqueless, and
slightly dispirited from the relationship of her conscientious budget to
an unconscionably overpriced market. She killed the extra time by
walking around the construction site of her new condominium, proj-
ecting her rust-toned loveseat against the Pink-Panther insulation, the
track lighting she had selected, against the strands of electrical—or
were they telephone?—cables.

Darlene could hear Dr. Chatterji the rental agent narrating a tour of
the model unit, six next-to-complete rooms hung like an art gallery with
the architect's renderings that portrayed the many decorator touches
included in the selling price. Through the doorless rooms of Darlene's
own unit, she heard two other female voices posing questions (many
she remembered asking herself) and the agent answering in the accent
that, Darlene admitted, conferred a quality upon the rooms that even
the artist's exotic shadings hadn't. ". . . luxuriating but affordable," Dr.
Chatterji said. ". . . it's only natural."

In each of Darlene's rooms, Quality Drywall had posted signs with their logo and the words "Pardon Our Dust," silk-screened in a chiselled typeface that made Darlene think the message wasn't intended as a bit of politeness but as an imperative like the Ten Commandments.

Darlene continued to imagine her possessions against the undifferentiated partitions as Dr. Chatterji described many of the accoutrements—open-hearth fireplace, appliance garage—that Darlene had thought were specific to her particular master-plan. "Much more than just a place to wash up," Dr. Chatterji said. "And rheostat-controlled lighting throughout."

Before both tours were concluded, Dr. Chatterji called to Darlene, knocking on the empty door frame that would hold Darlene's security system and dead-bolt lock. "I wonder if you'd mind my showing off your splendid view of the course?"

"My house is your house," Darlene said, introducing herself to her potential neighbors, two women she imagined to be her daughter Jacqueline's age.

Her three guests pressed against the sliding door, obscuring Darlene's view of the thin stands of trees and the tended greens whose silence seemed organized between the traps of sand and water, each shaped like a quotation mark. Something about looking through the three figures, posed like vertical blinds at the glass, caused Darlene to imagine a scene she had heard about, repeatedly, but had never watched. Somewhere, at opposite end of the course, her son and a husband she must have been happy with then, were driving buckets of golf balls straight at her window.

The garage sale netted over twelve-hundred dollars and a garage that Darlene described to everyone as "empty as a college boy's brain." It also entitled her to a threateningly counterproductive time until the move. It wasn't just the emptiness that distracted her, she was confident, but the things that the emptiness refused to relinquish, that it framed like the dull grey outlines of paint where the family portraits had hung. Packing as much of her remaining essentials as possible did help upset the idea of what was missing. But the furnishings that Darlene still feared might crowd the condominium looked diminished in the large rooms of her four-bedroom ranch. The Parson's table looked flimsy. The loveseat looked too small for even one person. And once it crossed her mind, each time Darlene passed the dining room, she couldn't dismiss how the emptied breakfront resembled a magician's box, nor could she keep from rehearsing the ridiculous scenario suggested by the lone andirons, where a magician would hypnotize Darlene, seal her inside the cabinet, seize the andirons, and then pierce the box over and over until it would be clear she couldn't be hiding anywhere in the breakfront. At last, he would click his fingers, and Darlene, amazingly unharmed, could continue her trip to the kitchen.

Darlene's condominium was finished a month ahead of schedule, in fact. And, as her real estate agent promised, her house, *priced to sell* like everything in the garage sale, didn't even appear in the August listings before a family of six had signed a contract for a thousand dollars above her asking price.

For the first week, Darlene appreciated the clarity of the colors she had chosen, and imagined, where the "Pardon Our Dust" signs had been posted, the names of the paints she and Dr. Chatterji had picked: "Rose Ash," "Simplicity Itself," an off-white, and "Warm Grey III." Nearly everything she had moved possessed a remarkably sharp edge against the new colors, a cleaner feel under sky- and tracklights. And, there was room, room for the first time since the children had been born, for her own things to sit in one place, undisturbed. "I won't tell you I'm completely settled," Darlene admitted to Nora over coffee, "but I have spotted several signs of my self, my *old* self, among all this clean living."

Darlene threw herself a housewarming party with the same fervor she had marshalled for the garage sale. A November Sunday, nearly every new and old friend in town arrived for dessert and mulled cider. Although she insisted "Presence Not Presents" on her invitation, an unreasonable number of gifts piled up on the island that divided the kitchen from the dining room as though her guests had unanimously and wrongly assumed its function.

"These are awfully big for gag gifts," Darlene laughed, hugging a couple who carried in one package large enough for a torchiere and another dozen wrapped in identical paper as if a set of something, "because I just got rid of a whole houseful of bad jokes."

An hour into the evening, the door bell rang, announcing to everyone but Darlene, the arrival of Jeanette, Paula, and Nora.

"Get the door, Darlene," more than one person called.

"OK, something's up, right?" Darlene said, walking toward the door. "There's a cake with a male stripper backed inside? Shelly's paying me back for sending that gorilla to her office," she guessed, opening the door.

"Trick or treat," the new arrivals shouted together, thrusting the contents of their arms forward and posing for Darlene's inspection.

"Trick or treat—I can't tell," Darlene said, holding the sides of the door jamb.

Jeanette wore Darlene's mother's mohair sweater stitched with the baby pearls, and bore her mother's silver tray laid with the porcelain tea cups that the two had collected since Darlene's birth. To one side Paula floated in the woven comforter Darlene had bought on her honeymoon in Maine. She bore a pair of Darlene's crystal champagne flutes and had draped an armload of the monogrammed linens over her arms like a sommelier. Nora balanced Jacqueline's antique-look plant shelf, crammed with pots of fresh herbs, and a bouquet of sweetheart roses that Denney and her daughter-in-law had sent from California.

"Now I get it, the stuff *was* haunted," Darlene said, still braced inside the door, blocking the view of the guests that had assembled behind her.

"We're friendly ghosts," Jeanette said, "like in *A Christmas Carol.*"

"We knew you didn't want *everything* to go to strangers," Paula explained.

"Just—just what, what else did you keep?" Darlene asked.

"I hope you can thank us later," Nora added, seeing the water in Darlene's eyes through the water in her own.

"Thank you? You'll be lucky if I can pardon you," Darlene said, receiving the clumsy embrace of blanketed arms. "Now hand over those goblets before you break one," Darlene said.

"Come on, Dar, aren't you going to open you *other* presents?" cried a man singled out by the beam of light above the kitchen island.

Amid the round of laughter, someone else called, "Yeah, Dar, move out of the way. Let them in already."

JERRY'S INSOMNIA

by Jack Heffron

Jerry's in there breaking things, slamming his fists into doors and walls, punching his own head, pounding it. Tomorrow his knuckles will be swollen like an old lady's, knuckles fat as walnuts and red with the skin split, a sliver of black dried blood ringed around them.

It's the insomnia that does it, makes him so crazy I don't know him, my own husband. I can't sleep with him anymore, and I miss that, miss our mornings when we snuggled, bodies cool and smooth against each other, legs all wrapped around, thighs rubbing, waiting to thump the snooze button, giving us ten more minutes together before we have to get up.

I have to sleep in the guest bed, which is where I am now, the room washed silvery white by the moon. It's too painful to watch him pace and fret and act all crazy and not be able to help. And I need my sleep—which is what I told him, though I don't get much, even in here.

"It's like a demon's inside me," he'll say sometimes. "A demon causing me to work against myself." But when he says it he's looking at me, burning his eyes through me, the blue bleached almost gray, the whites dingy, and it sounds like he's blaming me—like I'm responsible for the demon.

I say, "It's just all your pressure right now, baby. Just relax and that demon will go away." I soothe his fine black hair off his forehead. He's under a whole lot of stress, with a new job, new mortgage, baby on the way, and he's afraid, at thirty, that he's already a failure and nothing will ever come of his life, because he's still searching for himself and for what he wants to do while all the time trying to get settled. I tell him not to worry about those things or about making as much money as my brother, who sells pharmaceuticals and lives in a nice house: four bedrooms and a Jacuzzi.

Jerry says he's not worried one bit about any of that shit, says worry has nothing to do with it, says his insomnia is inherited from his dad who couldn't sleep worth a damn either. "One more curse that prick put on me," he'll say, then give himself a hard whack on the head, maybe keep whacking it until I start yelling, "Stop it, now, just stop," or "Quit calling him that," meaning his dad, who really wasn't so bad.

But he was a nervous, troubled man with a bad temper, and sometimes strapped the kids long and good with a belt over hardly nothing. More often he hurt them mentally—particularly Jerry, his spitting image, same lean face, same wild black hair falling free across his forehead. Jerry has a brother who's kind of weird from all of it, lives by himself and doesn't go out with girls, barely speaks to anyone. His sister has been a few times in a mental home and takes pills for manic depression.

Jerry's always been the strong one, the leader, especially since his dad died a few years ago, right after we met, but I think he's afraid this insomnia is the beginning of some kind of mental sickness. And he *has* changed, saying all kinds of crazy things.

"I smell different," he said the other day when he came home from work—said it during supper like a secret, leaning across the kitchen table to turn down the TV, staring at me, nodding, like it had some kind of hidden meaning. "When I sweat, I stink in this real funky way, not like regular sweat."

"Baby, you always smelled like that," I said. "You just never noticed till you quit smoking," which he did three months ago. I smiled and hoped he would laugh, or roll his eyes in this cute way he has, like an actor in a silent movie, real big and crazy when he rolls them, always making me laugh.

But he didn't. Doesn't ever laugh anymore. He just stared at me a second, or stared through me, like he was considering the possibility, then shook his head. "It's a different smell. Real rank and bitter."

"That's my baby," I said, still trying to carry off the joke, though not trying very hard by this point.

"And my piss smells different, too. Putrid. And I can smell it on me all the time. I'll be working and all of a sudden smell my own piss, or that piss smell coming out of me but doesn't smell like my own, and I wonder can't everybody smell that. 'Can't they smell that?' I think to myself."

I just stared at him, not knowing what to say, frightened, hating when he starts talking like that. He got that spacey look again, then turned up the TV where the Skipper was whacking Gilligan on the head with his captain's hat.

My overnight bag is already packed, squished back in the corner of the closet next to my bed. I can see it peeking out behind a box of winter clothes, and laying here listening to him bang and slam stuff around I'm thinking of grabbing it and just getting away. Twice this week, since things keep getting worse, I've taken it down, gripped the handle in my hand and got ready to walk out, to just be gone when he gets home from work, leaving him a note, of course, saying I'm sorry and I love you so much but we have to think of the baby and all, and telling him I'll call you and I really am sorry.

But then I see him reading the letter, the look on his face, and I can't bring myself to do it. My mom says I should, says I'm crazy to stay with him when he's liable to do anything. "Don't get me wrong, I like Jerry," she said, and she's not lying, she likes him fine, though she's always thought he was kind of weird—dark and full of moods she couldn't understand. Which, of course, he is. Sometimes he laughs at things she doesn't think are funny and sometimes says things in a way that you know he isn't serious, that he's pulling her leg, but she isn't sure what he means.

Before I got married she asked me did I think for sure it would work, didn't I see the potential for problems down the road. I said I did—and I did, but nothing like this, never thought anybody's life was this crazy. I knew Jerry was smarter than me, more complicated, but then he wasn't so unhappy all the time, except about whatever job he was doing, full of regrets about not finishing college but too stubborn to go back.

Mom says if I loved him I'd leave because now I'm only helping him stay sick, and that if I threatened to leave, maybe he'd get help. Tough love, like with an alcoholic.

His beating his head reminds me of Gracie, who lived next door when I was a kid. A mongoloid they called her then, what they now call a Down's Syndrome. She beat herself so much she had two bluish-purple welts on her forehead, an inch or so above her eyes, purple mounds of bruise the size of fists.

"Stop talking," she'd say, sitting by herself on her porch, a fierce look on her face. "Shut up shut up!" then wham, she'd give herself a hard crack. Her mom would fix her up pretty—new dresses and patent leather shoes and white anklets—but Gracie slouched around, stalked, like a bully ready to fight, and she couldn't keep herself neat. Always looked kind of gross and sick.

My friends made fun of her, called her re-tard. I felt bad, but I was afraid of her, like she was possessed by the devil. Maybe my friends were afraid of her too. She never noticed anyway, always in her own little world.

Mostly she stayed inside, but you'd see her when a school bus would stop to pick her up. The bus would be full of these mongoloids, some as old as my parents, staring out the windows with empty eyes, mouths sagging open. Gracie'd come stomping out in that silly walk she had.

Other times you'd see her at Mass, brown bangs combed over her forehead to hide the big purple knots. She'd punch her head, but her folks had trained her, I guess, to not yell, "Shut up shut up shut up," like she did at home, sitting alone with a doll that was beat to rags, the legs hardly more than strips of cloth hanging down.

When the head punching got real bad, her mom put a helmet on her, like old-time football players wore: soft leather with no face bar. You'd see her on the porch with that helmet, black strap pinched tight under her chin, and she'd still bash herself. They ended up putting her in an asylum. The doctors said she was schizophrenic and heard voices inside her head. She was trying to stop the voices by hitting herself.

I wonder, sometimes, if Jerry hears voices, but I'm afraid to ask him. I'm afraid to think of it, really, so I don't. It's stupid.

One thing I know bothers Jerry, adds to his stress, is the baby. Our first. We've been married a little over two years and been thinking about it for a while—me more than him, I guess. But he'd agree whenever I'd bring it up, even point out cute kids at the grocery store, say, "Get me one of those, would you," and I'd pretend to write it down on my list, and we'd laugh together.

But when I came home with the news his jaw dropped like a bag of cement kicked off the back of a truck. Then he smiled and said, "Great," but it sounded phony, with no enthusiasm or joy. Later he kissed me and said he was really happy and that he hadn't looked it at first because he was shocked, not thinking it would happen so fast after we started trying.

So the demon he talks about being inside him is really inside me, growing and nursing while her dad (I'm sure it's a girl) is having fits at four in the morning, knowing he has to get up in two hours for work. I'm afraid all the craziness and stress will hurt her, even cause me to miscarry, so when things are bad and Jerry's acting crazy, like now, I sing to her and rub my belly, and I tell her, "Your daddy's a little confused right now, but by the time you're born he'll be good as new, I promise."

I hear him walking around, the floorboards down in the living room creaking under him. There's other voices, too, soft and muffled: TV. Sometimes if he has a few more drinks while he's watching, he'll fall asleep. But then he's tired and hungover the next day, making him incompetent at his job. He forgets and loses things, his boss will tell him an order and just that fast he can't remember what it was, like he didn't even hear it.

He works for a chemical company that cleans out factories—he's the foreman and safety supervisor. Since it's his job to make sure that the men are safe, he blames himself for the time, a month ago, when one of the guys turned a wrong valve or crawled into a wrong vent pipe or something, and the guy died, leaving behind a wife and two little ones still in diapers.

The company investigated the accident and decided it was the guy's fault and there was nothing Jerry could have done to prevent it, but Jerry doesn't believe them, says it's just the company's way of protecting their own asses.

"Don't blame yourself," I told him. "You'll go crazy blaming yourself."

Jerry said, "Don't play shrink with me."

So I didn't. I made an appointment for him to see a real shrink who could maybe find out what's wrong with him, why he's so quiet and sad all the time and why he can't sleep at night. I'd begged him for the longest time to do it, but he'd always say, "It won't do any good."

And he was right.

He went a few times until the doctor said there was nothing really wrong, just a lot of stress right now, and a bit of "situational depression" because of the guy dying at work. He gave Jerry some sleeping pills but not valium or anything like that—just mild ones that don't hardly work—saying he didn't want to risk getting Jerry addicted when insomnia was just a nuisance.

"A nuisance?" I said when Jerry told me about it. "Did you tell him it was driving you crazy and maybe something else was driving you crazy and causing the insomnia?" He said he didn't. Didn't tell the doctor about his family history or hardly anything else that would have been helpful and maybe given us some answers.

I've known Jerry three years and I know what he did. He sat there all polite and charming and convinced the doctor there was nothing wrong, that his worry-wart wife was making, like always, a mountain out of a molehill. But if they could see him at four in the morning, beating his head, cursing and crying and threatening to kill himself, they'd know there *was* something wrong.

So I called the doctor myself and told him just that. He said it was just that Jerry's been through a few jobs, didn't feel settled yet, had a new house and a baby on the way and that, in terms of stress points, he totaled about ninety on the chart, just less than death-of-a-spouse stress points.

I said, "Thank you, sir," and hung up, knowing he wasn't going to be a bit of help with his chart of stress points and smooth voice, talking like he was Jesus or somebody, with all the answers and knowing more about Jerry than I did after all of three bullshit sessions.

Jerry scares me most when he walks in his sleep, which he's never done before in his life, and which says, to me, something is really wrong. When he does, it's like he's possessed. I think of Gracie.

It happens when he's drunk too much, gulped down a bottle of wine or a pint of Jack Daniels. The booze puts him to sleep, but a half-hour later I wake up to see him peeing in the closet or trying to get out the front door, or yelling something that doesn't make any sense.

"Where's the opening?" he yelled at me one night, standing at the foot of the bed, eyes wild and glazed. "Where's the fucking opening?"

"What opening, baby?"

"The opening," he screamed at me, grabbing my T-shirt and yanking me out of bed. "Where'd you put it?"

"The door?"

"The opening!"

Other times he's gotten just as violent, which is why I'm here, sitting up listening to him roam the house, wondering if he'll walk in his sleep.

He'd never hit me when he was awake. Sleepwalking, I don't know. I lock the door.

I can feel his presence not more than five feet from me. He's right on the other side of my door, trying to hear if I'm awake. I'm balled under the blankets, barely breathing, pretending I'm asleep. If he knows I'm awake, he'll want to come in, maybe to talk, which I'm not ready to do. He jiggles the doorknob once, then squeezes it a half-turn real hard, then lets go.

"Peg, you up?" he says in almost a whisper. I don't answer. There's been nights when I'd let him come in and lay by me, and I'd stroke his forehead to soothe him and he'd almost be asleep, then jolt straight up, fling my hand away, paddle the air like he was on fire or like some demon was tickling every nerve end in his body with a feather. "Peg?" he says again, and it's a long time before I hear him walk away.

The final straw, the thing that drove me into this room here, was when he broke the ceiling fixture. It was about one-thirty in the morning, a few weeks back, and I was laying there, only half asleep because Jerry was up and down, turning the light on to read, then off ten minutes later, ten minutes after that bolting out of bed, cussing.

He went downstairs to fix another Jack Daniels, hissing, "I've had enough of this shit," which always signals he's reached wits' end and decided to put his lights out with three or four long swallows off the bottle.

A few minutes later he comes back up, then I hear the fixture above me shatter—explode—fat chunks of glass flying everywhere, little tiny pieces shining like diamonds as they fly and big daggers dropping down, some shaped like pieces of pie, some like icicles.

He'd flipped his robe over his head but instead of just slamming on the floor, it snagged on the fixture, yanking it right out of the ceiling. I turned away and started crying while he bent down to pick hunks of glass off the bed and the floor. I felt helpless, like he'd finally gone totally crazy.

"You could have killed our baby," I screamed at him. "If I was on my back with no cover and one of those big pieces fell—"

He was shaking his head, his eyes wide and wild, scrambling around on his knees to find the smaller pieces twinkling in the light of the naked bulb on the ceiling. "I know, think I don't know?" all said in almost a whisper, and fast, like he was telling a last minute secret before running out the door. I'd never seen him look so ashamed.

It's like that memory has come to life again when I hear glass shattering. But I'm safe in bed and he's downstairs, somewhere.

"Fine, okay?" he's hollering at somebody, probably himself. "Just fine," and more glass shivers into pieces. "So go ahead then," he shouts.

I bolt out of bed but hesitate before opening the door, thinking that this time he's over the edge—dangerous. I run to the closet, grab my overnight, then leave it on the bed, open the door to see him standing in the middle of the dark living room, alone, my fancy mirror all busted to pieces around him, the gold swirly frame in splinters.

Blood leaks from his hands, loops like candy stripes down his bare arms. It rolls in long lines down his chest and stomach, pooling and turning brown in the white elastic waistband of his underwear. He looks up at me, like a baby almost, mouth hanging open a little. Then he sinks to his knees, bows his head, squeezes it between his elbows, and his whole body is heaving like a drowning person coming up for air.

I hurry down to him and cut my foot on a jag of glass, which all of a sudden makes me mad, so I yell, "You go see a doctor and get help, goddamn you. You can't let this hurt the baby." I stand right in front of him but he keeps his head bowed. I grab my belly, saying, "This is the baby now. You're not the baby anymore. You've got to grow up, be the daddy. Be the daddy, Jerry."

He looks up at me, surprised, I guess, though his face is fuzzy somehow, out of focus, like he's looking past me at something he sees a long way off. I kneel down next to him. "You gave me this baby and you'd better not be giving up," I say, and grab his arms, which are soaked with blood, to see if he's cut his wrists.

He yanks away from me. "I'm not giving up."

"Then what is this?" and I swing my arms to take in the whole room.

He looks around at the glass all over the floor, twinkling in the wash of light from the streetlamp outside. He sees the blood on himself, discovering it for the first time, all of a sudden, like coming out of a dream, and he sees himself kneeling on the floor bleeding in about five different places at almost three in the morning, then says, "I wish the fucking thing would die."

I stare at him, hardly believing what he said.

"We made a big mistake."

"But you said—"

"I wanted it, I know I did, and I do." He wipes back a lock of hair that fell across his forehead. "But I'll fuck it up like my dad did me."

"Baby, you learned from his mistakes."

"There's no learning and there's no getting better. The kid'll turn out just like me."

"Would that be so bad?"

He spreads his arms to offer the room as Exhibit A.

I tell him it could be worse, tell him about Gracie and that he should be thankful he's not like her, tell him I worry about the baby turning out wrong—handicapped somehow—because of all this stress when I'm pregnant.

He says he worries about it too.

"Is that what all this is about, then? The baby?"

"Of course not."

"Then what? Tell me." The job, the not being settled, the new house, the guy who died at work, I mention everything I know that could be bothering him, even ask if sometimes he hears voices.

He keeps shaking his head, no, and looking at me like I'm stupid for not knowing, for even asking, so I say, "Fine," stand up, pick my way through the glass and back upstairs, pull on my jeans and boots, grab my overnight, but then Jerry's in the doorway, blocking it. He doesn't say anything but it's clear he won't let me pass. His arms, roped with blood, are folded across his chest.

"Let me by," I say, trying to sound tough, though I'm already crying.

Then he says, looking away from me, like he's talking to someone else, "I'm just in general fucked up, you know?"

Which makes me cry even more, but I don't answer, don't say anything.

"This is me now," he says. "I think this is who I am."

He looks at me, and I want to say it's just temporary or say I don't care if it's permanent, I'll always love him. He needs me to answer, to say *something,* but while I'm thinking he turns away, heads down the hall. The bathroom door closes and water gushes in the sink.

I spend a half-hour dabbing his cuts with peroxide, blowing on them to take away the sting. He doesn't hardly flinch, though some are deep with glass splinters I have to gouge out. It's like he's taking his punishment for breaking my mirror. I'm not mad anymore and he isn't either, but we both know the moment when I could have said the right thing has passed. We don't talk.

The house is quiet now. I heard his bed squeak awhile back and it hasn't squeaked again, so I guess the battle's over for tonight. My room is dark except for the moonshine coming through the window, turning the white sheets blue. On the clock, red numbers say 3:39. I rub my belly, rub my baby, and sing songs to her, softly.

DISASTER

by Judy Doenges

One July weekend in Chicago, twenty-four people were murdered. The exact number appeared on the TV screen the following Monday night under the face of the most recent victim, an elderly black man. I was eight years old and up past my bedtime. We were deep into hot weather, but I was able to watch the news reports while huddled in a blanket because it was during this summer that my parents had had a financial windfall, bought central air conditioning, and closed up the house.

All of the murders confirmed what I'd been told all along. Danger was everywhere outside; it wasn't safe to open the door or talk to anyone new. Fresh air was suspect. My parents told me stories of children kidnapped on the way home from school; of fast cars; of false friends who lied and stole toys; of branches that fell from trees without warning. I took their word for it and ran straight home from school every day. In class I remained stubbornly quiet so nothing I said could be used against me.

Outside my house I imagined a limitless space filled with random terror, accidents, and the screams of millions of strangers. Closer to home things seemed more manageable, possible to touch and smell—like leaves, and the persistent stench of the fungus on the maple trees in my front yard. The things I liked best were closest at hand: my toys, my furniture, the television set.

The dead man's face hung on the television screen that night, smiling and innocent, oblivious to fate. I learned that these murders were part of a trend. Just two weeks earlier a schoolteacher in my suburb had been stabbed. The murderer had shoved his knife right through the screen door. The schoolteacher had thought he was selling something.

After the teacher was stabbed my mother said, "I can see it now. Kids will be drawing pictures in school of bloody teachers. Children are always drawing pictures of what they are really afraid of. You just keep drawing trees, Lindy, like you usually do, so I don't have to put up pictures of bloody teachers on the refrigerator."

My mother put her hand on my forehead and pushed up my bangs, smearing them back over the top of my head. I had secretly cut my hair one day while hiding behind the big living room chair and now I looked rakish. My mother insisted I had to suffer for my silliness. She refused to take me to my regular barber shop, where I was the only little girl among hair tonic ads and men with cigars. I now suffered with my mother's hand on me. She smelled of cigarettes.

After the murders I gave up the trees and drew mug shots instead, using men and women from the news and game shows as my models. I also drew the faces I had seen on the "Most Wanted" lists at the post office, where I went every Saturday with my father. Only on these trips was I not afraid, but excited. I made a point of watching the men we passed on the street in case they might be criminals. The idea of catching a crook was invigorating: I would yell "That's him!" and my father would rush me off to the police station for a statement under his arm, my eyes agog. I especially liked the idea of my face in the paper— a crook catcher—wearing that expectant look I always saved for rare moments of self-confidence. I drew the mug shots in the classic front and profile manner, two drawings side by side, and tacked them to my bedroom wall.

"Where are your nice tree pictures?" my mother asked a few days after the murders. She peered at my drawing of the twenty-fourth victim. "Now who is this man?"

"He was on TV last night," I said.

"I don't recognize him from any show."

"He's dead."

"Oh. What was he famous for, do you know?"

"He was on TV."

That night I pulled the small television into the bathroom so I could watch the news while I took a bath. The city had quieted down after the killing weekend. Mayor Daley promised summer job programs for the poor, and a couple of kids drowned in Lake Michigan. While in the bathtub, I imagined Mayor Daley's mug shot, fat face forward and to the side.

"You'll electrocute yourself!" I heard my mother call through the locked door. Her knuckles sounded polite on the wood.

"I'm okay," I said.

"Dry off in the tub after you let the water out," my father said. Ice cubes clinked in his glass.

I was so close to danger, just a few feet away from zapping myself, from sending my crooked hair into ecstasy around my head. I splashed water on the TV but nothing happened.

"I heard that," my father called. "Keep your hands in the bathtub."

I turned back to the TV set. A golfer had been hit with lightning during a tournament. He was rolled away on a stretcher, his feet in cleats flapping to the sides as they installed him in the ambulance.

"Come out of there now," my mother called. "We're having dinner. Be a good girl."

I closed my eyes and saw golf clubs, or lightning bolts, or something more hard and tangible and unbreakable shoot down on my parents. They went up in smoke outside the bathroom door.

My father, hoping with all his heart that I was technologically inclined, taught me to operate the stereo system in the living room. I sat on the living room floor that summer with my elementary science book, listening to *The Best of the Ink Spots*. I read about infinity.

In my book, infinity was a one followed by a hundred zeros. Dutifully, I counted them all. Scientists were not sure infinity was real, but they needed it to know the size of space. My father pointed to infinity when he showed me stars out the window. Infinity was as endless as Chicago and as stuffed with peril. My mother passed by the window as I looked up from my book; she was wearing a scarf, holding a garden trowel in her hand. She traveled through infinity, weeding, going to the store, and still she avoided disaster. She waved and smiled.

The doorbell rang. When I opened the door I saw an orange-haired girl about my age standing stiffly on the other side of the glass storm door. She had a puffy and serious face, crammed with freckles. I didn't know her from school.

"I live over there!" she screamed, waving her left arm down the block.

I craned my neck to see where she was pointing, but she seemed to be indicating our garage.

"I'm Margaret!" she screamed.

"Be more quiet!" I yelled back.

"We've got a pool!"

"Okay!" I screamed at the top of my lungs. Margaret looked surprised. I closed the heavy front door, then ran to the big picture window in the living room. Margaret walked by slowly, like an insulted Miss America, glaring at me through the glass. I ran from one room to the next, watching as she circled determinedly outside the house three times, the last time running at full speed. She fled from the front yard yelling, "I put a spell on you!"

I put a mug shot of Margaret up on my wall. Hers was the first drawing of a real person I knew. I wrote "Margaret" under her picture and drew a small blue heart next to her name. Under this I wrote "pool." The background of the drawing was strafed with a rainbow of curly lines; this, Margaret's home, I labeled "infinity."

"Well, at least you've got someone your own age up here," my father said. He peered at Margaret's picture, a drink in one hand, some papers from work in the other.

I was nervous about the heart on the drawing. Maybe it was too much. I concentrated on how the glass would feel in my father's hand, cold and slimy, and the weight of the papers, light and thin like a dead bird I had once held.

"That's a nice one," my mother said, as she entered my room. She smiled at me and patted my head. The moon-shaped streetlamp shone outside the window. My mother quickly snapped shut the curtains.

I worried over the next few weeks whether Margaret's spell meant trouble and if I would survive it to live on into old age. Perhaps she planned for my house to blow up, or a plane to crash into my back yard. I tested my stomach for queasiness, a sure sign of tragedy, but felt nothing. I decided that it was a friendly spell and hoped it would make my mother pregnant, or bring other good fortune.

Then, more worry. My parents told me they were going away for the weekend and a reliable next door neighbor boy would stay with me. He was eighteen and had many friends who spit on the sidewalk and swore a lot. He mowed our lawn, occasionally turning his sour face to me, sitting safely inside. Alan, the boy, insisted on calling me "Kid."

"Please," I said, always polite, "call me Lindy." I was watching through the picture window while my parents drove out of sight.

Alan laughed and pulled my braids.

It was Saturday afternoon, so I switched on the TV to see if the lightning-struck golfer had returned to the tournament. He had, and he got rounds of applause at each hole he played. The natural phenomenon hadn't hurt him any; instead, he seemed more powerful than ever. The movement of his swing was like an eye snapping open.

I turned off the set and sat across from Alan at the kitchen table. He worked on math problems for summer school while I read about Venus's-flytraps in my science book. I imagined one of these plants in Margaret's garden, under another one of her spells, its mouth closing around my finger, gripping hard.

Alan made hamburgers for dinner. He ate three and I ate half of one, with a whole bun folded around it like a blanket. Alan had a huge head with an enormous mouth. I imagined gears clanking while he ate. Thick, straight hair, like grass, fell in his eyes.

By the time the after-dinner game shows came on, Alan was sipping his second beer, the phone receiver pressed to his ear. I understood that boys were coming over and only hoped they wouldn't spit in the house. I sat at the kitchen table. A mug shot of Alan lay to my right, drawn a week earlier from what I had seen of him through my window. I was now revising, making his head much larger.

Soon boys were coming through the front door. At Alan's request I had turned on the stereo, and played the Ink Spots record until he told me to take it off. I found The Beatles on the radio and everyone seemed happy. More boys came.

"Kid," Alan said at one point, "let's have a party."

"Okay," I said, not looking up. We were all crammed in the living room where I worked furiously with my crayons and paper, drawing mug shots. Boys with big heads.

The music grew louder and everyone danced, spilling drinks and beer on the carpet. About a dozen boys flailed around the living room, trying out the Twist, tossing their crew-cut heads around in the hazy air. Alan sat smoking a cigarette and coughing, his eyes closed. I glanced around to get exact facial features for my drawings, but ignored the mess. My parents couldn't blame me as I would have been in bed.

I couldn't draw because everyone was dancing and their faces blurred as they moved. Watching TV was out of the question. I looked out the picture window at that point and saw an orange globe skim the tops of the shrubs. It was Margaret, spying. Her head looked a little like the drawing I had in my room of John Glenn's fiery spacecraft re-entering the earth's atmosphere. Her pale, dotted face rose over the bushes and scanned the living room. Margaret's eyes fastened on me and she scowled, fiercely. She had escaped from her own home! I stared back, marveling at Margaret's bravery. She was a member of that flock of irresponsible children who glided by my house every day on foot, and on bikes and trikes, dodging tornadoes and train wrecks, looking under rocks and through mud for even more danger and chaos. I watched these kids through my bedroom window as if I were witness to a funeral march. Margaret's head retreated, the orange globe slid on. No good would come of her visitation, I was sure.

I wandered into the kitchen and nibbled some potato chips I found on the table. Alan was on the phone again with some boy beside him who kept trying to take the receiver away. Alan kissed into the phone. Now girls were coming over.

A softball whizzed by my head. The boy near the phone caught it and threw it back out of the room. He saw me, smiled, then picked me up and sat me on his shoulders. We jogged into the living room.

"Kid!" some of the boys shouted.

I smiled and waved, dizzy from the great height. The boy who held me was doing the Twist and I felt queasy every time he rotated down and up. When he stood straight my head grazed the ceiling.

A man delivered four pizzas to the house and Alan set them on the coffee table. He handed me up a piece with olives. I picked them off and dropped them in the boy's blond hair, which made a perfect launching pad: every time he gyrated up or down the olives spun out from his head. I was starting to have fun.

But then a fast song came on the stereo and the blond went wild. I had to duck to avoid getting a concussion; my braids were flying. Now my neck would surely be broken, as my parents had often predicted. I screamed at the top of my lungs.

The boy set me down. I dashed to the end of the hall, sat down, and cried, running my legs in frustration against the carpet. I imagined Margaret in my situation. She would have handled things differently: A cartoon swashbuckler in high boots, striding through the house tossing boys aside and growling at them until they picked up all their mess. Instead, someone bounced a basketball in my room. A couple of boys wrestled in my parents' room. Two boys stood at the linen closet, looking down the laundry chute.

One of them turned and said, "Hey Kid, where does this go?"

"Lindy!" I cried. I was exhausted. Boys danced in the living room, ate pizza, called girls on the phone. Sports were going on all over the house. Everyone called me "Kid."

"It goes to the basement," I said. The basement was where my father kept out-of-season things like my sled and skates and his shovels and the long pole with the metal half moon that he used for breaking ice. These dangerous articles waited patiently for winter, like trolls under a bridge.

One of the boys threw his empty beer can down the chute. It clattered onto the basement floor. The other took off his tee shirt and threw it down. More boys from the living room wandered up to the closet, peered down the chute, and threw in their beer cans. Alan tossed the Ink Spots record. Soon everything was going down the laundry chute. Alan sent some of his friends to the basement to wait at the bottom. They tried to throw things back up. The boy I had danced with put me back on his shoulders and we joined the others. When I tried to see the end of the chute I was faced with a swirling darkness, and shouts coming from the bottom. The softball came back up.

"Let's see if the Kid'll go down!" Alan yelled.

"Yeah!" all the other boys said.

Before I could scream, Alan took me off his friend's shoulders and pointed my head down into the laundry chute. I felt my shoulders go in and then the rest of me. Someone held my feet. Like a torpedo primed for firing, I started to shudder. All I could picture was an expanse of dark space and millions of stars, and my body shooting through it all. This was the stuff of my nightmares—the loneliest place in all infinity. I was up against exactly what I had been trying to avoid. I was sure my parents would be interviewed on the news after my disappearance, my mother crying, my father shaking his head and staring at his fingernails. Alan would get in big trouble for losing me. I screamed.

They brought me up and held me upside down, my braids dangling to the floor. Way down the hall I saw someone's small bare feet skid across the tile from the front door to the kitchen and then disappear. The boy who was holding me began to sway from side to side. This ding-donging increased my screams. The boys just laughed.

Suddenly, I saw two short legs in spaceman pajamas come charging down the hall, each step full of strong purpose. The legs squared off at the knees of the boy who held me and kicked him hard. He howled and dropped me. It was Margaret, her face a furious red. Without even looking back at the boys, she grabbed my arm and dragged me from the house. We raced down the hall followed by sound of the boys' protests.

Once in the yard, we stopped. Rock and roll music blared behind us, but no boy moved outside the house or made a sound. The sky around us was clear of clouds, the moon a crescent. Tree branches waved, the neighbors' houses were dark. No one shouted, nothing fell; no sirens. I shuffled my feet on the rough grass. The night breeze felt like quick hands around my legs. The wind rose and moved the ends of my hair.

Margaret took my hand and we ran down the warm sidewalk, past the empty garage, on to the next block. I saw the two of us in a newspaper photograph come to life: Wearing matching baseball caps, our faces brown from the sun, Margaret and I would trot down the street in time, waving to our cheering game show audience. Now Margaret brought me to a redwood fence where I looked between the slats at the water in her pool, shining and shifting in the light from the streetlamp.

Margaret opened the gate and rushed to the side of the pool. I walked up behind her. She didn't bother to take off her pajamas, but simply dropped into the shallow water.

She stood neck-deep and brave in the pool, squinting up at me and giggling. I couldn't see the bottom, but I imagined something down there holding Margaret up to me. If someone were to draw me now I would be a flash of bright light, an arc of fire from the sun, lighting up the dark.

Margaret punched and pinched at my ankles. "Come on, Scaredy Cat, jump in," she said.

Dizzy from the witchcraft of my true name finally uttered, I laughed and threw myself forward, diving headlong into the dark water.

ON VACATION
by Richard Kraus

Shivering in the pre-dawn chill, she pulled her robe tight around her, the thin shaft of cold air reminding her that he had tunneled through the plaster again. Two months it had taken this time. His fingers were growing longer and stronger. Beyond the edge of the carpet she could feel the particles of broken plaster cracking beneath her bare feet. She could hear it, too, and the infinitesimal sound accentuated the blessed silence. Though she was cold and bone tired, she would not trade the peace of the moment for warmth or sleep; her ear was still tuned and her mind distracted, waiting for the signal that would end it.

She opened the door and went out into the yard, putting at least that much more distance between her and the upstairs. Through the darkness she could see the pond, a bit of moonlight flickering off the surface. The cold morning dew squished between her frozen toes. She put her hands flat against the wire fence, then her face. Her left hand climbed the fence, rested on the bolt latch, slid it back, then forward, then back again, playing with the latch, not idly but with deep concentration. She stopped, leaving it open, and raised her eyes, staring for full seconds. She could feel the tears on her cheeks before she knew they were coming. To stifle the sobs in her throat she threw herself on the grass and buried her face in the wetness, pounding her fists into the soft earth. When she was spent, she rolled over onto her back and lay looking at the lightening sky. She was soaked through her robe, through her nightgown. When she got to her feet she thought she could hear the crooning begin. She started back to the house, then remembering, turned and locked the gate.

It was still quiet as she eased up the stairs, keeping to the right to minimize the squeaking of the wood. In the bedroom she removed her robe and slipped the wet nightgown off. Naked in the darkness she could feel her body bulge with goose bumps. Then she heard the stirring from across the hall. Not yet! She lurched across the room and climbed in to bed, on George's side, trying to force room with her own body. He was too heavy to budge, and for a moment she lay perched precariously on half a hip bone.

"Geez," he said, "you're all wet."

"Just thinking of you, honey," she said.

"Yeah, yeah," he said, laughing awake.

This time she could hear the crooning begin, and to drown it out she sank beneath George's body and crooned her own song trying to accompany the beat of his body and obliterate the sound of the song from the other room.

She waited in the pickup, watching them disappear into the school, George's back like a moving wall shielding her from the sight of him. She had forced George to go in. She could not face Mrs. Murray, this morning, or yesterday. She had not read Mrs. Murray's note, nor would she let George tell her what was in it. "I don't want to know," she'd said to him. "Consider me on vacation. You know what that is, you're a Union man. Two weeks, I'm taking. Two weeks off!! Don't tell me. You take care of it. What I don't see I don't want to know about."

George had taken her into his arms. She felt his power, like a huge motor idling within the bulk of him, and it enraged her. It was so useless, and he as helpless and idiotic as the rhythmless tapping of his big hand against her shoulder.

"I'll take over for a while," he said, "you need a break."

From the pickup she watched the children assemble; clustering by twos and threes and more; talking, their voices singing in the wind that carried words she could comprehend. She closed her window, leaned across the seat and closed George's, trying to shut out the words. But still the voices came, undeterred by mere glass; names and songs and high pitched insults, happy and funny and cruel. Human sounds, unmistakably human.

Through the windshield like a picture on a TV screen she watched a tangle of children make a kaleidoscope on a giant jungle gym. Arms and legs and vari-colored torsos wriggled and shifted like the parts of one beast and the ragged chorus of laughter was its voice. She wrenched her eyes away, focusing on a small boy in a red plaid shirt. He stalked a tall girl with a long dark pigtail that moved like the pendulum of a grandfather clock, back and forth across her back as she walked. The boy, slapping from underneath knocked the girl's books out of her arms. The girl's voice cut through the glass:

"You . . . you LITTLE SHIT!"

She nodded her head.

She could see George smiling as he came out of the building, a piece of notebook paper in his hand. The building itself seemed to give George hope. It was an ordinary school for ordinary children. If they let him stay in a room in a building for ordinary children then there was hope, some officially sanctioned hope. She watched George pause in the doorway to look at the paper. She knew what it was, some ragged clutter of lines and shapes that Mrs. Murray made George believe was a drawing. Mrs. Murray was a magician, she whispered magic words in George's ear, "operant conditioning," "positive reinforcement," "mainstreaming." She stood him before George and shaped some word or two in careful full rounded tones, and drew from his throat one or two strangled sounds. "Words," Mrs. Murray declared and translated them, laying them before George like rabbits from some top hat. George stared at the paper, grinning like a surprised child. When he looked up toward the pickup he looked pleased and pregnant with good news. She could see him framing the sentences; she could even hear them. Before he could reach her she slid over into the driver's seat and drove off, watching the smile fade from his lips in the rear view mirror.

The road took her home against her will. While her mind struggled for a destination the pickup dropped her between the twin birches that led into the driveway beside the house. Because the door couldn't open without her volition she sat clenching the steering wheel. She was still sitting there ten minutes later when the cab pulled up to let George out. The ground seemed almost to shake as he moved to the pickup. When he yanked open the pickup door,she hissed at him, "Get away from me. Get away." He held the door open, foolish, his anger dissipating like air out of the unpinched mouthpiece of a balloon. She slammed the door shut again and hunched down over the steering wheel until he went away.

On his way to the house he stopped, hopped sidewise to avoid something in his path, went on to the garage and came back with a small spade, half a dozen of the chickens following in his wake. He scooped it up on the shovel and carried it to the ragged patch of dirt beside the chicken coop and buried it. She half expected him to put up a marker. It was his patience that broke her heart and enraged her.

When he came back to the pickup, she opened the door and climbed out.

"Again," she said; "Even the dog's housebroken."

"He hasn't done it for a while," George said.

"Not since yesterday," she said, ". . . you should see the wash I've got."

He nodded.

She was still ironing past midnight. Her arms and neck ached from scrubbing floors and ceilings. George, unwilling to leave her, was asleep in the easy chair. The TV flashed shifting images of Johnny Carson and a parade of people selling things. She'd turned down the sound as soon as she saw George doze. She took up her laundry basket and counted the remaining pieces. Nothing left but underwear. She ironed it all. Once George told her how impressed the guys at the plant were that he had a wife who ironed his underwear. She ironed both of their underwear. A good wife was one who ironed her man's underwear, and her children's. As she neared the end of her task, she searched her mind for something more, furniture to move or walls, anything physical to tire her, or at least to make her bones ache. There was nothing like a good long-lasting hurt somewhere in her body. It turned her head inward to the throbbing place, to a pain she could endure, knowing its cessation was out there in the foreseeable future. She held up the last pair of small shorts, searching for brown stains, before she ironed it.

In the morning she had her pain, a wracking migraine that put her out of commission. She swallowed aspirin, suffered helplessly as she listened to George getting him ready for school. She was certain he would look a mess. George couldn't tell play clothes from school clothes. Desperately, she tried to pull herself out of bed. He could not go out of the house without clean and ironed clothes. Though he would come home with them ripped or soiled with paint and mud and food and his own shit, he could not be allowed to leave until he looked right. Every morning she would let him go, washed and combed and ironed. She had to catch him before he got out of the house. By sheer effort of will she dragged herself out of the bed and hurried downstairs just in time to see the pickup turn out of the driveway. In his bedroom she saw the outfit she had laid out for the day, still folded neatly in a pile on the chair. She burst into tears.

She could feel the vibrations through her bed, and she lay there counting the thumps . . . five-six-seven . . . twenty-two. . . . She felt the bed spring upwards as George jumped out. She lay still, listening.

"Okay, okay, okay," George said. Through the walls she saw George engulfing him, burying him against his huge frame, restraining him until the rage or whatever it was subsided. This time George stayed a long while after it was quiet. She lay waiting for him, her view of the next room obscured by the silence. She tried to sleep, but without George the bed was empty and lonely. When she could bear it no longer, she got out of bed and crossed the hall. Standing in the doorway she caught the silhouette of the large head bending down over the smaller. She could see the shadow of George's lips pressing against the dark round shape. Inadvertently she coughed once, not loudly, and the small head came up violently and the shadow of George's head snapped back.

"Ouch," he yelled.

When George came back to their bedroom, he was still rubbing under his eye.

"He really nailed me," George said, "I'm going to have a shiner."

"What were you doing so long?" she said.

"Holding him. I thought he was asleep. I like to hold him when he's asleep. You ought to try it some time."

"I have," she said. "I've had my share of shiners, more than my share."

"I didn't mean it that way," he said.

"Of course you didn't," she said, "you just said it to make me feel good."

"Have it your way," he said wearily.

Grimly she brought it up again. "How long do we go on; how long, George?"

"I don't want to hear about it," he said doggedly. "I don't want to talk about it."

She lay awake in the darkness, her mind ticking like a clock. It was too hard to love a saint. She'd married an ordinary guy, a big easy going guy with a quick temper who loved a good time, and she'd ended up stuck with this sponge. How much could he take? Tossing and turning and unable to find any road into sleep, she swore she'd find out.

Somewhere near dawn chickens screamed in her sleep, but she shut them out and hunched deeper into her covers. The voice in her head that always drove her across the hall to get him ready for school nagged at her, but she turned it off. She was already exposed. Yesterday he had gone to school in the stained, torn blue jeans and the faded blue T-shirt that said, "Who? Ray! Hooray!" Let George get him ready again. Let George do it. Let George do everything. He'd made the decision. No, he'd decided there was no decision to be made. Coldly she made up her mind, and dropped off to sleep. When she awoke the sun shone bright through the tiny crack above the shades. She hadn't even heard them leave. Like a lady of leisure she went downstairs, made herself a cup of coffee, drank it, had another. Back upstairs she took a long bath, combed her hair, put on a clean shirt and a fresh pair of jeans and went out into the yard, carrying a copy of *Better Homes and Gardens* with her. She sat and read for a while, the spring sun warming her back. Then she walked over to the gate, slid back the bolt and went to stand at the edge of the pond. It was filling with water lilies, bright yellow flowers sitting on their wide floating green leaves.

On her way back to the house her eye caught the still white shape against the wall of the chicken coop. She went over to it. Its wrung neck flopped over her arm as she lifted it. When the dead neck touched her skin she flung it angrily toward the house. In the back of the coop she found two more dead ones. She remembered hearing the screaming chickens.

Last year, last week, the day before yesterday she would have been out the door before he could get near the chickens. She looked inside the coop. The rest were alive. She gathered the dead fowl and dropped them into the kitchen sink, debating whether to cook them for dinner or save them to show George. Seeing them in the sink, she decided to cook them, regretting having taken them from the yard. She should have left them where they lay; she should not have moved the corpses until George found them.

After filling a pot with water she realized she had no vegetables for a soup. The idea of going to the store suddenly seemed pleasurable. It seemed ages since she had talked to anyone, ages since she'd set foot in her Chevy. When George bought it for her, he'd promised they'd put a minimum of 10,000 miles a year on it. After two years the speedometer read 8,000 something. It was damn near brand new. Periodically George asked her why she never used it. As if he didn't know. She stayed home, monitoring the telephone until school was out.

When she pulled out of the dark garage into the bright sunlight she saw the upholstery on the passenger's side. Near the door there was a hole nearly as big as a saucer, and the seat and floor in front of it was covered with flecks of yellow foam rubber. She slid under the steering wheel across the front seat, opened the passenger's door, and climbed out. Furiously she swept the debris off the seat with the edge of her hand. She stepped backwards, her foot landing squarely in the middle of something soft. She didn't even look. She knew what it was.

Before going to bed that night, after being certain that George was asleep, she went out into the yard and opened the latch on the gate that led to the pond.

When her head hit the pillow she dropped into an easy sleep from which she did not wake until the sky had already begun to lighten. She lay bolt awake waiting for fuller light and the sound of the song from across the hall. When she heard it she burrowed more deeply beneath her covers, and still more deeply when she heard the squeaking of the stairs.

"You still on vacation," George said, anger, not sleep, in his voice.

"You bet your sweet life," she said.

The cold air hit her back as George surged from the bed. She felt the vibrations set off by his weight on the stairs. The whole house seemed to be shaking. Without haste she got out of bed and went over to the window. It was full daylight and she could see the gate, nudged slightly open by a substantial breeze, and beyond it the yellow flowers floating on the pond.

She saw George burst out of the house and make straight for the open gate, saw him swing it shut and fix the latch in place; heard his voice, loud and frightened; "Ray, Ray!"

From her window she saw the small golden head appear from around the corner of the house. It bobbed unrhythmically as it moved across the field of her window pane, and she could hear the tuneless song spiraling up to her as the small shape disappeared into the heart of his father's body.

THE RED SEA

by Constance Pierce

Brenda was standing at the window, spying on her two daughters, who were supposed to be raking leaves in the yard between the house and barn. They were blond and slender, nearly the same size. One was twelve, the other thirteen. They were moving z-shaped, jabbing one rigid hand forward, the other behind, and making languid snake-like motions with their heads to the music from an enormous radio blaring from the grass. The radio had been the self-selected birthday present of the oldest girl. It was the size of Brenda's microwave, bigger than the computer she used to keep the farm's accounts. It had an alien look, like something from another planet.

Her daughters' plaid flannel shirts were swaying above their jeans and Pumas. Suddenly, the girls froze to a hesitation in the music, and Brenda saw them, not as her daughters, but as stylized Egyptians in a frieze: Painted on the red barn arching behind them.

She shifted to clear her eyes of this odd vision. Out in the field beyond the yard, the bay gelding Jim had bought the girls was nosing its way across the bright green grass, its tail swatting at something. It was an in-between season, with things still alive that ought to be dead or hibernating. She wished it would get cold, just to get things settled. Maybe the leaves would blow off somewhere, and at least Jim could put the horse in the barn and she wouldn't be reminded every day that the girls never rode it.

I thought young girls were supposed to love horses, she thought. All her girls cared about was junior-high social life, music, expensive play shoes. She'd wanted them to be responsible farm kids, smelling like horse-sweat and hay, with hayseed in their hair. She had thought they would be in 4-H, that they would husband animals and win prizes at the State Fair. She'd imagined them streaking across the field, doubled up on the horse, their hair bright and flying. They were wearing simple plaid shirts and jeans in her daydreams, but in life she was lucky if they'd even dress like that to rake at the leaves.

The song finished and the girls fell on the ground, red-faced and laughing. Every few seconds one of them would sing out "Ee-i-oh!" in imitation of the women on the record, the Bangles. Brenda watched Millie, the youngest, unbutton her shirt and fan it against her bare chest.

"Stop that!" Sadie yelled. Millie hesitated, and then she rebuttoned her shirt, not looking at Sadie. "You're too much," Sadie said with disgust.

Then there was another song on the radio and they were both on their feet again, pawing at the grass with their soft shoes and swinging their arms from the elbows, busily snapping their fingers.

Brenda watched them a little longer. Am I going to be able to take this? she wondered.

Sadie had been wearing a bra for less than a week, and not quite needing it, and already she was making Millie self-conscious. Twice Brenda had come upon Sadie scrutinizing the figures on the tape measure wrapped very loosely around her chest, maybe even around a couple of fingers too, the contents of the sewing box strewn on the carpet in the spare room. How much progress could women have made?

Brenda turned away from her daughters. Through another window she could see their old orange cat, Chloe, ambling across another square of lawn, heading for the barn. A snatch of lyric, odd as her daughters frozen on the barn, ran through her head: Joe MacDonald had a farm.

She watched Chloe stop, as if blasted by the heat from the girls' music. The cat put her ears back. If she were human, she'd be frowning, Brenda thought, frowning herself. Country Joe and the Fish? She hadn't thought about them since the days when she used to go to rock concerts, decked out in an Indian headband and bellbottom jeans with a peace sign sewn on the tailpocket, her other pockets stuffed with sunflower seeds. Life. Now she had a flagpole in a bed of peonies on the front lawn and flew the flag on Flag Day and the 4th of July, like folk art.

The cat gave the girls one last indignant look and changed her course, her white-socked feet breaking into a run for several yards.

"I'm going," Brenda called to Jim, who was watching the Bengals and the Colts fight it out on the tv, in between feeding the cattle and feeding the cattle. He was trying to get them ready to sell. When he didn't answer, she stepped into the living room and saw him sleeping on the sofa, sitting up. And this was a game he'd been waiting for all week.

She tiptoed over and turned up the sound. He was exhausted, she knew, but he'd feel worse if he missed this game, and the last thing he'd want was for her to catch him sleeping in the afternoon. She wished he'd give himself a break. If she had known how hard life was going to be, on all of them, and if she hadn't loved Jim, she'd have married somebody in another line of work, or just kept on living in town and teaching school.

"Don't let them cut it too short," he mumbled suddenly, his eyes still closed. It gave her a start, like he'd heard her thoughts.

"I thought you were sacked out," she said, digging into her purse for the keys. "You could give somebody a heart attack like that."

"I'd like to give you a heart attack, Baby," Jim said, opening his eyes and flirting with her.

"Well, it wouldn't take much these days. I'm too old for this."

"Too old for what," Jim said, turning back to the game, where the Bengals were slaughtering the Colts. Brenda watched the Bengals' bright tiger-striped helmets against the turf.

"Breasts," she said.

Jim gave her a puzzled look.

"Loud music, expensive fads, dates." She found her keys and strung her purse back on her shoulder. "Cranky moods. Sulking."

"You need some interests," Jim said.

"Yes," Brenda said. "Maybe I'll start riding Tony-the-Pony. They're never going to ride him." She paused. "I thought they'd ride him," she said, looking back to the tv set where her husband had fixed his eyes again too. "I thought they'd wear their jeans and Dingos and ride across the hayfield like little Calamity Janes." She could feel herself near tears.

"You ought to figure out what's bothering you," Jim said, sitting forward a little to follow a play.

"Mummy!" Sadie's scream brought Jim to his feet. Brenda turned as her daughter burst into the room, her face glowing.

"There's a big lizard out there," Sadie said, excitedly. "Millie raked it up with the leaves."

Jim sat back down.

"Well, are you scared or hot-to-trot?" Brenda asked, giving her daughter a look. "I can't tell with you anymore. Where's Millie?"

"That child," Sadie said, suddenly calming down, sounding about thirty years old. "She's hiding in the barn."

"From a lizard?" Brenda said.

"Well, it might be a snake," Sadie said indifferently. "It's out in the yard crawling around. Are you going to shoot it?" she asked her father, in the new world-weary voice she used these days.

"If it's a snake, I guess a hoe'll take care of it," Jim said, looking longingly at the football players rolling around in living color.

"I'll do it," Brenda, her heart beating faster.

Jim looked at her.

"Really. I've killed a snake before," she lied. "Get me the hoe, Sadie."

"Don't cut it too short," Jim said, looking back at the tv.

Brenda was confused. "The snake?" she asked.

"Your hair."

"Lisa cuts it however she wants to," Brenda said irritably. "I don't seem to have much influence with her. Or anybody else."

Outside, holding the hoe like a club out in front of her, both her daughters on her heels (Millie snuffling, Sadie walking in a contemptuous silence that could be felt), Brenda approached the area where the animal had last been seen.

"You let it get away," Sadie said, as they stood on the empty lawn, looking around. "Daddy should've come."

"I see it!" Millie yelled, shrinking back toward the barn.

"Where?" Brenda asked. Then she saw it. "Oh," she said.

"Kill it," Sadie said.

Brenda lowered her hoe. A snake-like lizard, a skink, was lying still in the grass about ten feet away. Brenda moved closer. It had about six inches of head and torso and six inches of tail. It had frozen in all of the commotion, its body stiff and raised slightly off the ground on impossibly tiny legs; but its eyes seemed to move a little, as if it were trying to assess the danger it was in without calling extra attention to itself. At its throat, a half-transparent ruff expanded in creamcolored poufs and then collapsed, a motion so regular and precise that Brenda stood transfixed for a moment, watching the wrinkled skin bloom in slow motion, the dull color of collapse swelling again and again to a taut luminescence, like a little dawn.

Is this the snake in my garden? she wondered. A small wary snake, poised to run?

"You girls are something," she said, finally. "That's just a skink."

"Well, kill it," Sadie said. "It almost bit Millie."

Already Sadie was drifting off in her head. Brenda saw her eyes disengage, watched her dig into the pocket of her jeans and bring out a barrette and begin to rearrange her hair.

"Can we have pizza for supper?" she asked Brenda.

"No. Bad for your skin and hair," Brenda said. "You're going to go bald if you don't stop pulling your hair up like that. It makes your skin look pulled back." Sadie was fashioning a wild new-style ponytail, pulled to the side. Brenda could see gold stars that looked like the ones she used to put besides the names of her best students on a bulletin-board chart, studding her daughter's earlobes, one of the several holes there dangling a golden half-moon. The stars and moon together looked like the logo of Proctor and Gamble, who bought all Jim's cows that got struck by lightning or just died, and made them into soap and shampoo. The logo was also an old symbol for Satan, some fundamentalists said. "They'd had P & G on the run, and Brenda thought she had read that the logo had been changed, but she couldn't be sure.

"Those animals are good for my garden," Brenda said, turning to squint at the skink, then urging it toward the bushes with her hoe. It moved several feet and stopped, its eyes frozen now, too, within their small pouches of wrinkles; even the miraculous throat seemed still. "Just leave it alone," she said to the girls, turning and heading for the barn to put away the hoe. "What kind of farm kids are you anyway?"

"No kind," Sadie said, glumly. Brenda stopped and looked back. Sadie picked up a small rock and tossed it near the skink. Millie was looking at the skink and then at her mother, then at the skink again.

Brenda resumed walking. She could hear Sadie's rocks landing in the grass with soft thuds, like a sluggish heartbeat. "Leave it alone," she said, not looking back. She felt Millie's clammy hand catch up to hers and tug on it a little before it settled in. Then they walked together to the barn, palm to damp palm.

Chloe was sitting, sphinx-like, on the walk when Brenda got home. "You old cat," Brenda said, affectionately, pausing to scratch the cat's head. She was going to miss Chloe, just as she missed her litter-mate, Cleo, who had died last year. Cleo had died out in the barn and had frozen up and thawed out half the spring, Jim said, before Brenda found her when she went out for her gardening tools. Cleo had been dismantling in bits out there, and Jim hadn't said a word. "Why didn't you take her out and throw her in the field," Brenda had asked, wiping away tears of fury at her husband. She'd had Chloe and Cleo as long as she'd had Sadie and Millie. She'd found Cleo only half-frozen at noon on the prettiest day of the year, a day when she'd been so happy, her pockets stuffed with seed packets, everything sunny and warm, bright blue sky, high clouds—and she'd ended up digging a grave, making a little casket for Cleo out of the straw she'd planned to put between her vegetable rows to keep down the weeds.

"I didn't have time to do it whenever I thought about it," Jim had said, shrugging. "Then when I had time, I never thought about it."

"Good old cat," Brenda said again, rising up. Chloe had a sagging belly with two lines of sagging tits, a broken fang, and a cloudy spot on her eye, two permanent bare spots on the back of her neck where the neighbors' male cats had left their vampire's mark for years. Chloe had a scar on her nose from fighting one of them when he'd come back to kill her male kittens, a losing battle. They always came back and killed the kittens. Did Chloe remember any of that now, the murky sea of kinship? Or had all the old battles, the many lost and the several won, receded into a haze deeper than memory? The stuff of life, gone, and yet you'd never know it, the cat seemed so content. It was like getting a little sun was enough now, that and staying out of the way of the girls, who never knew where anything was except themselves.

Brenda lingered, touching her haircut. She wondered if there would be a time when everyone she knew now would be lost to her, when they would be only thin surfaces of themselves in their relations with her, like most of her own old selves. Sometimes it seemed like you survived life because nothing much accumulated.

She looked out across her yard, feeling the soft fur of Chloe against her leg, aware of the winding-down clock inside the cat, contradicted by the wound-up motor purring. The yard was a sea of red leaves now, and beyond, the field was circled with red trees, burning as if in their finest hour. Tony-the-Pony broke into a little trot at the field's edge, then settled down quickly and began to graze again. Probably the last of the bees or a fly on its last wing, Brenda thought, breathing in the queer mixed season, shaking her hair out, which was not too short, she had reassured herself all the way home in the rearview mirror. She'd been pleased with how she'd handled Lisa at the beauty shop. It had seemed a small engineering of Fate, which she imagined as a vast ectoplasm, scrunching invisibly on the horizons of her life. How could you do much, when everybody else was going through stages? When love fell on you like a disease, leading you into a life you weren't trained for. When business, and trends, and adolescence, and death disrupted households all over the world, and your muscles and bones began to separate within you, nothing you could do about it.

Was all this what was bothering her? She didn't think that was all of it. She couldn't seem to get at all of it.

"Oh," Sadie said, stumbling out of the door, onto Brenda and Chloe before she slowed down. "Sorry." She looked at Brenda a moment. "Your hair looks nice, Mummy."

"Thanks," Brenda said, smiling at her daughter, who had exchanged her raking clothes for a soft pink sweatshirt, against which her little breasts, absurdly high on her chest, pushed like two crabapples. "I told Lisa to pay attention to me for once. It seemed to work. Where's your Dad?"

"Feeding the cows," Sadie said. "Where else?"

"Don't be smart *every* chance you get," Brenda warned, already weary of Sadie's pouty, whiny voice, which she knew she'd be listening to for the next four or five years, until the girls came back into the human world. "Where's Millie?"

"Who cares?" Sadie said. "I wish I could get a new haircut."

"Why don't you?" Brenda said lightly, feeling a sudden release of her daughter's weight, which she'd been carrying around inside her head for months, she realized, as if her brain were a womb and Sadie was back in it. "Why don't you do whatever you want to do to your hair? Wear anything you want, eat junk? Rake the leaves or don't rake them. Kill skinks." Brenda felt her face loosening in the loss of tension. She didn't have to struggle with these kids every step of the way, over every little thing.

"I did kill the skink," Sadie pouted.

Brenda felt a shock. Chloe's fur, still against her leg, gave her a creepy feeling. "What do you mean?"

"I didn't exactly mean to," Sadie said. "But I hit it with a rock and stunned it a little, and I just couldn't quit."

"You stoned it to death?" Brenda said, looking at her daughter in horror of all she was that her mother didn't know about. The cat got up and walked to the edge of the walk, swishing her tail.

"Well, so what?" Sadie said, pushing past her mother. "It was just an old snake with legs. It almost bit Millie anyway."

"I think that's the worst thing you've ever done in your life," Brenda said, and meant it. "Where is Millie anyway? Did she help you?" Brenda almost reeled with the possibility that both of her daughters were propelled, inside, by something darker than what was inside herself, or in Jim, who never hurt anything uselessly, even if he did forget about things that weren't business sometimes.

Sadie scoffed. "Millie cried about it. She's about five years old, if you ask me. It was her that almost got bit."

"And you're about a hundred," Brenda said, relieved that Millie, at least, hadn't crossed beyond the pale. "I want those leaves raked before dark or you can just forget about a haircut or junk-food, or radio music or skink-hunting or anything you like to do."

"I plan to rake the leaves," Sadie said, indignant. "Why do you think I came out here?"

"Yes, in your spiffy clothes," Brenda said. "What did you do with the skink? Hi, honey," she said as Millie came out of the house, still wearing her raking clothes, her face drawn into a knot. Brenda held out her arm and let Millie walk into its circle, as if under a wing.

"Sadie killed the skink," Millie said.

"I know," Brenda said. "Just try to forget it."

"That's what *I'm* going to do," Sadie said, walking toward the rakes still lying on the lawn, making Chloe jump out of her way and disappear into the safety of the shrubs along the house.

"No, you're not," Brenda said, gathering steam against the facts: that her daughters scared her, that the next four or five years would decide, one way or the other, how and how much they would stay in her life, for the rest of her life. And how and how much she would want to stay in theirs, she asserted now, knowing it was a lie. She would want to stay in theirs, whatever happened. "You're going to go over there and pick up that animal and carry it out in the field and cover it up with something," Brenda said. "I'm not going to have it rotting out here on the lawn."

Sadie and Millie both gave her a horrified look.

"Did you think I was going to do it?" Brenda said. "Or your Daddy? Those days are over. Come on. We'll all go."

"Oh, Mummy, no," Millie pleaded. "Then I won't be able to forget it."

"Well, maybe I was wrong to say you should forget," Brenda said. "On second thought, I think it's something you both need to see, close-up: an act and its consequences. Which will give you some idea of what really growing up is all about."

"I wish you wouldn't preach all the time," Sadie said over her shoulder, already fuming toward the dead skink like a steam engine, kicking up a spray of red leaves.

Is that true? Brenda wondered, as she and Millie followed. She thought about it for a moment. Maybe I do preach. Maybe I'm just pretending this is something they have to see, to make an impression on them, any way I still can.

At the edge of the yard, the skink lay in a thin wave, as if it had just stopped and would be scooting off again any moment. Brenda could see the small white line of its underbelly. It's undersized legs curled against its body like tiny question marks.

"Maybe he isn't dead," Millie said, letting go of Brenda's hand and moving closer to the skink.

"Well, he is," Sadie said. "Look at his head."

Brenda saw its head for the first time, a little mound of disconnected tissue, mashed up like berries or fruit. "You beat his head in," Millie said, reproaching her sister.

Sadie picked up a thin forking limb nearby and poked at the skink, flipping it over and then back on its stomach. Brenda could see now the small tears in its body where her daughter's rocks had found their mark. The ruff at its throat was limp now and the throat itself slack and dun-colored.

Millie, wide-eyed and fearless with sympathy, was crouching down by the skink. Amazed, Brenda watched her put a finger on its back. She felt a deep chill, in spite of knowing what it said about Millie. She felt like she was finding an orphan-child in the bulrushes—one much more noble than herself.

"I thought it would feel slimy," Millie said, her voice miserable. "It feels like my felt board."

"You make me sick," Sadie said. "Get up so I can do what she wants me to do."

"What's going on out here," Jim said, coming up on them.

"We're having a sermonette," Brenda said, struggling for the banter he expected. "We're learning about Paradise Lost, and growing up. Life. And Death."

"Well, you sure let him have it with that hoe," Jim said. "It's nothing but a skink, though."

"I didn't kill it," Brenda exclaimed. "Your daughter Sadie stoned it to death in a fit. She sounded possessed. She said she couldn't help herself."

Jim looked at Sadie.

"I just want to forget the whole thing," Sadie said, her mouth a pout the color of her pink sweatshirt.

"Mummy says we shouldn't forget it, Daddy," Millie said. "I'll never forget it. Its skin felt like felt."

"Well, you'd better do something with it, Sadie," Jim said. "They say that a dead reptile's mate will come and wrap around it and stay there. You don't want two dead lizards on your conscience."

"She hasn't got a conscience," Millie said solemnly.

Sadie began to lift the skink onto her tree-limb. Brenda turned away, pulling Millie with her. She felt like somebody had died. She wished Jim would notice how well Millie was behaving, though.

"I don't want to walk back through those leaves," Millie said.

"Why not?" Brenda said.

"Because the skink's mate might be there."

"I thought you'd made your peace with the skink," Brenda said, disappointed. This would be the story of the rest of her life, this constant shifting around, always having to put a new face on things.

"Daddy?" Millie said.

Jim bent down and swung her up on his shoulders. "You're getting your last piggyback," he said. "You're too big."

The three of them headed back. "You should have raked the leaves," Brenda said to Millie. "Then you wouldn't have to worry about hiding places for skinks. Is that true?" she asked Jim. "About the skink's mate?" The idea moved her.

"I've always heard it," Jim said. "About snakes, anyway. But I've never seen it. I heard a skink will brood its eggs just like a chicken—that's rare for a lizard. I've heard a scared lizard would drop its tail, too, and that it would grow another one in its place."

"Really?" Millie said.

"It's called regeneration," Jim said. "I read about it in *The Progressive Farmer.*"

"Will the tail grow another body?" Millie said.

"I don't think so," Jim said. "But you never know. They're always shedding whole suits of skin and growing new ones, snakes anyway."

"I think that's creepy," Millie said.

"I guess so," Jim said. "Dead things ought to stay dead. It's natural."

Brenda looked at her husband and Millie. Their heads were close together, Millie's arms around Jim's neck. Millie still looked a little scared, and Jim looked a little tired, but otherwise they looked normal as apple pie.

"Regeneration is natural too," she said, to nobody. It was. A natural miracle, for a few chosen creatures of the earth. The rest just had to reproduce, something different from themselves.

Sometimes *very* different. She looked back at Sadie, out in the field, scraping doggedly at the ground with a stick. She wondered if Sadie would hold in her mind the day when something ugly had welled up inside her and taken over. Brenda hoped her daughter would remember the smell of the earth, getting ready to die for a while itself as she dug into it, the moment when she committed the skink back to earth, the private funeral. She hoped that it all wouldn't be sloughed off, or lost, like Chloe's forgotten babies.

But maybe she'd even forget it herself, until it surfaced after thirty years, like that blast-from-the-past this afternoon, Country Joes and The Fish. Recalling a few minutes out of all the minutes of life. Where were all the others?

"I like your hair," Jim said.

"Good," Brenda said. "Who won the game?"

"The Bengals," Jim said.

"Watch out, Daddy," Millie warned as they headed into the leaves, Brenda slightly ahead, her hair stirring in the breeze.

Brenda walked slowly, sneaking looks back toward the field, where Tony-the-Pony was a grazing shadow behind his shadowy fence—content or lonely and tormented by flies, who could know? She couldn't think about him now. He was a backdrop for Sadie now, a lesser mystery. Brenda was looking for something in the posture or gestures of her prodigal daughter to reassure her. She could see Sadie lifting the skink up on her tree-branch out on the deserted field. She seemed rigid, stoical, like a prophet of old.

Brenda stopped looking back. Walking through the leaves, she suddenly felt scared too. You never knew what lay ahead of you. It would be nice if you could know, unless you couldn't do anything to change your course. When she was young, she'd imagined that all the time:

how awful it would be to live your life over and know everything you knew now and not be able to warn anybody or change the course of things. She had concluded that that was God's Fate, and she had thought, Poor God, unable to warn his creatures, and had even prayed for him.

She felt a gust of wind whip by them. A moment later it attacked the leaves, blowing them out of their path, a brief happy accident. Chloe seized her chance and darted by, then disappeared into the shadows. The bright green grass seemed to stretch out like a narrow carpet for about a dozen feet as the red leaves rolled back before piling up again. Neither Millie nor Jim had noticed. For a moment Brenda felt herself suspended—how to use it: a lesson for Millie or a joke to lighten her husband's load?

She decided not to mention it. "Come on, Sadie," she called over her shoulder, but looking straight ahead. "Just cover it enough to keep the cat from digging it up. Let bygones be bygones, for now. She was lost in a desert herself. She would take the parted leaves as a small, good sign, like Chloe had. Wily old cat. Wily, and doomed anyway.

"Let's go make a pizza," she said. It's getting cold out here." She sped up, determining to lead her people, if just for this evening, out of something too big for every living thing.

POOR CONDITIONS
by Laura Yeager

My boyfriend drives a towtruck. He told me that once he pulled up at the scene of a horrible accident. A husband and wife had been killed by an oncoming car. In a bush, squirmed a small child with no forehead.

"The thing still made noise," he said.

I was struck by the fact that I could do nothing to ease his pain except to say, "Death is death. You can't get away from it." Tony's two years younger than me, and sometimes I feel justified to give him such profound advice.

"No one noticed the kid," he said. "If I hadn't heard it, I don't know when it would have been found." For a moment, he felt like a stranger to me. He'd seen people going places, waylaid by mechanical errors, human mishaps, accidents, flat tires, bad batteries.

My boyfriend, Tony, has been to car war, yet he refuses to get out of the business. His ex was, ironically, killed in a car accident, but he didn't have to haul her car away, and for this I am grateful. He's a man with a kind of post-traumatic stress disorder.

Because of this, we have devised a code to aid us in communication. Code A means "I have a secret." Code B means "I just don't want to talk, shutting down, no problem." Code C means "I *really* don't want to talk." Code D means "lick my feet, you gas station dog," or "yes, I want to make love."

Tonight, on the eve of Tony's father's first visit to Ohio, I'm thinking of those secrets which drive us, for tonight I feel secretless. My past has been levelled by him.

His father has never visited the house. The visit is even more complicated by the fact that Tony's father deserted the family when he was eight. My father deserted me. Suicide. We are both abandoned children.

My boyfriend is worried that his father will not respect him because of the condition of his home. His place, like mine, is owned by an old man who has never thrown anything away. Our backyard is full of old toilets,as well as stacks of couches and chairs rotting under tarpaulins. I'm sure our landlord would invent a way to dry out the furniture if he ever needed it. He's taken six neighborhood homes and turned them into apartments. I live in the side apartment in the main, 150-year-old farm house, on the first floor. My boyfriend lives next door, six feet away, in the remodelled garage.

The whole place, in two words, is falling down. My apartment has no storm windows, little heat, three kinds of carpet in two rooms, a fireplace that's plugged with a gas heater, which I never leave on at night for fear of explosion, and radon poisoning. The one beautiful thing about it is the front room and its crank windows which let in the morning light.

My boyfriend's house, as I said, is actually a garage. It's dark and predominantly brown with a cement bathroom floor. I don't know what Tony is worried about. It's not the house's structure; it's his decorating.

One of the reasons I like my boyfriend is that he takes me for long drives, and driving is how I came into the world. My mother would take me for long drives. She could not stand to be cooped up and survived our childhoods by touring Akron in search of a place to stop for a Coke.

The joke is still used by me at school. "What are we going to do on Friday? my students ask. "We're going for a Coke," I say. One industrious student (before he was shipped off to Saudi Arabia because he joined the Marines) brought in a whole 24 pack of Coke on Friday. He also brought in a MRE—a meal ready to eat. We all had to take a taste of two-year-old beef stew. The army doesn't print the expiration date, but they say it's two years.

While we are waiting for his father to arrive, we drive off in his jeep and get lost in the movement and the closeness of the small, steel box. Tony forgets the image of what cars can do, and I enjoy the movement of the road. I am not moving, the road is; the world is passing. I think of our short history.

How I came to know of Tony is I moved in next door to him. He appeared one night as noises in the dark—the rattling of keys, the swinging of a door, footsteps. He scared me in the beginning because he was arriving home so late, and *I* could have been the only respectable person living in that dump. But no, he simply worked nights—drove a truck.

At first, our relationship consisted of saying hello in the morning. He worked both nights and days—took the truck home. I kept my drapes shut, but little did he know I used to make myself come by raising the window blind just enough so that he could see in, if he were looking. Our lives are the constant formation and destruction of secrets.

Our first official date consisted of going to a tractor pull at the Lakeland County Fair. He was, I would have formerly said, not my type. The city—country deal? Blue collar, white collar? It didn't make any difference. The point at that time was we both lived on the other side of the tracks.

And today is a beautiful day. Somehow we got over a communication gap, and we're now zooming along in the jeep. We open our eyes wide to take in our twenty minutes of sunshine to prevent SAD, and we drive the little vehicle down the road.

We stop at an antique shop in Peninsula where he purchases eight green, hand-painted, Italian glasses for $8.00. They are the most perfect liqueur glasses I have ever seen.

Tonight, we'll toast the lady who once owned the glasses, after scraping the labels off the bottoms. She never used them.

"If you had to pay tribute to the lady, what would you say?" I'll ask.

"Rest in peace," he'll answer.

We wait for his father. I would so like to see my father materialize before me. Perhaps if I tell my father I forgive, him he'll appear. But I hold on to the resentment because it's all I have of him.

We've gotten word that Tony's father will be a day late.

My mother and I drive to Tony's place of employment—the shop. We go there at night so that I can get my forgotten stuff out of his jeep. My mother says, "I don't like it back here." The place has all the classic features of a dangerous place—darkness, dirt road, old junk cars scattered around, rusted fences, and yet it is entirely safe. "Are you sure there isn't a big junk-yard dog out here?" my mother asks.

"Mom," I tell her, "you'd invent something to fear even if there was nothing to fear," but I have no empathy for her. I've forgotten that this place once scared me. Poor conditions? This terrain is the safest place I know.

Since my father's death, my mother has gone a little crazy, as if she killed him. She won't talk about it. What would she say if she did? That if she would have stopped trying to make him come to his senses he might be alive now? He went to bed for a year before he did it. What might have happened if she would have simply left him alone? She seems to think he'd be alive. He would have had nothing to fight then. She seems to still be in love with him.

Looking into the jeep, I see Tony's bow and arrow on my good skirt, which I'll now have to drop off to have cleaned. I gather the skirt, a coat and bag of long johns, and leave my mother in the car while I pop in the shop to say, "Hello, I'm taking my stuff." Tony isn't there, but one of his co-workers greets me. I do not look like someone running with Tony. They don't know what to make of me.

We drive away through the dark night back to my mother's house, where I run a bath to wash away Tony's kisses, so we can begin loving again.

I ask my mom from the sanctity of the tub, "Have you seen a change in your students?" I ask her this about every three years because she would know. She's been teaching 23 years. I want to know if it's bad all over.

"Yes, I have seen a change," she says. "In the last three years."

"What is it?" I turn on more hot.

"I've noticed, it's a very subtle thing, that people enjoy watching other people's pain."

"The kids?"

She says nothing, but I know that by "people," she also means me.

Tony's father arrives. He's the image of Tony, only older, with a squinty face because he made all of his money in the crane business, working in the sun. We go to dinner at the hotel he's staying in, but on the way from his room to the restaurant, we get lost. The place is huge.

"First floor doesn't connect to the restaurant," I say. "You have to go outside."

We take the elevator up to the second floor where we enter a long glass bridge, which is leaking. Water sits in puddles on the floor. Some-one has tried to clean the water up, but the towels are sopping. The rain refuses to stop. We step around small, white bath towels. The place is a cold, leaking green-house, with nothing of value inside—an experiment that didn't work. I feel sorry for the designer of the place.

"Where are we going?" I ask, as we drive down some back roads. It's dark out here.

"Dad wants to see the house."

We pull up before the remodelled garage.

His father never says a word about the place, but only wants to see more—where his son works. We drive to the shop at night—the large, dark tow truck garage. I'm back in that terrain again—the dangerous-looking area which is actually safe. It is only here that I can understand how much everything is worth and decide that, if I had to, I could give it all up. From this neutral place, I can move.

Tony's father, strangely enough, seems impressed. He tells me, "Bring Tony and come out to Iowa for a visit. We'd love to see you."

"Tony has a hard time getting off work. We'll try to make it."

We drive back to the hotel, all three of us in leather jackets. A leather jacket was Tony's Christmas present to me. I feel as if we are a strange tribe of primitive people, all clothed in identical skins. I guess the reunion is a success.

Tony says his knees ache.

"Why?"

"My father wanted to wrestle."

"Did you?"

"Yes."

"Who won?"

"I did. He wanted to have a foot race."

"Did you?"

"Through the hallways."

"You loved your father, didn't you?"

"I worshipped him. He could do anything, hunt, ski, ride bikes, shoot."

"A man's man."

"Yes."

I lie in bed, wondering what a visit from my father would be like. I'd cook him pork and mashed potatoes. He'd lie on the floor, talk to the dog and watch TV. My father would like Tony. He would be charmed.

No, he'd recognize something in him he could never be—everpresent, sturdy, alive.

I am creating my own secrets. I sigh at the bigness of my predicament, for I can see me telling my child when she asks me how I knew I'd marry Daddy, "I just knew." And none of us would go anywhere. We'd stick it out, sick with responsibility, awful with burden, but determined not to make the same mistakes our parents did.

"My father is smooth, isn't he?" Tony says.

"Yes."

"He's good."

"*I* can work around him."

"I'm sure you can. I'm sure you can."

My boyfriend is still haunted by the child in the bushes. So am I. I think the child is him, left to fend for himself. He must pick up that faceless baby. And I must cradle him. This is no longer a secret.

THE WAY IT COMES BACK TO ME

by Ellen E. Behrens

The bowling center in Novi, Michigan: Flat bricks the color of winter sky, and as cold; angles sharp as cutting edges. Damp asphalt leading the way. Sixty lanes in two lines of thirty thin-stripped wooden alleys, and balls shiny as billiards but soft down the lanes like rubber wheels against the wood, crumpling white-painted pins as promising as picket-fence dreams.

She's slight, even in the front-pocketed apron; hair pale brown, frayed at the edges. She's holding that wedge of pizza, that slice of dough and pepperoni and bloodred sauce.

Your stance belies your intensity. The smile your mask. She can't hear your nervousness as I can. You tug the fifty-dollar bill from your vinyl wallet. The bill is crisp in your tight fingers. "If you'll just pose," you say. "We don't live far. When do you get off shift?"

She backs away. "I don't think—" The pizza on the designer paper plate becomes her shield. Lion tamer's chair. She glances at me but can't see me in the shadows. I look away, watch a graying, big-bellied man drop a fourteen- or sixteen-pound ball down the lane to pick up a three-pin spare, and despite her oversprayed bronze hair and rolls of skin above her bra line, I want to be his wife when he hugs her.

"Really, your eyes are beautiful," you say, and the waitress blushes. The pizza is in your hands now and you offer it to her. "I know it's crazy, but would you kiss it?"

She tries to read my reaction but I am invisible. Then she leans, touches the center of a pepperoni circle with her lips.

"I've got to get back—they'll be upset," she says. Her face is flushed, her hands in her pockets, then out again in quick, old-movie jerks. "Two-fifty for the slice and pop."

The ice in the cup I hold has melted. You ask if she has change for a fifty.

The closet in our last apartment: Large, walk-in. Alone, you have no one to organize you. Heaps of dirty jeans and shirts and uniforms, and you in the attached bedroom, and I find the box—tall, narrow cardboard—and you beg me please not to open it. You've protected yourself for so long. Defying you has always angered you. Defying you has become revenge.

I rip box open, dump out the contents of your secrets: ropes and handcuffs and a vibrator and a stuffed grizzly with a bib that says: "I love you so much I can hardly bear it."

"Where are the letters I sent?" I ask. My fingers clutch laundry, toss it aside, feel in the room I can no longer see, the closet I used to share. "The cards? The stuffed animals *I* gave you?"

You want me to stop. I ask again. "I threw them away," you say. Your words have no sound but I hear you anyway.

Faith Lutheran Church, Farmington, Michigan: Rain against the windows echoing in the empty sanctuary, and the telephone rings from the minister's office. I hold my breath, hoping he won't interrupt the ceremony to answer it, hoping this isn't a bad omen. No one to give me away. Your look is even, steady, your words strong, "I do," and the minister's wife and daughter witness. I've heard rain on a wedding day is good luck and I see you smear away a tear before you start the car and I know it is lucky while the rain pats the car in congratulations.

Third apartment, Westland, Michigan: Front door torn off its hinges, sliced through with an axe. We shiver on the sidewalk, chilly October air cloudy with smoke. I worry about the birds, but a firefighter tells me they're okay.

Her first-floor apartment takes the bulk of soot and smoke. Walking across her living room blackens our feet. Touching countertops blackens our fingers and palms. We ask her to stay with us.

She is your second. I awake in the middle of the night and she is on top of you, beside me. In the morning you find me on the living room floor, shivering under a spare sheet.

My room in Shorney Dorm: Window curtains pulled against winter sun, you huddle in the dark corner of the bed, of the room, my pillow with brown and beige flowered pattern hugged against your chest, warding off my roommate. You want me to send her away, I do, and you tell me it's the acne, the plague, your own curse. I hold you, reach to touch you, but my fingers are pulled from your face. "Don't," you say. "It only makes it worse."

You don't want to go out, can't face people, you say, it's a bad day, and we stay in the room so long the girls down the hall newspaper us in. I laugh but you whisper close, "You're the only one who understands," and I think I do.

Our last apartment: The cold porcelain tub, standing in clipped hair and biting air, naked, my eyes clenched shut. "Turn around," you say, your fingers pressing into my arm. "Not that way, dammit." You jerk me in another direction.

I feel my hair falling against me, an itchy fleece. I want to scratch my shoulders, my breasts, but I know you'd scold me.

When you finish and rage out of the bathroom, swearing that if I hadn't moved the cut would have turned out fine, I close the door behind you. I soften the click as best I can. I turn to my reflection and pull my fingers through my cropped hair, trying to pull the length out of my head, as if between my ears all I had were wadded hair, waiting to grow, like on the dolls I had when I was little.

A motel inside the eastern border of Colorado: The cold tile unforgiving beneath my cheek, the water dripping in the sink, shattering against the bowl and the silence. It is our honeymoon. You're in the next room, glossy slickness of women spread open across your lap. Through the door I clicked shut between us I hear the pages turn, the moans. Listen to the water drip.

Our first apartment, Canton, Michigan: Green sculptured carpet, three water stains marring the living room floor, camouflaged by potted plants. Delicate cane and bleached-wood furniture. Our first anniversary you bring home an albino parakeet, a cake, two different kinds of ice cream. We crawl around the room, coaxing the bird into perching on a stick. In another hour it's on my finger, tiny talons prickling me, tiny beak pulling on my fingernails. Mayonnaise, I name it.

Any apartment we shared: Early morning, automatic sprinklers jetting water against the window, or snow filtering onto the balcony. You awaken and shove me. "Bitch," you call me. "Slut."

"What?" I blink, wonder about the time, your mood.

"Sleeping with other men."

I realize it's that dream you have. "No, honey," I say, reaching out to touch you. "Honestly. It was just a dream."

"Still . . ." You brush my hand away and you don't look at me for hours.

Our fourth apartment, Southfield, Michigan: Corner fireplace burned cold and a half-bath downstairs, but we are upstairs, me sitting on tiny tiles bleached white from my toothbrush scrubbing of them, and you in the tub, cool water to your neck. The floor tiles and wall tiles echo the noise of our words but maybe it is an echo from the last apartment, or the one before it, and you there with the knife pushed against your arm, bending the pale skin under it, just a nightmare image from the last apartment too, but I feel the tiles, trace my finger into the grout between them, and hear you say, ". . . to set us free, the only way."

Naked in the water, your hair flattened, wet, against your head, you look small, like the Cleveland man in the clipping my mother sent who murdered the little girl in his neighborhood. I hid the clipping, didn't know then why she sent it, neither of us knows the man, the girl, but now I remember there were murders in the trailer court where you lived before me, remember the neighbors there suspected you because you didn't look the type, so Young Republican, so fresh, always smiling.

The skin bends but the blade is unyielding. "Don't," I say, but it is a whisper that maybe you hear or maybe you don't, the knife pressing into blood and for a second I wish it would press harder, cut deeper, because maybe you are right, but I grab the blade away from you and later I nurse your arm, my hand, and wonder at the clear brown of your eyes.

Northville Charley's Restaurant, Northville, Michigan: Canopies and imitation gas lamps across from Northville State Hospital. Signs a quarter-mile in each direction warn against picking up hitchhikers.

Maroon brick, this hospital, multistoried, a top level with paneless windows and no roof, making it look like the blasted remnant of a war that never reached Michigan.

We eat but I stare at that top level, waiting to see a white-gowned figure appear in one of the open window frames. Waiting for it to leap. Like the screams I strain to hear when we drive past in the summer with the windows rolled down, the leap never comes. The figure in white never appears.

I eat quietly.

Our last apartment: Luvs diaper boxes from the grocery store, flaps open, stalled at half full, the sticky, smelly tape my fingers reek from reinforcing them, all in the second bedroom that days ago was my home office. I confine signs of my leaving to this room, pulling a few plates, glasses, forks, spoons, and canned goods from kitchen cupboards to carry here, careful and quiet like a stowaway. Photographs strewn around the floor: your arms around me in Cave of the Winds, you feeding a squirrel by hand, a family cluster of friends, and I tuck these into a box, pull them out again to leave for you. Who was closer to this family? Who's likely to see them again? My arm scrapes the corrugated cardboard.

And then I find the note; hold it in one hand while I rub the red of the other arm deeper into me. "I miss you—will you call?—S." Not my handwriting, not my initial, but I know her, have seen her, have turned up the stereo loud some nights to block out the murmur of your voice on the phone to her, and I crumple the note and seal the boxes.

The family room in a friend's house, Canton, Michigan: A jewelry party and you've made a surprise appearance. You ask who's ordering and flip through the catalogue and make funny remarks. The hostess says it's time for a drawing. She has a tray with slips of paper on it. She'll be giving away a gold locket but there are stipulations: whoever wins the locket must hostess her own jewelry party.

It's a challenge you can't resist: will you pick the winning slip? You tell the hostess you want to play. She re-explains about the party, but you want to win the locket, and you do.

"Here," you say to me, "let me hook this." You turn me away from you and I feel the tiny necklace around my neck.

"You won this for me?" I ask, and everyone laughs.

"Well, *I'm* not going to wear it," you say, and everyone laughs again.

I'd thought you wanted it for someone else, for the woman who'll cohost your party, maybe, but I don't say that. I just touch it, and kiss you, and feel my eyes burn, and hear the women coo at us.

My apartment, Troy, Michigan: Borrowed burgundy print sofa and fringed tweedy pillows, a bentwood coffee table with cut-glass candleholders, long white tapers I light every few nights, sitting in the weak glow, my shadow dancing but me not moving, barely breathing, alone. You call in the dark, surprising me out of my present and into our year-ago past. "Are you okay?" I ask, knowing the answer to all the questions, now.

"I miss you," and your voice breaks, although I don't need the evidence to believe you, can hear the truth from you and know I will not act on it. "I was so wrong," you say. "You were the only one who stayed, the only one who put up with me, and I was so bad to you."

The summer heat no longer warm enough, I pull an afghan my grandmother made around my shoulders, the yarn twirled around invisible cores into crocheted patterns of yellow and red and orange. "No," I say into the telephone, "you weren't," and finger the locket around my neck.

You tell me you've bought a rifle, have calculated the angle, and I start to speak but you tell me not to say anything. "The only bad thing you ever did," you say, "was to talk me out of it."

My ear burns, bruised from pressing the receiver hard against it, listening for clicks, bangs, pops, screams, cries, a disconnection. But all I hear is you telling me good-bye.

It will be years, maybe never, when I hear from you again.

LITTLE NIGHT CREATURES
by J. Patrick Lewis

Her voice bleats out of a billboard-sized menu lit up like a bowling alley. I'm in a bad mood anyway, and the last thing I want to hear is this Debbie person asking how she can help me. We both know there's nothing she can do to help me so why pretend. Somewhere in the seventies, I think, they decided waitresses should come on with the la-di-da speech about to burst into song. Here's one customer says no, it's just not working.

Eleven o'clock now, the Saturday night of the worst wedding reception I ever attended. Two hundred guests sleepwalking around a textbook case of hopelessness. Merciful God, I wanted to say, annul this thing before it festers. I believe I did say it to the bride's uncle, a first generation Latvian who kept burping into his fist, then tapping his chest. heartburn, he winced, mistaking me for a relative, for ten *seconds* you should have this heartburn. I expect seven, eight more wedding receptions in my lifetime, none as incredible as this, the night of the waltzing dead.

But Bruce and Darlene are a whole different story. They say a woman can get married after she hits thirty-five about as easily as she can win Super-Lotto. But Darlene miraculously beat the odds and invited every other name in the phone book to meet the guy who punched her ticket. Bruce, okay, is a doozy of a glad-hander, but I'll give him this, tonight he was also the only shred of humor in the entire Sheet Metal-workers' 1066 Union Hall. He must have hired a practical joker to make the wedding cake because it contained microscopic chips of something it shouldn't have. After the top layer had been cut away and frozen for all time until the divorce, a two-foot sparkler popped up through the icing and self-ignited. Breathtaking, burped the Latvian. With the chops and the sparkler dots, the cake tasted like sweet radiation, but nobody had the moxey to call it awful.

Which is why I'm sitting in the Gremlin with Bud and Andrea, giggling their asses off in the back seat, and my wife, Liz, laughing so hard she can't lift her forehead off her knees. We couldn't go straight home, no, the comedians decide they're hungry for shakes. And we're sitting here in wet suits because two months ago, on the first June day the temperature rockets to 95, the air conditioner decides to go kaplooie. Right now, if it was up to me, which is like saying if the sky were chartreuse, Bud'd be driving his knockout baby-sitter home the long way and I'd be closing the books on one more yawner of a weekend.

On top of the heat and the boozed-up company, what ticks me off as much as anything is the gall of these fast-food whiz-kids, these absentee franchisers, dining at the Ritz, knowing that forty-one cents of every food dollar is spent eating out, and snickering into their escargots about the idiots who actually drive up, sit here in their Gremlins, and listen to the blinking scoreboard. Just when you think this is it, the Great American Menu has been completed, they add something truly inspired like ice cream workbenches and salad bars with forty vegetables when everybody knows there aren't forty vegetables in the entire Western Hemisphere. So it's not the girl's faulty she's made to act brainless. I'm sure she'd rather spend her Saturday nights with her girl friends or with some yay hunk wide receiver back of the high school. But here she is and here we are and someone is doing a Chinese gong number on my right temple.

We sit in a track that could have been designed by a carwash engineer where you take your hands off the wheel and let it pull you through. It's almost that bad. A four-inch high cement ribbon bites at the tires if you get out of line. I try to think away the headache by staring without blinking at the Big Boy dumpster directly ahead of us that we'll just miss when the car veers left up alongside Debbie. Beyond the Dumpster is the Redhead station and three blocks beyond that is Liz and Jerry's dread house, missing, this endless night of lunacy, Liz and Jerry.

But gong, gong, gong, the Chinaman won't quit. Here comes Debbie again: "How may I serve you?" she radios through the car window, doing her whiny best to imitate a Barbie doll. I try to imagine what she must look like but it's no use.

"Okay, whatya gonna have?" I say this with a nonchalance that surprises even me. After twelve years of marriage, Liz reads the anger without any problem.

"Je-he-he-sus," Bud sputters, rollicking front and sideways in the back seat. He can barely get a sentence out. "Did you get . . . a loada . . . Aunt Frog? Was she alive, or what? Her eyes didn' close. Hey, listen, Brucie gets kissed by Frog-woman, it's ribbet, ribbet . . ."

Andrea's hoarse from laughing and two packs of Camels a day since she was sixteen. The sound coming from her side of the back seat blends with the Gremlin's broken muffler. Something like "Nunh-unh, nunh-hunh."

Liz'z turn: " I couldn't believe those people. And that minister! A Hare Krishna, for Chrissake, wasn't it?"

"Nunh-unh, nunh-hunh."

"Sir, what would you like this evening?"

"Hey, look, the girl wants to know. Do you want something or not? She's waiting for the order."

"Jerry, I wanted to, so help me God," Bud wheezes. "Almost stuck my hand down Froggie's cleavage to the goddamn elbow. One more of those goddamn spritzers, I woulda . . ."

"Oh right, Mr. Mastroni, movie star," Andrea says, scraping thunder from her lungs. "And while you were dallying in the decolletage, whadyu plan on doing with your teeny weiner?"

Pandemonium. The damn Gremlin's shaking. Bud says stop, he's gonna pee his pants.

"I'd be happy to take your order, sir."

Getting nervous about Debbie, more about the lengthening parade of cars behind us, I feel a tiny pool of perspiration collect on the plateau just below my sternum.

"Liz, for God's sake, you want a chocolate, strawberry shake, what? Bud? Andrea?"

"You wanna be a shit, Jerry, fine," she says. "Just don't spoil it for the rest of us."

"Hey, Debbie honey," Bud shouts through the back window. "Andy here'll have a Jack Daniels straight up, Lizzy gin and ton-ton, prune juice for Jer babes, and get old Bud a Bud." He turns to Andrea. "Buda-bud, I like that. Andy call me Budabud from now on in. Budabud . . ."

"Debbie," I whine, ready to apologize for every drunk-infested Gremlin she's had to put up with over the air waves. But the idea of apologizing to a bank of electricity is unthinkable. "Make it three chocolate shakes and a coffee, black." I spit the words out like liver.

"Would you please repeat that, sir. Use the microphone."

"What in the hell're you doing, Jerry?"

"In case you hadn't noticed, there are six cars behind us, Liz."

"Six, sixty, six hundred fucking sixty doesn't make a particle bit of difference. We were here first, in case you hadn't noticed. And I want a butterscotch sundae. At least have the decency to ask Andy and Bud what they want."

"I did, Liz. What they want Big Boy doesn't sell. What they need is sleep. Let's call it quits, huh?"

"Where the hell do you get off telling people when to go to bed? You know, Jerry, you have been a king-size pain in the ass since this morning. No, it started last night, didn't it? With that paper boy."

"Okay, Liz, just drop it, willya?"

"Sir, I'm sorry but the cars are backing up onto Rosedale. Could I please ask you to place your order now?"

"Cheeseburg, babes, the works," Bud sputters against my neck. "Hold off on the mayo, Jer. Tell her, tell the girl, no mayo."

"He's lying," Andrea pipes in. "Marchello here really wants a hot dog. He hasn't had a hot dog in weeks, have you, Budabud? I should know, shouldn't I?"

The joke's over. Nobody's laughing now. A yellow VW convertible honks a horn in back of us—one of those sick heifer jobs. A Jeep and a van join in. The domino effect. A regular symphony.

Bud reaches over my shoulder and punches at the horn.

"Gotta show 'em who's boss, Jer."

I do nothing to stop this, and he keeps hammering away in a frenzy. Then, as if the horn has suddenly become electrified, Bud bolts back in his seat, sticks his head out the window and vomits.

The honking stops.

Even the blue zap lights seem to go quiet as the bugs sense someone else's disaster.

"Unnnhh, Jesus, Bud," Andrea groans.

"Jerry, do you think it would be possible for you to get your ass out of the car and help him?" Liz suggests thoughtfully.

The billboard crackles. "All right, that's it. You're going to have to leave. We won't be serving you this evening!"

Now this has to be the voice of some paper-hatted oyster-sucker's lackey who's apparently grabbed the mike from Debbie because he's afraid he's going to lose one goddamn carwash full of quarters. A toady of a manager who couldn't arrange his own sock drawer. He can't see any of Bud's mess, and I can't see him, but I'll bet anything he's got Debbie in tears.

Bud's gone green, his head hangs out like a rag doll's, eyes focused on Asia. I figure, well, I don't know what I figure at this point, except maybe Bud can take care of himself, which he's done, more or less, for thirty-eight years. Liz'll stew, simmer, boil, pop her lid, and start the same routine next Saturday night. Or Thursday. Or Monday. She'll lock up the dark country for a few days, a couple of weeks, thinking what better punishment, and she'll be right again.

But it's Debbie I'm worried about now, so what happens next nobody who knows me, Jerry St. John, assistant postmaster going on ten years, father of a brilliant Brownie and two great little Webelos, could possibly believe. I'm out of the car, that much I know. My body's out of the car, except maybe for the eyeballs which feel like they're rolling on the dashboard watching 6'2" me approach the drive-in window in my new Madras sportcoat.

Unglued, disconnected.

And there she is. Standing behind her porcine manager, Debbie is as plain as a brown paper, her blond hair up in two buns. I bend over to the screen window, look up at her like the good gray monsignor and say, "Are you okay, Debbie? Everything all right here?"

She nods sweetly, terrified.

Like a drill sergeant barking orders into his walkie-talkie, the manager heaves with the feeling of power. He doesn't even hear me talking to Debbie. He's just arrived at the clincher, the part about what I can expect the police to do when they get here momentarily. I don't bother to lift the screen but shove my fist through it and grab him by the tie with the double Bs all over it. The Madras coat rips to the forearm. I pull him over so his face is flush against the glass window. His pressed nose has a silly broken look to it, though I know he is perfectly fine. There is a ten-dollar bill in my left hand and it's waving in front of his face.

"Do you see this?" Though every word I speak escapes through clenched teeth, I am amazed at how well I conceal this absolutely alien violence.

"Ummhunh," he mutters. He can do little else.

"One butterscotch sundae, one cheeseburger, everything but mayo, two chocolate shakes, one black coffee. Get it ready, Now. Or you just bought yourself a whole shit wagon full of bad advertising. Do you understand me?"

Yes, he understands. I loosen the hold on his tie and tell him to keep the change. He unruffles himself, memorized my face and turns to get the order. Debbie nods again and smiles as if she's being remotely controlled. She's okay, I know she's going to be okay. It occurs to me in the flash of a half-second that the shit wagon remark will not stand tall in court.

Honking has resumed. A dozen or so customers in the restaurant have come outside to get a look at what's going on. I glance back at the Gremlin where they've reeled Bud in. He'll be asleep soon on his wife's lap. Liz and Andrea look at me as if I'm some alien invader on a drive-in movie screen. A space of forty feet separates us; a distance of years.

It widens

My mind's remarried my body. I take off the jacket and fling it over my shoulder. My shirt is sweat-stuck to my back. Now this is the second part no one will believe. No waves, no thrown kisses, no good-byes, I walk away from it. A block down Rosedale Avenue I break into a slow trot, off the main drag, past the high school , into the woods and the dark. By the time the old B. & O. tracks come into view, I've been at a full bore sprint for five minutes through the fields and the trees and am as wet as a mother's womb.

Exhilarated, exhausted, I plunk myself down on the railroad tracks. After a while little night creatures come to find out who I am and what I'm doing here. It depresses me to think that I have never consciously listened to animal sounds—the hums and clicks and hisses of night. Sounds so insistent that when I close my eyes I imagine I can make out the dark messages. It's way past midnight when something jolts me out of this trance—mosquitoes peppering my legs, tow cats screeching through the bug percussion. the lights over town have all but disappeared. I get up and walk carefully along the rails, dimly back-lit by an egg of a moon. It doesn't matter if it takes until three in the morning to tightrope the half mile home. One wrong step and I'm a goner, onto the railroad ties and the cinders, four inches down. If I fall here, I think I'll fall forever.

TWILIGHT OF THE GODS
by Joseph G. Cowley

When their son Frank died of a heart attack at the age of sixty-two, Florence and Bernie had not been able to attend the funeral. Almost ninety, both of them, they didn't have the strength to make the trip north to New York. So they stayed in Florida in the July heat, staring out from the air-conditioned comfort of their apartment in Bal Harbour at the bright sunlight shimmering on the white sands and the blue sea, grieving alone.

Finally Florence, letting the blinds drop, turned back to the pale, muted atmosphere of their livingroom, to the deep-pile beige rug, the overstuffed sofa, and the color-splashed paintings on the cream walls, her grief mixing with the ennui that had gradually wrapped itself more and more tightly about her these last few years, years she thought of as their endless dying as Bernie became more and more incapacitated.

But frailty was a poor excuse, though valid enough this time, for not attending their son's funeral. The truth was, they had never been close to their children, not since they had grown up, all three of them, and left home. All she and Bernie had ever needed was each other. In fact, it suddenly occurred to her, they hadn't seen Frank since his divorce two years ago, four years after his wife Morna had run off at the age of fifty-six with a poet much older than herself, some kind of aberration, obviously, of her middle years.

She and Bernie hadn't even attended the wedding last year when Frank remarried, a widowed schoolteacher named Laura Taylor, a thin, bony woman, or so they had been told by Jerry (all Evelyn had said was that she was very nice), having decided, even then, that another trip north was at last just too much for them. They had never met the woman, though Frank was planning to bring her south when he died, and now they were never likely to. Which perhaps was just as well. What was the point of becoming involved?

In the beginning, when they first moved to Florida thirty years ago, Frank used to fly down regularly with Morna and the children and would play golf with his father, and they would all go to the beach together. But in these last few years there hardly seemed to be any point. Bernie was blind because of the diabetes, and incontinent, and his mind was gone, and the visits of anyone, especially their children, only upset their routine and left Bernie restless and unhappy when they were gone.

She herself no longer seemed to care, not really. She had liked it, of course, when the grandchildren used to come, but they had stopped making the trip, or made it only under duress, once they were in their teens. And her own children, as old as they were, could sometimes still be troublesome to her, especially when they assumed she had the strength to share their problems. The truth was, their endless picking at the sores of life, at the scabs of wounds they felt had been dealt them in the past, irritated her, and depressed her, and she was glad enough when they stopped coming so often.

She would never have admitted this to them, or to anyone, for that matter. Not that she was the only one who felt relieved. She sensed that one reason they stayed away, other than their total involvement in their own lives, was to avoid the prick of conscience such visits might have aroused at their not being more concerned about their parents now that she and Bernie, it must seem to them, had passed beyond the point of redemption into what they could only view as an indecent old age.

The truth was, she was happy playing bridge every afternoon at their social club after the beach in the morning, looking up from her cards from time to time and staring over them at her partner, ready to make an acerbic comment on whatever she considered a misplay, while Bernie nodded and dozed in a chair in the corner of the club, the stripes of afternoon sunlight moving slowly across his bald, florid head, the wisps of white hair delicate as gossamer in the light, as the game was played out over the endless hours.

Her mind, unlike her husband's, was in no way dulled by time. She was quite capable of second-guessing the bank's managing of their

money, and from time to time she might send the children a scathing
letter commenting on their management of their lives, or their management of the small chain of clothing stores in Westchester they had
mostly turned over to them, or, taking a larger view, on the President's
mismanagement of the country. The world was so filled with idiots and
incompetents it distressed her to even think about it. And so, mostly,
she didn't.

She was just as glad she wouldn't be around when the debacle came.
Still, when you came right down to it, she clung to life, while there was
yet breath in her body, with a kind of secret glee. One of the things that
kept her vibrantly alive was the knowledge that, having made the mistake of investing heavily in an annuity in their middle years, they had
managed to screw the insurance company by living far beyond the sta-
tistical death the mortality tables had prescribed for them. And she was
determined, if she could, to live another twenty years, even if it meant
they had to feed her intravenously to keep her alive.

If necessary, she would scold the nurses, as she did now, sending
them scattering down the hall on errands, aware she was extracting
from them their energy, their youth, their life, even, to extend her own.
But it didn't matter, their sacrifice, as long as she was alive and could
feel, along the white painted window sill, the coolness of February
nights, the nascent sunshine of Florida dawns splashing the white
beach with its still-damp rays and splashing against the pale pink stucco
of this expensive nursing complex on the beach she sometimes sneer-
ingly called "home."

She watched with mocking eyes the young doctors who tended the
infirm and elderly, which was all of them, come and go, except for Dr.
Linscott, who managed the place and who was probably as old as the
rest of them, and who would probably die there, too. She knew in her
heart she was going to outlive them all, but she was surprised, and it
came as a shock, not only the death but her grief, when Frank, her son,
died. While others might die, she had expected her own children to
outlive her.

When the telegram, signed Laura, came from the Western Union in
Scarsdale, she couldn't, for a moment, place the name, and she
thought there had been a mistake. She still thought of Morna, who was
the mother of their grandchildren, as her daughter-in-law, and couldn't
get used to the change. She asked her husband, before the answer
came to her, who Laura was. But he only nodded at the far wall with

vacant eyes and asked if Frank had come home from school yet and would she let him know the moment he came in.

Though Bernie had his lucid moments on occasion, she knew right away they were too old, too weak, to make the journey north. It was senseless to even ask the doctor for his advice. But when she tried to call their son's home in Scarsdale to explain, all she got was busy signals, and, finally, after the call went through, there was no answer.

After hanging up, she sat on the sofa feeling helpless and with the beginnings of rage, due to the frustration at no one being there to take her call, and wept icy tears that no one else could see or understand for lack of caring. Bernie sat beside her drooling (it was hopeless to try to reach him at the moment), his empty eyes wandering about the muted room with its thirty-thousand dollar furnishings and Bracque paintings on the wall, unseeing.

The pain surprised her.

She should have known that to be alive was to feel pain, but somehow she had forgotten. In these last dozen years or so she had known only physical pain, which might make her think briefly of dying, but which had no capacity to cause her any mental anguish, especially as the "home" provided them all with a daily diet of pills to keep such pain away. Only occasionally, when she thought of her children, or of hers and Bernie's almost seventy years together, would she get a twinge in her heart or a pinch of sadness. But that was perhaps only to let her know her emotions were in working order.

Even so, she would brush such feelings aside if she could, or, if not, take one of the tranquilizers the doctors were ever ready to prescribe. Deep in her soul lurked the idea that mental and emotional pain was somehow a sign of weakness, a "trivialization" of her essential self, and that she should be above such things. Such feelings belonged to ordinary people, the vulgar masses she so despised. How could she be expected to identify with them when their stupidity revolted her so?

Feeling the way she did, she tried even to avoid reading their newspapers or watching their television. Such outlets were for the feeble, and feeble-minded, as she was well aware, especially living as they did among people euphemistically called "senior citizens." Besides, aside from the news or an occasional movie, there was little to watch. And she hated the commercials most of all, with their huckstering of oven cleanser and dental powders and clean breath, not to mention bodily ills and other, more private, orifices of the body they felt needed redeeming from God knows what awful scourge. She thought to divorce herself from the world, as one might divorce oneself from a drunken sot one had made the mistake of marrying in one's youth, and the media were part of that world.

Of course, there was no way of totally avoiding the rabble and its vulgarities, not even being old and with money. Even at the beach they infringed upon her world in the guise of doctors and nurses and attendants, nibbling at the fringes of her reality. One simply had to endure a certain amount of life's hideousness, but she learned to avoid trips outside the club, the beach, and the apartment complex, though she might occasionally go into town to shop or go to a play or movie or concert with Bernie, or with one of her acquaintances if he was not up to it.

Even so, she found Miami mostly a cultural desert, with its influx of foreigners, Cubans especially, giving it the appearance of an alien world. But, the Cubans aside, it was still a wasteland. And when she wrote to family or friends in the north, or shared her feelings with the privileged few among the other residents, she said it was "shocking, simply shocking," adding, "But what can you expect? There are so few people of refinement and taste left."

Naturally, it made her want to withdraw from the world. A younger person, of another generation, especially considering the way they were brought up these days, might have said she "didn't give a shit." But she wasn't vulgar and didn't think that way. Besides, a younger person, living her life, might have died, or taken up booze and drugs in order to hang on, dying slowly instead of all at once.

She was more stubborn, and had her own way of surviving. Part of that tenacity, though she would never have verbalized it, even to herself, was the desire to extract full value for payment made, payments made long ago when the children, Frank, Evelyn, and Jerry, were young, and she played the role of a Westchester matron while Bernie built the store they had started out with into a clothing empire.

"A clothing empire!" That's what she called the chain of six stores when she spoke of them to the other residents and wanted to overcome her sense of shame for what Bernie had become now. For she saw him as he was, a hustler, a dynamic businessman, with charm and personality, and she wanted others to see him that way, too, and to know that it had not been easy, especially for her, when it seemed all Bernie's energies went into the business.

Now she had a sense of loss, of neglect, of having suffered pain, though she had difficulty recalling specific incidents that might have caused such suffering. But she must have suffered, especially considering her sensibilities and the struggle they had gone through to achieve such success, else why would she feel the way she did? What she did not consider was the fact that she had never been one to face pain, and so did not know what someone less complicated, less sensitive, would have known instinctively, that pain rewarded as well as demanded payment. And so she had not received any reward, and, growing old, had not become wise, nor truly happy.

Now, in the stillness of the room, the bright sunshine softening outside the drawn blinds in the late afternoon, she wept alone, for Bernie, in the end, though she tried to communicate the news to him, could not remember who this grown person Frank was. And what she, Florence, had finally had to face was that the burden of the past was hers alone to bear. It was not something she could share with any of the other residents, not even with the doctors or nurses, for she had developed no intimate relationship with any of them, and thus there was no one who might hold her in their arms until the pain abated.

The tears streaming down her lined cheeks, she gasped, the pain in her chest so like a knife she could hardly breathe in the stifling silence of the room. The blinds drawn against the heat locked them into their air-conditioned apartment, and she was alone, unable to share her agony. She felt as if a huge ocean wave had knocked her down and was drawing her, frightened and out of control, into the depths of the sea, until, as if by a miracle, her feet touched the ground andq, struggling toward the shore, she knew she was going to be all right.

How long she had tossed in turmoil she didn't know, for she had lost all sense of time. But twilight must have come, for the light behind the blinds was dimming and the room was growing dark. She reached up and turned on the lamp. Across from her, in the corner of the room, Bernie was asleep in his armchair, breathing quietly, spittle caught in the corner of his wide mouth. He suddenly smiled, and his legs twitched, like a dog asleep, dreaming of younger days when it ran with the pack.

How frail and old they had become, she thought, thinking not only of Bernie and herself but of Frank. What difference did a few decades more or less matter? Whatever would Frank have accomplished with his life that he hadn't already accomplished? To live like them in an air-conditioned prison, however minimum the security, to suffer the indignities of old age, the frailties that took away whatever freedom they had had, to suffer even more of life's senseless tragedies than he already had?

She remembered the night his youngest daughter, Kathy, had died in an automobile accident on Christmas Eve, driving home around the reservoir above White Plains in her boyfriend's car. She and Bernie were on a Caribbean Cruise and the radiogram came on Christmas day, late in the afternoon.

How helpless she had felt! She knew Frank must have been suffering, but there was nothing she could do about it, no way she might reach out and make his hurt go away, beyond cabling how sorry she was, how sorry they both were, so she tried not to think about it. They were in the middle of the ocean and there was no way they could get back for the funeral, and it didn't make sense to let a tragedy they could do nothing about spoil a vacation they had paid so much for.

Still, at the captain's table that evening, she had not been able to eat well, and she left Bernie and went out and stood at the ship's railing, searching the sky whose light was dying in pale shades of pink and mauve with anguished eyes, for what she didn't know, finding it neither there nor in the wash of the dark green waves that hissed along the bulwarks of the boat.

When Bernie came out after dinner, lighting a cigar and leaning on the railing beside her, she complained of indigestion. He suggested she might be grieving, but she didn't quite understand what that had to do with her stomach and she thought he didn't understand. Of course she was grieving! Any mother would. She felt very sorry for Frank and could certainly understand the terrible pain he must be going through.

But this tragedy, Frank's death, was quite something else, and she didn't know what to do about it, how to get in touch with Laura. She felt so confused. It was only after they had come back from the diningroom and had turned on the light, and she was standing by the bookcase in the front hall while the nurse was putting Bernie to bed in the room opposite hers, that it occurred to her to call Jerry or Evelyn. Of course! She would be able to explain to them why they couldn't come north and they would be able to get in touch with Laura and offer her a mother-in-law's condolence.

Pleased to have thought of it, she went into the livingroom and turned on the lamp. When she dialed the number, the call went right through. She heard it ringing at the other end in the summer house the family shared on the lake up in Putnam County when the weather was nice. The thought occurred to her, too, that she must remember to ask how the children, Frank's children, were taking it. But when the phone was at last picked up and Jerry answered, she found herself so choked up she couldn't speak.

"Hello, hello," he kept saying.

After a long while she managed to whisper his name.

"Jerry? Jerry?"

She started to cry.

"Mom, Mom?" he said. "It's all right. He didn't suffer. He went quick, just like that. We were down there today and everything's okay. We just came back up here to the summer house to pick up some things and lock up. We're going back tonight. The funeral's all arranged. It will be on Wednesday."

But that's not what she wanted to hear.

"Do you love me, Jerry?" she cried.

He hesitated, and she could hear him breathing into the phone.

"It's okay, Mom," he said at last. "He didn't suffer at all."

VERY EYES

by Sally Savic

Nobody sings like Minnie. I could pick her voice out of a chorus of hundreds like the only black feather on a white chicken. Reedy and complaining, it tumbles lazily into the street where I hesitate, listening, before I turn the corner into the alley. I peek around the brick wall and spy on her, watching her sweep butts, sno-cone paper hats, and chicken bones into a big pile between the Barbecue Palace and Darla Sue's Beauty Barn. Minnie is singing *Danke Shoen,* a peppy number she's turned into a dirge. *Danke Shoen* is her favorite song. Erla, the shampoo lady at Darla Sue's, thinks you can tell a lot about a person from their favorite song. She's always asking the customers what their favorite songs are, making judgments and drawing up personality profiles like a psychic on a phone-in radio show. "I can tell you're the sorta person who likes to buy pretty things," she might say if someone tells her their favorite song is *Love For Sale,* or, "You're kinda the romantic type, arentcha?" if a customer fancies *Moon River* or *Night and Day.* But Minnie's preference for *Danke Shoen* has Erla stumped. "Maybe you was from Germany in another life," she ponders, shaking her big, precarious hair at the mystery of it. Though it's as simple as this: Minnie has a thing for Wayne Newton. She loves his skinny, anchovie mustache, his Kewpie doll voice. Each night she puts herself to sleep with dreams of Wayne calling her on stage to belt out an encore or Wayne taking her by the elbow to a coffee shop after the show. To speak ill of Wayne in Minnie's presence is to blaspheme a god.

I watch Minnie sweep and sing as I push a hank of damp hair off my forehead and notice a foot of toilet paper trailing from the bottom of one of my pumps. Tissue that has, no doubt, been tailing me like a stray dog from the Ladies Lounge of the country club. Every Wednesday I meet my mother-in-law, Delphine, at the country club for luncheon and bridge. First thing she said to me today was, "You're punch drunk." Why is that, I wondered, and took out my compact to look in the powder-dusted mirror. I had a mascara bruise beneath one eye and my lipstick was a little crooked, but I've looked worse. I followed her gaze and looked down at my feet: I was wearing two different shoes, one black, one navy with heels uneven in size. Often Delphine is disgusted with me, but she gets a certain amount of satisfaction from my fashion blunders. She's storing up these boners for divorce court, hoping her testimony against me will clinch the deal, as though some judge would condone a divorce on the grounds of a lackadaisical make-up job or a ladder in my pantyhose.

To punish me for the mis-matched shoes, Delphine paired me with a woman named Paddy who teaches bridge at the community center. Delphine gave me bridge lessons with Paddy for my birthday one year, so Paddy already knew about my bad bridge skills and was no happier than I to be partners. Paddy always wears a sleeveful of red, white, and blue plastic bracelets that clack with fury when she shuffles the cards. She's a cut-throat player and claims to be pen-pals with Omar Sharif— they share bridge tips, winning strategies across intercontinental phone lines. Paddy scares the hell out of me. I hate her bracelets and the too-pink lipstick that seeps into the wrinkles around her disapproving mouth and sticks to her yellowing teeth when she sucks her upper lip in concentration. She refuses to lose and kicks me under the table when I make a stupid bid. After a few hands, I made some noises, felt my forehead in a worried way, and escaped to the Ladies Lounge where I hid until I was sure they'd gotten fed up with waiting and had found another fourth for bridge.

When I came back to the table, Paddy and Delphine were aloof. They had no sympathy for my feigned illness and were peeved because they'd had to pull a fourth for Paddy off the golf course, a yakkety woman named Sylvia who Delphine suspected was Jewish and there-fore untrustworthy as a bridge opponent. Sylvia wore a short white skirt with orange golf balls appliqued across the front. She still had her cleats on though it was strictly forbidden in the Garden Room.

"You're going to get senile," Paddy snapped. Paddy believes bridge is one's best defense against the vagaries of aging.

Gingerly, I pick the dirty toilet paper off my shoe. It's curious that

Delphine didn't notice it. She usually notices things like that: food stuck between teeth, a skirt hitched up in back, a wig on crooked. And she takes her time before telling you about it. She'd rather let you walk around for a while with the world laughing up its sleeve at you.

When Minnie's finished the last chorus of *Danke Shoen,* she sits down on an empty fruit crate and rests the broom between her bony, doorknob knees. She takes a cigarette from behind her ear and lights it, shaking the match with a flourish. This ritual accomplished, she turns, her lips pursed in a perfect "o" and blows a tiny, tottering smoke ring. Darla Sue taught her how to do that. She teaches her something new everyday: the capital of Arkansas, a recipe for tuna surprise, how to fold paper airplanes or cut out paper dolls from the classified section of the newspaper.

Minnie always wears a black hair net Darla Sue gave her which cages her downy, reddish hair, and she looks like a war collaborator, someone who's had her head shaved as evidence of betrayal. She wears the same clothes everyday: hand-me-down nurse shoes two sizes too big from one of the shop customers, and a faded school girl's plaid dress beneath a pale green smock. Darla Sue buys Minnie's clothes at the St. Vincent de Paul's, choosing dated frocks for her childish frame that belie her true age, though nobody knows Minnie's age. She could be twenty-five or forty. From behind you might mistake her for a colt-legged grade-schooler on her way to the bus stop.

Starting down the alley, I skate through a puddle of barbecue sauce as slick as new ice. I skid down on one knee, scraping my shin bone. I think I've broken something and I hear Minnie call, "Hallo, Miz Platte!" in a merry voice. The pink silk skirt Delphine gave me for Christmas is splattered with sauce, my pantyhose torn. Silk is impossible to clean. This promises to escalate into an ugly situation if Delphine finds out. "What in God's name have you done to my skirt!" she'll drawl in her languid, haughty voice like I did it on purpose. Delphine always speaks slowly, carefully, as though her words are heavy gold nuggets, as though you'll want to pocket them and take them out to admire later. She loves to give a gift, but all of her presents are apparently on loan, since she retains a proprietary interest in them and insists they be displayed and enjoyed in her presence. Under the stress of Delphine's impending disapproval, I forget where I am, press my palms against the concrete and allow myself to enjoy that freedom. Lately I've been experiencing these blackouts. I wake in the morning and don't know what bed I'm in, how old I am, if I'm living or dead. It's not an entirely unpleasant sensation.

"Ooooops!" Minnie hollers after the fact as she watches me struggle to get up. She blows another smoke ring and tamps out her cigarette on the side of the crate, putting the butt into the pocket of her smock. Why she puts it in her pocket is a mystery since there's a pile of butts and other garbage at her feet. But Minnie's moments are guided by curious and arcane rules, maddening in their absurdity. I don't know if she's actually retarded, but getting used to Minnie's quirks has gotten me back in touch with some dormant Christian principles. I'm proud that I've learned to be patient with her without feeling pity or irritation anymore. This is, perhaps, all you can do for people you can't love. And maybe, I ponder sometimes, it's enough. Maybe it's all anybody can really hope for.

The screen door to the beauty shop slaps open and Darla Sue and Erla step out. Darla Sue tosses a plastic bag of hair clippings near Minnie's feet. Minnie gapes at the bag in alarm, her face blushing up to her scalp. Instantly, Darla Sue realizes her error and brings a pale, dry hand to her mouth in mock fear, the other hand reaching to take the bag back.

"You done it now," Erla smirks.

"You know better'n that," Minnie scolds with a tinny shriek. Minnie saves all the hair clippings for Mrs. Amstutz, one of Darla Sue's customers, who weaves sweaters and wreaths from the dead hair. Even in the heat of summer, Mrs. Amstutz wears a coat she made for herself from the shed fur of her sister's Angora cat. Minnie snatches up the bag and presses a dark look on Darla Sue before she flounces back into the shop. Darla Sue owns one of Mrs. Amstutz's hair sweaters but she's never worn it. She told Mrs. Amstutz it made her too sad, seeing as how she could recognize which customer's hair had been used in the sweater's weave and two of those customers were dead. In truth, Darla Sue thought the sweater was creepy and smelled funny, though Mrs. Amstutz considered the dead customers an acceptable excuse and offered to make Darla Sue a new sweater from the hair of an anonymous and live dog for a nominal price.

"You're in trouble now," Erla needles. Erla likes to make waves. She loves practical jokes and enjoys teasing Minnie. She pretends to call Wayne Newton on the phone or she'll flip a gob of shampoo at the back of Minnie's head as she passes. Once, when Minnie fell asleep in a chair beneath a hair dryer, Erla tied her shoelaces together. Darla Sue undid them before she woke up.

"Mrs. Moon is coming in for her blue rinse in a bit," Darla Sue tells Erla. "Why don't you go in and set up for her?"

"I got to take my cig break, don't I?" Erla rebels and sets her thick bottom down on the arm of an old easy chair someone from the Barbecue Palace left out in the alley. Darla Sue pushes Erla's hip out of her way and sits in the chair, stretching her long legs, turning out her scuffed yellow sandals splay-footed.

"Sit over here," she says to me, pointing at the fruit crate, the tips of her fingers stained bloody with henna. She raises a hand to shield her pale eyes from a spear of late sun cast down between the bleakness of the buildings. Dutifully I come and sit and examine the barbecue on my skirt. The stain is the size and shape of a rabbit's head; not a dry cleaner in town will tackle it. I try to remember what store the skirt came from. Maybe they'll still have it in stock and I can replace it with Delphine none the wiser.

"How you gonna get that clean?" Darla Sue wonders aloud. She looks like a tropical bird. She's got on a yellow sundress beneath her green smock. Bright plastic bananas dangle from her earlobes to match. In the hot, trapped air of the alley, she smells of peroxide and lemon verbena. Darla Sue is a striking woman despite a total, almost purposeful, disregard for her appearance. Strangers stare at her, wondering how and why the puzzle fits, the proud Caesar's nose, the plump, purplish tulip lips, the wide-set sulfurous eyes. The mere sight of Darla Sue makes me thirsty for something: I feel a quickening, a small lust, a desire to get in a car and drive willy-nilly into a stranger's future. I appear to myself not so parched and paper-made with Darla Sue as my mirror.

A long brown cigarette droops between Darla Sue's unpainted lips, trailing smoke in her eyes as she squints at me. Her eyesight is going bad, but she won't see an eye doctor. She's a penny-pincher. She keeps track of every cent she's ever made, taking notes each time money leaves or enters her palm in a small leatherette book she keeps in her pocket. I suspect she's the sort of person who has thousands stashed in flour cannisters, beneath floorboards, squirreled away in the toes of old shoes in her closet. Her customers are always giving her things or leaving her things when they die: old cars, fur stoles, boxes of musty cocktail dresses, record collections, and one customer even willed Darla Sue her cleaning supplies (old scrub brushes, cans of Comet, and half-full bottles of Murphy's Oil Soap).

"What are you doin here today?" Erla says to me, blowing smoke through her nose. Erla's eyes are a muddy hazel, and set wopper-jawed in her tiny face. Her skin is the color and texture of oatmeal. It's hard to look Erla square in the face, so you can never remember what she looks like or you're afraid to remember what she looks like.

"Don't you usually drop by on Thursdays?" Darla Sue says. Darla Sue and Erla are always asking questions that never get answered. They answer them themselves or go on to something else before you can respond—unless you're gossiping. Then they're alert and quiet, leaning in on you, all hot breath and heavy weight like puppies that want to be petted. They enjoy descriptions of Delphine's idle life, so I tell them about lunch and bridge at the club. I am fortified by Darla Sue's low opinion of Delphine, and though she has never met Delphine face to face, I'm certain of her victory in a battle of arrogance and wit. Darla Sue is equally as certain of herself as Delphine.

Neither Darla Sue nor Erla has ever been to a country club, and they like to speculate about "country club life" as though there is such a thing and it happens on another planet.

"All those ladies in new shoes," Erla murmurs, lighting herself another cigarette. Erla thinks women who frequent country clubs never wear the same pair of shoes twice.

"What's Del bought this week?" Darla Sue wants to know. "Del" is a nickname my mother-in-law would never stand for. She hates nicknames and won't even call her son Harry though the rest of the world refers to him that way. Delphine is always buying expensive, useless things for herself and "Harold," and sometimes for me. Though less often for me. Usually she buys me the same sort of gifts she buys for her housekeeper, Mabel. Cooking lessons, floral arrangement classes, bridge instruction, and once, a seminar in scarf-tying at a local department store, educational opportunities meant to "civilize" Mabel and me.

"She bought sheepskin car seat covers for Harry's car and a diamond tennis bracelet for herself," I tell Darla Sue and Erla.

"I hear those sheepskin covers are real nice," Darla Sue says, "but I don't understand about those tennis bracelets. Who needs a diamond bracelet to play tennis in? And Del don't even play tennis, does she?"

"Delphine doesn't do anything more strenuous than take out her credit card."

"That's right," Erla caws as though she and Delphine have had an acquaintance for years. Darla Sue is irritated by Erla's laugh which is loud and raucous and too close to her ears. She frowns and squints at Erla before she says, "Why don't you go in and get ready for Mrs. Moon? You know she hates to be kept waiting."

"Why don't you?" Erla mutters just loud enough for Darla Sue to hear. Because Erla is older than Darla Sue, she feels she can talk to her like this every once in a while. Darla Sue scratches an itch beneath her eye and blows out a big breath. Even Erla doesn't want to see Darla Sue get mad. Everybody's scared of her when she gets mad. Though she doesn't actually do anything when she's angry. She's just a menacing presence, and she closes down, pulls the shades, turns in on herself and smolders, her anger evidenced in little gestures of impatience that send Erla and Minnie scurrying to please her. After a moment of weighty silence, Erla does the wise thing and goes back inside, careful to keep the screen door from banging behind her.

"I'm gonna fire her when she turns sixty-five," Darla Sue says. "It's almost five o'clock and Betty Moon's our last customer. You'd think Erla would want to get this day over with."

Since it's five, I think about dinner, what I'll make for dinner. Something magical that will appear neither pre-packaged nor canned. Delphine doesn't believe in food that isn't fresh and she's confided in me that pre-packaged food is an affront to Harry's finer sensibilities. But Delphine doesn't know about the convenience store microwave burritoes and pink coconut cupcake wrappers I've spied beneath the seats of Harry's car, the odor of burned beans and bad beef lingering long after they've been consumed. The preparation of dinner is my main job besides taking care of the laundry and the house and Harry himself. Unambitious tasks I take little pride in though sometimes I feel good about polished furniture that mirrors my face or I feel territorial about the nap of a freshly vacuumed carpet. But racing home to prepare a palatable meal for a man who secretly prefers burritoes and pink cupcakes seems a terrible fate. I imagine Harry, surely on his way home by now. I see him driving up to the house, locking his car, taking the brick walk around the side of the house to the back door where the clematis hangs heavy on its trellis, its deep purple flowers starched and pressed flat like the collars of Harry's shirts when they come back from the dry cleaners. He lets himself into the kitchen and calls my name. The kitchen is clean and sterile, the smell of pine disinfectant still fresh on the counters. Harry's shoes make black scuff marks on the tiles like fat commas punctuating wordless sentences. This is one of my pet peeves, these scuff marks, perhaps because they mean the work I do, the work I take little pleasure in, is forever and endless.

But Harry is alone in our house which is strange for him. He doesn't believe it for a while. He tours the rooms, calling my name. The house is too big for the two of us, four bedrooms furnished with beds and bookshelves and nighttables from Harry's childhood, Delphine's furniture that came to us when she moved into a condominium. Delphine's life has become ours, her furniture a presence more powerful than mine. Harry doesn't know what to do with himself without me quietly orbiting his daily rituals. It doesn't feel the same to find himself a beer and sit down with the sport's page without me there in the background like white noise. Soon he'll call his mother to see if she knows where I am, and Delphine will tell him about my bad behavior at the country club. For Delphine, it's a crying shame her son wasted his life in marriage to me. "What does she want?" she often says to Harry as though I'm sapping him dry with my mysterious demands. For a moment, I feel guilty and afraid imagining Harry alone in our house. How will he manage? He seems fragile, even sad. What *do* I want? Perhaps Delphine is right to ask, cunning in her suspicions about me. But it's a delicious and secret pleasure to be at Darla Sue's Beauty Barn where nobody can find me. Harry doesn't even know Darla Sue's Beauty Barn exists or that I've come here every Thursday for almost two years after shopping excursions with Delphine, and now I'm here on a Wednesday, too, which must mean something . . . though I can't say what.

I came to the Beauty Barn the first time when the cab I was riding in had a flat tire outside the shop. The driver told me to find someplace to call another cab and I walked into Darla Sue's. There was nobody in the shop that day and Darla Sue sat like a queen in one of her chairs, smoking cigarettes and telling jokes. I bought a bottle of shampoo and laughed at Darla Sue's jokes as I waited for my cab. The next week I went back, mostly to look at Darla Sue again, to see if she was real, to see if her eyes were really gold. I asked her to give me a new style, and it was a sad affair. In truth, Darla Sue is a lousy hairdresser. Together we surveyed her handiwork in the mirror and even Darla Sue knew she'd done me wrong. "Oh, well," she sighed, "it'll grow back." A lopsided cut, the bangs short as a Marine's, the curls singed with her curling iron. Darla Sue has been a beauty operator for over twenty years, but she hasn't learned a new technique since 1967. She offers her aging customers marcels, pink and blue rinses, old fashioned perms. Even Erla has never let Darla Sue touch her hair. Erla has her hair done at the Fashionette Beauty College downtown by young students who balk at the outrageous, out-dated fashion Erla has been insisting on for most of her adult life, a style that lies somewhere between a Texas beehive and a sixties flip. She explains this hair-do by pointing out the smallness of her face, which is, in fact, stunted and petite, like a perky little otter's face, and belittled further by the size of her hair. Though Erla believes her hair-do distracts on-lookers from her miniature, wrinkled face, and in some Samson-esque way, gives her a certain power she'd lack if her hair lay flat against her head.

All of Darla Sue's customers are senior citizens and have been clients since she opened her shop. They no longer seem to care that they look worse when they leave than when they came in, but they're crazy about Darla Sue. They lie in her cracked leather chair, their eyes lolling back in their heads and listen adoringly to Darla Sue's no-nonsense chatter. Curiously enough, Darla Sue's forte is beautifying cadavers in funeral parlors for memorial service viewings. By her own admission, she takes more care with the dead than the living She hates to be criticized, and she says a dead person stands still better, doesn't fidget or peer over her shoulder in the mirror making judgments. "Dead ladies aren't so persnickety," she tells me, though I can't imagine smoothing setting gel on a floppy, lifeless head or patting pancake make-up on the pliable skin of a corpse. Almost all of her customers have clauses in their wills asking that Darla Sue pretty them for God when the time comes.

"What's your husband look like?" Darla Sue wants to know. She has never asked me about my husband before, and there's a slight edge to her voice, a small blade of malice buried in the harmless words. Darla Sue was married once to a traveling vacuum cleaner salesman who went to Indiana one day to learn about a new vacuum model and never came back. Darla Sue still remembers his sales pitch by heart and entertains Minnie and Erla with it when she's in a good mood: "Hello, madam. I know you to be a homemaker with a myriad of responsibilities, but let me take a few minutes of your time and change your life forever . . ."

"Harry's got a mustache," I tell Darla Sue, wondering why I've chosen this detail to describe him, this scruffy brush of hair on his upper lip to serve as Darla Sue's first mental image. Perhaps it's because I've never seen Harry without a mustache. He had a beard, too, when we first married, but he shaved it off one day without giving me warning. I didn't recognize him when he came into the room; how odd he looked, chinless, his bottom lip fuller than I knew it to be. He became a stranger right before my very eyes. For days, even his personality seemed altered in subtle ways at once ominous and diabolical.

"Funny, I don't see you with a mustached man," Darla Sue says. "I see you with a hairless guy, a baby-faced type."

I note the cool edge in her voice again and brush it away like a gnat.
"No, he's dark and sort of tall and he used to have a beard, too."
"How come he doesn't have it anymore?"
Delphine can probably answer that better than I. Almost everything
that has happened in our married life boomerangs back to Delphine
somehow, for she is the hinge we oil together to avoid hearing its inevi-
table squeak. Delphine thinks men with beards are hiding something: a
disfigured face, a lack of character, a clandestine past. She must have
given Harry her lecture on personal duplicity, impressing upon him the
need for honesty in appearance. This lecture has been part of my education, too, though it generally has something to do with why I should
wear a string of pearls with a certain dress or a different colored pair of
hose than the ones I've put on. How hose and pearls give one integrity
is lost in the labyrinths of Delphine's baffling code of social behavior.
Like Minnie, she has reasons of her own not to be challenged by logic.
But if I admit all this to Darla Sue, I'll be implying a weakness in Harry's
character, an inability to stand up to his mother, a fear I bury myself
time and again like a pesky bone. To excuse Harry's lassitude, I tell
myself it's not so much that he's afraid to cross his mother, but that he
hates confrontation and is wise enough to choose his battles carefully.
I can't always make myself believe this. But I do pity Delphine. She's
alone in the world without Harry and me. Harry's her only child and
it's natural for her to want to control his waking hours. Delphine rarely
drinks, but when she does, she tells Harry and me how meaningless
her life would be without us. She includes me for once, draping a be-
jeweled arm across my shoulders, her breath smelling of the anise liquor she drinks, and I'm placated by her solicitude, short-lived and
alcohol-induced though it may be. This doesn't seem the sort of senti-
ment Darla Sue would have any patience for.
     "I don't remember," I say quickly, reaching for one of Darla Sue's
cigarettes. I light the wrong end and toss it into Minnie's pile.
     "You got lipstick on your teeth," she advises me. I scrub my teeth
with a finger and study her. Her face seems white and cold and unknow-
able as the inside of a porcelain bowl.
     "Is it gone?"
     "Yep. There's something wrong with you," she admits in a suspi-
ciously weepy voice, her sentence rising to a quavery finish. I'm confused by the uncertainty in her tone and I watch her face for clues to
some hidden unhappiness. She blows smoke at the sliver of sky and I
follow her gaze up past the tops of the buildings where pigeons coo

and gobble and fly into the last light of day. When I look back, her face seems normal again, the lips not strung so tightly, and I think I must have imagined the damp in her voice. What is wrong with me I wait to hear though I've sensed it myself, have felt its presence and seen it flitting past the corner of my eye like a bat trapped in the house. Wrongness taking on a shape and weight though not an articulate import as yet. Something is changing; I'm overcome by a strange sensation especially in the evenings, my heart chugging like an off-beat wind-up toy as I stand at the kitchen window over a sinkful of dirty dinner dishes watching the early summer sky fade to the color of a crocus. I have no time, no patience for looking at the things I've always looked at: the rooms of my house, the newspaper and television, my husband's face. I don't say much to Harry these days. He is busy with his thoughts and I with mine. Sometimes I'll try to tell him a story, something that happened during the day, and he'll watch my lips with concentration, but then he'll interrupt me, ask me something extraneous: "Did you see my mother today?" "Did the trashmen come this morning?" "Are we having dinner with the Brown's on Friday night?"

But I don't feel dissatisfied so much as primed, ripened, ready, and impatient to fall like the last apple on the tree. In the middle of the night I wake drenched in sweat, my mouth watering for something sweet and cold, watermelon bought at a stand on the side of the highway, a brand of soda pop I've never tried. I want to throw up the sash and shout into the pristine stillness of the suburbs, I live, I am here in the world, a thing to be reckoned with! But I'm thirty-four years old for chrissakes, ten years married, and I have never been a thing to be reckoned with. I haven't been shaken up, turned upside down and inside out, surprised by the newness of fire and water and air for decades. The things I've been learning are quiet, serious lessons, grandmotherly wisdoms, unfailing in their boredom and rightness.

"What's wrong with me?" I cry finally in a meek, panicky voice.

"Maybe you're pregnant," Darla Sue says, a smirk lighting briefly on her plummy lips.

"Maybe I am," I blurt, and know at that moment it must be true. The insight perfect and a complete surprise like when Minnie chirps out a pure and flawless observation, something the rest of us with our cluttered, competent minds have overlooked. I won't tell Harry. Not yet. I'm angry with him and I'm not sure why. He doesn't love me enough, I'm thinking. He lets his mother run my life, and lately he becomes irritable if I criticize her or ask him to intercede for me. It used to be different, when we didn't live in the same city as Delphine. We had a life of our own. We had friends that didn't have to have Delphine's stamp of approval. We talked to each other. I know we did.

When I look up, I'm shocked to see Darla Sue's face has crumpled like a paper bag and she's brought her thin hands up to cover her shame. Her hands like fragile moths fluttering around the light of her eyes. I've never seen Darla Sue cry. Perhaps I'll be punished for it. But I'm mesmerized by her tears, can't take my eyes off of her even out of politeness. I haven't watched anybody cry in years, maybe since the death of my mother when my father stumbled on the front step after the funeral and stayed there weeping in full view of God and everybody for over an hour. Twenty years ago, at fourteen, locked outside my father's grief, my mouth propped open, unhinged by fear and a gathering doom, wondering what could be done with all of his tears, what purpose they could serve in a world where purpose is everything, just as only months before my mother and I while folding the laundry wondered what could be done with those endless flannel blankets of lint the dryer manufactured, how we could make ourselves rich on some crazy discovery—insulation for houses? stuffing for winter coats?—yet finding ourselves not as ingenious as Mrs. Amstutz who dreamed up something productive to do with a wasteland of shorn hair.

A noisy, hiccupy sobber is Darla Sue, her whole body loosed and wakened, surrendering itself to sorrow like a child. I feel my lower lip pout in sympathy. The fruit crate I sit on seems suddenly capable of collapse, and my eyes are damp, my mouth disturbed into an uncommon shape by a misery not mine to claim. Maybe it's just a day for weeping, an evening for sadness, the breezeless night lying down upon us like the shadow of a lost lover, the soft music of the world beyond these walls too sympathetic, too redolent of something dear and once cherished and never to be recovered.

Abruptly the sobbing stops, the air grows still as glass. Darla Sue stiffens, surprise and irritation colliding on her brow as she struggles to bring her face back from the edge of sadness.

"Ahh," she sighs, wiping her nose with the back of her wrist. She gazes wistfully at my feet for a moment before she says softly, "Why do you come here?" Her words slow, clipped, measured in teaspoons.

"What?"

"What are you doing here?" More strident now, a mild hysteria lapping the edges. "Why do you come here? Every week, for almost two years. Like Minnie, you just showed up and stayed . . ."

A spider of fear creeps along my spine as the words sink in. That's a low blow comparing me to Minnie. I look at my knees, the barbecue stain on my skirt, anyplace but in Darla Sue's yellow eyes where it's fearsome to be, the chill of gold, obstinate metal, no longer a mirror for my better self. For lost minutes, I am Minnie, as hopeless as Minnie, cruelly caught in a life I never asked for like a firefly trapped in an airless jar. I have to look down at myself to see it isn't so.

"What's wrong?" I say, hoping Darla Sue will take it all back, hoping that her anger and misery does not begin and end with me.

"Lookat that skirt!" she cries, almost weeping again and pointing at the ruin of my pleats. The damn skirt! If only I hadn't worn it, too many troubles this skirt has brought me today.

"Maybe you could use the money you stole to get it cleaned," Darla Sue sniffs, her proud nostrils flaring.

I stare at her, my eyes won't blink. I dig a small voice out from deep inside, let it rise and squeak, "What money?"

"The money you stole from my petty cash drawer," Darla Sue says. "Erla saw you take it. Minnie did too, but I don't count on Minnie's word."

"Why would I take your petty cash?" I am thinking about Erla, wondering why she would lie.

"I don't think you're laughing at us," Darla Sue is saying, pushing hair from her eyes with the heel of her hand. "No, it's not that . . . but what could it be, I ask myself. Why does she come here? I don't do her hair. She doesn't even buy a two dollar shampoo, and Erla's good at shampooing. She's got magic fingers, she puts the ladies to sleep."

Could Erla be mad that I don't ask her to wash my hair? Perhaps I've insulted her without knowing. Darla Sue leans back in the ratty armchair and lights another of her endless brown cigarettes. I sneak a look at her, wondering why she would believe something so absurd. I venture a sigh and think about how suddenly things can go awry. It's so wrong-headed to march merrily along thinking things are swell, thinking you have love and friendship and a place to lie down when it might not be so. A human being is a treacherous, mercurial animal, and every moment of life pivots dangerously on a lie, the truth always swimming upstream through the gray depths never to be caught on a hook and held up in triumph like a prize fish.

"I didn't steal your money," I insist, but it feels like a lie. I *have* stolen something, if not money than something else, something more personal. Yet it's funny how the truth can ring so false, can convince you of its duality. Liars must be privy to this magician's trick, severing their victims in half yet making the world see them whole and intact. And maybe I did steal Darla Sue's petty cash. Even this I can picture myself doing, my hand rising furtively from the till as I peek over my shoulder to make sure no one sees me. Or maybe I'm losing my mind.

"Didn't you?" Darla Sue says smoothly, her eyebrows raised, the lines around her mouth, small parentheses, calming as though she might believe me.

"It was wrong, probably, my coming here all the time. I see how I look to you now," I babble, though I don't see and will probably never see the true reasons for Darla Sue's resentment and her wrongful accusation. Yet Darla Sue seems confused now, too. She takes a pair of bifocals from her pocket, glasses bought at Woolworths which don't improve her vision, but perhaps she needs something to hide behind. Pity rises sourly in my throat. All my life I've had the misfortune to be moved by the embarrassment or shame of others, to wear it on my own face, my cheeks flaming in empathy. Stirred by a classmate's wet pants, a murderer's horrific childhood, a drunk's absurd posturing, I see the world washed in gray and never in black and white. But if Darla Sue claims my pity now, it will diminish her, make her small as a chickpea. Even now, I don't wish this fate on Darla Sue and couldn't bear to see her grovel.

"I didn't steal your money," I say again, fearing I might be saying it to someone, anyone for the rest of my life, in my sleep, in my daydreams, defending myself from the indefensible. "I won't come back here anymore." I feel pitiful saying this, but it's part of the drama, the script demands it be uttered.

"Aw, don't be that way," Darla Sue moans, itchy to be out of this dog sweater she's woven around herself.

All the things I'll miss about Darla Sue! But it's a revelation that she cares so little about me when I seem to care so much about her. And though she could not possibly know it, she gave weight to my life. Perhaps what I stole from Darla Sue was a small bit of her confidence, weaning from her a little of that self assurance for myself as a secret weapon against Delphine.

Erla sticks her head out the door. "Betty's getting cranky," she hisses, tapping the door impatiently with her blood-red fingernails. "I got some of that blue dye in the folds of her neck and she's mad."

Erla is irksome and mean-spirited, I think, staring for the last time at her big, stupid hair, a "do" I would have hated more if only I'd known what she had in store for me, a lie as big as Texas, and what for? Jealousy, craziness, or just her spiteful nature?

I look back in those yellow arrogant eyes of Darla Sue's and recognize the indifference, the wild insouciance of a cat. Finally no one can touch her. Not Darla Sue who has prettied the dead, who has ushered porous bones and withered flesh to God's door.

Darla Sue waves Erla back inside and keeps her eyes locked with mine, unashamed to be caught in such a true light. I enjoy the pin-prick of hate; I have been wrong about Darla Sue. There's nothing to admire in this cold, stubborn woman.

"I'm just havin a bad day . . ." she begins, but doesn't finish, doesn't offer excuses as piddling as alms. Unlike me, she has no allegiance to guilt. I would buy guilt at the store if it were for sale; I'm naked and souless without it. Guilt is the stuffing that shapes me, the weapon I carry to battle. But Darla Sue knows nothing of guilt. And the guiltless are free, the guiltless survive.

I stand to go but linger unfinished, a cartoon without feet drawn to carry myself away on. Thoughts bumble and buzz inside my head. There are so many things left to say, things I will think of hours, days, months and years later that will do me no good in the future. I want . . . what? . . . the last word. The "last word" my father used to say was something I was never allowed as a child. The last word, the only true gem in a crown of anger. But I can have the last word if I want it now, not a girl any longer, I can stand here all night fighting Darla Sue for it. But the last word is elusive as smoke. If only I was one of those people who can think on their feet, know how they feel at any given moment and give vent to their rage.

"You come back next week and Erla will give you a nice shampoo," Darla Sue hollers after me. It makes me smile. I turn back then, memorize Darla Sue sprawled in the old chair, a leg thrown comfortably across one arm as she gazes at the sky and blows smoke rings. Like Lot's wife, I have to look back, needing to see where Darla Sue goes when she's no longer mine, but just a woman alone in a alley, any woman, nobody to know.

"Wish me well," I command, startled by my cold tone, the words I've set loose without knowing they were loitering in my heart. Darla Sue's face rises, a moon flushed dark and amber with wonder. I watch her lips purse, holding back the words, reluctant to give this last gift.

"If wishing could make it so . . ." she whispers, and she rises then, as if to salute me, waving a pale hand in the air like a holiday flag.

DISTANCE
by Eve Shelnutt

Already someone will have put him on the train in northern Iowa—
the boy who will remember to buy the flowers.

And, there, it didn't rain unexpectedly, drops falling as fast as wishes
from a gray-painted sky. Someone would have fed him something
warm, a person old enough to have a vision of his narrow face pasted
to the window, and miles of grass bent flat by wind. Dry wind almost
silver through grasses never reflecting the sky.

The note pinned to his shirt pocket gives him away, not because he
is not beautiful or bright enough—all boys of that age are beautiful from
pride and the urge to run away. It brightens their eyes, even when they
keep them calm and hooded. Simply, in a scrawl on blue: "You can
have him. He was not really mine anyway." But what does that mean?

And who instructed him carefully about the flowers, fixed the oatmeal so that he would travel on its warmth; let him pet the cats a final
time, and did not want him to cry?

From the platform, she must have seen the thin, pale stalk of his
neck jutting just above the train's window. Maybe only that, the shade
half-drawn. Saw the muscles of the neck push his head back against,
almost into, the seat, his eyes (unseen?) looking straight ahead as if he
imagined he would die and, like a bird or a flower, didn't know to ask
for mercy.

Then the train moved, moved once, held back, moved. A jerking, accumulating—a connotation for the word *train,* as her smell would have connoted for him *mother* or *woman* or whatever she was to him.

He should have gotten off then. But his pride was of the opposite sort, not to have her face grow wild when it was now set. She must have seemed fragile, something showing on her without precedent in his life that held him back. Or everything he had seen being around her coalescing at once.

And a boy's body does not call what it does a revelation; it moves or it stays put, implicated in some unnameable embrace, feral. He must think that he leaves *for* her, her sake, for some mysterious life that had only been suggested—a raggedness of movement. It wasn't there now; he looked once.

Suppose he relaxed, alone but for a small, tinted flame, interior.

Or maybe the note in his pocket was more normal, whatever that may mean in the context of sending a boy to live with strangers. He had lost the note or letter by the time he got to Kalamazoo—read it and thrown it away; read it and held it in one hand—not for the words' comfort but for being simply something of her—held it until it crumpled from his sweat. Maybe, even then, when he was eight, she was partially educated, reader, say, of Blake by some accident, and was propelled to explain as evenly as possible.

"He's mine, but you know that, and because he, at least, has done nothing disgraceful, I trust you will take him in before I taint him in some way, like teaching him my fears." Sitting at the kitchen table— the only table—where she wrote the note, a single bulb hanging over it, creating (if she could have known, standing back observing) a lovely picture, she might have listed to herself what seemed like a plethora of fears, and shivered. Well, they included almost everything in the modern world, did they not?

He slept, then, in the next room, blissfully unaware. She was certain that his intelligence, what she thought it indicated of his potential, was far greater than hers. "His father was much older than I, and died soon after the birth. He has been around a few men, but how, still going to school as I am, would I meet men like your husbands to bring home?"

In fact, her men were usually musicians, or at least young men who played musical instruments—Spanish guitar, flute, mandolin, music a kind of promontory leading to her; it *got* to her in some way she was ashamed of. They were like artist-princes, drifting, pretending. "He's almost old enough to see it all."

See what? If this is what the boy read, what would he understand of the phrases? It was comprehensive, what she said. Reading it, he may have felt exhilarated by its opacity: something to discover, later. For seconds, even for minutes, he would have felt older, more capable, and sat up straighter in the seat, noticing the nubby brown of the train's seat covers, how faded the sun had made the green shade.

During the first day of his travel, after driving home alone, she would have arranged the cans on the kitchen shelves, to keep herself from running outside in a frenzy of panic which, having imagined it hundreds of times when she had thought he was in danger, her body had memorized as proper response. To let go voluntarily the boy for whom she would have killed: "I have thought it through, many times, and I have decided that I want him to have what all of you can offer him. Now, before it's too late."

And they knew he was on the train—the conductors, both decent-looking men, and an older woman whose job it was to rent pillows until 9:15 when the train pulled up next to a closed depot and let her out to meet a man in a beige truck that was parked near the tracks.

Asking for special treatment, since he was so young, she had lied, saying she herself had no money for a ticket (that much was true), only enough for the boy, whose father, much older than she (also true), lay dying in a veterans' hospital in Kalamazoo, Michigan (where there was such a hospital), and he was asking to see the boy a final time.

Did the boy hear this lie about his father and ride, then, with an image of him under sheets, waiting? Faceless, inert?

And what could they say but, disapprovingly, yes? And the boy's father *had* seen the boy; then, soon after, fallen, breaking bones in his rib cage and hips; and died soon after, when she had convinced herself he was invincible, because he had wanted to be.

But he had been in no war; there was no pension—the tiny house was rented. She had the car, she had her health, and she had a confidence in fate, now. Sometimes, when he was still very small, she had looked at the boy puzzled, as if trying to remember how she had come to have him, the new unnaturalness of a child with no family. "And that is my point: *I* am not, by myself, a family. I see that now, or I've seen it all along and am now acting on it."

He, the husband, would have stopped her. And that, for all of the boy's seventh year, had been the stupefying part: her husband's voice seeming to say, "But we can work this out. We're not incapable people, you know." It ran—his voice—like a tape recorder through her head, and only lately had she begun to argue back. You aren't *here.* Or softly:

You aren't here. Simply, seriously, each time more quietly, which meant that, daily, the boy was in more danger of being sent away.

The cat had slept in his room, on a wool blanket in a corner—*his* cat, the other one being hers, now both hers, he may have thought to himself, but skeptically since he did not believe an animal could be so simply handed over. If he had the thought, it was a prophecy, except that someone must voice a prophecy or it remains dormant, simply a fate whose time is coming. She, his mother (had he known, would a shared thought, however differently worded, have drawn them more together, cemented them?), had thought, whenever she read, that all words were prophecy, announcements that kept fate tamed, quiet, coming only softly on him, yellow legs. How many times before he died had Blake said his own death, how many ways?

Afternoon of the day the boy departed: it began to rain, the serious rain of fall, with its promise of cold (but not nearly, there, the kind of cold the boy was headed toward—Michigan's snow, sleet, wind, blueness in a sky brittle with cold). Then, she had gone out, driving around aimlessly until parking to watch a bike race, the racers, one of whom she knew, going over a hill, disappearing, then reappearing so quickly that it made nothing of the road she and he had walked many times. Watching him fly past four times, she knew she was through with him. Or imagined she was, until that night when she let him in. Whimpering almost as soon as he had closed the door. . . .

The boy had, on getting on the train, put his off-white canvas bag on the seat beside him; it contained his food as well as the clothes; a few books. She thought he would be calm enough to read. His *body* appeared calm—it was a trait he had learned while watching her: she stopped, shook her shoulders, looked around slowly, breathed in, and opened wide the fingers of each hand, even if he happened to be holding her right hand. His would fall, her fingers spreading.

With her, was nothing natural? Opening the door that evening (he was still in his biking clothes, the ones that seemed to shrink him, making him look too young, too small to make love to anyone), she felt she was in two places at once, inside herself needing him before she broke from the pain kept slightly aside all day like something parallel and too familiar to need looking at, but also she seemed to stand back observing herself opening the door and, as the whimper bubbled up, throwing herself at him. A traveling back and forth of herself. Even a third position: herself coolly thinking, considering it pathetic—her gestures of remorse that had to take into account his arrival, the open door, the rain on his jacket, the wind blowing her blue stationery from the table where two cans she hadn't known where to place in the cabinets were sitting.

She wished, now, he hadn't come, a wish she was free to have now that he had. A promise, in fact, extracted from him two days before when she had begun to imagine the scene at the train, not her feelings, only the picture of the boy in one place, her in another, and a white, blank space behind her, a precipice, unless she filled it imaginatively with her house and some activity in it.

Well, he would stay—why not, whatever transpired between them beside the point. She knew, now: activity would have this edge: to be gone through only as if to get to the other side, each action accompanied by a sensation of restlessness for real life to begin again.

Ah, so this was the difference between what death ended and choice ended. The boy and she still had volition, still occupied space pushing forward with them encased in little envelopes of time. Her son might reappear at any moment: the possibility had a kind of logic despite her quite clear instructions: "He should be raised as if all four of you are his parents. He will grow up feeling doubly lucky, and he will forget eventually since he's so young."

So, obviously, given the contradictions of her thoughts, she hadn't considered everything. He took off his windbreaker and shook it while she sat on the edge of a chair. "You should have gone with me to the train station."

"But I was in training all day," which she pictured—a blurred smear of bike and person while, it seemed, they, she and the child, stood motionless.

"Still, it would have made a difference. In what he saw. Since you encouraged it: 'Are you sure he's sleeping?' and 'Shush, he'll hear you.'"

"I didn't 'encourage' it."

"It was when I felt the most dangerous, you know. When you said something and I agreed in some way, even when I didn't say anything."

How true, she thought, but she was aware, too, of what they said filling the room in the way she had anticipated its being filled when she had made him promise to come regardless of how tired the afternoon race had made him. So she had gotten what she had asked for. And, later, after whatever explosion of feeling was gotten through between now and then—something building in her indictment and in how casually he answered her, in the disjunction between their two states—they would make love because, so late, there would be little else to do or because, so late, for her to refuse would incite another panic, distracting her.

Left uninstructed, the boy would have eaten all of the food in the brown paper bag inside the canvas one, an activity since the books inside the canvas bag seemed to have no relationship to him, simply there on one side of his clothes. Unrecognizable, almost.

But she had stooped in front of him, twice, once in the kitchen before leaving and again after she had locked the car doors at the station. Both times, she had taken his narrow face between her hands and recited the rules for the trip (and beyond, far beyond into the limitlessness of his entrustment to someone other than herself), waiting between each for it to enter his head, wedded to the steadiness of her eyes looking directly into his. She had learned this gesture from her husband, his hands taking hers over the white sheet, his eyes uncommonly clear: "Promise me you'll *do* something with yourself," whatever it had meant; the tone had substance, a gravity meant to impart a kind of serene will that could function as a benediction. And much later she would compare the occasions—his, hers with the boy—to what she had learned of the way children, especially children, were given no similar opportunity to receive instructions at Buchenwald, Auschwitz or, for that matter, anywhere events disallowed calm, final instruction, even if the words themselves were not applicable.

The boy drank the orange juice, and then both bottles of the apple juice, afterwards carefully zipping the bag closed with the bottles restored to the space he had taken them from, in a slowness of order uncommon for him.

Now the grass in the moving fields outside the window was almost invisible, then, suddenly, gone as lights above each window of the car came on. He saw his face and the face of the old woman across the aisle reflected in the glass, unless he leaned forward and put his face flat against the window. Then, in the distance, farmhouses came and went, with their barns, and the lights shining from tall poles making visible fences and the moving shapes of penned animals.

He slept, or his legs, hanging unsupported halfway to the floor, numbed and drew the rest of him into a semi-sleep, his clean hands opening to form a shallow cup on his navy cotton pants.

This may have been the picture of him she had had, beyond mentioning since it was for herself and not for him—a steady shadow moving forward.

Already, one having driven with her husband across town to be with the other, the two aunts were inspecting a final time the room that was to be his—not his mother's sisters but *her* mother's, the one who had died leaving this mess which their capabilities (she *must* have counted on it) would fix. The room was anything anyone could want, put together with the dredged-up impulses and memories from the long-past era of their fertility, when *they,* not, for heaven's sakes, the niece at age sixteen, should have had their children. And now these rays of love, directed so long in the controlled ways of women who, without children's having cemented them to their husband, loved, seeing to the upkeep of their bodies and the small rituals of couples, with enough money to back them up, to support these thousand acts of maintenance.

They switched off the light and joined the men for whom so much had been considered and inserted into time so that it would pass well. All four would go, of course, to meet him although anything could have happened on the way, which the aunts kept unspoken. Possibly a fear leaked out in their movements, too bustling, but their movement would not be a betrayal unless the other one, or their husbands, mentioned it. And they were all careful people; it was what, in her mind, had recommended them to the mother, having been in their homes once, briefly, when she was fifteen.

The fathers—both the boy's mother's and the boy's: well, one disaster led straight to another, did it not? Unless someone with will intervened, providing order and space for thought—an atmosphere conducive to thought. Possibly the aunts considered climate a factor, and here the pristine days of winter were coming, to be deliberately arranged into season's rituals, colors, even something so simple as giving the boy hot chocolate after he came in from sledding with his friends.

"My trouble," the mother may have written in the note that would disappear during the trip (lodged between the double seats or, when the boy became restless, torn apart in his fingers' unconscious movement as he gazed out the train window) "is a feeling of not experiencing his childhood, and I think it must feel the same to him, as if he's living simply adjacent to me when I'm unable to spend what must be the necessary time—time slowed down—to look into *his* life. I feel a guilt, as if he's a visitor, you see. It isn't easy to explain, but I have told myself, to no effect, that I should recognize that this is *his* life, not only mine, happening now. I can't seem to *inhabit* him, and keep seeing him as both mine and not-mine. If he isn't standing next to me, I think about

what I should do, should be doing, have done and haven't done to recognize his life. Every thought seems self-conscious, almost unnatural,
as if the *way* I go about thinking prevents any possibility of what the
thought is from ever coming to fruition. And this awkwardness only
disappears when he's with me, next to me in the car or on a walk,
for instance."

But maybe these were only sentences she had thought; possibly
other words framed them, words that, in daily exchanges with the boy
would have been, somehow, communicated to him, to make his rights
as a child seem paramount to her, even if she were, day by day, accru-
ing reasons to give him away. Either these words in a letter or similar
sentiments conveyed as they did things together—the effect of them
would have been to give him something while taking it away, in her, the
giver. A tension, not a strain of feeling but an irresoluteness. Possibly it
made him feel careful, almost as if he had been sick, sometime earlier.

At 9:00, the woman with the pillows had passed through what was
the train's last occupied car, and, making no sale, had gone through
the vacuum-operated door, turning back to look at its two passengers,
wondering why the boy had been put there, away from the others, but
maybe the old woman was the boy's grandmother, too old to be
trusted, on a separate seat to give them sleeping room.

Having had the three bottles of juice, now he had to find the bathroom, and he walked, holding on tightly each time he moved forward,
to the next car, half-full, and through it to the next, where men sat
drinking and playing cards.

Making love that night, what she had felt was the racer-musician's
insubstantiality, although he was as he always was, exactly the same,
no more or less attentive, considerate, the same in every way, only
now, in bed with him for the first time when he would not need to leave
at dawn so as not to give a wrong impression to the boy—now she felt
as if her back, spine, were exposed to the door, to the possibility of its
being opened by some thief or murderer or bum, when, never once,
while the boy slept in the next room, had she imagined the possibility,
after she locked the door for the night. The pile of clothes on the floor
seemed insubstantial, hers dwarfing his not because she was larger but
because he wore so little, as if he never looked at them to find them
ridiculous.

It could be that, then, she closed off from him, no matter that she
rested her head on his shoulder, with one hand between her legs made
wet by him—not separated from him in such a way as—like a frozen

lake—to see him through some thin sheath of self-protection until another desire, another nature in herself asserted itself like a warming. Simply, because she wouldn't give him up easily, she felt older than he, though, chronologically, age twenty-seven, he was three years beyond her. Her sudden dislike startled her, his *name:* "Gene." She would rather have said "Eugene" as a way to give him weight, if that were possible. And all of this too was a distraction, a way of reinserting herself into some racket of ordinariness by which the radical nature of the morning would subside through noise.

The train's bathroom was nothing like her description; she had said it would be similar to those on Greyhound buses which they rode every year when going to put flowers on the grave of the man who had been his father, she said. This was a small room, separated from the card players by two doors and a small hallway with a red light inside a dome fixed above the second door. Inside were seats in a row under the window. A man sat on one, sleeping, snoring with his mouth open, his hands over his stomach, partially exposed because his pants were unzipped and the shirt partially pulled out.

When he was finished, had zipped his pants inside the cubicle, and was washing his hands as she had reminded him to, the man woke up or had been awake. He noticed it and almost jumped back when he reached up for the paper towels. The man wasn't moving, only winking at him, first one eye, then the other, a game.

His mother had been wrong about the room and had also said nothing about a car with tables and a set of machines for crackers, or men drinking in the car from paper cups. He had to step around the man's feet to put the wet towel in the bin. And now, when he stepped around them again and began pushing the door open, it slammed open, seeming to fly from his hands as if, accidentally, he had pushed it too hard, when it had seemed heavy.

Then he was being lifted up by one arm, up and twisted around in one motion, to the man's face. "Is *this* what they're sending us these days—my God, is *this* what we've got"—slamming the boy back against the wall opposite the open door. "Well, keep it"—he put his fingers on the boy's cheeks, pressing, until his lips formed a pucker. "God! A runt!", dropping the boy and slamming the second door behind him.

So now, having waited and then walked with his head down through the roomful of tables to his own car, he sat breathing steadily, one short breath deliberately followed by another until his chest began to feel normal. He knew, now, that he would not eat or drink what she had packed, would not leave his seat unless he had arrived.

She had been wrong about the bathroom, she hadn't known about the car with tables. . . . And he couldn't fall asleep since the woman was asleep and too old to help him if she were awake. Help him how, against what? It was what he didn't know, what *she* hadn't imagined, except that he was not to talk to strangers, and he had obeyed.

When he was asleep, he cried to himself, except he saw when he brought his shirt tail out to wipe his face and then stuffed it back in that he hadn't been asleep, had been pretending with his eyes *almost* closed, because he couldn't sleep; now, it wasn't allowed.

She said, upon waking, that he was almost there and soon she would be able to call, not to talk to him—as she had explained, now it would not be good to talk since he would make a new life there, going, oh, to drawing lessons at the art center (a brochure had advertised them, its work with young children a specialty of the museum) and of course school and to the park across from the museum and all the other things boys did—wherever, too, the aunt's husbands thought to take him, having to do with sports, "which I've neglected for you." But the aunts, or one of them, would say he had arrived: "He's right here beside me."

And then life would begin again, she would be in her class in order to resume removing what had been her husband's superiority in knowledge that had made her envy him, given her the sense that it was the one thing to possess now that he was gone, some guarantee against anything whole being wholly ruined again. A corner to turn; in class, she approached it slowly, hopefully, full of a kind of faith that was unexplainable except in how she had absorbed his final words, when he had been cold and nevertheless caressable and had caused an ache between her legs. And memories not much changed but driven inward.

It was the aunts who noticed the beauty of the morning, its light made more brilliant by the clearness of the sky seemingly purified by a sudden drop, overnight, in temperature. Light pouring into the windows in what was to be the boy's room, which the aunt in whose house the room was described to the one across town, also restless until the train was met.

But none of them was free to see the day apart from its meaning to them, the weather's pragmatic registering on them, except possibly the boy. Not the mother, since "Gene" or "Eugene" was still there, a new event requiring accommodation around her inward focus, but seamlessly because she felt or thought she should feel some gratitude, and because it would be only later that she sent him away from her, got rid of him, extracted her life from his, to whatever extent the two had meshed.

He had watched all night what light there was and, early, when it was still pale, had moved slowly, pulling one leg up, to take off his left sock and remove the money she had given him for flowers. He put it in his shirt pocket, where the note had been, and he sat still again waiting while the scenery changed to include towns and all that went with them, the train slowing, sometimes coming to a full stop, then picking up speed again as the sky lightened.

She must have asked about the flower-seller, called and known and told him what was true even now. The woman came through after one of the train's stops, so he was able to buy the carnations, six of them, three for each aunt, as she had said, since she had not wanted him to know that, without them, how would the aunts know who he was?

He tore the thin green paper wrapped around them into half and wrapped both sets of three into the paper—his own decision—and held them together in one hand.

When she called from a pay phone, because she didn't have one in the house, she chose the one inside the drugstore, with its doors and little fan, which she cut off in order to hear better.

"He's here," the aunt said, flatly, and she waited for more, listening to her aunt's breathing, then: "What more do you want? We agreed. He's *here.*"

So she had promised, in her note or by telephone when making the arrangements. And to herself, a sub-vocalization within a litany of promises—she wasn't to talk to him. What did she want now, a description?

She wasn't to hear that the boy, standing on the metal steps of the train and while climbing down with his canvas bag in one hand, the carnations in the other, a porter waiting at the foot of the steps, had begun to wet himself and that it streamed down the inside of his pants. That he had begun to cry when he felt it, and that he hadn't been able to stop himself from crying even when the aunts rushed up, crying, "Baby, hush, hush, it'll be all right, everything's all right, you're fine, you'll be fine now, you did just fine, it's all right," over and over. The husbands standing back, taking the bag, the flowers, and then taking out their cigarettes while their wives talked to the boy and smoothed his hair, got a sweater from the canvas bag and put it on him.

And she wasn't to know that, in the red car, both aunts in one, the uncles in the other, with him in the front, one aunt behind on the back seat, they began—between pointing out to him all there was to do in Kalamazoo—they began to talk about her, the mother or whatever she was to him now.

Somehow they saw on him what the trip had been like, saw, he imagined, even the man in the bathroom, what it may have meant. And couldn't say (not to him but over him) enough about the disgrace such a trip for someone so young had been—its unthinkability in an unsafe world, its typicality as a scheme from the atypical part of the family, how anything, anything at all might have happened, when he was precious, truly beautiful and quiet and obviously intelligent to have remembered the flowers, surprising though it was that *she* had remembered to tell him, that she *had* any money to give him for them. . . .

It seemed to animate them, excite them, to say what might have gone wrong, to imagine all that she had not imagined, and then to recite his state not minutes before. While he, in order to listen without their realizing he was listening, turned around in his seat to look at the town where he would live.

So straight, so soon, so fast, before his memories and hers changed?

In bed, after his hot chocolate, with a stuffed bear beside him, given by one of the uncles, as he watched the light through the shade, he began to sense an unfairness or at least something wrong or something slipping away as if it were finished, like a train's view. Or it was a stubbornness he had felt many times before, with her, over some small thing, rising now, here, but connected with her, greeting him not against her but with her attached, an almost hot sensation, of pleasure, each time it came—when he turned in the covers. It, it was a kind of travel, unknown to the aunts or the two uncles, or to her.

It wasn't *her* fault—the sentence he managed and that impregnated him. A weighing, against what *was* her fault (the description of the bathroom, for instance). And he began to feel (because the aunts talked on the phone and went over again her crimes of ignorance and neglect and pure youth and breeding and waywardness and no-doubt sexuality and choices connected to it) over several weeks a sifting through of truth from distortion, as if a drape covered one and, like a piece of clothing, encased it next to him.

She went around carefully then, moving carefully as though she had been released from a hospital and could not be sure of the sharpness of alien objects in the places where she moved. "I know I will miss him," she may have included in her note, "but that will be my concern," which it was, but more than what may have been a blithe accounting of it in a note prepared for her.

Dutifully, he went to the new school and brought from it a boy to play with him, and he ate what the aunt provided, waiting but uncertain for what. A redress of an imbalance? And how would it come when, now, they never said her name, mentioned her at all?

She talked about his father often, a shadow brought to the table when they ate or went walking or, as he grew, when similarities between them began to be apparent to her, where the memory rested.

And to her teachers who asked, to the man at the meat counter where she shopped, to a neighbor, even to Gene, she brought the boy out, explaining where he was and why, but how many times could she do that, sucking from a bare fact a repeated need for its repetition?

She let his room stay as it was and this, too, was one of the differences: death demanded a disposing because the face came up even in objects to admonish: You're still looking at me. When it had been a husband: somehow sexual and thus indecent. But this. . . . Maybe his things were like ornaments.

Did he return?

Suppose, using all of his intelligence, he got back, having stolen the ticket money from one of the uncles and, from what he remembered of the note—something he learned from it—learned how to say what a ticket-master, a conductor would require.

And, coming flowerless, found her several weeks later drinking coffee alone in a cafe in town, in the afternoon between classes.

Would he have been the same, the same boy and she the same mother?

Their mutual panting after a second of disbelief locked together in a purer uniting than a birth, then each explaining at once, the words colliding, how they had not been separated at all, not at all. And then the reckless laughing, holding on, laughing because, between them, they had outmaneuvered the world this time and hence forever—my God, you can hear it, everyone turning to watch, how they are outshining everything. . . .

Whose business, then, would it be, when they are seen taking their walks or, much later, buying him a first suit or brown shoes or picking out a second cat to replace the one that ran away: Whose business is it that, now, to anyone taking the time to watch, to evaluate, they appear uncommonly close, that in their smallest sentences and manners and inaction and silences—then, *almost* imperceptible, some suggestion of death or its surrogate hangs about them and, for the young, the uninitiated, makes them, as a pair and sometimes individually, hard to look at, hard to love?

FUNERAL PLOTS

by Jack Matthews

Sitting on the patio after dinner, Walt Thatcher sensed that his wife
was preoccupied. The two of them hadn't spoken for perhaps five or
ten minutes, although it was becoming increasingly difficult for him to
estimate time accurately. Still it must have been something like that.
Perhaps fifteen minutes, but surely no more. It was late summer, and
the cricket songs were pleasantly loud and rhythmic, emanating from
the hedges at the rear of their two-acre lawn and in the thick under-
growth beyond.

Walt could also hear music from somewhere inside the house, although he couldn't identify the composer. Mid-nineteenth-century, perhaps; maybe Schumann, maybe Brahms. It was a piano concerto, he
thought; but couldn't be sure. His memory had begun to do odd things
to him since his stroke several months ago. A year? No, he didn't think
that long, but it had been some time. Months and months. *Several*
months, whatever that might be.

Often they were quiet after dinner, and he thought of this quietude
as a kind of beautiful peacefulness, knowing even as he thought so that
for Doris it might be the most terrible sort of boredom. Why did he
brood so much these days over how she felt? There had been a time
when he could have felt assured of their essential sympathy, a time
when she'd enjoyed their silence together as much as he. Only, lately,
he sensed that the character of her share in that silence had changed.

And yet, to take the long view, hadn't their ten or fifteen years of marriage proved warm and satisfying?

Because it hadn't been built upon the typical infatuation of a man facing his middle-age crisis . . . it wasn't as if Walt Thatcher, at the age of sixty, had married a twenty-five year old. Doris had been a mature, divorced woman of, what, forty, at least. Maybe forty-five. Only the other evening he had asked her, and she had answered—surprised that he could have forgotten—but she had answered, anyway. Still, the answer she had given had gone gulping down the drain of forgetfulness, like so much.

This evening they were sitting on opposite sides of the table, each in a wheeled padded lawnchair that rolled easily on the flagstones. She was looking at a catalog advertising women's clothing, and he was simply sitting there, letting his thoughts drift, vaporous as veils of rain in the distant sky.

The evening air continued warm from the heat of afternoon, but the lengthening shadows cooled and protected them from the slanting yellow rays of sunshine that struck the lawn about twenty feet on this side of the hedgerows that bordered their lot. Maybe twenty-five feet. The crickets sang, pulsing their ancient shrill song of summer grown old, and the shadows loomed darker against the bright minty green of the well-tended lawn at the far edge; and he sat there comfortably, wondering if Doris had been forty or forty-five when they'd gotten married all those years before, he couldn't remember exactly how many. But whatever that mystic number was, she was still a handsome woman of middle age—sixty-something, but beautifully groomed and with a cheerful countenance and a good, firm figure.

So this, he heard himself recite somewhere inside his head, was old age. "But then, thou must outlive thy youth, thy usefulness. . . ." Proud that he could remember Milton, he tried to remember the rest . . . but it wouldn't come. A stanza that ended, "fall, like ripe fruit, into thy mother's lap," anyway. The mother being earth, of course; a most uxorious—or at least, female-loving—image for Milton, who was supposed to have been something of a misogynist.

A soft breeze came over him, bristling the hairs on his arms, and the old lines of poetry sifted out of his mind. Perhaps it was better this way, he often reminded himself, and remembered doing so; for when you die at an advanced age, there is not so great a loss, since so much of what you were has already departed through the small silent attritions of the years.

"I was wondering," she said.

He lifted his face and looked at her. "What?"

"You weren't listening."

"Sorry. I didn't hear you."

She nodded and carefully laid the catalog on the table between them. "Not surprised," she said.

He had not heard the first of that, but he knew what she must have said, and nodded.

"Walt, I have something to show you," she said.

Something in the way she said it, something in her expression, alerted him. What had she been leading up to? Surely, she had been chatting about something, for there was an odd and disconcerting air of conclusiveness in the way she'd said it.

"I said," she said slowly, "I have something to show you."

"Like what?" he asked.

"Something you should look at. And think very seriously about."

"Well, I would assume that."

"Would you really?" she asked, tilting her head and smiling at him. It was a very small smile, and in some way not entirely humorous. There was something almost old and tired in it; it occurred to him that it was an expression he could not at the moment remember having ever seen in her face.

"Well, let's see it, then," he said gruffly. "Bring it out, whatever it is. Another new dress? Some extravagance you haven't told me about, Doris?"

She shook her head no. "No, you'll have to come inside. It's something you should look at inside."

He thought about that a moment, then nodded. "All right, if you want to be mysterious. We'll see if the old legs will get me out of this damned thing."

"And don't forget your cane."

He looked at her. "Of course I won't forget the cane. How could I? The first step or two would remind me."

He pulled himself to an upright seated position, swinging his legs to the side so that his feet rested on the flagstones. Then he slowly and painfully pushed with both hands on the sturdy aluminum edge of the lawn chair and eased his weight onto his legs and finally lifted himself to his feet. Then he leaned over and picked up the cane that had been slanted, notched between the arm and the chair.

"All right," he said. "I'm ready. Where are we off to?"

"The bedroom."

Walt nodded. "Ah, the bedroom! She's going to try to see if she can get a rise out of the old gentleman, after all these years."

She laughed distantly. "Oh, no: nothing like that, I'm afraid."

"Why 'afraid'?"

"Oh, I don't know. You figure it out. You've always been good at figuring things out, haven't you?"

He paused after one step. "I'm not sure I want to answer such a question when you ask it like that."

She motioned to him, wiggling her index finger. "Come on, come on. There's nothing to be afraid of, after all."

"What do you mean, 'after all'?"

"Just come along like a good boy, will you?"

"I'm not a boy—good, bad, or indifferent. I am an old man, which I would guess means indifferent."

"Really? I'm sure I hadn't noticed."

He stepped carefully over the threshold of the sliding doors and said, "What in the hell's gotten into you, Doris?"

"Not a thing. Just come along. We have something very important to discuss. Even critical, you might say."

Saying that, she walked at a spritely pace into the bedroom, and he followed, plodding forward with his cane and favoring the numbness in his left leg. "It'd better be important," he grumbled.

"Oh, you'll see that it is."

He was a little surprised that she'd heard, but that was all right. And by the time he reached the open door of their bedroom, he was feeling downright curious. It wasn't like Doris to play games, so he reasoned that this game must have a very special significance.

But his brief surmise did nothing to prepare him for what faced him when he entered the bedroom, for he saw that she had hung two of his favorite old suits side by side on hangers from the door of their big, walk-in closet. One suit was black, and the other was a very dark gray. Both a bit old-fashioned, but representing the very best English tailoring and made of one hundred percent wool, of course. The dark gray had been the suit he'd worn, oh, ten or twenty years ago, when he'd represented the Rawlings Corporation in a local property dispute, shortly before he'd retired.

"Why do you have those two suits hanging there?" he asked.

For a moment, she didn't answer. She had her back toward him, and she stepped forward and caressed the sleeve of one of them, as if the arm of the man he'd once been might still be inside.

"All right, I give up," he said. "What's this all about?"

She turned back to him, and, smiling, asked, "All right, which one would you like to be buried in?"

For a moment his mouth got dry and he couldn't have spoken if he'd wanted to. Then, gradually, he eased himself over to the upholstered chair in the corner and sat down. "I see," he said finally.

"After all, it's something I should know," she said practically. "Things being what they are."

"I see," he muttered.

"You *do* see, don't you?"

Gazing at her, he saw her entire body ripple, as if she were no more than a reflection in water that had been mildly agitated by a dropped pebble. He took a deep breath and said, "You know very well that all of this was decided long ago, Doris. We agreed on everything when we were married."

"Two innocent lambs we were, weren't we?" she said, smiling still harder. "How well I, for one, remember. You a widower, and I a divorcée. You were the lucky one, though; better to have a mate die than have him leave you."

"I don't suppose you have the authority to say that unless you've experienced both."

"Well, no doubt I will before long."

"My God!"

"Let's not be maudlin, shall we? I asked you a very simple question that requires a very simple answer: which suit would you like to be buried in?"

"You know perfectly well the answer to that: neither one."

"Come, come, Walt: we can't be shown in the casket in our birthday suit, can we?"

"What in the hell has gotten into you, Doris? I've told you a hundred times I don't want any *viewing,* as they call it. I don't want to be embalmed, even. But even if that's the state law, I still want to be cremated. Right away. I never could tolerate the thought of those barbaric rituals. *Never!* I've always felt that way, and you know it. Even Rita knew how I felt about such things."

"Well, isn't it a shame that poor perfect Rita had to die and leave you to little old me."

"Don't be such a bitch, Doris."

"Oh, it comes easy, if the stakes are high enough. And if you hear the name of Rita often enough. As I have through the years, God knows!"

"What are you talking about? I hardly even mention Rita's name."

"Oh, *don't* you, now! Why, it's 'Rita this, and Rita that, and Rita kiss my nose'!"

"Doris, where in the hell did you get such nonsense? Have you been drinking too much already?"

"Only the honest truth. And the sound of Rita's name ringing like a bell for more than two decades would have driven most wives away . . . but, as you see, I've stuck it out. And will continue to stick it out to the bittersweet end."

He shook his head and pushed down on his cane, trying to lift himself out of the chair. "I don't know what you're talking about, Doris!"

"Oh, I think you do. Your memory is bad, all right; but it's not *that* bad!"

"Well, tell me, then. Come right on out with it, if you've got something to say."

This time he did manage to lift himself shakily to his feet, and, step by step, leaning heavily on his cane and clearing his throat so he wouldn't hear her, he began to work his way out of the bedroom. He had gotten halfway down the hall when he heard Doris walk up behind him. "Don't you walk away from me when I have something to tell you!" she hissed.

"I'm going back to the patio. It's cooler out there."

"We can turn the air conditioner on."

"No, I like fresh air. Especially at this time of evening."

"Listen, you're going to be awfully sorry if you don't listen!"

"Just leave me alone, for God's sake! I don't want to hear any more."

He opened the sliding screen door and moved slowly out onto the patio, feeling slightly vertiginous, as if he had stepped onto the deck of a ship rolling in a slow swell.

When he had seated himself, he looked up and saw her sitting in her own chair, gazing at him. The top button of her white blouse was hanging by a thread, and in view of her compulsive neatness this suggested a shocking, even sinister, neglect.

"I want to be cremated," he said. "No ifs, ands, or buts. Any other option is abhorrent to me. Question closed. It's in my will."

Doris spread the fingers of her right hand and studied her nails. "Let me put it to you clearly: by the time they read the will, my dear, there will have been a viewing, and you'll be wearing one of those two suits. I can see nothing more reasonable than asking which suit you prefer for the occasion."

He stared at her a moment without speaking. Finally, he inhaled and said, "You know that would be foolish. When the will is read and they find out that you didn't abide by my instructions, you'll forfeit everything I've provided for you."

"Everything you've provided for me!" she whispered contemptuously, glaring at him. "This house and an executrix fee and, what, five hundred dollars a month for as long as I live?"

"Plus the furniture, don't forget. And five hundred dollars should be ample, considering the income from your own investments."

"Why, it's only a token, and you know it."

He nodded. "Yes, it is only a token. But according to our agreement when we were married, we weren't going to mix our estates. We agreed that it would be unfair to our children if we did so."

She smiled slightly. "Walt, I'm impressed by how much you seem to be able to remember when the issue is money . . . *especially* when the issue is money that *I* might inherit!"

"I do have my lucid moments."

"I suspect it has to do with how important the issue is. But you seem to rise to the occasion."

"What is it you want, Doris?"

She closed her eyes a moment, then opened them. "When you changed your will two years ago, I was led to understand that you intended to change it to my benefit."

"And so I did. The house, the conventional executrix fee—which is only fair, I don't mind saying—and the monthly stipend."

"Five hundred dollars a month won't even keep me in clothes."

"Then perhaps you'll change your spending habits. Perhaps you'll draw on some of your own income, which is getting fatter all the time. I see nothing unreasonable in that."

"What is unreasonable," she said carefully, slowly, feeling her way with the words, "is that I have four grown children—all with families of their own, along with the natural expenses of raising them and sending them to college—and you have only two grown children, one not even married."

"There's no reason to bring that up, now."

"There's every reason to bring it up now. Four is twice as many as two, in case you've forgotten your arithmetic."

"Doris, don't be so goddamn insulting. My memory may be faulty, but my reasoning powers are not all that diminished. What's your point, anyway?"

"My point is that, whatever so-called 'agreement' you may think you remember about our marriage . . . whatever the terms that may or may not have been part of this so-called agreement, they were never put in writing; and the fact is, I don't remember it at all as you state the matter. All I can remember is one evening we talked about how 'it would be nice if we could keep our estates apart'—it was all very hypothetical and theoretical, as I remember it. And whose memory do you suppose will be judged more reliable, yours or mine?"

"In this case, mine. I remember very clearly."

"Well, as efficient as you were then—and such a brilliant and distinguished attorney, I'll remind you—why wouldn't you have had it down in black and white? After all, the way you're referring to it, it was nothing more than a verbal contract . . . and as you've told me many times, a verbal contract is no contract at all."

"I've always insisted upon the term 'oral contract' to distinguish it from a written contract, because in one sense *all* contracts are verbal."

"I stand corrected."

"You will never stand corrected, Doris; I'm afraid you are simply, hopelessly incorrigible."

"Well, we'll see. Or, *I'll* see. Because we're losing sight of the present issue, which is which suit you choose to be wearing at the viewing."

"You really are a disgusting bitch, aren't you?"

"I knew you'd get around to saying that, and it doesn't really bother me. But for your information, no, I am not; I merely have my own priorities as a mother, as well as a woman who has a certain amount of personal pride and resents the humiliation of your settlement. If you'd really done something worthwhile when you changed your will two years ago, this question wouldn't even be coming up now, and those two suits would not be hanging from the door. So what's it to be?"

"You know I can't bear the thought of having my corpse filled with formaldehyde or whatever they use and then have it stuffed inside a coffin."

"The way I see it, there's only one fair solution: slice your estate right down the middle. Not only would that be simple justice, it would be a very small price to pay, considering all I've done for you during the past twenty-two years . . . how I've nursed you and taken care of you. Not to mention what I've had to put up with; how I've kept silent all this time; how I've kowtowed to your every whim and notion."

"You sound as if you came to me in rags and I kept you that way. You were far from being poor, you know. And you're even more comfortable now, because you've been living off me. Nothing wrong with that, but it's allowed your own estate to grow in ways it couldn't have grown otherwise."

"No, I wasn't poor. And I admit I'm not poor now. But I can feel the financial burden of my children—I wouldn't be a decent mother if I didn't; and considering the way I've had to take care of you all this time, it isn't fair that *your* two should receive more than my four, especially when mine need money far, far more than yours."

"Rick doesn't."

She nodded. "No, that's true. Rick is doing very well, and I'm proud of him. But what about the others? They're all struggling in debt, to some degree or other."

"Letty and Ron are trying to live beyond their means, that's what *their* problem is."

"Oh, yes? Well, just tell me this, Walt: who's to decide what's beyond their means? You?"

"No, the fiscal realities of the world they live in. It's relative, of course; but the test is, are they happy or not? And if they're not living at the starvation level—which I'll remind you they most emphatically are *not*—then the trouble's not in their income, but in how they handle it . . . and how greedy they are for more."

She made a face. "Don't talk to me of greed and fiscal realities. I've had to listen to too many of your lectures, and I'm not about to tolerate another."

"Actually, I've never understood why you haven't filtered some of your own dividends off to them, if you're so worried about them. You've got plenty to spare."

"I've got my old age to think of, don't forget. You're practically past all that; you're almost safe at home, you might say; but I might have twenty or thirty years left. And what if something should happen to me? I don't ever, ever want to become a burden."

"You're already a burden."

"Well, aren't we witty this evening."

"Fifty-fifty, you say?"

"I ask you, what could be more fair?"

"Now let me get this straight: if I don't change my will, you'll have my body embalmed and put in a goddamn casket so it can be 'viewed' by friends and relatives and enemies and any passing ghoulish types who might have developed a fondness for such ceremonies?"

"I'll promise it will be a very, very handsome and expensive casket, along with a fine headstone, if you wish. I'll even see that it bears a favorite inscription of yours, if you want. Something from Milton, perhaps? You used to quote Milton a great deal, as I remember."

"My will already specifies that I choose to be cremated . . . and you're right, I suppose: if it's important enough for you to forfeit what I've left to you, then you could go ahead and have my body embalmed and laid out in a casket. But what if I call my lawyer and make a specific point of having my wishes followed?"

"I assume you're talking about Pete, who drew up your last will. Well, Pete's a good old boy, and no doubt as obedient as hell . . . but stop and think a minute. Who's going to be with you when you croak? *Me,* that's who. Your loving and faithful wife. And I'll have you embalmed and in your suit before Pete even knows you're dead. And if he asks me, what do you suppose I'll say? Why, I'll say that you told me you'd changed your mind and had talked about getting back to him so that he could put your most recent wishes in a codicil; because you wanted to be buried like everybody else, including your old momma and daddy, whose bodies are still rotting away in their caskets, the way God meant for them to rot away."

"Stop it, will you?"

"No, I won't. And as a matter of fact, I could even go in the opposite direction and say you were so crazy even two years ago that you couldn't have made a sane decision. Even if they don't agree with me, what do you think they'd do? You say I'd forfeit my inheritance, such as it is: I say that's nonsense—I'd take it to court, and win, and pay the expenses out of the estate . . . because no *sane* man gives a damn about what happens to his body after he's dead, because everybody knows it doesn't matter. And do you think they're going to take a widow to court over such a sad and silly business as that?"

For a long moment he was silent. Finally, he said, "Well, you've learned something from living with me, I'll say that."

"*I'll* say I have!"

He shook his head solemnly. "To think it would come to this; to think you would ever blackmail me like this."

"Actually," she said, "it would be more accurate to call it extortion, if you'll excuse my correcting a man who was once said to have such a fine legal mind."

"That's right, extortion."

"But I'd say a more proper term yet is simple justice."

"You probably would," he said, and closed his eyes as he took a deep breath and exhaled.

"So what's it to be? Do I phone Pete and ask him to come over so that you can make a new will? Or do you choose which suit you want to wear in your casket? Or do you want me to choose your suit for you? It wouldn't be the first time . . . although it would certainly be the last."

For a moment he was silent. It was getting dark out, and the crickets were louder than ever. "All right," he said. "Call Pete."

She nodded. "Good. I'll call him right now, at home. Maybe he can come tomorrow. Considering who it is, he'll drop everything else. I'll stress how urgent you feel it is that you make a new will right away. You do agree that you feel urgent about it, don't you?"

"Yes," he said. "I guess I do, under the circumstances."

"Actually, I think what I'm asking is very modest. And it's not as if *your* two need money, is it?"

"No," he said, "they're doing pretty well. And as for you, you're a model of temperance."

She laughed and told him how pleased she was that he understood and was willing to be realistic about the whole thing.

Then she went inside and phoned their attorney, Pete Schreiber, who agreed to come to their house on the afternoon of the next day with all the necessary legal forms. He itemized these, emphasizing the complexity of the transaction because of the size of the estate; but Doris hardly listened.

When he finished, however, she thanked him, said good-bye, and returned to the patio, where she informed her husband that all would be taken care of the next day. "Now whatever you do," she said, laughing, "don't die tonight just to frustrate me."

"I'll do what I can, Doris," he said.

"And when it all works out the way it should be, I'll promise that you'll be cremated and your ashes scattered over the flower borders, just as you wanted it."

"So you do remember."

"Why, of course I remember," she said. "Every single word."

It was almost three-thirty the next afternoon when Pete Schreiber
arrived. Although he himself was no older than Doris, his firm had been
formed by two lawyers from Walt Thatcher's own law office shortly
after Walt's retirement, and Walt had retained a close and cordial personal relationship with the younger firm.

Pete rang the bell, and the Thatchers' maid, Imogene, admitted him
and let him go back to the family room at the rear, where Walt and
Doris were waiting. Pete was a large bald man with a large shapeless
nose and a drooping ginger mustache. He was the son of Tom
Schreiber, who had been one of the founders and senior partners of
the branch firm; only Tom was partially retired, and Pete took care of
most of his business. This afternoon, Pete was wearing a light tan
open-necked shirt that showed a cluster of red hair at the top of his
chest. He wore a diamond ring on each hand and a solid gold Riscotti
handmade watch on his left wrist.

Doris greeted him and asked if he wanted a drink, which Pete de-
clined, saying it was a bit early for him, but please go ahead if they liked.

"We do like," Doris said in a festive voice, picking up a Bloody Mary
and holding it high for him to see, "and we have already taken your
advice. Pre-facto, if that's a word. If not, well, pre-facto anyway."

Grinning, Pete turned to Walt and said, "Well, Doris is in rare good
humor today, I see; and it looks like the party's begun. And how are
you doing?"

"I've been worse," Walt said in a faraway voice.

"Well, glad to hear that, anyway. What's this business about changing your will again?"

For a long moment Walt merely stared out at nothing.

"Walt?" Doris said.

He lifted his head, and she said, "Surely, you heard what Pete asked
you just now. Why didn't you answer?"

Walt stared at Doris a moment and then turned to Pete. "Hello,
Pete," he said.

Pete laughed nervously. "Hey, I just came in and we all greeted one
another. And Doris asked me if I wanted a drink. Remember? You probably didn't recognize me because I said no."

"Why are you here, Pete?"

Glancing quickly at Doris, Pete turned back to the old man, who was
leaning slightly to the side as he sat in his chair. "Hey, are you all right?"
he asked.

"Of course I'm all right. What is it you want?"

Doris said, "His hearing isn't all that good." Then in a loud, angry voice, she said, "Listen, Walt, I called Pete last night and asked him to come on over because you wanted to change the will. Surely, you remember."

Vaguely, Walt nodded.

When he didn't say anything, Pete said, "So you want to change your will again. Is that right, Walt?"

"Yes," Walt said. "Rita wants me to change the will."

"Who?"

"What in the hell are you talking about?" Doris yelled.

"Who's Rita?" Pete asked. "Wasn't that his . . ."

"You know damned well who it was," Doris whispered. "And so does *he!* Rita was his first wife, and she died thirty years ago."

Pete shook his head. "Hey, maybe we'd better put this off for the time being."

"The time being, *shit!* He knows goddamn well who I am, and I'm not about to be taken in by his sick little games!"

"Sick is the word," Pete said in a low voice.

"No, I didn't mean it that way," Doris said. "He's just trying to get even with me."

"Get even with you for what?"

Doris blinked and thought a moment. "I don't like to talk about it."

"Well, if you don't talk about it to me, and I'm your lawyer, what do you expect me to do?"

She nodded. "All right. Walt promised me several months ago that he wanted to change his will and divide his estate right down the middle, which is only fair, as anybody could see. Anyway, he said he wasn't comfortable with the will he had you draw up two years ago because it obviously *wasn't* fair—especially considering how much would go to his own children, and how little would come to me, or to mine. Especially after I'd, you know, done so much for him, and everything all these years. Also, as a protection in my old age."

"I see," Pete said.

"You can see how it is," Doris said. "Listen, that old man is as sharp as a tack. His memory may be a little funny now and then, but he hasn't lost an ounce of his intellectual ability, and I'm in a position to know. What he's doing now is just having his little fun. He's been awfully bored lately, and entertained himself with some pretty far-out jokes."

In a louder voice, Pete said, "Is that right, Walt? Do you want to change your will again?"

"Whatever Rita says," the old man muttered, waving his hand at Doris.

For a moment no one spoke. The clock was ticking, and Imogene was making distant noises in the kitchen, preparing dinner.

Doris suddenly got up and went over to him. "Listen, don't think I don't know what you're trying to pull, and don't think you'll get away with it!"

"I think I'd better be going," Pete said in a low voice to her. "I didn't have any idea he was this bad."

"I didn't either," Doris muttered.

"Well, I guess I'd better be going then."

Doris took him by the arm and led him to the hall entrance. "All right, it's probably best you shouldn't witness any more of his skill as an actor. I'll only point out to you that I am as certain as I am that you're standing there that he's just putting all this on."

"Why on earth would he want to do that?" Pete asked.

Doris shook her head vigorously. "Oh, never mind, Pete. We've all had too many Bloody Mary's, that's the problem."

"You mean, Walt's been drinking them, too?"

For a moment she paused thinking; then she said, "I'm afraid that's only the truth, and this early in the day. As you can see, I joined him. But Imogene took his glass back in the kitchen right before you came. He gets like this when he's been drinking."

Pete shrugged. "Well, whatever, it's no time to make a new will. If I can help, get in touch."

"You'd better believe we'll be in touch," Doris said.

Pete frowned a moment, then patted her on the shoulder and left.

When she went back into the family room, she said, "Well, I suppose you think you've been awfully goddamn clever, don't you?"

When he didn't answer, she stared at him more closely. "Did you hear what I said?"

"I heard," he said finally.

"And in case you really are slipping your gears, I'm not Rita; she's been dead for thirty years. I'm your wife, Doris."

"I know goddamn well who you are," Walt said.

"And I still have to figure out what suit you'll be wearing, unless you decide to change the will, as you promised."

Walt shook his head and handed her several sheets from his private p.c. printer. "I wouldn't bother, Doris. Maybe you noticed I was busy in my study all morning. Well, here are the fruits of my labor. I suggest

you look at it very closely. You will see it's an instrument referring to
my wish to be cremated, explaining that, frequently, throughout the
term of our marriage, you have been fully informed of my preference
for cremation over burial; and if you do not follow my instructions regarding cremation, not only will you be immediately discharged as executrix, but in view of your willful meddling in my long, constant, and
undeviating choice to be cremated, you will be sued by the estate. I will
remind you that the estate is a legal entity, and will remain so long after
my death; it will be a corporation, of sorts; and whoever your successor
might be (I suspect it will be Pete himself), he will be legally obligated to
sue you. And supposing he himself is corruptible—which I don't think
to be so, but believe you will try him, anyway—I have sent copies of
this will, along with suitable retainers, to various other agencies which
I will not name, but which will have an obligation to see that the intention of my will in this regard is carried out."

When he finished, Doris sat down in an upholstered chair, staring
distantly at the remains of her Bloody Mary, which she finally decided
to finish. Then she licked her lips and said, "Very clever, but it won't
work; Pete can testify that you're bonkers."

"Irrelevant. This instrument, which I intend to execute tomorrow (reminding you that copies have already gone out—Imogene and the
maid next door, what's her name, were witnesses and each signed six
copies), will simply reinforce what is intrinsic to all of my previous wills,
for the clause about cremation is in all of them—a fact to which I give
great emphasis, of course. So my present mental state is irrelevant as
to substance, but representative of my passionate concern over this
matter, and enjoining the estate to seek restitution if cremation is not
carried out as I have determined. I might also add that, like Sophocles
of old, the character and precision of my prose speak volumes, in a
manner of speaking, concerning my mental alertness and perspi-
cacity."

Doris nodded. "You say you're going to have this done tomorrow?"
Walt nodded.

"Well, we'll just see about that, won't we?"

"We will," he said. "But I will remind you that copies have already
been mailed, so you haven't a ghost of a chance, Doris. I'll be burned
or I'll be damned."

Walt Thatcher not only survived the night and did as he had promised the next day, he lived for just over a year, dying in his sleep late in

November with the season's first snowfall. Doris had accepted her defeat rather gracefully and good-humoredly, cautioning herself that whatever happened, she should not do anything so foolish as get sued. Not at *her* age, certainly.

So, immediately after Walt's death, she saw that he was cremated, just as he wished. And at the special services at St. George's Episcopal Church, where they had been accustomed to attend services at Easter and Christmas and were regular supporters of the Mission Fund, Doris proved to be a pleasantly sorrowful but dignified widow.

In spite of all, she had been quite content with how things had gone, and she realized that her memories of her second husband would not remain altogether unpleasant. In fact, they might turn out to be rather cozy. After all, Doris herself was getting old, and she might as well face the fact, although she knew there are almost as many ways of facing facts as there are facts, and she planned to do it in the right way—because she was still an attractive woman, when she dressed up, and had not lost all her ability to charm.

She admitted to herself that Walt had not really been a bad husband, as bad husbands go, although she thought it was something of a shame, and a bit ironic, that most of the lucidity of his last two years should have been concentrated upon foiling her plan to inherit more of his estate. Still, she had accepted the fact and had not tried it again. She had consoled herself with the memory that she had given it a shot, it hadn't worked, so it was best to forget about it and go on living the life she had to live. And even though Walt had spent most of his last year in various states of confusion, Doris tolerated it all very well and took care of him.

After his death, she sold the house and contents for just over $685,000—more than she had dreamed it would bring. She moved to a small, comfortable, rather exclusive condominium in Arizona, set up a trust providing for escrow accounts, along with annual gifts of $9,999 to each of her children, and took care to phone all of them twice a week.

She was quite happy, for she had her health and her independence, along with her eye on several quite eligible old gentlemen in the neighboring condos. She would see what she would see. Time would tell. Meanwhile, memories of her life with Walt would prove to be memories she could live with, which was important for her. And was certainly more than you could have said about her first husband, that son of a bitch, who'd left her, so young and vulnerable, for another woman.

CONTRIBUTORS

Lee K. Abbott is the author of five short story collections: *The Heart Never Fits Its Wanting, Love Is the Crooked Thing, Strangers in Paradise, Dreams of Distant Lives,* and *Living after Midnight.* A professor of English at Ohio State University and a frequent recipient of NEA fellowships, Abbott was recently awarded a major fellowship by the Ohio Arts Council.

Ellen Behrens is the fiction editor for *Mid-American Review,* has been published in *Fiction, Paragraph,* and other small press magazines, and is included in the anthology, *What's a Nice Girl like You Doing in a Relationship Like This?* from Crossing Press. She is a writer-artist in the schools with the Ohio Arts Council, serves as a writing consultant to educators, and lives in Clyde, here she is working on a novel.

Julie Brown currently lives in a twelve-room farmhouse built in 1859 in Bristulville, Ohio. She is an assistant professor at Youngstown State University, where she teaches creative writing and women's literature. Brown has published over a dozen short stories in literary journals, such as *Michigan Quarterly Review, Hayden's Ferry Review, Southern Review,* and others. She also has published twenty children's books on topics ranging from dinosaurs to exploring outer space. "Home" won the Chris O'Malley Prize for best short story in the *Madison Review* in 1991.

Robert Canzoneri is professor emeritus of English at Ohio State, where he developed the creative writing program and directed it for many years. His books of nonfiction, fiction, and poetry include *"I Do So Politely": A Voice from the South, Watch Us Pass, Men with Little Hammers, Barbed Wire and Other Stories, A Highly Ramified Tree,* and *Potboiler: An Amateur's Affair with La Cuisine.* His play *Siege: The Battle of Vicksburg* was published in 1991.

Jaimee Wriston Colbert is originally from Hawaii and a former resident of Columbus, but she now lives on the coast of Maine teaching writing and communications at the University of Maine, Augusta, and she is the writer-in-residence at the Maine State Prison. Her fiction has been published in various journals, including *Triquarterly,* and most recently *Snake Nation Review, Nahant Bay, The Incliner, Chaminade Literary Review,* and *Pacific Coast Journal.* She has published an essay in *The Incliner.* She was a finalist for the 1991 Katherine Anne Porter prize in fiction, and she has a chapbook, *Final Light,* recently published by Bootleg Press. She won the Zephyr Publishing Prize in 1993, which published her short fiction collection.

Joseph G. Cowley is the author of the novel *The Chrysanthemum Garden,* published in 1991. His short stories have appeared in *The Maryland* Review, *Prairie Schooner,* and other publications. He moved to Ohio in 1985 with his wife, Ruth, to be near their grandchildren. He now writes plays and for computer knowledge-support systems.

Judy Doenges is a teacher and writer now living in Tacoma, Washington. In 1990, she was awarded a major fellowship in fiction writing by the Ohio Arts Council. In the spring of 1991, she was an artist-in-residence at Headlands Center for the Arts in Sausalito, California. Her fiction has been published in *Permafrost, Nimrod,* and *The Valley Women's Voice* and her nonfiction has appeared in *The Progressive.*

Robert Flanagan's stories have been anthologized in *Best Ohio Fiction* and *The Norton Book of American Short Stories,* and his short fiction collection *Naked to Naked Goes* was chosen by the *Cleveland Plain Dealer* as one of the best books in 1986. *Maggot,* a novel about the Marine Corps, is now in a twelfth printing from Warner Books. Flanagan is director of creative writing at Ohio Wesleyan University.

Abby Frucht's collection of stories, *Fruit of the Month,* won the Iowa Short Fiction Prize for 1987 and has been released in paper by Graywolf Press. The author of the novels *Snap* (1988) and *Licorice* (1990), she was visiting assistant professor of creative writing at Oberlin College. The story "Throne of Blood" is part of Frucht's new novel, *Are You Mine?.* Frucht has received fellowships from the National Endowment for the Arts and the Ohio Arts Council. She now lives in Oshkosh, Wisconsin, with her husband and children.

Mary Grimm teaches fiction writing at Case Western Reserve University in Cleveland. She has had several stories published in *The New Yorker;* they **were** collected with some others in a book published in 1993. Random House published her novel, *Left to Themselves,* in 1993.

Jack Heffron lives in Cincinnati. He is a graduate of the writing program at the University of Alabama. His stories have appeared in *Ambergris, Beloit Fiction Journal, The Chariton Review,* and *North American Review.* His reviews have appeared in *Black Warrior Review* and *Utne Reader.*

Richard Kraus began teaching creative writing at Denison University in 1966 and retired in 1991. He has won three Hopwood Prizes, a Breadloaf Writing Fellowship, and a Wallace Stegner Writing Fellowship. His story "On Vacation" won *The Gamut* tenth-anniversary creative writing contest and was published in the spring of 1990. He is currently working on a collection of short stories and is looking for a publisher for his novel *Weddings.*

J. Patrick Lewis's stories and poems have appeared in *Ner/B1, Gettysburg Review, Dalhousie Review, New Letters, Sycamore Review,* and many others. He was a 1991 Ohio Arts Councils artist grant recipient in poetry. His children's poetry books have been published by Dial, Knopf, and Atheneum.

Paul Many reversed the common wisdom and ran away from New York City to the Midwest to find his fortune. His fiction has appeared in *Special Report: Fiction, The (Ohio) Journal, Exquisite Corpse,* and *Paragraph,* among other publications. He has recently completed his second novel, *Free Grace,* and is seeking a publisher.

Jack Matthews has published novels, books of stories, essays, and poems. His short stories have been reprinted in various issues of *The Best American Short Stories* and the *O. Henry Prize Stories* annuals and his novels have been widely praised. The Dramatic Publishing Company has published two of his plays, a new interest for him. He and his wife, Barbara, live in Athens, where he is distinguished professor of English at Ohio University.

Constance Pierce is the author of *Philippe at His Back,* a poetry collection, and *When Things Get Back to Normal,* a book of stories. Her work has appeared in *New Virginia Review, Michigan Quarterly Review, Substance, Alaska Quarterly Review,* and elsewhere. She has been the recipient of two fellowships from the National Endowment for the Arts. She teaches in the creative writing program at Miami University in Oxford.

Michael J. Rosen's most recent books are *The Company of Cats* and *The Company of Dogs,* two anthologies of short stories to benefit animal welfare agencies nationwide, *The Kids' Book of Fishing,* and *Home: A Celebration of the Home to Benefit the Homeless,* a collaboration of thirty-one children's book illustrators and authors in support of Share Our Strength's fight against hunger and homelessness. He has been literary director of The Thurber House in Columbus since its inception.

Sally Savic is a graduate of Tulane University and the Iowa Writers' Workshop. She is also a recipient of three grants from the Ohio Arts Council. Her first novel, *Elysian Fields,* was published by Scribner's. She lives in Columbus.

Anne Shafmaster, originally from Massachusetts, now lives with her husband and two children in Yellow Springs, Ohio. She received her master's degree in creative writing from Antioch University in 1991. She is currently working on a collection of short stories.

Eve Shelnutt is the author of three story collections: *The Love Child, The Formal Voice,* and *The Musician,* as well as three poetry collections: *Air and Salt, Recital in a Private Home,* and *First a Long Hesitation.* Her books on writing are *The Writing Room: Keys to the Craft of Fiction and Poetry, The Magic Pencil: Teaching Children*

Creative Writing, and, as editor, *Writing: The Translation of Memory, The Confidence Woman: 26 Women Writers at Work,* and *My Poor Elephant: 28 Writers at Work.* Shelnutt is a professor of English at Ohio University and a consultant on teaching writing to children.

David Teagle's stories have appeared in *Prism International* and *El Nopal.* A graduate of Antioch College, Teagle currently lives and works in Tijeras, New Mexico.

Laura Yeager's work has been published in *The Paris Review.* She was born in Akron, Ohio. She's a 1989 graduate of The Writers' Workshop at The University of Iowa.

Jon Saari teaches in Antioch University's Weekend College in Yellow Springs, Ohio. He also advises creative writing students in Antioch's individualized graduate program. He is a book review editor of *The Antioch Review*. He holds a Ph.D. in English from Bowling Green State University; a master's degree in American studies from Purdue University; and a bachelor's degree in American studies from Michigan State University. He and his wife live in Yellow Springs.